**Praise for Kate R⟨...⟩
Her Prior Novel *The Baby Plan***

"Smart and funny, *The Baby Plan* is irresistible! A winner."
—Susan Mallery, #1 *New York Times*
bestselling author

"Described with arch humor and a loving attention to detail seldom found in fictional depictions . . . Top-notch women's fiction."
—*Kirkus Reviews*

"Heartwarmingly real and hysterically a little too real. I laughed, cringed, and cried—sometimes all at the same time. This book is emotional perfection."
—Sarah Watson, executive producer of *Parenthood*
and creator of *The Bold Type*

"Kate Rorick's exploration of modern-day parenthood is razor sharp, hilarious, and acutely true to life. I couldn't put it down."
—Beth Harbison, *New York Times* bestselling author
of *One Less Problem Without You*

"Rorick's prose is witty, engaging, and delightful, introducing us to characters who are relatable—and whose mistakes we've probably made ourselves. Recommended for fans of Marian Keyes and Jennifer Weiner."
—*Booklist*

LITTLE WONDERS

Also by Kate Rorick

The Baby Plan

LITTLE WONDERS

A Novel

KATE RORICK

wm

WILLIAM MORROW

An Imprint of HarperCollins*Publishers*

P.S.™ is a trademark of HarperCollins Publishers.

LITTLE WONDERS. Copyright © 2020 by Kate Wilcox. Excerpt from THE BABY PLAN © 2018 by Kate Wilcox. All rights reserved. Printed in the United States of America. No part of this book may be used or reproduced in any manner whatsoever without written permission except in the case of brief quotations embodied in critical articles and reviews. For information, address HarperCollins Publishers, 195 Broadway, New York, NY 10007.

HarperCollins books may be purchased for educational, business, or sales promotional use. For information, please email the Special Markets Department at SPsales@harpercollins.com.

FIRST EDITION

Designed by Diahann Sturge

Preschool Newsletter art © Robert Kneschke / Shutterstock, Inc.
Social media art on pages 61, 63, and 357 © Maksim Ankuda / Shutterstock, Inc.

Library of Congress Cataloging-in-Publication Data has been applied for.

ISBN 978-0-06-287721-5

20 21 22 23 24 LSC 10 9 8 7 6 5 4 3 2 1

To my family, for the chaos.
To my friends, for the calm.

Little Wonders Preschool
October Newsletter

Hello, WONDER-ful Parents!

September and new school jitters are behind us, and fall is officially here! Which means preschool is in full swing—and it's about to get super fun! ~~Buckle up buttercup, this is gonna be intense.~~

Ms. Rosie in the Tadpole Room has asked that we remind everyone that Share Day is every Friday, and the kids should bring only ONE toy, preferably organic, and no branded products. ~~So no, you can't bring the entire Avengers squad. I don't care if your kid cries. Don't ask.~~

Also, as the days grow shorter, we will be moving the chicken coop into the barn for the winter months, so don't worry if you don't see Cherry, Jelly Bean, and Candy Corn, they are nice and cozy inside!

Theme days this month are Sports Day, ~~you better not send your kid in Yankees gear we are in the playoffs,~~ Favorite Cuisine Day ~~but still means no peanuts for anyone who decides to bring Thai food I'm looking at you TERRY~~, and of course, the big one: Halloween!

The Little Wonders Happy Halloween Parade will be at 4 PM on Friday, October 30th, followed by a rockin' Dance Party in the Multipurpose Room. We look forward to decking the place out in Halloween gear and food, and hope that we can rely on families to help with the decking! ~~We want money.~~

Finally, our Parent Association president, the ~~domineering pain-in-the-ass bitch-on-wheels~~ indomitable Quinn Barrett, would like to remind everyone that the volunteer boards are up for the Halloween parade! Everyone loves to help out on Halloween, so to make it organized, you can sign up to volunteer via our Facebook group, via the portal on the Parent Association website, or go old school and sign up on the posters in the lobby. The information will be consolidated. You don't need to sign up more than once! ~~And you know who gets to consolidate it, right? Yup, the Parent Association secretary. Cuz I don't have enough shit to do.~~

Parent volunteers are what make the Happy Halloween Parade and Dance Party work, so let's do everything we can to make it a special event for the kids. ~~And if you don't, you're a horrible parent.~~

We can't wait to see the costumes!

Together in Parenting!
Suzy Breakman-Kang
Parent Association Secretary
Little Wonders Preschool and Child Development Center

P.S. As a reminder to those parents ~~TERRY~~ who brought up their concerns again at the last Parent Association meeting, the hens in the chicken coop on campus are NOT diseased. They are molting, as they do every fall. There is no need to worry. ~~Seriously, people. Google.~~

CHAPTER ONE

In dark moments, when Quinn Barrett looked back and analyzed what caused the destruction of her entire life, she should have known that it would happen at the Little Wonders Preschool Happy Halloween Costume Parade (and Dance Party).

Not that the Little Wonders Preschool Happy Halloween Costume Parade (and Dance Party) was in any way apocalyptic. No, it had been a perfectly executed Quinn Barrett production from start to finish.

But, if she was being honest with herself—and in those dark moments of wine-fueled reflection, Quinn could be nothing but honest—the entire day had been full of hiccups that stacked one on top of the other, until she'd felt like she had when she was six and she'd drunk five root beers at McDonald's and everything exploded out of her, into the playspace ball pit.

The day had begun as usual. Her internal alarm—once she started using the Parcel Method she no longer needed an external one—went off precisely at 5:45 AM. Dividing her day into Parcels—basically fifteen-minute segments—had been an organizational godsend that allowed her to "take the reins" of her day—or at least that's what the motivational book she'd adopted it from claimed. Her first fifteen-minute block was delegated for either 1. a solid mile and a half on the treadmill, 2. frothing some coconut milk for a decent cappuccino, or 3. a shower *with* shaving legs. Since she would be running around all day at work at the Beacon Hill house followed by the Halloween parade setup, she could skip the treadmill. And since she had gotten a full five hours of sleep last night, she didn't need the caffeine shot. Thus she could indulge in smooth legs.

So, shower. One of complete luxury and solitude. She was even contemplating a decadent exfoliating scrub, when the first hiccup occurred. She heard the fast, hard footfalls that heralded the arrival of one sleepy, grumpy three-year-old boy. Who was awake six minutes ahead of schedule.

"Mommy, I'm all wet," her son, Hamilton, said, and sat down on the bathroom floor in his pee-covered pajamas.

Her heart broke even as she sucked in a steadying breath. She should have opted for coffee. "Oh, sweetie, again?" Quinn said, as she quickly rinsed the soap out of her hair (no time for conditioner, and shaved legs were laughable at this point). Ham had been using the potty—*really*, he was!—for several months now. But he still had problems at night with wetting the bed. (. . . And, there were those times during the day that the teachers would find him crouching behind a chair and pooping in his pants.) But Quinn insisted he was completely potty trained. Because he knew how to do it. He just . . . didn't. And now, she had less than five minutes to get their morning back on track before the next Parcel started.

"Okay, hop in," she said. Stepping out of the shower, Quinn efficiently stripped him out of his wet pajamas, and got him in the shower to wash off. She ignored Ham's screams of having to be under the water (really, you'd think he was melting like the Wicked Witch of the West). Then she got him out (naturally, after thirty seconds in the water, now he didn't want to leave), dried him off, and used the remaining four minutes of her Parcel to strip the sheets off Ham's twin bed and replace them.

Even with the plastic mattress protector a vague pee scent permeated his room. She would have to leave Alba a note to see if she could do anything about that.

By the time she dug out that one pair of summer slacks that sort of worked for fall, she was running seven minutes into her next fifteen-minute Parcel. Time to pick up the pace.

"Yaaaaaaaaaaayyyyyyy!!!! Mommy, chase me!" Hamilton cried, running away, toward the master bedroom, for no apparent reason other than he was three years old and didn't need the coffee that Quinn dearly wished she had made.

"Ham—Hamilton, come back here!" she hissed, but never underestimate the speed and slipperiness of a wet three-year-old.

There was a dive, and a crash, and then a wailing cry.

"I. STUBBED. MY. TOE!!!!"

As she rushed over to console the victim, another grumpy voice, one she'd hoped to avoid rousing, sounded through the master suite.

"Aw come on," the voice whined, in a state of cranky stupor. "Ham, I need my sleep."

"Hey, honey," Quinn said soothingly, to both Ham on the floor and to the rumpled pile of sheets that was groaning in the bed. "Sorry, but Ham wet the bed and then stubbed his toe and—"

"I was in surgery until midnight, Quinn," her husband,

Stuart, groaned, not even opening his eyes. "And I have to be back in the OR again today. I need my sleep."

"Right. Sorry. Come on, sweetie," she said in a hush to Hamilton. "Let's let Daddy sleep."

She managed to scoop Ham up and tiptoe out of the room, shutting the door behind her. By now, the stubbed toe was forgotten, and she ushered him to his room where she began to ruthlessly dry him off and get his clothes on.

Stuart was a wonderful dad, like she told everyone—but God, was he grumpy when he woke up.

Like father, like son, she supposed. Not everyone was a morning person. By biology, or necessity.

"Come on, Ham," Quinn said as she wrestled her son into clothes, rooting around in her mind desperately for something to motivate him into cooperating. "You have to get dressed so . . . you can be my special helper today!"

She was now nine minutes into her next Parcel, and it looked like the whole morning was going to be shot if she didn't do something to get things back on track.

"I'm Miss Rosie's helper this week—I get to feed Nemo."

Ham was immensely proud of the responsibility of feeding Nemo, the class goldfish. Not to be confused with the goldfish in the other classes, all named, like all preschool fish, Nemo. To hear Ham tell it, he had a special bond with *his* Nemo—maybe this was the beginning of Ham being responsible enough for a pet? A dog—ugh, but Stuart would say no. That conversation wasn't even worth starting. Especially not in the morning.

"Yes, but I need you to be my helper, too."

"Why?"

"Because it's a very special day! It's Halloween!" Rather, it was the Friday before Halloween, but when you're in preschool, Halloween was more of a weeklong spectacle than any one event. "And we have lots to do before the parade, so we have to hurry hurry hurry to get to school. Got it, buddy?"

"Halloween? My costume!" Ham's little eyes lit up and Quinn felt the warm glow of a three-year-old's joy. And no small amount of pride at what she had been doing until one in the morning the night before.

Ham thundered down the stairs. Where, in the center of the impeccably decorated living room, by the vintage gray tufted couch she'd agonized over, sat . . .

"What's that?"

"That's your costume, sweetie! Your spaceship!" Not just any spaceship. It was hand-crafted papier mâché and shaped corrugated cardboard, with vinyl sheeting for windows and actual working LED lights. It was a feat of engineering and silver chrome spray paint. And it was what Ham had said he wanted to be for Halloween—not a space man, not an astronaut, but a *spaceship*—for the last month.

And Quinn Barrett did not disappoint. Especially not her son.

"It doesn't look like a spaceship," Ham said, dubiously. All of the good feelings Quinn had crashed down around her.

Hiccup Number Two.

"Sure it does!" she said, and she was about to give him the rundown of all the amazing things the spaceship could do (Lights! Sounds! A smoke effect that she wasn't allowed to use in the parade but would be employed on Halloween night!) when her watch went off, reminding her that the latest Parcel was up, and she NEEDED to get breakfast ready.

"Okay, honey, time for you to go use the potty and get your clothes on, while I make mini-quiches!"

Ham was left eyeing the spaceship dubiously, while she trotted off to the kitchen.

A healthy breakfast was the best way to start the day, and luckily, she had made the egg white, spinach, and mushroom quiche cups in advance and frozen them; all she had to do was pop them in the toaster oven. (Microwaves were not allowed in her household since she'd read that study on developing brain waves and concentration.)

The steaming quiche cups came out of the toaster oven, delicious and tempting, and—

"I'M A FIREMAN!!!!"

—and they hit the floor, as one of Ham's toy fire trucks hit her ankle.

Damn. Damn damn damn damn. That was the last of the mini-quiches. Also, Ham was somehow naked again.

"Too loud!" came the grumbly voice from above stairs.

"Sorry, Mommy," Ham said, contrite. Whether he was contrite about the fire truck to the ankle or about again waking his father, she didn't know, but she didn't have time to guess, she had to plan B a healthy breakfast, pronto.

"Got a sorry for Daddy, too?" Stuart said, as he plodded down the stairs, looking rumpled and gorgeous with a morning beard. He came up to Ham, and they did their usual greeting. Tiger claws and growls.

"Grr!" Ham said.

"Grr!" Stu said back; he cocked an eyebrow at the spaceship. "What's this thing?"

"It's my fire truck!"

"It's a spaceship, buddy. You wanted to be a spaceship."

Stu's eyebrow remained cocked. "You made that? When?"

"Here and there. It wasn't hard." She aimed for breezy, but

her fractiousness at the loss of the mini-quiches was showing through. It was too early in the morning for her to entertain a fractious moment, she thought as she rummaged in the cabinets for what to sub in for breakfast. They were low on almost everything. She would have to leave Alba a list.

"Muesli mix!" she said triumphantly, finding some in the back. It was usually reserved for the weekends (high-carb breakfasts on weekdays were generally a no-no, but when needs must) and with Ham comfortably ensconced at the kitchen's marble island, chomping away, she could rush upstairs and finish getting herself dressed.

She threw on the dress shirt she had thankfully had Alba iron yesterday, her favorite high-heeled ankle boots, and was so grateful for the tousled, chin-length cut she'd had her stylist implement. Sure, Stuart bemoaned the loss of her midback tresses, but if she could save herself one Parcel of time in the morning on hair care, then all the better. Secretly, she loved the way the cut framed her face and brought out her eyes. But she didn't tell Stuart that. She told him that she'd grow it back out once life got a little less hectic.

Plus, for special occasions, she could put in some extensions.

She trotted back downstairs, tucking her shirt in as she went.

"Mommy, I want green juice." On the one hand she was thankful he was into his vegetables this morning, on the other, she was already a full Parcel behind. And their fridge was desperately empty.

Also, Stuart's fancy blender defied her.

"I'm sorry, Ham. Alba isn't here, so she can't make you a green juice. Go on, time to go get dressed."

She shot pleading eyes at Stuart—*Go help him get dressed!*—but . . . well, it might have been too early for Stuart to get such complex signals.

"Go on, Hamilton," Stuart said, not looking up from his own bowl of muesli.

Ham hopped down off his stool and went to his room. Quinn shook her head. The chances of a three-year-old actually getting dressed by himself were approximately the same as a shark marrying a nubile young skinny-dipper, but Stuart didn't seem to understand that.

"What?" Stuart said. "What's that look?"

"Nothing!" Quinn replied, letting her eyes fall to her watch (vintage Cartier, her push present from Stuart). "Where is Alba? She's not usually this late."

Alba had been Ham's nanny since he was born, but now that he was at Little Wonders, she had transitioned to being their housekeeper, and general all-around lifesaver. Alba proved the adage that behind every woman who has it all is a middle-aged domestic helper making everything work.

"She's in Puerto Rico," Stuart said, filling his mouth with muesli as he spoke.

Hiccup Number Three.

"*WHAT?*" Quinn couldn't help but let out. This time, she couldn't help but let her fractiousness show.

Stuart kindly swallowed before he replied. "She's in Puerto Rico. For her daughter's wedding?"

"When did that happen?"

"She called my office a couple of weeks ago, asking for the time off." Stuart shrugged. "I told Charlene to email you."

"That's not something you have your scheduler email your wife about! That's something you put on the family calendar! That is something you—"

That is something you tell me, and we discuss it, and we figure out what our game plan is going to be.

"Oh, now, don't give me that look," Stuart said, a sly half grin on his face, looking up from beneath his lashes. He got up from his stool and came over to her. "I'm sorry, okay? I was running from one OR to another when Alba called, that's why I asked Charlene to email."

"You didn't think to mention it to me when you got home?" Quinn tried her damnedest to maintain her justifiably pissed-off face, but Stuart slipped his hands to her hips in that way that he did, and well . . .

"Honestly, it completely slipped my mind until now." He gave her a grin that romance novelists would describe as "saucy," but that Quinn could only describe as "trying to get away with it and succeeding." His lips lightly grazed her neck. "It's just for the weekend. Is it really that big a problem?"

Was it really that big a problem? Alba only made it so their household functioned. Beyond the grocery shopping, the cleaning, the green juices she somehow convinced Ham to love—she was Quinn's backup and life support. She was supposed to come help with the Halloween parade today. She was supposed to come help hand out candy (and help with Quinn's visiting mother) on Halloween night tomorrow.

Alba never asked for time off. She worked whenever Quinn had an emergency, or she and Stuart needed a night out in the city. Now Quinn was left without a backup for the madness of dealing with a three-year-old's Halloween weekend . . . And for her to leave without telling Quinn—purposely calling Stuart's office instead—it just about cracked Quinn's psyche in half. What did it say about how Alba viewed her?

But there wasn't time for a cracked psyche, not today. She could handle this. She was Quinn Barrett—she got shit done.

"No, it's fine," she said, sighing. "You and I will just handle my mother on our own tomorrow."

Stu let out a groan, and pulled away, back to his muesli mix. "You really know how to kill a mood. And to think, I was all ready to show you my gratitude for the snack when I got home last night."

Quinn's brow furrowed. When did he think she had time to enjoy his "gratitude"? Did he think she took a shower with half-shaved legs that morning for his benefit, and not the benefit of the hundred people she had to interact with that day?

But no, she was getting irked. She couldn't get irked. Or fractious. Or have a cracked psyche. Not today.

"What snack?" she asked instead.

"The one in the green Tupperware," Stuart said into his cereal.

A shiver of annoyance ran down her spine. "You mean Ham's lunch?"

Stuart didn't have time to reply, or to give her a romance novel saucy grin and save himself. Because at that moment, Stuart was saved when his son bounded down the stairs, wearing a fireman's hat, one sock, and nothing else.

Her alarm beeped. Another Parcel gone.

"Fireman!!!!!!" Ham yelled as he zoomed around the room. "Let's go to schoooooooool!!!!"

By the time they trotted up past the sign on the front door that read "Needleton Academy for Potential Prodigies" and "Little Wonders Preschool," Quinn was back on her Parcel schedule by mere seconds. Once she got to work she would get a more comfortable lead, but for now, she plastered a serene smile on her face, as if Ham's Halloween costume, a bag of Ham's spare clothes, her Parent Association clipboard, and the six cellophane-wrapped raffle baskets she lugged weighed a mere feather.

Luckily, Ham had decided to be helpful that day, and carry his own (hastily assembled) lunch as he rushed ahead, eager to get to class, Miss Rosie, and Nemo.

"Hamilton, remember what we talked about," she sing-songed as they made their way through the yard. "Walk perfectly straight please."

For once, Hamilton did as he was asked. And while she was laden with the entire contents of a craft store, Quinn still had the wherewithal to walk with perfect posture (she'd killed it at Pilates during her lunch breaks) and do the smile and nods to every other parent she passed.

There were the twins, Charlie and Calvin, running at a breakneck pace through the yard and toward the primary-colored playground structure, followed by their extremely tired moms trying to corral them inside the building. There was Jorge, who managed a lucrative investors' fund (and Quinn had to remember to hit him up for Parent Association donations), yelling numbers into his phone while his little Javi trailed sullenly behind. And there was Shanna, leading her little Jordan—her nose as high in the air as her mother's, as if they smelled something foul—toward the front doors.

"Hold the door, please!" Quinn called out, not altering her pace at all. Shanna paused long enough for everyone around to know that she heard Quinn, and thus, could do nothing but hold the outer door.

"Thank you," Quinn said. "Thank you!" Ham piped up, making Quinn preen.

"You have quite a bit of stuff there," Shanna said by way

of conversation. "Jordan honey, make room for Hamilton's mommy. She's very . . . wide today."

"What is that?" Jordan said, looking at the spaceship dangling from its shoulder straps on Quinn's arm.

"It's Ham's Halloween costume," she replied, and enjoyed the stricken look on Shanna's face as she gently shifted the bag behind her that no doubt held an Elsa dress or something equally banal.

"No it's not!" Hamilton cried, but he was interrupted by Quinn's watch beeping. Her next Parcel was up, she needed to get moving.

"Shush, honey, of course it is," Quinn said, and then managed, with more grace and strength than she usually had at that time of the morning, to wave and sail into the school.

She was dying for a coffee. Or any food, really—it was only then, carrying all that crap, that she realized she'd skipped breakfast.

Her empty stomach was the cause of her annoyance right now, she told herself. And her armload. Once she put everything down and got a nondairy latte, she'd be her usual cheerful, competent, Get-Shit-Done self.

She felt her smile becoming a touch more honest as they entered the main halls of the historic building that was the Needleton Academy for Potential Prodigies and Little Wonders Preschool.

She loved it here. One of the town founders' original barns from the early eighteenth century still stood on the grounds, but the preschool itself was a late-nineteenth-century building—with graceful lines, but appropriate security and plumbing upgrades. She loved the idea of Ham being so close to history. And she loved the teachers, the Reggio-play-based learning curriculum, and even the annoying welcome song that started off each morning. She felt safe leaving Hamilton there every day, certain he would be cared for, educated, loved.

Another checkmark in her endless score of being an awesome parent, she thought to herself. Choosing Little Wonders. *Ham is lucky to have them. And they are sure as hell lucky to have me.*

Hamilton lit up the moment he saw Miss Rosie, his teacher.

"Hamilton, my friend!" she said, a welcoming cry that greeted every child who walked through the door as if they were the most special person in the world—which, when Miss Rosie locked eyes with them, they were. "Come, my helper! Nemo is so hungry, it's time for his food!"

As Hamilton rushed forward, very intent on his important job of feeding Nemo, Quinn managed to hand over his lunch and his costume.

"Is this Hamilton's fire truck?" Miss Rosie asked.

"No—it's a spaceship. He's been asking for a spaceship for a month."

Miss Rosie cut a glance at Hamilton, but otherwise said nothing.

"And here's more pants and underwear."

Miss Rosie took the bag of comfortable, easily-pulled-down-for-potty-training pants and space-themed underwear with a gentle sigh. "Mrs. Barrett, I know you want Hamilton to wear big boy underwear, but yesterday was the fourth time this week that he had an accident. Maybe just for nap time, we keep him in the pull-ups—"

"Nonsense. He knows how to do it. And he will." Her stomach was grumbling. Damn, she needed a coffee. The gift bags were getting heavier and heavier. "Ham, honey! Have to go!" Ham nodded solemnly, as she blew him a kiss—

without using her hands, because of the raffle baskets. Her heart broke a little, walking out the door, the way it did every day. But she had too much to do. The Beacon Hill house was waiting. She quickly ran by the underutilized supply closet that she and Jamie had petitioned to have converted to a Parent Association room and dropped off the raffle baskets, ducked her head into the front office to update everyone on when to expect the pop-up tents to arrive, and the food trucks to come, expecting to check those things off on her trusty clipboard.

And then came Hiccup Number Four.

"Didn't they tell you, Mrs. Barrett?" Ms. Anna, the school's principal said. "The food trucks were canceled."

"*WHAT*?"

"The town said that since we are a historic landmark, we couldn't have food trucks."

That goddamned prehistoric barn, her mind flared angrily.

"The food trucks would be in the parking lot! Are you telling me that the parking lot is a historic landmark?"

Ms. Anna simply shrugged. "I spoke with the town council, but they said no food trucks. We can have catering brought into the cafeteria . . ."

"No. We had food trucks last year. We are having food trucks this year." Everyone—*everyone*—said that the Halloween-themed organic taco truck was the highlight of last year's parade. This year she had not only booked the taco truck but the snow cone truck with a special request for monster-themed agave syrups. It had cost them an extra 10 percent for that. No way was she canceling the food trucks.

As she marched out the door, she sent a quick series of texts. To Sutton at the office, saying she was taking a personal day, and to text her every hour with updates on the Beacon

Hill house kitchen fixtures situation. To Stuart, telling him that she was going to miss their usual Friday lunch date. And to Alba—but no, Alba wasn't there. She quickly shifted the Alba text to "Hope you're having a great time! Congratulations to your daughter! When will you be back, Monday?" and hoped her tone was collegial and not angry and desperate. She added one of those smiley emojis just for flavor. Then, she shifted her car into gear and drove straight for the town hall.

Last year they'd had food trucks. So, by God, this year they would have food trucks.

But last year, Quinn had had Jamie Stone at her side. And Jamie had arranged the food trucks. She thought wistfully of her partner-in-crime on the Parent Association board. They'd been copresidents, a dynamic duo, running the show and making it fun. But then, last year Jamie had decided to give up the stay-at-home life and go back to work. And of course Quinn, a working parent herself, could not begrudge the decision. But it also meant that Quinn was now alone as Parent Association president.

Not everyone was as Get-Shit-Done as she was. But Jamie was a Needleton native and had relatives on the town council. No doubt that was how they had gotten the food trucks past the landmark barrier. Quinn's thumb hovered over Jamie's number on her phone. But no. She was going to do this herself. It would take no time at all, she told herself. And then she'd get a freaking coffee.

It had not taken no time at all. It had taken almost the whole day.

But, it had gotten done. She had permission from the town

council. She used the Instagram picture of Ham's Halloween costume as guilt fuel, and it had worked. She had uncan-
celed the food trucks (for another 10 percent markup, damn
them) and she'd fielded incoming texts from work while she
did. And Stuart, of course, who didn't get her lunch text. As
he was in the cell phone dead zone of the surgery floor.

Stuart: Where are you? You said you got us a res at Bocca?

Oh, Bocca. They hadn't been since before Ham! She'd
made the reservation ages ago, it was one of Stuart's favor-
ites. She'd been dreaming of their panna cotta for weeks.
Quickly, in a text, she explained the day's craziness. Then
she followed with a plea.

Quinn: Is there any chance you can come early and help
   do set up?

She hoped with her fingers. But she pretty much knew the
answer.

Stuart: Sorry, Hon. I have a surgery right after lunch.

Quinn: But you'll still make the parade, right?

Stuart: It's an appendix, should be quick. Hold a chair for me.

Quinn: You got it. Enjoy Bocca. Bring a dessert home for me!

But he didn't reply. The thought of dessert made her stomach grumble.

But once she got the Little Wonders Happy Halloween Parade (and Dance Party) up and running, everything would be fine.

Admittedly, when she first faced down the prospect of doing the parade by herself without Jamie, she'd considered hiring an event coordinator. But that would be too unQuinn. And really, it should be simple. All the work had been done in advance. Now that the food trucks were sorted out, it was easy peasy. The tents and tables and raffle baskets and tickets had been dropped off. The rented decorations for the dance party in their little auditorium were laid out and waiting to be hung. The popcorn machine was stocked. The parent volunteers had signed up on the sign-up sheet weeks ago, and now, all she had to do was direct them where to put things and how.

But then the volunteers were late.

And then they all acted like gerbils who had never opened a folding chair before.

And the food trucks didn't know where to park, and she had to get six people to move their cars out of spots she had specifically marked "RESERVED FOR FOOD TRUCKS" in the school's parking lot.

It was as she was dictating to Elia's dad (one of Ham's classmates, the little girl who hugged too much) exactly how to open a pop-up tent that the parents began to arrive.

Starting with Shanna Stone.

Of course she would be first. Quinn left Elia's father to actually read the instructions for himself, pasted on a smile, grabbed her clipboard—the most important accessory for exuding authority—and forced herself to slow to a leisurely pace to greet the new arrivals.

Shanna's eyes were hidden by massive sunglasses that covered practically half her face—and were completely unnecessary on this slightly overcast fall afternoon. But still, she swanned about in her athleisure wear, as if she were on the porch of a Nantucket beach house in mid-July, as at ease and ready to be waited on hand and foot.

"Quinn! Oh, Quinn!" Shanna called out, waving her over. And much like the reverse from this morning, Quinn couldn't pretend she hadn't heard.

"Shanna, how lovely to see you," Quinn said as she approached, pretending to check something off on her clipboard. Thank goodness for that clipboard—it acted not only as a badge of authority, but as a body blocker from those who might air kiss—as it looked like Shanna was about to attempt.

"You're very early," Quinn chided.

"Well, now that I'm at home full time, I don't have to rush from the office. It's so freeing."

"Yes, I recall Jamie very much took advantage of that last year." And it was an advantage that Quinn herself missed.

"Hm. Well, Jamie's so much happier now, back in the office. He just loves it. He'll be here when the parade starts."

If Quinn could undo anything in this world, it would be to have her partner-in-presidenting Jamie *not* also be Shanna's husband, Jamie. But there they were.

Last year, when Quinn decided to run for Parent Association president, there had been fierce competition from Shanna's husband, Jamie—until they decided to run the show together. Quinn had all the organizational skills and experience, while as a stay-at-home dad Jamie had the time to implement their decisions. Not to mention, he was a decent handyman and good at fostering connections with local vendors and could set up a pop-up tent all by himself without having to have the instructions dictated.

But at the beginning of the school year, Shanna and Jamie had decided to trade places. Jamie went back to work, and Shanna stayed home.

And Shanna . . . Shanna didn't do pop-up tents.

"I would have thought at least the chairs would have been set up by now," Shanna was saying.

"Well, that's what happens when you arrive early."

"Not that early. We stopped by the Tadpole Room, I had to drop off Jordan's Elsa wig—it's a professional wig and I didn't want it getting ruined by sticky hands through the day. All the kids are in their costumes." She gave Quinn a decidedly pointed look. "Well, most of them."

"Oh, I wouldn't worry. Ham knows his costume is special, for the parade." She snuck a glance at her watch. Yes, still way too early for Ham to be in his spaceship costume. Absolutely.

"Hmm. I saw your Instagram post. It looks . . . very involved. You certainly know how to do Halloween."

"Oh, you follow me on Instagram?" Quinn said, and watched Shanna's face harden, knowing she'd missed a trick. "That's wonderful, I'll have to follow you back."

Quinn mostly used her Instagram for her work as an interior designer. It was a crucial tool in showing her skills and design sensibility to potential clients. (Plus, she loved impressing random people on the internet with her color schemes.) But sometimes Hamilton pictures snuck their way in there, especially when they were ridiculously cute, or ridiculously amazing—and the spaceship qualified as both.

"Hey, Shanna, I found them," said a breathless young

woman with alarmingly blue hair who came up to them, hauling four chairs under her arms. "They were in that closet place, like you said."

"Excuse me," Quinn said; this girl must be a mother's helper to Shanna. God knows Shanna would hire someone hapless to boss around. "But you can't just take our chairs. Parent Volunteers will be placing them out shortly."

In fact, she sent the world's fastest all-caps text to Elia's dad to tell him to abandon the tent and get on the chairs, toot-effing-sweet.

"Oh, I'm a parent," the young woman said, awkwardly putting the chairs down in a jumble so she could extend her hand. "So I volunteer. I'm Daisy."

"Have you two not met yet? I've been so remiss," Shanna tutted. "Daisy is Carrie's mom. She joined the Tadpole Room a few weeks ago."

Quinn's eyebrow went up. Of course she had noticed the new little girl in Hamilton's class. She was hard to miss, with the bright purple glasses and the mop of dark curls. But if *this* was her mom—with the electric blue hair, completely tattooed arms peeking out from the pushed-up sleeves of her cardigan, and a discreet silver hoop threaded through her septum—Little Wonders must have been hard up for enrollment (which she knew by the waitlist was not true) . . . or a rather big favor was called in.

"Jamie and Daisy's husband, Robbie, are cousins. Practically brothers."

Ah, and there was the answer.

Quinn turned a short but polite smile to the newcomer. "Nice to meet you. I guess Shanna hadn't yet explained that parents have to volunteer to earn their hours, and that sign-ups happen far in advance."

"Oh . . . ," Daisy replied. "I guess I can put them back . . ."

"Daisy, don't be ridiculous," Shanna said. "Besides, it's not good for me to be on my feet too long. In my condition."

As much as Quinn wanted to ignore that conversational cue, she couldn't, not with the way Shanna's hand lightly grazed her perfectly flat stomach.

"You're pregnant?" she asked.

"Two months. We're very excited for Jordan to have a little baby brother. Or sister."

"Well, congratulations." Oh thank GOD, Elia's dad and another father were bursting through the doors that moment, pushing the flatbed with the folding chairs. "I have to go, but next time," she said turning to Daisy, "sign up on the volunteer board in the lobby or on the Facebook page. Or on our Slack."

"Little Wonders has a Slack?" she heard the blue-haired Daisy say, bewildered, as Quinn walked away.

The tents got set up. The chairs got set up. The decorations in the auditorium/multipurpose room were hung—twice actually, because the first time the volunteers went for "charmingly askew" and missed wildly. But she'd dug deep for her inner patron saint, Martha Stewart, and fixed it with serenity and poise. The Little Wonders Happy Halloween Parade was going to happen, and it was going to happen through the sheer force of Quinn's will.

She hadn't eaten all day. Coffee was a distant dream, why even bother at this point? But it would all be worth it to see the Tadpole Room march in the parade, with Ham in his picture-perfect spaceship costume.

Oh, the pictures were going to be amazing on Instagram.

Then, she got the text from Stuart's scheduler, Charlene.

Charlene: Hello, Mrs. Barrett. A complication arose and
Dr. Barrett is still in surgery. He won't be able to make it
to the parade.

Disappointment filled her chest. Disappointment for Ham,
for herself. She took a moment and stepped away to the far
side of the historic barn in the corner of the school yard,
giving herself a little privacy. She pinched the bridge of her
nose—annoyance and sadness mixed to give her the begin-
nings of a wicked headache.

And then . . . Hiccup Number Five arrived.

"Mrs. Barrett," Miss Rosie, Ham's teacher said, approach-
ing. "I'm sorry, but Ham wants to wear his fire truck costume,
and he says this isn't it." Miss Rosie held out the spaceship by
its sparkly elastic straps. Behind her, Ham stood, grasping
Miss Rosie's leg. He wasn't dressed in his space suit; he was
in a well-worn firefighter's hat and coat from the classroom's
dress-up box. He had that miserable and stubborn look on
his face that usually appeared only when she was trying to
cajole him into using the potty.

"Hamilton," she said, perhaps a bit more harshly than she
intended, "your costume is a spaceship. You wanted a spaceship."

Hamilton just wrapped his arms about himself and shook
his head.

"I think, with the excitement of the parade and party . . . ,"
Miss Rosie was saying as she knelt down next to Ham, "that
he's a little overwhelmed . . ."

"Nonsense," Quinn said, huffing out a breath. This was
the last thing, the very last thing, that she needed. "Hamilton
loves Halloween. Don't you, sweetie?"

This time, Hamilton stuck his tongue out at her.

"Mrs. Barrett, I—" Miss Rosie was glancing over her shoulder. Across the yard, peeking their heads out of the door, was a line of small children, ready to show off their wide range of Elsa and Marvel superhero costumes.

"Go," Quinn said. "I'll get him in his costume." She would. And by the time the Tadpole Room marched by, she would just add him to the end of the line. Like Santa Claus at the end of the Thanksgiving parade—he would be the closer, what everyone remembered.

After Miss Rosie trotted away, Quinn knelt by her son. "It's time for the parade."

Head shake.

"All your friends are waiting."

Tongue out.

"We can't go to the party unless you wear your spaceship."

A full-on raspberry.

Quinn's voice was rapidly losing its softness, leaving behind only the angry steel. She huffed a breath out of her nose.

"Hamilton, I've had enough of this." She rose to her feet. "Mommy has had a very long day. Very, very long. It's Time. To. Put. Your. Spaceship. On."

"No!" Hamilton yelled. "I. Want. A. *FIRE TRUCK!*"

The last word was screamed so loud, it echoed across the yard, flitting over red and gold treetops and no doubt reaching the International Space Station. Pity he wasn't interested in space.

Maybe it was Hamilton's tone, so similar to her own. Maybe it was the headache that was quickly sweeping beneath her eyes and throbbing toward her temples. Maybe it was the hiccups. But for whatever reason, that was the moment that Quinn Barrett Completely Lost It.

"You don't want the spaceship? Fine! FINE!" The space-ship that had been sitting delicately on the ground next to Quinn was picked up. Not by Quinn—no, surely it wasn't she who picked up the cardboard, LED lights, and chrome paint masterpiece and tore it in half like the Incredible Hulk. It couldn't have been Quinn who then flung the silver remnants to the ground. And surely it wasn't Quinn who proceeded to stomp on said masterpiece.

"I did"—STOMP—"All of this"—STOMP—"For you!"—STOMP—"The parade!"—STOMP—"The party!"—STOMP—"The freaking food trucks!"—STOMP—"And if you"—STOMP—"Don't want it"—STOMP—"You don't get to have it!"

Her hair had flown about wildly. Her stiletto boot heel had gotten caught on the spaceship, and she had to windmill to keep herself from falling. Her breath fell out of her in wild, hot pants.

And Ham was staring at her like she was a snarling beast—the villainous creature in his book of fairy tales that he always made her skip over.

Shock settled over her bones. What the hell did she—the one and only Quinn Barrett—just do?

Shock seemed to hold Ham still too, as she knelt in front of him. "Oh, sweetie, I'm sorry, I'm—"

A long, thin cry built up from inside his chest, and broadcast itself out like an air raid siren.

"*aaaaaaaaaaaAAAAAAAAAAAAAAAAAAAAAAAA!!!!!!!!*"

Tears started to rain down Ham's little face. Snot from his nose. Little gulps of breath the only punctuation to his cries.

"My spaceship!" he despaired. "MY SPAAAAAACCCCEEEE-SHIIIIIIP!!!"

"Oh, Ham," she said, practically hyperventilating. "Oh,

sweetie, I'm sorry, I'm so sorry." She folded him into her arms. He allowed her to hold him while he cried. Which was all that she could do.

Because she was the world's worst mother.

Just, the absolute *worst*.

On the other side of the historic house, she could hear the Halloween music she had picked out playing over the loud-speaker. Elia's dad had moved on from making a hash of tent setup to making a hash of MCing the parade.

"And now, here comes the Tadpole Room!"

The parade went on. No one had noticed that they were missing. Or if they had, they didn't care. Because everyone had their own kids in costumes to coo over.

Ham was now on the downhill side of his upset, his left-over cries perfunctory, tapering out.

She chanced pulling back, to look at his face. He still wouldn't meet her eye.

"Ham, do you want to be a fireman in the parade?" she asked.

Slowly he shook his head. "I peed."

She looked down and noticed the dark patch on the front of Ham's trousers. He'd wet himself.

Oh hell.

"Oh, Ham . . . do you want to clean up, then skip the parade and go get ice cream?" She felt awful. Truly, like she needed a crater to crawl into and then let the earth swallow her whole. That was what she deserved. How could she have done this in front of her sweet little Ham? He was only three. She was supposed to be the grown-up here.

Ham nodded fervently, his tears drying very quickly at the mention of such a special treat.

She picked up the mangled remains of the spaceship and picked up Hamilton. She ducked around the historic house to see if anyone was looking.

Nope. Everyone had their eyes on the parade, their cell phones out, recording their own kids, locking in their cuteness for posterity.

She minced quickly around the edge of the yard and slipped in the school's door. She ran to the Parent Association closet and grabbed her purse. They could figure out how to throw a kids' dance party and break down everything by themselves.

She loaded a now completely fine Ham (he was babbling about the kind of ice cream he wanted) into the car, and then threw the spaceship into the trunk. As she did, she found herself staring at it. Her beautiful Instagram spaceship. Covered in her stomp prints. There were even little holes where her stiletto boots stabbed their way through.

She shut the trunk, and a small hysterical giggle escaped her lips.

If anyone had seen what she'd done to the spaceship, they would have her committed.

But luckily, no one had.

Thank God for small miracles.

CHAPTER TWO

*O*h. *My . . .*"

Shanna's voice was coated in delicious scandal. So much so that Daisy couldn't help turning her head. Years in Los Angeles traffic had beaten the rubbernecking instinct out of her, but suburban New England must have made her rusty, because she immediately looked.

And saw what could only be described as the preschool equivalent of a Maserati spinning out on the 101 Freeway.

"Is that . . ."

Shanna nodded, her eyes wide.

Quinn Barrett, the president of the Parent Association, and having-it-all motherhood motivation poster, was having the mother of all meltdowns.

Daisy and Shanna were sitting on a little rise by the rotting "historic" barn. Shanna had said it was the best spot to watch the parade, although now Daisy wished she had insisted on the front row. She'd wanted to get good footage of Carrie in her costume. Rob was rushing from work—she could see him in the tracking app she had on her phone, willing him to magic his way past all the horrible Massachusetts drivers (apparently in Massachusetts drivers' ed they taught signaling was optional).

Carrie couldn't be more thrilled to be in the parade. Her daughter was a round little bullet train, ready to barrel through anything with a big smile and a type of joy that, previous to parenthood, Daisy didn't know existed. The first day she had come to the Needleton Academy for Potential Prodigies and Little Wonders, she had walked up to three kids in the Tadpole Room, said, "Hi! I'm Carrie. I like *Star Wars* and dragons. You're my friend now."

And all three of those kids complied. Falling in behind Carrie and playing castles and dragons and Jedi knights while Daisy watched, completely astonished.

She'd planned to stick around, to ease Carrie into her first school experience. But her kid was more ready for school than Daisy was.

"She'll be fine," Miss Rosie had said, patting Daisy's shoulder as Carrie practically pushed her away. Daisy quickly found herself sitting in the Little Wonders parking lot, heaving loud sobs.

And now, at the Halloween parade, she found herself pushed to the back again, but this time it was against the crappy old historic barn that only housed vermin and the school's chicken coop. Shanna had settled into a folding chair next to Daisy's, but almost as soon as her Lululemon-covered butt hit the chair, she jumped up again.

"Oh! There's Cass and Rebecca! They're Charlie and Calvin's moms. I have to go ask them something about the next Parent Association meeting. Hold our seats, okay?"

And just like that, Shanna had danced across the yard toward two women whose smiles could not mask the bone-deep tiredness of having twin boys.

Daisy pulled at the sleeves of her cardigan—since the move she had been the recipient of a half dozen cardigans, pea coats, and puffy jackets, mostly from Robbie's well-meaning family. Everyone thought that as a transplant from LA, she'd be ill-equipped for a New England winter. But the sun was fighting its way through the clouds—and she missed the sun. The cardigan felt lumpy and unnecessary. So she shed it.

Daisy had beautiful arms. It was one of her favorite features. Perfect, strong shoulders, tapered wrists, muscles born of carrying her daughter around for the last three years. (The rest of her body had turned into Play-Doh, but her arms were in *amazing* shape.) Her tattoo artist loved them—she'd cried when she finished Daisy's sleeves, because she couldn't work on such great arms anymore.

It felt good to let her best side out, for once.

She'd sat in the sun for some minutes, letting the mass confusion of a preschool event wash over her. She scanned the crowd for Shanna. There she was, now talking to . . . oh god, which dad was that? He was setting up a sound system and doing it wrong.

Daisy was half a step from leaving their chairs to go tell him how to fix it. She knew her way around AV cables. But then she stopped. Shanna wanted her to save these seats.

Normally, she would have marched over and cheerfully offered her assistance. But she was still learning the landscape. Of Little Wonders. Of Needleton. Hell, of the entire northeastern quadrant of the United States. So, she stayed where she was.

Suddenly, there had been a commotion. The parade was starting up. A tiny little Captain America was peeking out of the doors of the school.

And everyone's phones went up, at the ready.

Daisy raised hers, too.

And on days when her daughter was dressed in her hand-made General Leia Organa costume, complete with headband ear buns, she was glad she had the convenient phone instead of the bulky equipment she'd used for work in her previous life.

As she raised the phone to eye level, turned on the camera app, and zoomed the camera in (gah, they were stupidly far away from the parade route), Shanna had approached from the crowd.

But Shanna hadn't been looking at her.

Shanna had been looking beyond her.

"Oh. My . . ."

And that's when it happened. Daisy whipped her head around.

She also whipped her camera phone around.

"Is that . . . ," she said in the barest whisper. Her phone auto-focused on Quinn Barrett, who stood around the corner of the ancient vermin shed, looking like she might murder the small child in the fireman's helmet she was standing in front of.

Then, they watched as Quinn picked up a (surprisingly cool and well-constructed) chrome-painted spaceship and tossed it to the ground. Then she had an epic rage-out, punctuating each of her words with a stomp on the poor silver cardboard.

". . . And if you"—STOMP—"Don't want it"—STOMP—"You don't get to have it!"

Daisy cringed at every word. But she couldn't tear her eyes or her phone away.

And when Quinn Barrett's foot got caught, and she windmilled to keep her balance—well . . . it was really, *really* hard not to laugh.

Daisy wasn't the only one who found it funny, because she heard Shanna, behind her, snort into her hand.

When the wailing cry of *"MY SPAAAAAAAACEEEEEE-SHIIIIP!!!!!"* went up, Shanna pulled Daisy back around the corner, hiding them from view.

"She's looking over," Shanna whispered. "Act cool, act cool."

Daisy hadn't been told to act cool since she was under the bleachers vomiting up the cafeteria lunch after one hit from her high school friend's itty-bitty joint, but she did as she was told, holding silent as a church mouse until Shanna moved, peeking her head back around the side of the historic house.

"They're gone." Shanna exhaled. "Ohmigod, did you get it?"

"Get it?" Daisy said, bewildered.

"On your phone. Did you record that?"

"Oh! Um . . ." Daisy looked down at her hand. Yes, her phone had been up. And yes, she had hit Record. So, yes, the thirty-five seconds of pure parental freak-out from one of the most uptight people she'd ever seen had been recorded for all posterity on her phone.

"Ohmigod, you have to email that to me," Shanna said, juicy delight in her eyes. "Not for, like, public consumption, but I *have* to show Jamie, he wouldn't believe it."

Daisy hid the phone behind her back. "Actually, I hadn't pressed Record yet, sorry." For some reason she didn't trust Shanna with something so damning. Daisy didn't have any love for Quinn Barrett—hell, she didn't even *know* Quinn Barrett beyond the fact that she was scary and made Daisy feel like a naive kid for having the audacity to move chairs without having signed up to do so—but giving it to Shanna seemed . . . cruel somehow.

Even though Shanna was her cousin-in-law. And friend.

A shiver ran up Daisy's spine.

"You cold?" Shanna asked, bending down. "Here, put on your sweater. New England weather will sneak up on you."

Daisy felt Shanna's eyes on her tattoos as she took the sweater from her. Everyone always stared. Usually they were her favorite conversation starter. But here, in Needleton, no one seemed to want to have that conversation.

But the sun had gone behind some big puffy fall clouds. She was legit chilly.

"Look, there's Rob and Jamie!" Shanna said, waving to the two men who looked more like twin brothers than cousins and who were waist deep in children as they cut across the parade route.

Seeing Rob in his work uniform of Red Sox hat, chambray shirt, and workman's pants sent a little zing through her heart. His eyes met hers, and he grinned wide, sending the zing shooting all over.

And just like that, the video, the incident, was all but forgotten.

"Come on," Shanna said, taking Daisy's hand, "let's move up toward the front. I can't see anything of the parade from back here."

That night, Daisy emerged from Carrie's room, stepping down into the basement of Rob's grandfather's house, where she found Rob snoring softly on the ancient plaid pull-out couch.

It had been less than a month that they had been crashing at Rob's grandpa's house, but damned if that couch didn't envelop Rob's body like an ex-lover. If it wasn't an inanimate object, Daisy might be jealous.

She smiled and lightly shook his foot, causing him to wake up with a jolt and a snort.

"Jesus!" he said, pressing his hand to his heart. "I thought it was an earthquake."

"Nope, sorry," Daisy replied. "This side of the country is quake free."

"Just another bonus of moving." Rob sat up and placed a kiss on Daisy's temple as she slid into the seat next to him.

"She go down?" he asked.

"Eventually," Daisy replied.

"I thought the parade and dance party would have taken it out of her . . . ," Rob replied.

"Not our girl—she feeds off other people's energy like a vampire."

They had come back from the Halloween parade and dance party in high spirits. Carrie had lead-jockeyed her way to the front of the line of the Tadpole Room and marched the parade route like a majorette with an invisible baton. (Thank God Princess Leia never wielded a light saber, else more than one person would have lost an eye.)

Then had come the dance party in their little auditorium. In which Carrie Organa Stone had taken the floor and did not leave it for two hours, only pausing to refuel on juice boxes and non-GMO popcorn. Rob had been her favorite dance partner and demanded that he do the *Dirty Dancing* lift (she had seen the ending dance sequence of that movie on YouTube, and it had quickly became an obsession), which set off a chain reaction of other little girls—and most of the boys—demanding their parents do the *Dirty Dancing* lift. Someone even managed to queue up the song.

Rob's cousin Jamie had jokingly said that he would send Rob his chiropractor bills.

Shanna chimed in, saying she would send along Jordan's plastic surgeon bills if Jordan got hurt.

Daisy didn't think she was joking.

Daisy and Rob fully expected Carrie to fall asleep in the car. Instead, Carrie brought the party home with her.

"Monster-mash dance!" Carrie had run around the tiny living room yelling. So they monster-mashed through the evening. Which was supposed to exhaust her, but instead Carrie was too keyed up for bed, so Daisy had to lie next to her daughter scrunched onto the "big girl" twin bed until she was 100 percent asleep.

When they'd moved east, they left the cribs and the baby gates behind, and let her sleep in the twin bed in Rob's grandpa's guest room. Which meant that if she wasn't 100 percent asleep when Daisy left the room, there was no obstacle to Carrie climbing out of her big girl bed to seek out her parents in their slim few hours of personal time, and then there was no alternative but to restart bedtime from the beginning.

"Today was great, wasn't it?" Rob said, stifling a yawn and giving her a grin. "Picture-perfect Halloween parade. Complete with crunchy leaves and a cool breeze. And not ninety-five degrees in October."

"Yeah," Daisy said, trying for the enthusiasm she didn't feel.

"I don't suppose you'd wanna do some monster-mashing with me," Rob said, leaning against her shoulder, giving her ear a kiss.

Daisy raised an eyebrow. "You can't even stand."

"I don't need to stand, that's the beauty of it."

Daisy's mind ran through all the stuff she had to do. Clean out the lunch box, clean the kitchen, run the dishwasher, get a head start on the laundry, email Carrie's pediatrician about that weird rash on her ankle (probably poison ivy since it grew in the woods behind the house, Rob said), make sure Carrie's soccer clothes were ready for tomorrow's practice, prep for trick or treaters, and search through a thousand listings online for a place for them to live that they could conceivably afford.

They couldn't stay in Rob's grandfather's basement forever.

Not to mention figure out how to build her career in a place three thousand miles away from her comfort zone.

But, she thought, as Rob slid a finger up her arm and then underneath her bra strap, letting it fall to the side, it *was* Friday night.

The lunch box and stuff could certainly wait until tomorrow morning.

HALF AN HOUR later, Rob was blissfully asleep, in that post-coital coma that he stereotypically excelled at. How he managed such boyish abandon after having sex in his grandfather's basement, Daisy did not know. He must have just simply felt at home.

Daisy stretched her neck, rubbed her eyes. She could have joined him in sleep. The fold-out couch was surprisingly comfortable, sunk into compliance by decades of use. And her body was certainly tired—completely wrung out by the day, week, month that she'd endured. But her mind would not quiet.

She had been so nervous about today. Not about Carrie having a good time—Carrie was her sweet, happy, interested girl who found a way to make almost anything fun. It could have thunderstormed and Carrie would have still had the time of her short life.

No—she had been nervous about herself.

This was something she would never admit to Rob. He thought the move from Los Angeles had been as smooth as cream cheese. He loved his new job. He loved being in Needleton, near his family. He even loved the freaking fall, from the foliage to the genuine need for knit scarves.

So what if Daisy felt like she was drowning in a sea of uncertainty every time she stepped out of this house?

Daisy didn't fit in—which, honestly, wasn't new. She had never even fit in with her own family back in Houston.

Her sister was a cheerleader. Her mother a penny-pinching homemaker. Her brother led their school to the state soccer semifinals. And Daisy . . .

She was the proverbial bespeckled nerd. She gravitated to the library, to comic books, to the tech crew of the theater department . . . and to the movie theater.

She loved movies. She lost herself in them, going to the theater two, three, four times in a row on weekends. She loved sci-fi best, and when, at eight years old, she'd heard that first blare of a trumpet in the *Star Wars* opening sequence, she fell madly, truly, and deeply in love.

Daisy did well in school itself. So, there was no question about going to college, not when it was the only thing her parents thought about, scrimping and saving so their kids would have better lives than they did. But Daisy didn't choose the nice, safe, state university her sister and brother had. She got a partial scholarship to USC and never looked back.

At first, Daisy thought Los Angeles was going to be basically the same as Houston: pretty people made of money, everyone trying to be—or at least befriend—a Kardashian. And there were those people. But Daisy also discovered a much larger side of the city—this wonderful, weird part of Los Angeles that reveled in nerdiness, celebrated your passions, and delighted in being different.

People who loved Funko pop figurines and then got to design them.

People who wrote twisted dark plays about humanity's grunginess and then Hallmark movies about a pair of rivals who fall in love at a harvest festival, with equal eagerness and delight.

People who spent their high school days doodling Wolverine in notebooks, and now drew X-Men comics for a living.

In LA, she found her tribe.

She dyed her dark brown hair—first time she went red, dipping her toes into the world of self-alteration, but quickly moved beyond natural shades to pink, aqua, and her favorite electric blue.

Her mom nearly had a heart attack when she came home for Thanksgiving.

She got her first tattoo. A Rebel Alliance symbol.

She finally took an interest in makeup—not because she wanted to "put her best face forward," as her mother had always called it, but because she'd started dabbling in cosplay.

She went back to Houston for her sister's very Houston wedding and came to the realization that Los Angeles was home.

In college, she played her first D&D game. By the time she graduated, she was Dungeon Master of her own game, which fired her imagination, played up her organizational skills, and catered to her love of masterminding from behind the scenes—thank you, high school tech crew. She combed through the 5e sourcebooks the second they were released like it was a lost tablet from Mount Sinai, containing all the secrets to running the world.

She'd even tinkered with writing her own *Star Wars*–based homebrew setting. Unlicensed, of course, but oh, so much fun living in that world!

And that was how she'd met Rob.

She'd been working in Los Angeles for a couple of years by then, having graduated from college and worked in TV production, going from job to job as a set PA, with a walkie-talkie on her hip and starry-eyed ambition. And as she did this, she met more and more people, some of whom played D&D. And everyone wanted a good Dungeon Master—someone to script and guide them through a game.

So, she started DMing campaigns on the side—mostly for fun, although sometimes she got paid. It was at one of these games that she'd met Rob. Among the players of her recent game was a newbie—a D&D virgin with a crooked smile and a Red Sox baseball cap who took one look at Daisy and claimed the seat next to hers. To "learn better," or so Rob had claimed at the time. Later he admitted to his nefarious scheme of trying to get her to laugh at his jokes.

Which she did.

Rob was funny. And sweet. And fun. A classic chaotic good, excited to take on the world. He'd come out to LA after college, like so many do, planning on being the next Steven Spielberg. Sure, he was working at a commercial production company at that moment, shooting close-ups of juicy chicken for Olive Garden commercials—but it was all a stepping stone, right?

They fell in love hard and fast. Rob had never been with anyone like Daisy, and vice versa. To Rob, Daisy was just so bright, so passionate, so interested in everything. And to Daisy, Rob was just so steady, so practical, so easy to be around. She just wanted to be around him all the time.

Their wedding was festive and silly, and she marched down the aisle to the Throne Room music from *Star Wars*. Both their families seemed perplexed, but his family seemed happy that he was happy with her, and when her mother had a drink or three too many, she confessed that she was just happy that Daisy ended up with a man. Because apparently Daisy's disdain for high school football players and her one camping trip to Joshua Tree had cemented her lesbianship in her parents' minds.

They settled into a little apartment and intended to work their way into the center of the Hollywood industrial complex. Rob got another stepping-stone job at an event company. Daisy freelanced her heart out.

But then Daisy got pregnant.

It wasn't planned. But they were both extremely happy. Rob's father had passed when he was still in college, so he was ecstatic to build a family. They'd spent weeks playing around with names, but as soon as they learned it was a girl, Daisy knew she was naming her daughter after Carrie Fisher. (The fact that the star of the new *Star Wars* franchise was a Daisy just made everything feel full circle.)

But as Daisy's work was all freelance, Rob's stepping stone of a job became their steady source of income and health insurance. Providing for those practicalities got in the way of Rob's ambition, no matter how many times Daisy told Rob she wanted him to do work that made him happy.

He always replied that Daisy and Carrie made him happy.

But she knew he needed more. She knew that the longer

he stayed at the event-coordinating job, setting up parties and press for other people's stories instead of pursuing his own dreams, Rob was getting more cynical. More unhappy.

And more and more, he talked about where he grew up. Needleton, Massachusetts. He told her the history of the town—how it had been founded around an ironworks that had ended up becoming known for manufacturing needles. (Hence, Needleton.) How the old buildings—the mill, the smithy, the town hall—all still stood, and always would.

He told her his childhood had been idyllic—playing in the woods for hours on end; building forts with the neighborhood kids; sports, games, and having space enough to breathe. Nothing like the hot, heavy air in the Valley. Not like the microyards and the dust that settled over everything. And any ambitions he had then were in the future, just waiting to be picked out of the sky. He missed home. He missed what family he still had, he whispered late at night before he fell asleep.

It didn't help his rose-colored hindsight that Daisy had been looking for work for a while. When Carrie was born, Daisy found herself out of the freelance production business for a time. And it was increasingly difficult to slide back in. Money was tight, and she could still DM games—but those were hours and hours long, sometimes whole days, and not very much money. Certainly not enough to justify all the work she put into it.

Then the Scary Thing happened.

And Daisy had been knocked off her axis of where she felt safe, and at home.

So Rob started looking at jobs back east in earnest.

Daisy honestly didn't know if Rob actually expected to get one.

Then, lightning struck.

An old contact worked freelance for a guy who sometimes helped out on a local Boston PBS show, *The Antique Home*.

This was Robbie's favorite show. He'd watched since he was a kid, in his grandfather's basement, on an ugly plaid couch thirty feet from his grandpa's amateur woodworking setup. They were starting a spin-off series—*The Brand New Home*, where they would build a house from foundation to faucets— and needed a film crew.

Daisy had a friend with a connection to *The Antique Home* and told Daisy to submit her resumé.

And Daisy told Rob to submit his.

She didn't mind, really, handing over the opportunity to him. Daisy had Carrie to think of. And it was Rob's show. It was Rob's dream. When you're married, she knew, you sometimes had to put your partner's happiness above your own.

And he got it.

"It was the best interview of my life, Daze," Rob had said on the phone. "After my interview with the producers I got to meet Jo-Jo" (Jo-Jo was the carpenter on the program, the son of Joe Senior, who had been the original carpenter in the seventies), "and I showed him pictures of my latest guitar and he said it had to be me! I'm the new production manager for *The Brand New Home!*"

So . . . they did it. Rob came back, gave two weeks' notice. Then, they packed up everything, said goodbye to their friends, and drove with little Carrie in their fifteen-year-old RAV4 across the country to Needleton, Massachusetts.

Daisy's Los Angeles existence, the first place she'd truly felt at home, was left in the rearview mirror.

The idea was that they would give it a year. Just enough time to decide whether Rob was a good fit for the job, if

Daisy was going to be able to find work, if Carrie was going to adjust, if they would find a place to live, if they would be happy. And if they weren't . . .

But Daisy knew within two days, with a sinking heart, that they were staying.

The job was perfect. Rob was so happy, actually making a show he cared about. And since it was public television, it paid an absolute pittance.

So, here she was. Carrie sleeping upstairs, Grandpa Bob snoring so loudly she could hear him two floors away, and a husband passed out blissfully, Daisy scrolled through the Needleton housing market, replete with new construction McMansions with tray ceilings and three-car garages, the familiar wave of helplessness settling over her like a scratchy old blanket.

Needleton, for all its working-class needle-factory roots, had evolved into a town filled with doctors, lawyers, and moneymakers who wanted nothing more than the protective bubble of a bucolic existence for their families. And were willing to pay very, very well for it.

And of course Daisy wanted that same bubble to protect her daughter—but jeez, even Grandpa Bob's hadn't-been-touched-since-the-seventies two-bedroom would go for many more zeroes than they had in their bank account.

Looking at all the fancy marble countertop kitchens and upstairs-and-downstairs laundry rooms made Daisy just miss their little apartment in North Hollywood all the more. Miss her job(s). Miss her friends. Miss . . . just fitting in.

Daisy had an unconventional look, she knew that. She knew she had created who she wanted to be, what she wanted to look like, and it was a source of confidence to her.

At least . . . it was in LA.

In LA, she fit in.

In Boston—or at least parts of it—she undoubtedly fit in. Heck, in suburbs across the vast swath of the country, she would probably fit in without much second-glancing.

But in Needleton—AKA colonial Stepford—she very much did not fit in.

She thought back to the parade that day, the way people glanced at her arms, and the number of cardigans she'd received since coming here.

The chill didn't come just from the weather. And it made her crave the LA sun all the more.

Just as she was feeling wistful enough to type "Los Angeles" into the real estate website's search bar, a message window popped up on her computer.

Sarah Prime: Hey, girl! What are you doing up?

Daisy's face spread into a wide grin. Sarah Prime was really Sarah Desantis—they had been friends since freshman year of college, on the same floor of the dorm. Over the course of the next several years, their circle of friends expanded to include several other Sarahs. But for Daisy, her first Sarah would always be Sarah Prime.

Darth Daisy: Me? What about you? Aren't your players supposed to be saving their village from hordes of orcs right now?

Sarah Prime: Danny had to go out of town for work and Martin's apartment is being fumigated for termites, so we decided to postpone the campaign until we could all be there.

Darth Daisy: Can't do without a ranger and a cleric for one
  measly week?

Sarah Prime: We are facing a three-headed gleeok next,
  so we need all our rangers and clerics.

When Daisy had left Los Angeles, she had handed Sarah
Prime the responsibility of Dungeon Mastering the end of
their ongoing campaign. She was a little confused, as she
hadn't had a gleeok dragon—let alone a triple-headed one—
in what she'd built. But it was Sarah's campaign now. She
can face off against however many dragons she wants, Daisy
thought reluctantly.

Sarah Prime: Besides, it's Halloween! I have a party or five
  to attend.

Daisy felt tired and sad at the same time. How she missed
going to all those Halloween parties! And how utterly exhausting it sounded!

Sarah Prime: How're the stiff upper lips of New England?

Daisy was about to give Sarah Prime the polite version of
how she was feeling (oh, it's very nice here, I miss you all so
much, but Carrie loves it, we're doing good) and she actually
got halfway through typing it, but then . . . she stopped herself.
    God, if she couldn't confess how she was feeling to her
friends, who could she talk to?

Darth Daisy: Well . . .

It all spilled out of her. The Halloween parade. Grandpa Bob's basement. Missing Los Angeles at Halloween—especially at Halloween, she loved the way LA did Halloween! Crazy decorations, kids packed on the streets, costume stores every fifty feet. And basically just feeling like the world's least impressive mom, behind the ball in everything, especially at Little Wonders.

By the time she got to the fact that Little Wonders had a Slack, Sarah Prime's entire message block was just filled with emojis that were either laugh-crying or fuming with anger.

Darth Daisy: I swear to god I've never seen people this uptight and crazy in my life. Needleton moms are no joke.

Sarah Prime: And you used to work in Hollywood! Seriously—there's no way they are more uptight than Vanessa.

Daisy and Sarah Prime's good friend Allie was personal assistant to one Vanessa Faire, star of *Fargone*, which had been Daisy's favorite sci-fi show until Allie started telling her all about Vanessa's diva-ish behavior. A few seasons ago, Vanessa had notoriously lost her cool while filming the season finale, while press was visiting the set. Ever since then, Vanessa had gotten more uptight, and in Daisy's opinion, the show had really gone downhill.

But Allie always had the most hysterical and exasperating stories about her boss. Hence, the barometer of crazy in their friend group was set by "Is this something Vanessa would do?"

Darth Daisy: Oh, I've witnessed things that can rival even Vanessa's craziness.

Sarah Prime: No way. Pics or it didn't happen.

Daisy snorted out a laugh. Sarah wanted pics? She had better than pics. She had video.

She went into the cloud and plucked the Halloween parade video out of her files. Then, she trimmed the edges—no one needed to see her bad camera work as she tried to capture the kids parading and the camera kept accidentally rack-focusing to Shanna or other parents. She set the start point at when Shanna said a juicy "*Oh. My.*" and the camera swung and found Quinn Barrett losing it on that poor misbegotten cardboard spaceship.

It was twenty seconds long, but that was all anyone needed to see.

Darth Daisy: Meet the head of the Parent Association at school.

Exactly thirty-seven seconds after she posted it, Sarah Prime responded.

Sarah Prime: OHMYGOD.

Then . . .

LOL!!!!! OMG that's hysterical

Darth Daisy: Seriously! That poor kid. And that mom . . . she's gotta live with the memory of doing that forever.

Sarah Prime: Are you kidding? Someone like that is just gonna take a Xanny with her cabernet and deny it ever happened. Hey, can I show this to Allie and Juliana? They will die.

There were no secrets in their tight little group, so Daisy didn't even think twice.

Darth Daisy: Of course.

Sarah Prime: Oh my god, did Allie tell you all about V's latest meltdown? Apparently, that asshole she's dating, Sebastian, well, he's got his kid for the weekend, and Vanessa loses it when the kid drops something on the rug—

As Sarah Prime began to download her on the latest secondhand madness of one particular rich and somewhat famous person, Daisy began to finally feel a little bit more like herself. As if they were sitting in Sarah Prime's squashy living room in Santa Monica, two bottles of wine in on that rare girls' night, unwinding with her friends. But then, Sarah Prime had a Halloween party to get ready for (though she said she'd wanted to talk to Daisy more than she wanted to party, which made her feel so warm and fuzzy and guilty) and quickly Daisy found herself alone again, in her husband's grandfather's basement, as everyone else in the house snored away. Content. Happy. Comfortable.

Everyone, except Daisy.

But now at least, she was bone tired enough to lie down next to Rob, let him throw a sleepy arm around her, warming her into sleep.

Little Wonders Preschool
November Newsletter

Hello, WONDER-ful parents!

Halloween is behind us and Thanksgiving is ahead, so we are all getting cozy for the holidays!

~~Thank effing God that's over. But seriously, you thought you were getting a break? You thought wrong, bitches.~~

The Thanksgiving play will be performed on Tuesday, November 24th—all the classrooms are working hard to make it a special day and parent volunteers are needed to help make decorations and costumes! Sign up online or in the school's lobby and get your glue guns ready! ~~We let the Target costumes go for Halloween, but we expect some artisan shit for Thanksgiving.~~

Please note, rehearsals will take the place of classroom yoga for November, as Ms. Jubilee will be on maternity leave.

While our hallways are going to be decked out with peaceful Pilgrims and harmonious Native Americans for the next few weeks, ~~don't worry your kids will get the real history in a decade or so, let them enjoy their childhoods for now,~~ we at the Parent Association are looking ahead to the big month of December. Our next meeting is this coming **Wednesday, November 4th** ~~which I bolded so you dimwits can't pretend you didn't see it~~ and we will be organizing, organizing, organizing! ~~Here, have another committee. You know you want it.~~

And of course, I know everyone wants to make sure the holiday season is one filled with laughter and learning. So we are going to be introducing an intensive holiday season primer for all classroom levels, showcasing different cultures, different traditions. ~~December isn't all about Santa, people.~~ Every parent should be prepared to contribute to the festivities, be it volunteering, or through you own special skills. We'd love to see how your family celebrates! ~~I mean sure, but really, we want money.~~

Also, our big event, the Winter Breakfast Party, is going to be lit! ~~I heard my niece say that and I assume it's cool.~~ We are striving to outdo last year's successes and look forward to hearing your ideas, to make it the most culturally diverse and fun party we can throw for the kids!

~~But yeah, Santa is totally going to visit the school, and this year, we'd like to spring for one with a real beard, so get ready to pony up.~~

We look forward to seeing everyone at the next Parent Association meeting! ~~Show up. Show up or you're ruining your kids' lives.~~

Together in Parenting!
Suzy Breakman-Kang
Parent Association Secretary

Addendum: this notice was composed previous to the startling realization that our Little Wonders had been brought to national attention, in a less than stellar light. This occurrence, as well as our usual holiday planning, will be under discussion at the November 4th Parent Association meeting. ~~Holy shit did you guys see that video?~~

CHAPTER THREE

Monday morning arrived as normally as possible.

Ham had slept in his Halloween costume for the second night in a row. He was happy to be a spaceman (sans spaceship, which had been unceremoniously trash-compacted as soon as they got home) once he figured out people would give him candy if he was wearing it. And bonus, while he was wearing the costume, he was super conscious of not wanting to get it messy, so he was incredibly aware of when he had to pee. They'd had a blissful weekend without a single potty accident.

And considering her mother had been visiting, and they'd survived that—without Alba!—Halloween weekend was nothing but a resounding success in the Barrett household.

Sure there was the inevitable, breezy evaluation by her mother—the arrangement of the décor, her giddy explanation of her latest hobby (she was opening an Etsy store), the lamenting of Quinn's bob-length haircut (again—it had been a year, for heaven's sake), and the puzzlement over why Ham wasn't wearing the "fun car thing you posted on Facebook," but that was all bearable with a rictus grin and the knowledge that once Ham went to bed there was a bottle of chardonnay with her name on it.

Thank God her mother got on a plane—back to Orlando and her Etsy store—Sunday afternoon.

But yes, all in all, a successful Halloween weekend.

But then came Monday morning.

"I WANT TO WEAR MY SPACE SUIT!"

"I'm sorry, Hammy, Halloween's over, we can't wear it to school."

"I don't want to go to school!!!"

Yup, just your average Monday morning.

Ham had been happy while getting dressed. Happy eating his organic eggs (thank god for food delivery services, since they were sans Alba) and happy while they piled in the car. But somewhere between pulling out of the driveway and the stop sign at the end of the street, he had realized he was no longer garbed in his shiny and somewhat smelly space suit.

But as Hamilton was strapped in his five-point harness car seat, there was little he could do about it besides cry. And as Quinn was running a half Parcel ahead of schedule, she had time for their Monday morning ritual.

"Hammy, it's Monday! What are we going to be today?"

". . . Spaceman . . ."

Quinn turned down the radio, which was going on about some new viral video or some such nonsense and caught her son's eye in the rearview mirror.

"Hammy, what are we going to be today?"

Ham sighed and recited their Mommy/Ham mantra.

"We're going to be good."

"That's right, bud. And what happens when we're good?"

"We get better."

"Exactly. And when we get better?"

"We get perfect."

"That's right! And there's nothing better than perfect."

"There's nothing better than perfect," he repeated.

It was a mantra she had come up with in college, but she had been working on it her entire life.

Growing up in the middle of nowhere Ohio, there wasn't a lot to do. But her mother, somehow, found every hobby under the sun, from ceramic arts to fabric dying to book binding to tango dancing. Each of these passions would last about six months, until she got bored and moved on. The same way she had with boyfriends.

Meanwhile, Quinn was left craving consistency.

It wasn't until she had escaped to college in Boston that she realized her mother hadn't gotten bored—she had gotten scared, reaching juuuust the point that it became challenging. So she gave up.

Quinn had been determined to NOT be like her mother in any regard, especially this. So, her mantra came into being.

First, I will be good.

Then, I will be better.

Then, I will be perfect.

And when she had met Stuart, a born and bred Bostonian med student, practicing his intubations and blood draws, he'd found her mantra almost as sexy as he'd found Quinn.

"Mommy's gonna try to be good today," she said to Ham as they drove. "So she gets better, and then gets perfect. I'm going to listen to my friends and the people at the office. What are you going to do, Hammy?"

"I'm going to listen to Ms. Rosie and my friends at school," Ham said, and this time he did it with a smile on his face. His missing space suit was forgotten, and once they pulled up to

Little Wonders, he hopped out of the car and merrily trotted forward, eager to start the day.

Quinn smiled at everyone she passed and tried not to smile smugly at their shocked looks. That's right—she had a three-year-old who was happy to go to school on Monday, while everyone else was dealing with clingers and criers. But when she walked into the Tadpole classroom, she herself was a little perturbed by Ms. Rosie.

"Oh! Mrs. Barrett!" Ms. Rosie said, staring at her like an owl. "You're . . . here!"

"Of course I'm here, it's Monday," Quinn said, bemused. Ms. Rosie looked so caught off guard, and then Quinn saw it—the phone in Ms. Rosie's pocket. Teachers were not supposed to be on their phones except on breaks.

Normally, Quinn would have frowned on that behavior. But class had barely begun, and she was still a couple minutes ahead in her Parcel, so she was feeling benevolent. But also a little cheeky.

"Catching up on the news after a busy weekend?" she said, letting her eyes fall to the pocketed phone. Ms. Rosie turned ghost white. "Don't worry," Quinn said, conspiratorially. "I won't tell if you won't."

Quinn bent down and gave Ham a big hug and a kiss (her heart only broke the usual amount at his "Bye, Mommy! Have a good day at the office!") and had turned to go when Ms. Rosie reached out and took her arm.

"Mrs. Barrett," she said, earnest. "We've all had those days."

Quinn nodded, a little nonplussed. Goodness, one would think she was the Gestapo, about to turn in her son's favorite teacher for something as small as an email check. She wasn't *that* hard-nosed, after all.

"You're right, we have. It's not a problem, but you probably should avoid your phone during work hours. Sound good?"

Ms. Rosie blinked twice, frowned, and then nodded slowly.

"Have a great day!" she called back, as she walked out the door, her peripheral vision catching a glimpse of her son playing with blocks with Elia, who was attempting to hug him, as per usual.

Really, someone needed to teach that girl about consent and personal space. Maybe she should introduce an "Understanding Your Body" initiative for the kids at the next Parent Association meeting.

She mused on that idea, dictating her thoughts into her phone's voice memos, while she drove into the office, finding that miracle pocket of no traffic to travel in and arriving at her desk in record time.

Heck, she thought, as she strolled through the main floor of Crabbe and Co. Interior Design services, her Monday morning had gone from "pretty normal" to "surprisingly good" in record time.

It wasn't hyperbole to say that Quinn adored her job. She'd landed at Crabbe and Co. directly after college, where her English degree was useful only in that she knew how to type.

But Jeremy Crabbe, the owner and son of the original founder, had seen her outfit, and decided she was chic enough to work in the front office. Quinn had absorbed everything she could, worked her ass off, got some attention from Jeremy.

Interestingly, her mother's slight interest in everything had given Quinn a solid foundation for design work—she knew just enough about sewing, just enough about color theory, just enough about carpentry to impress Jeremy.

He'd let her work on sites. Doing installs, adding touches

to the design. Then she got her first client of her own to do a small job, and she'd been a designer there ever since.

Crabbe and Co. was as much her home as Hamilton and Stuart were.

Every morning, when she walked into the office, she felt that little punch of pride that came from being good at her job. And she knew too that she was envied.

"Good morning, Sutton," she said, passing her young co-worker's desk.

Sutton, who was staring at her computer with her hands on the back of her head, holding back her long hair in the hungover posture of someone who looked like she might puke at any second, did a double take when she saw Quinn.

"Looks like someone didn't make it to spin class this morning," Quinn said, with just enough bemused admonishment for a mentor to deliver. She had taken Sutton under her wing when she'd first interviewed her for an assistant gig nearly two years ago. Everything that Jeremy Crabbe had done for her, she tried to do for Sutton. And it had paid off, as Sutton had just been promoted to working on Quinn's design team instead of for it.

It felt good to be beneficent with the youth, Quinn surmised. Noblesse oblige. Even when said youth had no doubt rolled into work hungover from a raucous weekend of Halloween parties.

"Oh! Oh god, Quinn!" Sutton said, jumping to her feet and smoothing her hair out of her face. She was alarmingly alert and flush—okay, so not hungover. "What happened?"

Quinn for a second was completely lost. "What happened . . . ?"

"Friday!" Sutton said in a harsh whisper. "There was the parade at Hamilton's school, right? You called out because of it?"

Quinn's eyes went wide. She hadn't been at work on Friday. "Oh god—did something happen? With the Beacon Hill house?" Sutton had been calling her with updates all day, yes, but after the parade she turned off her phone for the weekend.

The Beacon Hill house was going to be the pinnacle of her career. Her calling card for the future. She was lead designer on the renovation of one of the most distinguished still privately owned residences in Boston.

It was what was going to turn Crabbe and Co. into Crabbe, Barrett, and Co. They were only a few weeks out from handing over the keys, and when all of her professional dreams would come true.

"No! The house is fine!" Sutton said in a rush. Then, "You mean you don't *know*?"

"Know what?" Quinn said, masking her impatience. Really, whatever amounted to drama in a twenty-six-year-old's life did not require this amount of anxiety. The poor girl was going to give herself wrinkles.

"You haven't checked your email yet!" Sutton was saying, practically smacking her forehead. "Because you don't do electronic devices on weekends?"

"Of course I haven't." Was that a good idea when she was working on such an important project? Maybe not, but Sutton had strict orders to call her landline if anything went wrong. Besides . . . it was for Hamilton's benefit that she maintain total presence in the moment. Even if her mind was on faucets and fixtures.

"Right—me neither. Because of your suggestion, I've been doing social media and nonwork emails detox on weekends, and I *just* saw it."

"Saw what?" What could have come through Sutton's email that had anything to do with Quinn?

OH. Oh NO. Quinn grabbed Sutton's arm back. "It's not the Martha Stewart article, is it?"

"No! I mean, the interviewer's questions arrived this morning for you to answer, but—"

"Oh! Oh, thank god," Quinn said, breathing a deep sigh of relief. If the Beacon Hill house was her greatest professional achievement, the *Martha Stewart Living* magazine article that was going to accompany it was more of a personal triumph.

Quinn *loved* Martha Stewart. When other ten-year-old girls were squealing about *NSYNC coming to Dayton on tour, she was sighing over Martha's latest magazine. In her distracted mother's house, Martha had become the ever patient, steady maternal force that had shaped Quinn's worldview.

So when *Martha Stewart Living* magazine had called and asked for a walk-through of the Beacon Hill house and its redesign plans, Quinn had nearly died. When they said they were going to do a six-page spread in their January issue of the finished house, Quinn required a defibrillator.

"They're here?!" Quinn said with glee. "The questions? Oh my god. Why didn't you tell me first thing?"

"Quinn, there's something else—you have to see—"

"Later, Sutton. I have an email from Martha Stewart to read!" She practically skipped to her office, leaving Sutton, and whatever drama was consuming her, in slack-jawed astonishment.

Quinn closed the door to her office and only then allowed herself to rush to her desk and boot up her computer.

It was then that the little red ball on her work email inbox caught her eye.

That couldn't be right—497 messages? Granted, she was in the final stages of the Beacon Hill house, with a million little decisions to be made and a million and one things that could go wrong, but that was still about four hundred more emails than she was expecting.

A dazzling thought occurred to her. Maybe her Instagram post with the spaceship costume had lots and lots of likes. Maybe it went "viral," as the kids said.

But . . . no, all of those emails would have gone to her *personal* email, not her work, and her personal email only had . . .

Quinn blinked. Refreshed the screen. How . . .

Her personal email had six hundred more messages.

For the first time, Quinn began to have a queasy, sour feeling in her stomach. Something very strange was going on, and her gut told her it wasn't good.

She went into her personal email first.

They were mostly social media notifications.

Strange, her social media was mostly limited to Instagram—just for photos of her design work and the occasional cutie-pie Halloween pic of Hamilton. She had Facebook, but didn't really give a fig about whatever high school acquaintance was pregnant, divorcing, or Republican. Twitter seemed filled with angry political activists and Snapchat was full of silly filters that made you look like an anime cat. Life was simply too short to get caught up in all of that nonsense. Quinn much preferred reality, being present in her own life.

So why did she have so many social media notifications?

She apprehensively opened up her Facebook.

The very first thing in her feed was a video. Called "Halloween Mom."

And there was a message under it. From one of her Facebook "friends."

Hey, Quinn—long time! When I first saw this I thought
it was you! Ha ha!

2d   Like   Reply   👍😊 25

The video started to autoplay.

It took several seconds for Quinn to realize what she was
looking at. She recognized the schoolyard first. The historic
old barn that loomed on one side of the foreground. Then
heard the voice.

"*Oh. My . . .*"

And then . . .

"Holy fuck," Quinn said.

CHAPTER FOUR

O h my god, Daisy—what did you *do?*"

The question had been running through Daisy's head for forty-eight hours straight. It had been playing on a panic loop from the second she opened Twitter on Sunday morning, hoping to see her friends' reactions to Carrie's Princess Leia costume. But instead of being greeted by the dopamine hit of hearts and likes to her picture series of Carrie, she found herself looking at a video.

Her video.

The Video.

On Twitter. How the hell was it on Twitter? Maybe it was a glitch, maybe her phone was malfunctioning, maybe she was still half asleep . . .

Although, she was very much awake at the moment. And that video . . . it was posted by a mommy blog she followed, that had reposted it from somewhere else. It had a caption beneath it: "Halloween takes another soul."

And of course, a ton of views. Somewhere in the vicinity of eighteen million. And climbing.

And then . . . there were the comments.

Who the hell would do this? People are awful!
1 10

What a bitch.
1 6 6

Someone call CPS?
4 7 24

When you need a coffee and a 47 hour massage, ha ha ha.
7 18 14

This kid's exhibit A in therapy, no doubt.
10 8 28

Halloween is a Godless time, and should not be celebrated, it should be condemned! At The Soul of Goodness Church, we–
28 41 59

The comments blended together after that, but Daisy got the gist.

She'd sprung out of bed. Everyone in the house was still asleep, thankfully. She typed a text into her phone—but in LA it was pre-dawn, and everyone would definitely still be asleep. But she couldn't wait. So she did the unthinkable, something reserved only for emergencies or the insane.

She called.

Sarah Prime had picked up on the fourth ring, sounding like a corpse resurrected from the dead.

"This had better not be some fucking robocall . . . ," Sarah croaked out.

"It's me, Sarah—what the hell happened?" she said in a whispered rush.

"Daisy?" Sarah's voice was immediately awake. "What is it? What's wrong? Is it Carrie?"

"It's the video!"

"The . . . video?" The grogginess was back.

"The one I . . ." The house heating system made a clunking noise, causing Rob to start, then roll over and go back to sleep. Daisy began to creep up the stairs, away from him. "The one I showed you. It's all over the internet."

"It's . . . what?"

"All. Over. The. Internet. Go online, check it out."

"Hold on," Sarah said, and Daisy waited impatiently, looking blankly into the fridge for some breakfast while Sarah got online.

"Oh! Uh . . . Morning, Daisy," she heard a startled Grandpa Bob say as he froze on his way down the steps. He was wearing a ratty old robe, which he was hastily tying shut to hide the tighty-whities he wore. Daisy turned quickly, but they both knew she'd seen.

"Erm, morning, Grandpa Bob," she said, "can I make you some coffee?"

"Ah, no, I'm okay. Just gonna get the paper." He ambled past her toward the front door, throwing it open to the harsh autumn air. As he retrieved his paper, and made for the bathroom just off the kitchen, he gave her a sheepish smile. "I, uh, forgot how cozy this house was, living by myself."

She smiled back as he shut the door. She willed herself to ignore the grunts and shuffles coming from that small room (*Turn. On. The. Fan*), as Sarah Prime's voice came back to her.

"I found it. Okay . . . so . . . it's online."

"It's not just online, it got picked up by a mommy blog I follow, that means it's going viral, and oh my god I just showed it to *you*, I didn't mean for it to go on the internet!" Daisy hissed. "What did you do?"

"Nothing! I just showed it to Allie and Juliana—"

"Why would you do that?"

"Uh, because you said I could," Sarah Prime bit out. "Just calm down, okay?"

"Calm down?" Everything spilled out of her in a rush. "I have to, like . . . live here now! That kid is in Carrie's class at school, that mom runs the Parent Association, and it's on the internet now!?"

"Daisy, I didn't post it!"

"One of you guys did!"

"None of us would do that," Sarah said, but Daisy wasn't so sure. They didn't know. They didn't get it. The delicate social balance of parenting that Daisy was blundering through. The high school atmosphere that permeated the parents of preschoolers. The need to protect, to be polite. Judgementalness came in the parenthood starter pack.

The baseline was that one of them thought it was funny and didn't think about the consequences. For Daisy. For Carrie. For the kid on the video. Even for Quinn Barrett.

It took her a minute because she didn't want Sarah to hear the quiver of a sob that would no doubt escape if she did anything other than breathe.

"Daisy, don't worry—we'll figure out what happened, okay?"

Daisy took another deep breath. "Okay."

And they did figure it out. Sarah had roused the troops. It was so early in LA, and still basically Halloween, not everyone had gone to sleep yet. Juliana was still out. Allie was still drunk.

And Allie's drunkenness turned out to be the culprit. She was the only one who'd shared the video.

"I'm soooooooo sorrrrry, Daze," Allie said, practically weeping on the phone. "I showed the video to Vanesssss . . . Vanessa . . . she was freaking out about being a good stepmom—like, she's not even married to S'bastian, she's not really a mom, you know? So I showed her your video, and then like, I was at a party last night—no, wait . . . two nights ago? Ugh, I was a butterfly, but like a cool one, Jules did my makeup, it was awesome."

"Allie, stay on point," Daisy clipped out.

"Right . . . right. I was at a party and Vanessa texted and asked if I could send her the video so she could show it to someone. I figured you wouldn't mind because you shared it with us, right? I thought she was gonna show it to S'bastard or somebody, not like . . . the world."

Daisy wanted to rail against Allie. But what Allie said stopped her. Daisy'd been the one to share the video with her friends. She didn't delete it like she'd told herself she would.

She could have laid into her friend, but that would have been passing the buck—and the buck belonged all to Daisy.

"Thanks, Allie," she said instead. The sky had been well awake by then, she could hear Carrie stirring in her bedroom, and Grandpa Bob's flush and fan (thankfully) switched on, indicating he was done with the paper. "I just need to figure out how to handle it now."

But as Sunday moved into Monday, she began to realize there was nothing she could do. It had been shared so widely, that taking one down—even the first one—wasn't going to do anything. Allie had said she'd try to coax Vanessa into taking down her original post (it tried for relatable with, "Found this online! We've all had one of these days, right, mommies and stepmommies?"), but Vanessa was incredibly touchy about being told she was wrong, as Allie said.

By the time she picked up Carrie after school on Monday, it was with the increasingly claustrophobic weight of knowing that everyone had seen the video, and she was the one to blame for it.

"Oh my god, Daisy—what did you do?"

Yes, Daisy had been asking herself that question all weekend. But this was the first time someone else had asked it.

"Shanna," Daisy said in a rushed whisper. "I don't . . . I can't . . ."

Daisy grabbed at Shanna's arm, and pulled her down the hall, away from the other parents doing pickup. Everyone else was talking in excited whispers with each other—no doubt having seen the video—so Daisy and Shanna went unnoticed. She opened a random door—it was that little closet-room place that was used for Parent Association storage. And it was blissfully empty.

For a second, Daisy couldn't do anything but stare at Shanna. And then she threw her arms around the other woman.

Shanna stiffened in shock, but then relented and patted Daisy's back. It was a small relief—in truth, Daisy had completely forgotten that she'd lied to Shanna and said she hadn't taped anything at the parade. But Shanna had no doubt sussed out that little lie the second the video hit her Facebook feed.

After a moment, Shanna pulled back. "Okay, that's more groping in a closet than I've done since middle school. Daisy, what happened?"

Daisy gave her the full rundown. Feeling isolated, talking to her friends late at night, and just showing them the video, and then someone else showed it to someone else and it got posted.

"And I don't know what to do now. How do I fix this? I have to tell her, right? I have to tell them it was me?"

"No!" was the immediate answer, so sharp that Daisy jumped. "You should have called *me* the second it happened," Shanna said, brushing a wisp of perfect straight blond hair out of her eyes.

"Why? Do you know how to get a video taken down?" Shanna was a lawyer or had been before taking leave to stay at home. Maybe there was some legal maneuver . . .

"Well, no . . . but I could help you strategize. Figure out what to say. Maybe call one of my colleagues. And the very last thing you can do is tell anyone!"

Shanna's whisper was so fierce that Daisy actually took a step back. And bumped into a large Tupperware container filled with what looked like balls for a ball pit. "Why?" Daisy asked. "What good comes from keeping it secret?"

"Uh, it protects *you*?" Shanna replied. "You don't know Quinn Barrett. I do. And if she's not calling her lawyers right now, trying to place injunctions and figure out who to sue, then I'm Kim freaking Kardashian. I don't know a ton about the internet, legally, but I do know it's basically the wild west when it comes to privacy laws."

Who to sue. Daisy hadn't even considered the idea. Oh god, could she be sued?

"Not to mention," Shanna continued, "I'm in the video. That's my voice. She could come after me, too!" Shanna took a deep breath. "You really, really should have called me."

Cold dread trickled down her spine. "You think she would do that?"

Shanna just shrugged, her face smoothing over noncommittally. "I wouldn't put it past her. She and Jamie were co-chairs of the Parent Association last year."

"They were?"

"And he used to say that he'd never known anyone more relentless than Quinn Barrett. He kept saying it like it was a good thing," she scoffed. "Honestly, he could have done that job by himself, in his sleep. He didn't need to get tangled up with her."

Daisy's brow furrowed. "Tangled up?"

"Quinn Barrett, and her demands for the Parent Association—for the 'kids,'" Shanna said, complete with air quotes, "dominated our lives for about a year. Every single day when I got home from work, Jamie was up to his elbows in something Quinn Barrett told him to do. Honestly, if Little Wonders wasn't the best preschool in Needleton I would have transferred Jordan out, to someplace that put her needs first, instead of one parent on a power trip."

Daisy took that in, not entirely believing Shanna. Ignoring the contradiction inherent in that claim, Shanna was the one who had raved about Little Wonders when Daisy and Rob first moved, and insisted that Jamie pull strings to get them in.

Life in Needleton was a lot of things—overwhelming, overstarched, overperfected—but Little Wonders had been an oasis of normal. A place that felt safe for Carrie. And ever since the Scary Thing™, that feeling of safety was rare and precious.

"Still," Daisy said, trying to steer the conversation back to her main problem, "relentless isn't the same as litigious. What did Jamie say about the video?"

At that, Shanna's eyes narrowed. "He said, 'Whoa, it looks like Quinn didn't have her coffee that morning.'"

"Did he talk to her?" Daisy asked. "If they worked together all last year . . ."

"No. They don't speak," was the clipped reply. Then turning it around on Daisy, Shanna asked, "What did Rob say? About the video. Oh god, don't tell me you told him you posted it."

"No!" Daisy said. Her heart jolted at the thought. "I don't even know if he's seen it. I spent the last two days avoiding his stare so much he's been asking if I'm all right, looking at me like I'm hiding something."

Which, to be fair, she was.

She was such a terrible liar when it came to Rob. But who knows—he was so busy getting situated at work, he probably wouldn't notice just one more layer to his wife's eternal discomfort.

"Good," Shanna nodded. "There's no reason he should ever know."

"Shanna, if Quinn decides to sue me, then Rob definitely is going to have to know."

"All the more reason to not tell anyone you took it. It can't be traced to you, right?"

She didn't think so, but . . . who knew?

"It's not just Quinn you don't want to know—all the other parents would hate you, too. To think you would post something so personal and awful online?"

"But I didn't post—"

"Does it matter?"

Daisy didn't even have to think about that one. No, it did not.

"You're still very new. People don't know how to relate to you yet."

". . . relate to me?"

Shanna's eyes flicked to Daisy's blue hair, to the sliver of swirling ink exposed from her sweater falling off her shoulder. "A lot of these people are stiff-upper-lip types. They haven't met many people like you. I don't think this video is what you want to be known for." Shanna bit her lip, her eyes filled with concern. "The school administration may decide Carrie would be better off somewhere else."

Daisy felt the walls of the tiny storage space closing in on her, crushing her like a garbage compactor. She had worried so much about herself, she hadn't even thought about how it would affect Carrie.

Shanna was right. Should the truth come to light, even if the school administration didn't kick them out, Carrie would still be ostracized. No birthday party invitations, no playdates.

Daisy had always been the outcast at school. It had hardened her, made her delve into the fantasy worlds that fed her soul. But she did not want that fate visited on her rambunctious, outgoing, joyful three-year-old.

"So what should I do?" Daisy's voice cracked in anguish.

Shanna put a gentle hand on Daisy's shoulder. "Don't say anything. It will all blow over, I'm sure."

"Really?"

"Of course. I bet you by the time the Parent Association meeting convenes Wednesday night, most people will have forgotten the video exists. And you'll have been drowning in guilt for nothing."

Daisy steadied herself. It felt like too much to hope for. But it was true. The average life of an internet meme was no longer Warhol's fifteen minutes. It was closer to fifteen seconds. By the time Wednesday rolled around, that video would probably have been relegated to the dustbin of history.

And, Daisy thought, as they both emerged from the storage

space, heading off down the hall, out to pick up their kids, Shanna would be proven right.

She would have been worried for nothing.

Daisy had not been worried for nothing.

Daisy had never been to a Parent Association meeting. She had thought they would likely be a sparsely attended affair—considering they were scheduled deeply impractically mid-week at five PM, considering most people had jobs to come home from or dinner to get on the table at that time. But judging by the absolutely jam-packed Little Wonders auditorium, such thinking was misguided.

"Jesus," she said under her breath. People, apparently, made the time for this. She pulled her bag closer up her shoulder and slowly walked through the crowd. She tried to smile and nod to people she recognized—although she knew no one's name, beyond "Elia's dad" or "Charlie and Calvin's moms," and desperately scanned the chairs for a corner to hide in.

She grabbed a handout at the door—the photocopied meeting agenda, listing the topics to be covered. Of course, nowhere was there listed "Video of Parent Association president losing her shit with her kid," but that didn't mean it wasn't under discussion. Everyone she passed was involved in the same whispered conversations that had occupied the halls of the school on Monday. But now they weren't whispering.

"I heard she's been in lockdown. Like a rehab. Is there a rehab for bad parenting?"

". . . the video I saw had a laundry detergent ad in front of it, so if she's not donating that money to the school . . ."

"I heard that Hamilton is a bit behind developmentally. Not even fully potty-trained. I guess now we know why."

"Hey, Shanna." Daisy pulled up next to her cousin-in-law, who was gossiping fiercely with a woman Daisy recognized as a mom, but she couldn't say whose.

"Daisy! Have you met Suzy Breakman-Kang?" The other woman held out a hand. She had a halo of gorgeous natural black hair, tan skin and freckles bridging her nose. She was wearing an anorak sweater and basically looked like a soap commercial.

Daisy tugged at her army jacket, with its rebel alliance and alignment chart patches sewn onto the pockets. Suzy Breakman-Kang was one of those people who no doubt found it "difficult to relate" to Daisy.

"Suzy's little boy Aiden is in the Rainbow Room—and she's the secretary of the Parent Association. Such an underappreciated job," Shanna said, placing an understanding hand on Suzy's wool-clad forearm.

"Well, this is one night at least I'm going to enjoy the hell out of recording the minutes," Suzy smirked. "I'd better get to it!"

Shanna gave Suzy a conspiratorial wink (what was that about?) and shooed her off to the dais, where there was an old wooden table—probably made out of wood from the Mayflower—a few chairs, and nameplates.

Seriously. There were nameplates. At a preschool.

"Let's find some good seats." Shanna's eyes were shining with anticipation. Daisy meanwhile felt like she was sinking into mud.

"What was that about?" Daisy asked, once they jockeyed their way to seats three rows up and on the center aisle.

"What?"

"You know," Daisy said, and gave Shanna a wink akin to the one that Shanna had just given Suzy Breakman-Kang.

"Nothing," Shanna said, dismissing it with a wave of her hand. Then, she turned her concern to Daisy. "How are you doing?"

"We had a slight weapons malfunction, but uh . . . everything's perfectly all right now," Daisy said with a slight bubble of hysterical laughter. She was not unknown to spontaneously quote *Star Wars*, especially when she was jumping out of her skin with nerves. "We're fine. We're all fine here now, thank you. How are you?"

Shanna blinked twice at her. "I'm great, thanks," she said with a blank smile.

Daisy bit her lip, and diverted attention away from her total geekitude. "I didn't think it would be this crowded. Is this . . . normal?"

"Oh my god, this is a packed house! Nothing like an internet scandal to bring the lurkers out of the woodwork. Not to mention the spouses."

So. Not a blip. Too much to hope for, Daisy figured. After all, according to the view count, the internet hadn't lost interest in the video either.

Suddenly, the pit in her stomach burbled at the thought of spouses.

"Should we save seats for Rob and Jamie? Rob said he was going to try to make it."

"Jamie's at work," Shanna said, pulling her phone out of her bag and flipping through it casually. "And if you look at the traffic, Rob's not going to make it either."

Shanna showed Daisy her phone, and the sea of red on the traffic map confirmed Shanna's opinion. Great. So her support system was going to be stuck on the Mass Pike.

It was as if she was the only person there who was aware of EVERYTHING. The way the lights hung from the ceiling. The tick of the clock on the wall. The clicks of the keys as Suzy Breakman-Kang typed on her computer from the dais, no doubt prepping for her notes.

Everyone knew what was going on, and no one knew. No one except Daisy.

"So I take it Rob's seen the video now?" Shanna said, in a whisper, breaking through Daisy's thoughts.

"Yeah. I showed it to him, after we talked last."

Actually, Rob, true to form, made Daisy feel a lot better. She had silently slid her phone to him while they were watching TV that night, the video all queued up. If she'd said a word, he would have known immediately. But as he watched it, he didn't say anything other than "Huh. That sucks."

"'That sucks'?" she'd asked tentatively. "You don't think it's . . . awful? Or funny?" Or worthy of being a mommy meme on the internet for all eternity?

"I can see how it'd be funny in hindsight. But awful? Come on, I've felt like that before. Haven't you? Like when Carrie wouldn't leave the *Star Wars* aisle of the toy store and it was closing time? Anyone who's ever been a parent will get it."

And this auditorium was full of parents, Daisy thought as she looked around, chewing on her lip. So, yes, the video was no doubt going to be on the list of meeting topics, but in the grand scheme of things . . . they'd all been there, hadn't they?

"Listen, everything is going to be okay," Shanna said suddenly, turning to look Daisy in the eye. "Just . . . trust me and follow my lead. Understand?"

Before Daisy could ask what that meant, a hush fell over the crowd. Because just then, Quinn Barrett entered the room.

She looked almost exactly the same as she had on Friday at

the parade: impeccably pulled together, with a swingy knee-length trench coat over a soft-colored dress suit and pearls. And of course, a leather business folder under her arm. Daisy pulled her patch-covered army jacket a little closer.

Quinn paused briefly, taking in all the heads turned in her direction. Then, she squared her shoulders, and headed up the center aisle, a serene smile on her face—like Meghan Markle headed up the cathedral to Prince Harry. Or was it like Marie Antoinette headed to the guillotine? Either way, she kept her head up, and her eyes on her destination.

She crossed the dais, took her seat behind the nameplate that said "President," and struck a gavel that had appeared miraculously from somewhere.

The entire place—already quiet, turned as silent as a yoga class held in a Protestant church. (Not that Daisy had been to yoga in . . . forever. God, what would it be like to have a waist again?)

"Come to order," Quinn said perfunctorily. Then, with a deep breath, turned her serene smile to the crowd. "I hope everyone had a memorable Halloween! I know mine was."

A slight chuckle rippled through the audience. Daisy let out a breath she didn't know she was holding. Next to her Shanna stiffened.

"We have a great many things to discuss at this meeting—a lot of upcoming events, so let's get to it, shall we?" Quinn said, then hesitated. "But first—"

This was it, this was the moment. Daisy could feel it. Everyone in the room leaned forward ever so slightly.

"First of all, I'd like to thank our principal Ms. Anna and the teachers who stayed late tonight to watch our kids while we have this meeting. They truly are the most wonderful thing about Little Wonders and deserve a round of applause."

Slightly confused, the room dutifully clapped. So, now wasn't the moment.

"And of course, the Parent Association does everything it can to help the teachers, and everyone up here truly hopes that it's felt by all the people in this room, and the kids." Quinn held out her hands, imitating Jesus at the last supper, encompassing the whole table. The man who sat behind the "Vice President" nameplate (who was that? Was it Jonah-the-booger-eater's dad?), the "Treasurer," who Daisy recognized from her workout attire and eco-friendly water bottle as Violet's mom, who dropped off around the same time as she did, and Suzy Breakman-Kang all shared a surprised glance, as Quinn led the room in another round of spontaneous applause.

"These people all work incredibly hard. And the winter events are going to be even more amazing than the fall! So, Suzy, what's first on the agenda?"

Suzy's eyebrow went up. ". . . First on our *official* agenda is the Thanksgiving play—"

"Yes, the Thanksgiving play!" Quinn said cheerfully. "Which takes place right on this stage—"

"But I think we should talk about what happened this weekend," Suzy interrupted.

And once again, the room leaned forward.

Quinn kept her smile pasted on her face. "That's not on the agenda. We'll have time at the end of the meeting for a recap of the parade, and what could have been done better, but—"

"But the agenda was written before." No one needed to ask "Before what?'" Everyone knew. "And as Little Wonders has been brought to national attention, I think it needs to be addressed."

"I . . . I . . . ," Quinn stuttered.

"I second the motion," said Vice President Jonah's Dad.

"I . . . All right. Fine," Quinn said, waving her hand. "No need to call a vote. I was hoping to address this later, but honestly, I'm glad so many parents are here, because cybersecurity is truly of the utmost importance in this day and age."

"Cybersecurity?" Shanna said under her breath, annoyed.

"Cybersecurity?" Suzy Breakman-Kang echoed from the dais.

"Yes." Quinn turned to the crowd. "I know that we all want to take pictures of our children, or . . . or video." She swallowed hard. "And share them with friends and family and sometimes online—and that's completely fine! We all love to get likes of our kiddos being cute. But it's Little Wonders policy to request that when such pictures and whatnot are taken on school grounds, of school events, that they be shared privately, or posted on our Little Wonders private Facebook group. Because especially in crowd shots, it's up to the individual parent to decide their child's level of media exposure."

Quinn took a deep breath. "And this past weekend, someone broke those rules."

A hush settled over the crowd. They all looked from one to the other. It was as if the entire room suddenly realized that there was a second half of this scandal. No one over the past five days had considered that one of the people among them had actually made and posted the video.

No one of course, except for Daisy. Who felt the weight of everyone's eyes like a thousand pebbles burying her.

"Are you serious?" came from somewhere in the audience. Daisy couldn't tell if that person was incredulous or worried, but she and Shanna exchanged a look, eyebrows up. Daisy could tell, even for Shanna, this came to an accusatory head much more quickly than expected.

"Who said that?" Quinn bit out, squinting into the audience—which struck Daisy as weirdly funny, because it wasn't as if she were onstage in a Broadway play—the house lights were all up. But she said it so harshly, and so dramatically, it was a scold that went across the room. And people reacted the way they do to scoldings. Clamming up. Defenses up.

And unsurprisingly no one owned up.

"Well, in answer to your question, whoever you are, yes, I am serious. Someone not only violated my privacy, they violated the privacy of our school, and our children. And . . . and I think they should come forward."

Quinn stood rigid on the dais. The silent crowd continued to glance suspiciously at each other.

"Come on. Who did it?" Quinn said.

No one answered. But a few murmurs permeated the crowd.

"Quinn, that's not exactly what I meant when I—" Suzy Breakman-Kang said, but she was cut off by a harsh glare.

"But that's what I'm talking about," she snapped. "If you want the gavel, Suzy, then you can direct this meeting." She turned back to the room at large, her eyes glowing with heat. "I can promise no repercussions for you or your child if you come forward. All you have to do is own up to posting the video, and take it down, and everything will be forgotten. But if you don't . . ."

The room hung on her every word. "If you don't, then I cannot be held accountable for what kind of reaction the school administration will have . . . or the Needleton police department."

The words were as effective as a slap in the face. The murmurs that had permeated the room before became louder, worried, rushed.

This, it seemed, was what the parents had assembled for: the drama, the speculation. The potential for cops to come in at that moment and put someone in handcuffs and whisk them away.

Daisy glanced over her shoulder. No cops. No handcuffs.

The noise was quickly reaching a fever pitch—even Quinn looked astonished at the rancor in the room.

She couldn't just sit here like a coward, Daisy thought. She had to do something. Quinn was right—she had not only violated Quinn's privacy—she had violated her son's, she had violated the privacy of everyone at the school. She deserved to be shunned. She deserved to be flagellated and driven out of the school. No, put in stocks! It was Massachusetts, after all—there had to be old-timey stocks somewhere.

But as Daisy sat there, getting up the courage to say something, next to her, Shanna silently stood.

"Quinn," she said, loud enough, and in her mom voice. They all had a mom voice. The one that was strong enough to penetrate a Disneyland crowd and bring a three-year-old to heel. And apparently it was just as effective on parents as it was on their kids, because the room immediately gave Shanna the floor.

"I know who's responsible for the video," Shanna said.

Cold shot through Daisy as the blood leeched from her face and pooled somewhere around her toes. She looked up at Shanna sharply. Oh no oh no oh no oh no. It was one thing to confess—it was another thing to be outed! Daisy opened her mouth, but no sound came out.

Quinn looked as surprised as the rest of the crowd. "You do?"

"Yes, Quinn, I do," Shanna said. Shanna glanced down

at Daisy—too briefly for anyone to notice. Then, she met Quinn's stare straight on. "It's you."

A guffaw of disbelief finally broke the silence.

"Me?"

"You," Shanna replied. She was effortlessly calm. In complete control. An utter contrast to Daisy, who was internally freaking out. "You are the one in the video, being horrible to your own son. Your actions are the reason it was posted online, and you are the one responsible."

Quinn Barrett must have been internally freaking out too, because for the first time at the meeting, she was set back on her heels.

"That's not the point—"

"Yes, it is the point," Shanna replied calmly but firmly. "When you google Little Wonders Preschool, the first hit is not the school's website. It's that video. And judging by the views, that's not going to change any time soon. You boss us around, act like a fool in the video, and now you have the gall to threaten us?"

"I'm not threatening anything, I am simply stating facts—"

But Shanna just continued. And Daisy noticed every eye in the room was on her. Shanna had control of everything. Not Quinn. And Quinn . . . Quinn looked terrified.

"Scolding us. Like we're the preschoolers, not our kids. Saying that the person had better come forward or run afoul of the police? *That* is a threat. And it is conduct unbecoming a Parent Association president."

"No, that's the *law*," Quinn argued. "My lawyers said Massachusetts is a two-party consent state and recording me without my knowledge is considered illegal wiretapping."

Shanna's eyebrow shot up. But rather than be taken aback,

she simply smiled. She'd been right that Quinn had consulted her lawyer. And Shanna was ready for that.

"I *am* a lawyer, and from my perspective, it *was* with your knowledge," Shanna said.

"What?" Quinn nearly screeched.

"It was a preschool Halloween parade. Everyone had their phones out. You said it yourself, that we all love to record our kiddos, get love on social media. You live for Instagram likes. You *knew* there were people recording."

"I didn't know they were recording *me*. And . . . and Ham," Quinn said, a faint gleam coming to her eyes, but she sniffed it away. "Besides, what do you know? You're a tax lawyer. Or, you *were*," Quinn said. Potent words that had every parent in the room bristling.

"I can still read a law journal," Shanna replied, smoothly. "And I chose to stay at home—just like so many other parents here." Several people nodded enthusiastically. "What I didn't choose was to have my Parent Association president losing her mind on my Facebook page."

"I didn't choose that either, Shanna," Quinn said. "Which is why I mentioned the police and the law. Which, if you were still practicing, Shanna, you might know."

Everyone in the room sucked in their breath.

"Um, actually, I'm a lawyer, too," Elia's dad said tentatively, from three rows from the back.

"Maritime law," Quinn scoffed, almost to herself. But nothing was to yourself when you were on a stage.

Elia's dad scrambled to his feet. "And at the very least, whether or not you knew, it's a legal gray area. But I'd be more inclined to side with Shanna's argument. There's no expectation of privacy."

A couple of other lawyer types in the crowd (Jesus, was

everyone who lived in Needleton a lawyer? Daisy wondered) started nodding and murmuring in agreement.

"Oh, shut up, Thomas—" Ah, thought Daisy, that was Elia's dad's name, "if you had some clue as to how to set up a pop-up tent we wouldn't even be here."

Elia's dad (Thomas) jerked back, equal parts struck and confused. As was the rest of the room.

"Um, can you guys slow down?" Suzy Breakman-Kang said, pausing in her finger clacking, which had been underscoring the entire conversation to that point, only to be noticed once it stopped. "I'm only as far as 'who I called when I saw my Parent Association president having a mental breakdown on Facebook.'"

"You're not seriously recording all of this!" Quinn said, aghast.

"It's my job, Quinn," Suzy replied. "And maybe . . . maybe you should back off. Leveling accusations and making snide remarks about everyone is not a good look."

"I don't care how it looks," Quinn said, enraged.

"You should. This meeting is public. And recorded," Suzy said, indicating her small dictation device, no doubt running out of digital space. She smothered a smirk. "With your consent."

"You want to dictate the meeting's agenda, Suzy?" Quinn said. "You want to do actual work instead of taking notes? Take on all the hard parts, the organizing, the calling parents and trying to cajole them into volunteering? Calling all the local businesses, begging for donations? Working with the city council for permissions and making all of it *fucking fun*? You want that, Suzy? Here," she held out the gavel. "Take it."

"I . . . don't want it," Suzy replied.

"Quinn," piped up Vice President Jonah's Dad, who had

been so very very quiet while the most epically insane of all preschool parent meetings occurred, "Maybe you should adjourn the meeting—"

"Why, Jay? So you can silently do nothing, conveniently at home? According to Bronwyn, that's your forte."

Gasps shook the room. Followed by quick titters.

Apparently, when Quinn Barrett lost her filter, she *really* lost it.

"Quinn, that is uncalled for," the VP said, turning Pepto pink. "And unbecoming to your role."

"Then take my role, Jay," Quinn said. This time she held out the gavel to him. "Want it? All the work and absolutely no glory? No? What about you, Therese?" she said to the treasurer. Who was smart enough to remain silent.

"What about all the committee heads, all the room parents out there?" Quinn said to the audience. "Who'll take on this job? No one, right? Because everyone wants the perfect fucking experience for our kids, but no one is actually willing to do the work to make it happen."

The room held its breath. And suddenly, Daisy's eyes found Shanna.

Shanna, who had been standing there, silent, letting the argument play out in front of her.

Shanna winked at Daisy.

And suddenly Daisy realized Shanna had been waiting for this moment and had been all along. "I will."

CHAPTER FIVE

In hindsight, Quinn knew what she should have done. She'd walked into that room believing that she had a plan. But that travesty of a Parent Association meeting wasn't it.

She would put the discussion at the very end of the meeting, so she could showcase all the hard work the Parent Association was doing . . . and when the moment came, she would be charming. Self-effacing. Up on that stage she would have been the bloody parenting Oprah, opening herself up *just* enough, throwing in a joke here and there about how her stiletto boots make great hammers in a pinch and that she and Ham pretended the spaceship got hit by a meteor. She would have turned on the charm, won them over—and the whole thing would eventually ebb away into nothingness.

But when she looked out at the sea of faces—and all she saw were people greedy for juicy gossip, people who wanted nothing more than drama, any one of whom could have been the video taker—she couldn't give them the satisfaction.

And the only thought that went through her head was . . . *How dare they?*

She was Quinn Barrett—and she ran the hell out of the Parent Association, to make Little Wonders and their kids' (not just Ham's!) experience the best it could possibly be.

The idea that they could be so gleeful about her trauma . . . it set something off in her brain. Something primal. And something, apparently, pissed off.

She turned into a raging bitch in heels.

No, not a bitch, she thought, long after the fact and three glasses of chardonnay in. An asshole.

Because bitches were women in society getting shit done. But an asshole? An asshole just lashed out.

And that's what she had done.

How dare people turn on her?

No, not *people*. Quinn's teeth ground and she took another swig of wine.

Shanna Freaking Stone.

Quinn remembered with scary accuracy the moment Shanna spoke her infamous words. The way her mouth moved. Her serenity, like she was the freaking Virgin Mary.

"I will."

She had been up on that stage, holding out the gavel like it was the queen's scepter. Daring people to take it. And nothing could have shocked her more than hearing someone take her up on it.

"You're obviously going through some things," Shanna had said, her voice demure, as if she was sparing the audience from the unseemly. "And this has become too much of a burden for you."

"A burden," she said, nearly choking on the words. "*A burden.*"

"And you have Hamilton, who is . . . three, and comes with those challenges."

"What challenges?" Quinn shot out. "What are you implying about my son? Hamilton is perfectly fine. This is not about him."

"But it is. Because, do you think you're the best mom you can be to Hamilton right now?" Shanna stepped forward, her gaze zoned in on Quinn.

The fact that this conversation . . . no, this *interrogation,* was taking place in public was horrifying enough. And Quinn could have challenged her. She could have guffawed and reiterated all of the work that she did to make the Parent Association function. But instead . . . she was just too tired.

God, she was tired.

Because the truth was . . . she had seen the video, too. And she had seen her son so afraid of his mother that he pissed himself.

All of her fight had completely vanished. The past five days had been hellish, online and off. This meeting, which she had planned and prepared for, had gone so far off the rails she didn't recognize the room, the people, herself anymore. In the beginning, the important thing—the only thing—she wanted to accomplish was to reassert who she was, smooth everything over, and get everything back to normal.

And now, she was too tired to care.

So she did the only thing she could do.

She stepped off the stage.

Shanna seemed surprised by this. Her eyes flicked to the woman she'd been sitting next to—her little blue-haired minion Daisy—as Quinn approached.

Quinn came to stand directly in front of Shanna. In her heels she was taller than Shanna, but not by much. And it gave her absolutely no psychological advantage over the soft serenity her adversary displayed.

Slowly, she flipped the gavel over in her hand. And held it out to Shanna.

"Take it. Have fun organizing the Thanksgiving play, and the Snowflake Breakfast, the goddamn raffle baskets—I'm sure with the support the parents of this school are famous for, you will do just swimmingly."

Shanna reached out, took the gavel. Then she leaned forward and whispered in Quinn's ear.

"Get some rest."

The bitchiest of bitchy things that anyone could say.

The only triumph Quinn could claim, as she stalked out of there, was that she held back from slapping Shanna across her smug faux-concerned face.

She collected Ham from Miss Rosie and the other teachers—they were having a mini dance party that Ham was loath to leave—and they got out of there.

There would have been a formal vote, no doubt. Someone—Suzy Breakman-Kang probably (the little instigator) who would've formally nominated Shanna for the position. Jay no doubt would have seconded—anything to avoid taking on actual responsibility. The board would vote, the whole coup would've been over in minutes and relatively bloodless.

She wasn't there to see it though. By the time the room flooded with congratulatory applause for their new dear leader, she and Ham were on their way home.

Which was where Quinn stayed for the next four days, licking her wounds, considering her options, and reliving every moment of the parent meeting's humiliation.

The video, and now the parent meeting—turned out she was getting used to humiliation.

If Stuart had been at the meeting, she decided, she could

have managed. He would have smiled at her, steered the conversation, pivoted her into showing off her softer side, the way he did when she showed him off to clients. But Stuart wasn't there. He was in surgery. And it was very very hard to argue for him to stop saving a child's life to come to a preschool Parent Association meeting.

Even if his wife was under fire.

Of course, by then Stuart was aware of the video.

She had told him as soon as he texted her back on Monday—which, due to his being in surgery, was several hours later. Quinn was on the phone with her own lawyer (Grayson & Grayson was one of the best and oldest firms in Boston—only the very best for the Barrett family) when Stuart emerged from a victory lap with a recovering surgical patient's grateful parents, thus in one of his best moods.

That good mood didn't last.

Honestly, his reaction had not been what Quinn had expected. She thought . . . she thought he'd at least flinch as he watched the video. After all, that was his wife embarrassing herself and his son who was getting the brunt of her temper.

"Okay," he'd said. They'd met for lunch. In a dive diner they both secretly loved and where no one they knew would be. Still, she didn't take off her sunglasses as she queued up the video and let him watch it.

". . . Okay?"

"Okay." He shrugged and returned to his bunless garden burger—even in a diner he insisted on keeping his meal as healthy as he could. Ever since he'd taken up spinning, he referred to food only as "fuel." Usually, she admired his sense of control—her lunchtime Pilates classes weren't for nothing. But right then, Quinn would have taken him being a little out of control. A doughnut with chocolate sprinkles would have gone a long way to showing her that he was as upset over this as she was.

"I see a lot of parents, and all of them are stressed out, and sometimes they lose control. I've learned the best thing I can do is step back and say 'Okay.'"

"Okay . . ." Quinn tried to understand. "And that's what you think is happening here?"

He was stepping back? When it was his own kid? His own wife?

"Obviously not to the same level as a parent of a child undergoing a lumpectomy or spinal reconstruction," he replied. "And to be honest, I've never seen you quite so . . . out of control."

"I know, and I'm sorry—" she began. Finally, something she was ready for—censure. That, she could parry. But he cut her off.

"But I know you'll fix it."

"You . . . you do."

"Quinn." He shot her that smile. The one that made her heart skip beats and inspired some truly impressive drunken karaoke. "That's what you do. It's what I love about you. You fix things. You wanted to become a designer, you did. You wanted to marry me, you made it happen, from the flowers to the honeymoon." He smirked at her. "You wanted to have Hamilton—I thought it would disrupt everything, but you make it work. And you'll fix this. You'll make it perfect." He turned his attention back to his burger. "I assume you already spoke to Grayson & Grayson."

She'd nodded, filled him in on the little they had said. He nodded and chewed. He didn't rail at her, or at the video taker—he wasn't mad on her behalf, on Ham's behalf, on his own behalf. Instead, he trusted her to take care of the situation.

On the one hand, it was perplexing. Here she was, living through the worst moment of her life, and he was . . . eerily calm about it. On the other—it was reassuring. He had complete confidence in her abilities to deal with it.

"There are worse things that happen to people every day. I know, I'm the one telling parents about them." He raised his hand for the check. Then, he turned his gaze to her, held out his other hand. She put hers in it—he squeezed. "Are you going to be okay?"

"Yes. I'm just surprised you're not more upset."

"Oh," he said, raising her hand to his lips. "I am upset for you."

"For *you*, I mean," she replied.

"Why would I be upset for me?" he said, cocking his head to one side.

"Because . . . people know it's me, and I'm your wife. Our families, your parents . . . my work, your work . . . it's going to be affected. At the very least, it's going to get mentioned."

He took a moment. His eyes turned hard, his romance novel look nowhere to be seen. He worked his jaw, as if there was a last bit of garden burger stuck in his teeth. Then, the check came back, and he swiftly removed his hand from hers. "Then," he'd said, as he ruthlessly signed the receipt, "I suggest you start fixing it."

Maybe that was why she had gone so hard at the Parent Association meeting on Wednesday. Maintaining her position there was the first step in "fixing it."

And . . . well, no point in rehashing how well that went.

The day after the Parent Association meeting, she forced Stuart to do drop-off at Little Wonders (he only grumbled a little, since he knew he was in deficit as he'd missed the meeting) and she called in sick to the office. Not that they expected her, anyway: Jeremy told her that Sutton was covering her appointments, and he was overseeing the miniscule final details of the Beacon Hill house himself. Thus, she "should do what she needed to do."

She also had to shut down her Instagram and Facebook, as all of her posts with pictures of Ham were loaded with the cruelest comments imaginable about her parenting.

Meanwhile, she watched the view count on the video go up and up and up. Slower and slower, but still dauntingly high.

Her lawyers had sent out cease-and-desist notices, but when the video had been copied and copied again, they didn't have much effect. One or two of the first posted videos disappeared, but her lawyers were right—getting them all down was going to be like playing whack-a-mole. And, annoyingly, her lawyers also agreed with Shanna—that the question of whether or not the recording was unknown was up for debate.

"We could take this to the state supreme court!" one of the younger ones said on the phone, a bit too eager to put Quinn's life on display (and bill her hours). Spotlighting the video with a costly and cynical legal battle did not seem like the best way to "fix it." She didn't want the Streisand Effect renamed the Halloween Mom Effect.

What she needed was to bury this.

Friday, wearing her biggest pair of sunglasses and braving drop-off, Quinn again called in sick.

She could continue to endure drop-off and pickup, she decided, at least until Alba returned. She could never take Ham out of Little Wonders. He loved it there.

Although a phone call from Alba that morning put the kibosh on that plan of having Alba start drop-off duty again.

"My daughter is having a baby!" Alba said via the spotty connection. "I'm going to be a grandmamma!"

"Congratulations, Alba," Quinn had said, biting her lip. "I'm so glad you got to spend this, er, unplanned week with your family . . . you'll be back on Monday?"

"Actually, Miss Quinn . . . my daughter, she's due sooner than we might have told the priest. I need to be here for her."

"For how long?"

". . . It's my first grandchild, Miss Quinn." Quinn could practically hear Alba shrug.

And that's all there was to it. Alba might be back in a few months—or she might not. It might have been because of the video—or it might have been solely because of Alba's daughter's lack of birth control. Either way, Quinn would need to find another nanny/housekeeper/all around lifesaver.

Ham was going to be devastated.

Yes, there was absolutely no way she could remove him from Little Wonders now.

So, Friday afternoon, she managed to corner the principal, Ms. Anna (picking up Hamilton at the absolute latest possible hour, avoiding as many parents as she could), seeking reassurance about his place in the school.

And for the first time in a week, she got a glimmer of understanding, and, dare she say it . . . hope.

"Mrs. Barrett, Hamilton is part of our family. We look forward to continuing with his education. Regardless of the recent incident."

"Really?" Quinn couldn't help but exclaim. Relief practically had her knees buckling.

"I realize that this has not cast the best light on you—or on the school, and I have fielded some phone calls to that effect," Ms. Anna said, and Quinn's stomach dropped again.

"But the school's legal representatives have assured me nothing in the video threatens our charter. And any bad light on the school will soon blow over."

Lawyers were being called everywhere, it seemed. Who knew a Halloween parade would spur such a rush of hourly billing?

"Although I think it is the right decision to take a step back from the Parent Association. So you can focus on Ham, and his reaction to the video."

"But—he doesn't even know about the video!" Quinn said, horrified. "I can't even imagine him seeing it." Her entire body was revulsed by the idea.

"He knows something is wrong," Miss Anna said. "Ms. Rosie says that he's been remarkably subdued for such an energetic boy. And he's had more accidents than usual."

She had done an awful lot of laundry this week, Quinn realized.

"Mrs. Barrett, children bounce. They are resilient. We are here to support Hamilton through this and will help you. And personally," Miss Anna continued, taking Quinn by the shoulder, "I have a grown son. And I'm just glad that my parenting occurred before the rise of YouTube. That's why I think the video went 'viral.' Everyone relates to you. If you saw that on a sitcom, you'd laugh along with the television, yes?"

And it was in that moment she realized that maybe she couldn't bury it. But maybe she could change the story.

MONDAY MORNING, SHE marched into Little Wonders at the normal time. Sure, some parents whispered, but most were dealing with the hassles of dropping off kids who clung like capuchin monkeys to their legs.

Not Hamilton though. They had one of their patented Perfect goodbyes, with a big hug and kiss (and a hand-off to Ms. Rosie of a new batch of pants and underwear)—then she hit smooth traffic and strolled into the office a full Parcel ahead of her normal schedule.

"Sutton—conference," she said, not even pausing as she passed her colleague Sutton's desk.

But instead of scurrying after her, as was usual, Sutton held up a finger, talking into her phone.

"Yes of course, Mrs. Chaffee," she was saying. "I'll have those prints brought over for you to look at right away."

Quinn came up short. Once Sutton extracted herself from the phone, Quinn pounced.

"Mrs. Chaffee?" Mrs. Chaffee was the grand dame owner of the Beacon Hill house. Off Sutton's surprised nod, Quinn continued, "What prints is she approving?" Quinn was adamant on involving the clients in every step of the design process, but at this point, with mere weeks until it was formally ready, she usually asked them to step back, and let themselves be wowed with the final product.

"Just a couple of family photos we are having blown up and arranged in the children's bathroom," Sutton said, rushing to reassure her. "Jeremy approved it all last week, and Mrs. Chaffee wanted to make sure she liked the photos we chose, so . . . I thought it would be okay."

She took a few days off and her entire project had shifted, she silently harrumphed to herself. But she didn't have time to be squeamish about alterations to her protocol. "I'm sure it's fine," she said quickly. "But come with me. We need to conference."

Sutton stood to follow, but just then, Jeremy stepped out of his office.

"Sutton. Oh, and, Quinn, good, you're here, too. Step in, please."

What on earth was Jeremy Crabbe doing at his namesake offices so early? Usually he had barely made it to the pastry counter at Dean & DeLuca by now. But Quinn steadied herself. She was ready. She had a game plan.

But she was not prepared to walk into Jeremy's office replete with all the Crabbe & Co. project managers, seated around his refurbished Edwardian coffee table.

"What's this?" she asked, suddenly.

"Quinn," Jeremy began, rather formally. "We wanted you to know, that we . . . as Sutton here would put it, have your back."

"We understand that this is an incredibly trying time," Sutton said. "And you've been such a mentor to me."

"We're all family here," Jeremy said, putting an arm around her. The other project managers nodded in agreement. "Everything is going to be fine. We'll get through it."

Quinn could not help but feel touched. She leaned into Jeremy's sideways embrace. He'd been there for every major moment of her career; the fact that he was willing to back her now was . . . well, actually, she expected nothing less, considering everything she'd done for Crabbe & Co., but still, it was very nice to hear.

"I'm so glad to hear that. Because I have decided that the best way to approach the current situation is to 'lean into it'—and to have your support means worlds to me."

Jeremy's arm lifted gently off her shoulders. "Erm, what do you mean, lean into it?"

"Just that," she replied, forcing a confident smile onto her face. "I am the mom in that video, there's no denying it. So,

I have to own it. Go on the morning shows, on *Ellen*, laugh it off as a moment every modern parent knows well."

"Morning shows?" Jeremy asked, weakly.

"Yes— and I know what you're thinking. That scheduling these appearances and flying out to New York and LA will get in the way of my work—but nothing could be further from the truth. In fact, I am going to go full throttle into all of my projects. The Wellesley Shingle house, the Nantucket retrofit, the Cuban-Thai restaurant, the Greater New England Children's Hospital Charity Ball, and of course, the Beacon Hill house. Every single project is going to exceed expectations. Perfect Quinn Barrett productions, from start to finish."

She turned her glowing smile to the room. Open mouths hung like heavy drapes on the faces of every single person. She turned to Sutton, who stared at her, in shock.

Obviously in shock at her brilliance, Quinn thought with bravado. Although even she knew it was a lie.

"Sutton?" Jeremy said over Quinn's head to her protégé. "Can you . . ."

Quinn turned to Sutton. Surely, if anyone would be able to articulate her plan to Jeremy best, it would be her young, media-savvy colleague.

"I . . . I'm sorry, Quinn," Sutton began, her eyes shooting from Jeremy to Quinn. "But . . . um, I don't think 'leaning in' will work.

"Why not?" Quinn asked, shocked.

"Well, first of all . . . a week has gone by," Sutton replied. "The video is old news now. And going on these shows . . . it would just bring it back up. Is that something you'd want? For Stuart? For your family?"

Old news? The video was old news? Quinn had to hold in a

hysterical giggle. Not to her it wasn't. Not to the people in the grocery store who whispered as she walked past. Not to the nail technician who snickered with her coworker in Vietnamese while salt-scrubbing Quinn's feet.

And definitely not to the other parents in the halls of Little Wonders who completely avoided her eyes since that horror show of a Parent Association meeting.

Although . . . yes, the number of views had slowed. Still racking up a few hundred thousand views a day, so obviously it hadn't died out, but it was not the top-trending video anymore, thank goodness.

And Sutton had mentioned the one thing that gave her some hesitation about her plan. Her family. Hamilton was still only three. How was he going to feel about this video, where his mother was so mean to him that he pissed himself, when he was thirteen? What about when he discovered a clip of his mother trying to laugh it off with Ellen DeGeneres?

And Stuart . . . Stuart very much wanted her to "fix" this. Somehow, she got the impression that bringing it back to national attention might not do that.

Sutton clocked her hesitation because she took a step forward and lowered her voice—why, Quinn had no idea, because everyone could still hear.

"And . . . I'm pretty sure that the shows you'd want to go on . . . they only like to highlight, um, *positive* videos. You know, grandmas who can rap really well, and little kids who ate a bunch of sprinkles. Not . . ."

Not yelling at your kid and then destroying his Halloween costume in front of his school and the whole world.

"Ah," she said. Disappointment hit her like a wave, rocking her back slightly on her heels. "I understand." She wasn't going to get to change the story. She wasn't going to get to own the narrative and overcome it and be the freaking parenting Oprah.

She had to live with how it was.

"Even better," she said with a smile. Regrouping. "Now nothing will get in the way of my giving two hundred percent to all of my projects. Making our clients happy will be my sole focus."

The room was still. Someone coughed.

"Actually," Jeremy said, and the dread settled over her. "We think it would be better if you took a backseat on the firm's projects. Just until the whole hullaballoo dies down."

Not her projects. The firm's projects.

"But Sutton just said the video is old news now," she countered. Jesus, she practically had whiplash from this meeting. "Apparently there is no hullaballoo."

"It might well have died down on the internet," Jeremy said, glancing uncomfortably around the room. "But it's still present enough in people's minds that . . . well, if you were to be recognized from it with a client, or a vendor . . . it's not the impression Crabbe & Co. wants to make."

"I see." She narrowed her eyes, noticed that most of the project managers refused to meet hers. "I thought you said you had my back."

"We do! Entirely. So, we all sat down, did some reorganizing this past week. Divide and conquer, as it were," he said. He motioned to those sitting around the table. "Frankie's got the most commercial experience, so he's going to take over the restaurant design. Maryann and Josh are taking on the Nantucket retrofit, and Nina's handling the Wellesley Shingle. Her first solo project!"

"I'm so excited for this opportunity, thanks, Quinn," Nina said.

"No problem," Quinn said weakly. "So happy my personal humiliation could give you a leg up in your career."

Nina's smile faded.

"What about the Beacon Hill house?" she asked, sharp. The magazine. The Martha freaking Stewart magazine was coming in two weeks to photograph it. She'd already done the preliminary interviews about the process, her design choices.

If this didn't happen . . . it would be like Quinn had personally let Martha down.

"The Beacon Hill house is yours," Jeremy said. "You've worked so hard on it, it couldn't be anyone else's."

"A Perfect Quinn Barrett production," Sutton said softly, giving her an encouraging smile.

"Besides, it's so close to finished. Sutton can handle most of the final details, and I'll take on Mrs. Chaffee, when needed."

Quinn's eyes shot to Sutton, who, for her part, looked alarmed. "We're just talking about invoices and stuff at this point anyway, right?"

Right. And Sutton did that kind of stuff all the time. But it was still galling. It still felt like Brutus stabbing Caesar. Or at least, she assumed it did—she'd never run an empire that spanned Europe. Or been stabbed.

"So what am I supposed to do in my backseat?" she asked.

"The charity ball, naturally!" Jeremy said. "Arguably the most important project on our books right now!"

And one that Jeremy didn't dare take away from Quinn— because she was the one who had brought it in.

Via Stuart, of course. A few New Year's Eves ago they had attended the Greater New England Children's Hospital Charity Ball, and she had been absolutely appalled at the décor. Basic hotel ballroom lighting, basic hotel ballroom chairs, basic hotel everything. She understood the trust's desire to be frugal—the money raised was for sick children, after all—but she also ascribed to the philosophy that a dollar spent here would yield ten there, and in this case tens of thousands.

She'd approached the trust, and offered Crabbe & Co.'s services, at cost. Their way of donating to the poor, sick children. Jeremy had been against it, saying they didn't do event planning. But Quinn had convinced him that it would be a showcase for their design capabilities, to exactly the kind of clientele they wished to reach.

And it had worked.

They'd done the Greater New England Children's Hospital Charity Ball every year for the last five.

"After the ball . . . after the new year . . . I'm sure everything will have died down enough for you to take on clients again," Jeremy was saying. "And you'll be back on track."

Back on track. Partner track, he meant, no doubt. Because goodness knows he needed someone in the office who could handle everything while he took another six-month shopping trip across Asia.

But not yet. No, she had to earn her way back. Earn her client list back.

And she would, Quinn decided.

She could forgive Jeremy, in time, she thought. No doubt he'd gotten calls from some clients the past week that set him back on his heels. So, she had to eat a little crow. But she would earn back his trust. Show him that the kind of ruthless tenacity, the pursuit of perfection, that the video had showcased . . . well, that was exactly what made her an *exceptional* designer.

She would show them all what she was made of.

This year's charity ball was going to be nothing short of stunning. Amazing. Incredible.

Perfect.

"Don't worry, Jeremy. Everyone," she said, pulling herself up straight and giving the room her most determined smile. "You can count on me."

CHAPTER SIX

"Shanna sweetie, how much longer on the turkey?"

Daisy looked up from her chopping to see Shanna about to explode. But the taller woman's calm, cool composure prevailed, and she simply said, "About an hour, Patty."

"Are you sure I can't help with anything?" was the hesitant reply from Shanna's mother-in-law. "I've made a pie or two in my time."

"And you've earned the right to relax," Shanna said, easy but firm. "I've got everything covered. Why don't you sit down, play with your granddaughter? Or have some more wine?"

Just not both at the same time, Daisy thought, pleadingly.

"All right." Patty sighed. As she drifted away, she turned to Daisy with a pointed look. "Honey, you have a strange girl on your hands. She wouldn't let me leave the playroom until she'd recited the entire *Star Wars*. Complete with sound effects."

"Abridged," Daisy said, quietly. She didn't let her three-year-old watch *Star Wars*, of course. She just told her the plot as a bedtime story. Complete with light saber and TIE fighter sound effects.

Besides, some people's "strange" was other people's "delightful."

"Thanks for helping," Shanna said, once Patty was gone. "I love Jamie's parents, but I swear, that woman burns water."

"No problem," Daisy said. Although, the traditional Thanksgiving meal wasn't really her style of cooking. Once she moved to Los Angeles, she shed her white-bread, casserole-heavy upbringing and embraced the city's culinary eclecticism. But none of it lent itself to a big New England turkey dinner with all the trimmings.

When she suggested to Shanna that she make a zesty gazpacho, it was as if she could feel the hard, cold stare of the Pilgrims, shaming her for adulterating their feast.

Thus, she was relegated to chopping.

And there was always plenty of chopping.

Currently, she was on brussels sprouts, cutting them in half and arranging them on a sheet pan for roasting.

Which was, according to Shanna, enough of a culinary departure for the Stones.

"All right, after the turkey comes out, the pies can go in, and they'll come out and cool while we are eating the main course. The table's been set, Patty has wine, Grandpa Bob has beer, the girls have their apple juice spritzers, oh . . . do you need a mandoline? I have one around here somewhere."

Daisy's mind reeled at all the details. And she was a Dungeon Master who usually reveled in details.

"Oh no, I'm good," Daisy replied, setting down her knife. "Honestly, I don't know how you do it all."

Shanna threw a quick smile over her shoulder. "This is my first year doing it all."

"Really?"

"Seriously. I was too busy with work before, billing hours so I could take off for the holidays. There was one Thanksgiving I just had catered. Last year Jamie decided he'd do everything. He tried to deep-fry a turkey." Shanna took a swig of her mineral water. "He is no longer allowed to deep-fry turkeys."

Daisy looked over the completely alive, messy, working kitchen. The double ovens cooking away, the three pots on the chef's stovetop, bubbling happily, and the tall, blond, three months' pregnant glowing woman on top of everything.

Daisy's eyes fell to her small tray of cut brussels sprouts. It seemed to be all she was capable of.

But Shanna—apparently Shanna could do it all.

"Honestly, after the madness of the Thanksgiving Pageant, I almost gave my caterer a call again. But if I did that, I'd never hear the end of it." Shanna nodded toward the den, where Rob, Jamie, Jamie's father, Greg, and Grandpa Bob were sequestered watching the Patriots game. The occasional "Yesssss!" and "Come on!!!" punctuated the low hum of conversation that emanated from that room.

Daisy didn't get it—Rob was easily a better cook than she was. And she wasn't a slouch either. And when he came out of the bathroom, she knew Grandpa Bob could make a mean plate of eggs and bacon. But the second they got there, Shanna swept Daisy into the kitchen, and Grandpa Bob and Rob were removed to the den.

Traditional gender roles were not dead on major holidays.

"I am soooo glad that's over," Shanna continued.

"The Thanksgiving Pageant?"

"Jamie thinks I'm taking on too much—he keeps saying, 'I was president, I know how hard it is!'"

"Well, I mean—it wasn't easy," Daisy equivocated.

It really hadn't been easy. At least not from Daisy's perspective. She'd volunteered to help out as often as possible—
which wasn't as much as Shanna might have liked, because
Daisy had gotten a job, at the Cranberry Boutique on Needleton's Main Street. It specialized in sweater sets. The job was
seasonal, with an option for more, but she intended it to just
help fill their bank account while she still sought production-
related work. However, it got her out of the house and meant
she could help Shanna with the pageant only when she didn't
have a shift—which was not as often as Daisy might have
liked.

Shanna had assumed the leadership position and all that
entailed immediately after the Parent Association Meeting
That Would Live in Infamy. She'd accepted the position with
grace and fanfare, and then dived into the business of showing everyone she *was* a good presidential pick. And the first
expression of that was the Thanksgiving Pageant.

From where Daisy sat, Shanna spent a lot of time on
the phone, smiling through gritted teeth, and asking Suzy
Breakman-Kang where the promotional flyers were.

The rest of the Parent Association board stuck to their
roles. The treasurer counted, the secretary wrote, and the vice
president . . . existed. That left an awful lot of organization
that fell in the lap of the president. And not a lot of assistance.

Daisy had been put in charge of costumes and makeup—
which, thankfully, she had some experience with, thanks to
her adventures in cosplay. Granted, none of the kids were in
the market for a realistic Sailor Moon costume, but the kids
dressed as turkeys and corn cobs and the odd carrot were an
absolute triumph.

The show was . . . traditional, to say the least, with the
Mayflower landing and the friendly natives offering food to

stoic Pilgrims. Telling toddlers about the horrors of coloni-
zation didn't make for a fun Thanksgiving memory, so it was
all glossed over.

Mostly, the kids behaved . . . except for Carrie, who'd been
dressed as an asparagus. And she had run away from the
stage, screaming, "I WILL NOT BE EATEN!!! FREEEEEE-
DOOOOOOOMMMMMM!!!!!" to much laughter, applause,
and Daisy's utter delight.

Rob had leaned over and whispered that was a Thanksgiving memory he would treasure forever.

"Okay," said Shanna, giving the gravy on the stove a quick
whisk, "so it wasn't easy, but it wasn't hard either." Shanna
smirked and gave a quick laugh. "Honestly, I don't know why
Quinn Barrett complained so much. Probably because she
was losing her mind."

As always, the mention of Quinn Barrett made Daisy's
stomach lurch. Though she'd almost gotten used to it by
now—that grumble and falter, the desire to panic-pee at the
name. There had been so much to do over the past three
weeks or so—the whole "Quinn Barrett" thing had sort of
faded into the background.

In fact, the entire video had sort of faded into the background. It had been big on the internet for a week. And the
juiciest local news in Needleton for a few days beyond that. But
since then, it had fallen into the annals of internet history . . .
everywhere, except Little Wonders.

Those primary-colored halls were alive and alight with
speculation, rumor, and innuendo. The parents of Little
Wonders reveled in the juicy gossip—all in their own special
ways.

There was the concern trolling, typified by the moms saying, "I just want to make sure she's okay, poor thing. Should

we set up a meal train?" which was followed quickly by, "I don't think we should even be focusing on the video—we should be focusing on the stress we put ourselves under to be perfect."

Terry Frasier, when he wasn't being overly concerned about the chicken coop situation, managed to break down the footage in the video as if it was the Zapruder film. He had analyzed every angle, determining the exact location of the person who filmed the video by walking through the big yard after drop-off, only leaving once Miss Rosie and Miss Anna kindly but firmly escorted him back to his car.

But he had put his observations into a post on the Parent Association's private Facebook page, which kept the whole thing alive even longer as everyone jumped at the chance to present their alibis.

Elia's dad had piped up first, saying that he was MCing the event . . . so obviously, he was in the clear.

"I wasn't even there until the parade had already been marched!" Jorge, Javi's dad, then declared, his demanding work schedule coming in handy for once.

Dian Qi made it well known that she was far away from the barn, because it set off her allergies, and began a petition to have the historic barn removed as a danger to the children.

Soon enough, everyone was piping up with their alibis. By the time Charlie and Calvin's moms reminded the Facebook group that they had taken over tent assembly and were not able to hold up their phones during the parade, Daisy's gut had been roiling. She was dead certain that someone was going to figure it out, simply by virtue of elimination. They were going to realize who hadn't been accounted for and turn their eyes to the new outsider and throw her and Carrie out of Little Wonders.

And then, Shanna popped up on the Facebook page.

I can't believe we are still debating this, she had typed. I don't remember seeing anyone around that corner of the barn, and Daisy and I had a really good view of it from the other side of the parade.

And suddenly, that was that. They had been down at the other side of the parade. No one questioned it, because everyone was too wrapped up in making sure their own asses were covered. Daisy had an alibi.

That's not to say that Daisy was free. Far from it. Because the rumors and whispers just wouldn't die, and in the fallout she had to pretend even more. Had to smile and laugh. Had to glom herself to Shanna's side to keep from listing.

And all the while, Quinn Barrett walked down the hallway, her head up, her sunglasses on, her heels clicking along the linoleum like the tick of a metronome. She wouldn't let it get to her. And that was the most amazing thing of all. She never turned her head when people's voices became hushed as she passed. Her gaze never veered when people's eyes followed her.

Daisy had never been gossiped about on the internet. So she didn't know, but she had to assume that being gossiped about in person was far, far worse. Daisy wanted to throw herself at Quinn's feet and beg her forgiveness. She wanted this horrible weight off her chest.

Instead, the times she saw Quinn in the hallways at Little Wonders, she kept her head down, her focus on Carrie, made herself as small as possible. Basically, the opposite of what Quinn Barrett did.

Sometimes Quinn had a bag over her shoulder bulging with folders, bearing swatches of fabrics and floor plans. She smiled serenely at everyone she passed, gave polite hellos, engaged in brief small talk with some parents but generally rushed out the door, apparently busy with her amazing career. She didn't have time for anything else.

And thank god for that. If she'd ever zeroed in on Daisy and said more than a murmured "hello" Daisy would probably confess on the spot.

One thing was for certain—Quinn Barrett sure as hell didn't seem like someone who had lost her mind.

Probably her association with Shanna saved Daisy from being cornered in polite chitchat. It was one of the few benefits of being Shanna's handmaiden. Drawbacks included problematic ethnic stereotypes in pageant work and being relegated to chopping vegetables.

"Shanna, honey, do you have another bottle of wine in the fridge?" Jamie said, sticking his head into the kitchen. Rob was right behind him, sliding a silent arm around Daisy's shoulders.

"Jamie. I thought you weren't drinking," Shanna replied with a pout, as she held up her sparkling water. "Out of solidarity."

"I'm not!" Jamie said in easy protest. "My mom wants another glass."

"Already?" Shanna blinked. "Dinner isn't even for another hour."

Shanna and Daisy met each other's gaze. If Patty was the only one drinking wine, and the first bottle was already gone, then maybe she shouldn't be the one to watch Carrie and Jordan at the moment.

Daisy blinked and raised an eyebrow at Rob.

"Maybe we'll go help Patty watch the girls for a little while . . . ," Daisy offered.

"Right," Rob said. "And then maybe we can talk about those Pats tickets, Jamie?"

"Tickets?" Shanna interjected, her eyes swiveling to Jamie. "You were going to find time to go to a Patriots game, when you are telling me that you're so busy with work that you can't help with the Snowflake Breakfast."

The Snowflake Breakfast was the school's nondenominational Winter Holiday event—thankfully low-key after the intensity of the Thanksgiving Pageant. But still, very much on the Parent Association's plate.

Jamie sent his cousin a look, then turned back to his wife. "Dude, I told you, work is crazy right now, I can't commit to a Sunday game . . . and I've helped you with the Snowflake Breakfast, Shanna."

"Giving me your files from last year is not the help I was hoping for—"

"No, you were hoping that I would be able to do all the stuff I did last year . . . and I told you I can't, work is awful right before the holidays—"

Daisy grabbed Rob's hand and backed quickly out of the kitchen before things could devolve even further.

"Jeez," Daisy breathed.

"No kidding," Rob said. "It sucks that Jamie can't make it to a game."

Daisy tried hard not to blink at his cluelessness.

"I know," he said, shooting her a look that said he understood his own cluelessness. "I just thought it'd be . . . fun. Like when we were kids."

He looked so forlorn that Daisy gave him a little hug. "I'd go to a, er, sportsball game with you."

"Sportsball? Man, you really must love me."

He kissed the top of her head, and they wordlessly made their way to the finished basement.

She was a bit wary of what she would find downstairs—a passed-out Patty on the couch while the girls played with matches flitted through her mind—but instead Carrie and Jordan seemed to be playing My Little Pony very nicely together, with Patty keeping a watchful—if glassy—eye.

"Carrie, honey, put on your glasses." Daisy said, noticing the purple band of glasses discarded by the side of the toy bin.

"Glasses are dumb," Jordan said, not looking up from Twilight Sparkle.

Daisy pulled up short. Carrie glanced up at her mother, but Daisy's eyes laser-focused on Jordan.

"Glasses help Carrie see," Daisy said carefully. Trying to not let the *don't fuck with my daughter* come through too strongly.

Jordan just shrugged.

"Yeah, they give Carrie her superpowers—right, bug?" Rob said, grabbing the glasses and sliding them over Carrie's head.

"Daddy, come play," Carrie said, holding out a green pony that Daisy didn't know the name of. Rob dutifully went over to the girls and began to bray and whinny and make them giggle.

Daisy gave Rob a grateful smile, and went to sit down beside Patty on the couch.

Truthfully, Daisy was glad to get a chance to watch over Carrie. She had seen her daughter and Jordan play together a few times and wasn't super keen on the way Jordan played. She didn't like to employ the word "bossy" as it related to girls, but Jordan was . . . adamant about her goals and didn't concern herself much with other kids' feelings. She'd even seen Jordan call another kid "Poopybutt" in anger—which, when she mentioned it to Shanna, was met with an icy stare and a regal "Thank you for letting me know."

Suddenly, Daisy was pulled out of her thoughts when she felt movement on the side of her head. She jerked to the side, only to see that Patty had a lock of her hair in her hands and was twirling it.

"I just love this," Patty said, with a loose smile. "It's so . . . brave."

People commented on Daisy's hair. On the electric shade, the shaggy length, the crazy waves. Back home, the comments were mostly of the "You look amazing!" variety. But in Needleton, the "I love" seemed to come with an unspoken "but."

"I love it, but . . . aren't you a little old for this?"

"I love it, but . . . aren't you a mother?"

*"I love it, but . . . do you really want to stand out *this* way?"*

Rarely, if ever, did someone's "but" come in the form of a feel-up of her hair follicles.

"Ahum." Daisy cleared her throat, and shifted her weight so she didn't exactly move her seat, but still moved just far enough away from Patty that her hair fell free of her hands.

She hoped Patty didn't notice.

"Well, what do you do, Daisy?" Patty asked.

What a delightfully loaded question. "Well, back in Los Angeles, I worked in film and television production. Nothing glamorous—coordinating paperwork, budgeting, that kind of thing."

"Oh, anything I've seen? I just love those *NCIS* shows. Mark Harmon is a dreamboat."

"Um, not *NCIS*, sorry," Daisy said. "Mostly low-budget, independent productions. One movie did pretty well at Sundance a couple of years ago."

"Oh, that's nice," Patty said. Obviously, she didn't know

what Sundance was and what it meant to do well there. Because here, in Needleton, it likely didn't mean anything at all. "There's not a lot of that kind of work around here, though," Patty was saying.

"That's true," Daisy said, her gaze falling to Rob, who was now letting Jordan and Carrie ride him like a pony. "I think Rob snagged the last such job in New England." As her job search attested.

"Then what are you doing for work? If Carrie's at Little Wonders, I just assumed . . ."

"I am currently looking for work in my field, but in the meantime, I am doing some retail. I have a couple of shifts over at a boutique on Needleton's Main Street."

"Which one?" Patty sat up—actually interested. In retail. Go figure.

"The Cranberry Boutique."

"Oh! I know the owner, Elaine! Say hello for me. We went to Wellesley together. A thousand years ago." Then her eyes narrowed. "Don't they pay on commission?"

"They do. But I'm mostly in the stockroom, doing inventory and helping to sort out their books," Daisy said. "Although I would love to get more hours, work up front and make a nice commission."

"Well, I can tell you why you're not," Patty said with a laugh. "It's that."

She pointed to Daisy's hair.

"My hair."

"Well, maybe if it was *just* the hair it would be okay—a cutting-edge style is something Elaine might be able to stomach. But combine it with the tattoos, and of course, *that*." Patty pointed to Daisy's septum piercing. Patty shrugged, as if to say, *Well, you know.*

Daisy was sort of in awe of what she was hearing. Most people didn't say it out loud. And she didn't have a reply. She shot a look in Rob's direction. He had reared up on his knees, watching the exchange. Jordan and Carrie clamored to get on his back.

"Aunt Patty," Rob said, half astonishment, half a warning.

"What?" she asked, nonchalant. There was no rancor in her voice, just matter-of-fact truth. "Elaine is old Needleton, and Needleton is *very* old. If you want more hours at the boutique—I'm just saying a regular hair color and a turtle-neck sweater would go a long way."

Daisy looked at Rob, Rob looked at Daisy.

The magnitude of her words hung in the air . . . but so did the magnitude of the truth Patty drunkenly spoke. Daisy didn't fit in. She knew it. She knew she was as welcome in this living colonial etching as an outbreak of cowpox among the milkmaids. Add that to the Quinn Barrett situation, it wasn't hard to figure out why she fell asleep at night trying to think of ways to get back to Los Angeles.

Hearing it spoken aloud by a drunken in-law at Thanksgiving was . . . well, it was the most stereotypical Thanksgiving thing ever, she thought with a little humor.

Before either she or Rob could break the silence, stomps came down the stairs. Jamie appeared, ducking his head down to be seen below the ceiling.

"There you all are. Come up here, would you?" he said. "Grandpa Bob has an announcement."

An announcement? What kind of announcement? Daisy was drawing a blank. From the look on his face, Rob had no idea either.

"Did Grandpa Bob say anything to you before we drove over?" Daisy asked Rob in a whisper.

Rob shook his head. "We talked mostly about the show, what sort of work we're doing to the house. A little bit about our apartment hunting. Hey," he said, holding her back for a second. "I'm sorry about Aunt Patty. She's just . . ."

What could he say? She's just . . . blunt? Inebriated? Right?

"She's family," Daisy said, saving him from having to finish the sentence.

Carrie and Jordan had scurried up the stairs the second Jamie had come down, with Patty close on the girls' tails, so when she and Rob finally joined everyone in the living room, it was like walking into a formal painting. Grandpa Bob was in an armchair in the center of the room. His son Greg, Jamie's father, stood behind him, his hand on the back of the chair. Patty was seated off to the side. Jamie and Shanna stood opposite them, his arm around her shoulders, curiosity on both their faces. No remnants of their fight in the kitchen could be seen.

The only movement to the family portrait was Queen Elsa and Princess Leia, struggling to get up on the couch.

"Well, well, well, finally made it, did you?" Grandpa Bob said from his seat. His face was grim, set, which was disturbing to see: Grandpa Bob always had a smile on his face, especially when he was looking at his grandson Rob, or playing with Carrie. But now, he honed in on the two of them, sharp and lean. "Been dawdling, have you?"

"We came up when Jamie called us, Grandpa," Rob said, bewildered.

"Not talking about that. I'm talking about your circuitous route to hanging out in my basement again. Across the country, working in California, and then suddenly finding yourself a job back here where you grew up. Although, I can't begrudge you the trip, especially when it yields rewards."

Grandpa Bob nodded toward Daisy, and Carrie. Daisy felt herself blush under this strange kind of scrutiny. Carrie was blissfully oblivious. Continuing to throw her body against the couch, while Jordan sat perfectly still, watching the adults—and taking notes, no doubt.

"But coming home hasn't been all roses. Has it, Daisy?"

"What?" Daisy said, her eyes snapping back to Grandpa Bob.

"You haven't been very comfortable here, have you?"

"I . . . I don't know what you're talking about," she said. And really, she didn't. She'd done her utmost to hide her discomfort in Needleton from everyone. Especially Rob, Carrie, and Grandpa Bob—whose generosity had been above and beyond. She sent desperate eyes to Rob.

I didn't do anything, I'm happy here, I swear, she tried to say with her eyes.

"Of course you do! Rack those brains I know you have," he said to her. "Perhaps, back to Halloween weekend? And an . . . overly exposed encounter?"

All of the blood in her body drained to her feet. Her eyes shot straight to a wide-eyed Shanna, who met her eyes with equal alarm. A single eyebrow raise asked the question, *Did you tell him?*

An imperceptible shake of the head was the answer.

How did he know about the video? Grandpa Bob had only just gotten the internet when they moved in! And why was he bringing it up now?

"I . . . I . . . ," she tried, but nothing would come out.

"So, it seems to me that some kind of adjustment has to be made," Grandpa Bob said. "An adjustment in our living arrangement."

Oh god. He was kicking them out. Because of her. Because of what she did to Quinn Barrett. She and Rob and Carrie would be out on the street, and Rob and his grandfather's relationship would never be repaired.

And it was all her fault.

"I'm so sorry," she blurted out. "I never thought it would cause so many problems."

"Daze," Rob said, softly, but not softly enough to hide his alarm. "What is he talking about? What encounter?"

"I'm talking about when she saw me in my undies in the kitchen, Robbie!" Grandpa Bob said, on a laugh, immediately dispelling all the tension in the room. Daisy sagged against Rob. Shanna practically drifted onto the sofa next to Jordan. When Jamie leaned down to ask if she was all right, she waved him away. "Just . . . pregnant."

"Uh . . . no," Rob said to his grandfather, a gust of breath spelling his relief. "Daisy never mentioned that."

"Don't say I blame her—my skivvies are better forgotten, lest they cause long-term trauma," he said. "But it's happened more than once"—Daisy blushed, because yes, it had happened more than once—"and it got me thinking about our living situation, and the fact that I'm not likely to live that much longer."

"Dad!" said Greg from behind him. "That's not something you should be thinking about."

"Son, I'm past eighty, the life I have left is pretty much all I think about. And how I want to spend it. I also think about what I have left to pass on. And it occurs to me that the main thing I have to pass on is the house."

"Dad . . . what are you talking about?" Greg said.

"Yes, Bob, what are you talking about?" Patty piped up, suddenly interested.

"Well, here's what I was thinking. And since it concerns everyone in this room, I thought it best to bring it up now. I have this house. It's too big for me by myself, but a bit tight for the four of us at the moment. In my will, it passes to my two sons. Since Robbie's dad is no longer with us," Bob managed to say with only a slight hitch in his voice, "it will go to you, Greg, and to Robbie here. And I thought, why not hand it off now?"

"Hand it off now?" Jamie asked.

"The house is in a trust, and I pass the trust on to the two of you. And, Greg, you agree to sell your half of the house to Rob and Daisy. At the family rate, of course."

For a moment no one spoke. And another moment. And another moment.

"Rob and Daisy need a place to live," Grandpa Bob said into the silence. "They can't stay in my basement forever. My master bedroom, however, is much more accommodating. And I know their budget. Rob, didn't you tell me that Needleton's gotten so expensive you could barely afford to buy half a house here? Well, here's half a house. But it all depends on Greg." He turned around and looked at his remaining son. "Greg, what do you think?"

"I . . . I don't like to think about you going anywhere, Dad," he said. "Where will you live? A retirement home?"

"Not my style," his father replied. Then, with a smile, "You know my friend Donna?"

Donna was Bob's "lady friend." She was in her late sixties and dressed in loud animal-print jackets and shiny pants. Daisy had adored her the few times they'd met. She'd brought a lot of color into Bob's life, ever since they'd met about a year and a half ago at Grandpa Bob's bridge club.

"Well, Donna decided she's done with Massachusetts snow. She's got a condo out in Arizona and has asked me to come with her for the winter. I was planning on going right after Christmas."

"You're moving to Arizona?" Rob blurted out. "But we just got here!"

"I'll only be gone till May. Which should give you enough time to convert the basement into a nice little grandparent suite," Grandpa Bob said. "I'm told you're a fairly handy guy—and you work with some handy guys, too. And when I'm there, I'll pay you rent, to help out with whatever outrageous mortgage Greg decides to soak you for."

Grandpa Bob chuckled to himself. Then, he turned to his son. "This is what I want to do, Greggy. Think you can help me out?"

All eyes turned to Greg, whose own eyes were a tad shinier than before.

"I don't like thinking about you dying, Dad. Even though I know it's going to happen. When mom passed, and my brother, you were the only person we had left. I want things to stay as they are. But," he continued, stopping any interruption, "I also want you to be happy. And, from a practical standpoint, when Patty's parents passed, it was traumatic dealing with dividing up the estate and putting the house on the market, and everything else. So maybe, it's a good idea to take care of a large portion of that stuff now."

"Dad, what are you saying?" Jamie asked.

"I'm saying . . . ," Greg said, with a deep sigh. "I think we can make this happen."

Finally, finally, someone made some noise in the room. Patty took her husband's hand in hers, kissed it, in a kind of red-faced, tear-streaked prayer. Jamie came over and clapped Rob on the back. But Carrie jumped up off the couch and said, "YAAAAAAAAAYYYYY!!!"—she might not have followed the minutiae of the very adult conversation going on in front of her, but she knew people were happy, and that made her happy.

"We will do it through a bank, so everything is above-board," Greg said, as he came over to shake Rob's hand, give Daisy a kiss on the cheek. "If you kids can get a down payment together, I think it would help expedite things."

"Yes, absolutely, Uncle Greg. Thank you. And, Grandpa Bob—you're the most amazing person I've ever known."

A house. They were going to have a house. One with seventies plaid wallpaper in the den, and appliances in the kitchen that smoked, and likely some foundation issues given the moisture that came through the basement walls . . . But! It was a house. Their very own house.

And it was in Needleton.

Daisy's stomach lurched. And not just because Rob had grabbed her about the waist and hugged her tight. What this meant was . . . they were truly staying. An apartment would have been a lease, for a year. And at the end of the year they could see if they really wanted to stay on the East Coast, like they'd planned.

But this house was . . .

This house was for the rest of their lives.

"Can you believe it? Grandpa Bob's house will be our house!" Rob was saying in her ear, then he let go of Daisy to lift up Carrie. "What do you think, sweetie—do you want to stay at Grandpa Bob's house?"

"Forever?" she asked.

"Forever," he replied.

Carrie threw her arms around her father's neck and squeezed him tight.

"Wow," Shanna's voice broke through Daisy's haze. "It looks like you'll have a house."

"I guess so," she replied, subdued.

Which Shanna honed in on. "Most of the time when people give you a house, it's a good thing."

"It is! It is," Daisy said. "It's just a little overwhelming. You know, there's all the details to work out with the trust, and . . . there's still the down payment . . ."

"A down payment on half a house?" Shanna said, a little scoffing in her tone. Then, "And, hello? Lawyer over here. I can help out with all the legalities of the trust. Right, Grandpa Bob?" Shanna called out loud to the room, but Grandpa Bob probably couldn't hear her over Greg and Jamie and Rob enthusiastically talking about the house.

"We'll take the basement down to the studs, repair any damage, vapor-barrier the walls before we put in new insulation—" Rob was saying as he balanced Carrie on his hip. "The show actually has all this extra equipment . . . Jamie, you can come by next weekend to check it out?"

"I wish I could, but work—I'll be there every weekend after the holidays, all right?"

Shanna's face pinched, but when she turned back to Daisy, she had a smooth smile on her face. "I think I need to go check on the turkey. Come finish all the vegetables for the ratatouille . . . when you get a chance?"

Shanna excused herself to the kitchen, leaving Daisy alone in a room full of people, talking above one another, ecstatically making plans.

Rob was happy. Carrie was happy.

Everything else was incidental.

Even a down payment on half a house.

Now . . . now they just had to figure out how to get the money.

CHAPTER SEVEN

The Thanksgiving table was a perfect Quinn Barrett production, from start to finish. The china was a hundred and fifty years old and handed down from Stuart's mother at their wedding (she had several heirloom china sets handed down through her family, so she wouldn't miss this particular Wedgwood pattern, or so she often told Quinn). The table runner was reproduction lace, in a Belgian pattern from the late 1700s. The centerpieces were a long row of seasonal plants and flowers in thematic robust colors but varying heights, allowing the eye to travel. Quinn had made the napkin rings with Hamilton out of card paper by tracing turkey cookie cutters, and they added a touch of whimsy. The candles were hand-dipped, and she had found a shop that made their own dyed cement candleholders, a splash of cutting edge to the traditional beauty of the set table.

Martha Stewart would cry if she saw this table, Quinn thought. She would beg to include it in the magazine's pages and ask Quinn for tips on how to put together the look.

Meanwhile, the kitchen was a wreck. Pots and pans caked in grease. Dirty dishes everywhere. But that didn't matter.

She would set to cleaning that once Ham went to bed. She couldn't leave it *all* for Gina, their newly hired housekeeper, who would be coming in tomorrow. She was the same age as Alba with the same grandmotherly charm—and best of all, Ham had taken to Gina with the same grand-nephew type vibe of reverence and adoration.

But she'd started just that week and didn't have the hang of everything yet.

Quinn could hear Hamilton and Stuart in his playroom, just off the dining room. Stuart was in there with him. Deep laughter punctuated Ham's boyish giggles.

Quinn's mother was due to arrive any minute, loud and garish and interrupting everything. Thank goodness she was due to return to her Florida condo to get warm and pretend she was a painter in pastel colors. Or take up quilting, or tropical gardening, or alligator rearing—whatever would hold her attention for a few months. And Stuart's parents would not be back in the States until they grew bored along the south coast of France, usually sometime around Christmas. So, for this brief moment, everything was perfect—as well as being picture perfect.

Instagram perfect.

Quinn had her phone raised and was choosing her format before she remembered that her Instagram was shut down, as well as her Facebook, and every other social media account she had. Sadly, she lowered the phone. It had been three and a half weeks without checking in. Without browsing the internet. Without knowing what all of her friends and family and colleagues were saying about her.

Three and a half weeks since her life had changed forever. And to be quite honest, those three and a half weeks hadn't been so bad. Like with any crash diet, the first week or so was absolutely miserable—the stares, the whispers, the in-person gossip that is so much worse than anything the internet could ever do to you—but she was used to it now. And then of course, there were all her responsibilities to fill her time.

Yes, true, she was no longer working on the Little Wonders Parent Association, and she was sidelined from all of her major projects at Crabbe and Co., but in a way, it was a blessing. Because without having to maintain a split focus (which she was absolutely capable of, and would have executed everything perfectly on all fronts), she would be able to execute what had been left on her plate even MORE perfectly.

And the first of those things was the Greater New England Children's Hospital Charity Ball.

She was determined that this was going to be the charity ball to end all balls. The very basics of the planning had already been in place—indeed, they'd been in the works since last year's charity ball. Now, she was determined to bring the charity ball into this decade and was spending Crabbe and Co.'s budget accordingly. Her invoices for red velvet alone would give Jeremy a heart attack.

But it was necessary. It would be her masterpiece. Her calling card back to the world. And once the Martha Stewart feature on the now finished Beacon Hill house came out, she would be completely redeemed—and the video all but forgotten.

Yes, redemption was within her grasp.

The second thing that Quinn decided to laser-focus on— which was really first in her mind and heart—was Hamilton.

She had been neglectful. She had not been the awesome

parent she knew herself to be. Because if she was an awesome parent, surely her son would be completely 100 percent potty trained by now. So, she determined to redouble her efforts.

So far, she had spent at least four straight Parcels—a full hour—every day after work reading potty books to him, talking to him about how to identify the heavy feeling in his bladder, going over basic gastrointestinal anatomy, and making up songs to be sung to the tune of the infernal earworm "Baby Shark":

> *When you feel, do do do do do do*
> *That you need, do do do do do do*
> *To go pee, do do do do do do*
> *Go Potty!*

The fact that "feel" "need" and "pee" did not technically rhyme irked Quinn greatly.

Her goal was to have him completely accident free by the time he crossed the stage to sing "We Gather Together" dressed as a Pilgrim in the Thanksgiving Pageant.

Which, he had been! For three whole weeks! Except for when he took the stage, there was that telltale wet spot on the front of his costume, and Quinn could feel, next to her, Stuart's jaw tightening.

It was at this inopportune time that she spied Shanna and Jamie across the aisle. Shanna kept her gaze forward, but Jamie . . . Jamie met her eye and gave her a friendly little wave. She ached to return it . . . but couldn't.

Excepting that small moment, the whole week before Thanksgiving had been blissful. Like a family vacation. It was just the three of them. Stuart only left the house to go to his spin class in the city. And when he came back it was to Hamilton, who practically glowed under his father's attention. When it began to snow, Stuart rushed out to the store—an hour later, he came home with a plastic disc sled. He and Ham spent hours going up and down the hill behind the house, coming in with pink noses. He did that several times— running out to the store and coming home with something that lit Ham's eyes up like Disney World.

During the week, Ham went to school Monday through Wednesday . . . and Quinn decided that she could easily place her orders for the charity ball from her home office. So she and Stuart had spent luxurious, stolen hours together.

It was exactly what she needed. What they needed.

And it had led to this perfect moment. Ham and Stuart in the playroom, playing. And Quinn admiring her handiwork, setting and decorating the table. Pots bubbling away. Before the guests arrived.

Why shouldn't she mark this perfect moment?

No reason she couldn't take a picture. Just a picture, to save the moment for herself. Not every picture she posted went on social media.

She moved around the table, trying to find the perfect angle.

Oh, but after a few clicks, she knew this was just so beautiful—the well-dressed table in the focused foreground, the father and son very fuzzy in the background playing together—it was crying out to be seen!

What if?

Her Instagram hadn't been deleted all the way from her phone. She had merely disabled it and could easily reactivate it. With trembling fingers, she went into the app.

Before disabling, she'd deleted every single post that featured Ham (or spaceships)—keeping it entirely design oriented. So there was no "parenting" post to take the brunt of the bile. And she'd always had blocks active on her phone, hiding the comments that were offensive, or violated Instagram's terms of use. But that was apparently so easily circumnavigated. Also, she blocked all commenters that weren't mutual "friends." But then people would tag her and just rag on her that way, so they knew she saw it in their feeds, if not on hers. So she logged on, trepidatious.

The first thing she did was search her name. And then searched the "Halloween Mom" video. And much to her surprise, she didn't find anything new. Nothing had been posted about it, or, really, her, that she hadn't seen before.

Maybe, just maybe, it had faded away completely. Or at least enough that she could post one Thanksgiving table and not make any waves.

She loaded the picture up. She wrote a quick description. *The wonderful calm before the storm.* Then she immediately deleted it. Surely some snarker would comment, *"I hope *you're* keeping calm!"* Or, *"Just don't storm all over the table like you did your kid's Halloween costume, LOL."*

In the end, she decided on something very simple.

This year's table. #thankful

Her thumb hovered over the post button. She closed her eyes.

And when she opened them, the picture was right there, on her feed.

Her breath froze in her lungs. She couldn't move. She didn't even blink, as she watched her phone.

For what felt like hours. It burned in her hand. And then, it happened.

A comment notification.

"Love it!" from an interior designer she knew from conferences.

Then a like popped up. And another.

Nothing extreme, nothing callous or mean. Just . . . people appreciating her perfect table.

Quinn's entire body relaxed.

Ham called out to her from the playroom doorway. He was wearing his special lab coat that she'd had monogrammed with his name, and his green plastic stethoscope. "Mommy! Do you have an ouchy?"

She put the phone in her pocket, and moved briskly out of the dining room. "Oh yes, my, erm . . . elbow has a boo-boo, Dr. Hamilton. Can you help me?"

Stuart and Hamilton smiled up at her as she entered the room.

Yes, maybe they had finally, finally come out on the other side.

Little Wonders Preschool
December Newsletter

Hello, WONDER-ful parents!

Ho Ho Happy Holidays! Welcome to that most magical time of the year—the winter season at Little Wonders! ~~Also known as the month you really should have saved all your sick days up for, because these kids are off more days than they are on.~~ Our little ones are all so excited for the arrival of ~~Christmas Hanukkah Kwanzaa Solstice whatever the hell you celebrate~~ the end of the year that you no doubt are enjoying the fruits of their crafting labors. ~~We know there's glitter everywhere. Take it up with Santa.~~ And to that end, we would like to remind you all that each room has an art supplies closet that they would love help restocking! ~~We want money.~~ Construction paper, glue sticks, safety scissors—ask your individual teachers what they need to help keep our kids in paper snowflakes and cotton ball snowmen! ~~Seriously, a Target gift card will go a lot further than cleaning all the Play Doh out of your craft drawer.~~ We know you are looking for a way to give back to our teachers this time of year, and anything would be appreciated. ~~GIFT. CARDS. If you're not giving your teachers and teacher assistants heartfelt handwritten notes with gift cards inside them, how do you look yourself in the mirror every morning?~~

And what would the holidays be without a holiday party?

After the success of our splendid ~~and uneventful, thank god~~ Thanksgiving Pageant, our new Parent Association president Shanna Stone has decided to make this year's **Snowflake Breakfast** something truly special. ~~If you are not up to date on the presidential transition we witnessed at the last Parent Association meeting, I have the minutes.~~ So we are once again looking for parent volunteers! Come get your volunteer hours in at the most spectacular, cozy, delightful event of the year! ~~Seriously, it's the end of the calendar year, and if you're short on your hours you're SOL after this.~~ We need organizers, decorators, setup/breakdown, cleaning crew, people to call for donations, and everything in between! ~~Oh, yeah. This is basically everything you do at your own house. So, it'll be super fun to do it at the school, right? No wonder we have to force people to sign up for these things.~~

The Snowflake Breakfast will be held on Friday, December 18th from 8:30 AM to 10:30 AM. Santa will be in attendance, ~~yes, with a real beard~~ as will his photographer elves.

Please note that the **school will be closed for the winter holidays from December 21st through January 4th**. So we hope to see you at the Snowflake Breakfast before we all settle in for our long winter's nap! ~~Two weeks. Two weeks at home. With your child. And no one else.~~

Together in Parenting!
Suzy Breakman-Kang
Little Wonders Parent Association Secretary

CHAPTER EIGHT

For Daisy, December wasn't complete without a big trip to the movies. Something you buy tickets for in advance and plan drinks and dinner around. Maybe something you even wait in line for several weeks to be one of the first to see.

While Daisy didn't have weeks to sit in line to be the first person to see a movie anymore, she did have Grandpa Bob babysitting for Carrie, a planned evening out in the city, and two tickets to the new *Star Wars* movie in her pocket.

Daisy had earned this night out. She'd been planning it since she learned the release date of the film. Obviously, her plans required adjustment when they ended up moving to Needleton, but she'd still had this date blocked off on her and Rob's shared calendar for months.

It was her Christmas, Hanukkah, and New Year's Eve all rolled into one.

Sadly, Daisy hadn't been able to go to opening night, as opening night was right before the Snowflake Breakfast, and Shanna might have had a nervous breakdown/murdered Daisy/binge-eaten all the olives in the greater New England area.

In fact, Shanna had threatened to do all three things.

"Daisy you can*not* go to see a midnight movie in the city eight hours before the Snowflake Breakfast! We have to be there early to take delivery of Santa's chair and the decorative full-size nutcrackers! And I need you to make sure Santa actually shows up—the agency promised me it wasn't going to be a drunk and that he'd have a real beard, but then I spoke to Suzy and she said her office ordered a Santa from the same agency and it turned out he was drinking whiskey the whole time! Oh, I could kill you—please, please, just wait till after the breakfast, okay? I know *Star Trek* is your thing or whatever but it'll still be playing in the theaters the week after, right? Where's my spreadsheet of volunteers? I need to sit down . . . I think I might be having a panic attack—or, no, the baby is hungry. Can you slide me that jar of olives?"

Shanna was just out of her first trimester now (as she was quick to remind everyone) and having "held it together" through the potentially tumultuous first trimester—wherein she did not display any of the morning sickness or uncomfortable symptoms that Daisy remembered with such clarity—she was entitled to indulge her unborn child in every demand it put upon her body.

Basically, this involved a lot of sitting down (understandable), olives (cravings, totally made sense), and relying on Daisy to help out with the proverbial heavy lifting as much as possible.

Which was actually not as much as Shanna would have liked. Because Daisy had managed to get a couple more shifts at the Cranberry Boutique.

In the most depressing way possible.

The color on the box said it was a "Caramel Brown"—she guessed that was pretty close to her natural hair color. It had been a while since she had last seen it. It took two boxes to completely kill off the electric blue but, in the end, caramel highlights swished through her hair. Maybe she could make this work, she decided.

But when Carrie saw it, she cried.

Carrie just wasn't used to it, Daisy told herself. She was surprised by the abrupt change. She wasn't the only one.

"You don't have to do this," Rob had said.

"You don't like it," Daisy replied.

"No! No—don't get me wrong, you look amazing. It's . . . just so different from what I'm used to. But Aunt Patty doesn't know what she's talking about—it's the holidays, they're going to need all hands on deck anyway in the boutique."

"Working the front, making a commission—it's a lot more money than just restocking and straightening out the books."

"We could rethink Carrie's school?" he'd suggested. "Reduce her days, or take her out and reenroll next year, once we have the down payment?"

This just exasperated Daisy. They'd talked circles around and around about school when they first moved to Needleton. And it had been *Rob* who insisted that Carrie attend Little Wonders, even though it took out a massive chunk of his salary. It was too good for Carrie, he'd argued then. And it meant that Daisy would have the time to figure out an East Coast version of her career path, which he was adamant the move would not hamper.

"She's only three days a week now. And we wouldn't get her in next year," Daisy replied, trying to hide her annoyance. "Shanna says there's a massive waitlist, and we only got in because of her and Jamie's connections."

They talked further, of course—theorized, pitched a bunch of "what if" scenarios, but come the Monday after Thanksgiving, Daisy removed her piercing, found a deep red turtleneck that passed as festive, paired it with her most respectable pair of high-waisted trouser jeans, ankle boots, a banal black pea coat, and made her way to the Cranberry Boutique.

But she put on her most massive pair of sunglasses, and with a small smile at the irony, tried to do her best Quinn Barrett walking down the hallways of Little Wonders imitation. She'd planned for a casual but firm entrance. She ended up closer to "hesitant mincing."

There was no one in the store.

"Hello?" she'd called out, as the bell on the front door tinkled.

"Hello!" came Elaine's voice from the back of the shop. She came forward, all scarves and perfectly streaked gray hair. Her scarf today seemed to consume her—it was decidedly Christmassy, a green and red plaid shot through with gold, and tied in the most intricate knot this side of a gentleman's cravat. "I'm sorry, you caught me still getting ready. We're not quite open yet."

"I know . . . I'm not late, am I?" Daisy said as she took off the massive sunglasses and her heavy pea coat.

A frown crossed Elaine's face, then, as she stepped closer—her eyebrows went up as her jaw went down. "Daisy?" she asked, incredulous. "Is that you?"

Fifteen minutes later, Daisy was behind the register, opening up the store, and working the sales floor. And by the end of the day, she was scheduled for shifts every day Carrie was in school.

Cosplay, she told herself. This was just cosplay. She was playing the character of Daisy, a young Needleton mom and wife, who picked up retail shifts for a little "fun money." Not Daisy the weird, nerdy girl who desperately needed to make some cash so they could put together a down payment for their very own home.

This Cosplay Daisy knew all the latest trends and designers. She knew what a good silk scarf could do for an outfit. She knew that your sister was just going to *love* that cashmere sweater, and just how adorable your six-year-old grandson would look in that polo shirt with a whale insignia on the breast pocket.

And when she got home, she was herself again. Sure, her hair was a different color, but she could change into a Chewbacca Is My Copilot shirt and d20 patterned leggings and Cosplay Daisy would disappear.

But Cosplay Daisy kept popping up in the oddest places. Target (so many more "can I help yous" from the red-shirted employees), the grocery store (someone ma'amed her. *Ma'amed* her). And the Snowflake Breakfast.

Daisy had gotten there early, taken delivery of the life-size nutcrackers and Santa's chair, smelled Santa's breath to make sure he was sober and ran his name through the sex offenders' registry. All was checking out, except the beard.

His beard was red. Not white. Not even gray. *Red.*

Shanna had been apoplectic. "I am calling the agency! I specifically said white beard—this guy couldn't even be bothered to dye it???"

Privately Daisy agreed. They could have put Grandpa Bob in a red suit and he would have had the time of his life, she'd whispered to Rob after it was all said and done. But this guy seemed so over being Santa—like he'd reached his limit of being peed on, cried on, pulled, or hugged that he was just phoning it in. He'd hoed his last ho.

While Shanna was off making that phone call, and hopefully getting 10 percent or so knocked off Santa's rate, Daisy was at the door, greeting people and directing volunteers from the list that Shanna had handed to her.

"Hi—we haven't met," said a volunteer, as he came to the door. "I'm Elia's dad? I signed up to bring pastries." He wielded a pink pastry box.

"Um, actually we have met," she replied. "Daisy Stone— Carrie's mom?"

She read surprise on his face, then his eyes flicked from her hair to her face (to where her septum ring used to be) and to where the barest hint of her tattooed arms peeked out at her wrist.

She realized then she was in Cosplay Daisy's clothes— headed to the Cranberry Boutique after the breakfast was over.

He blustered for a minute about how she looked different— good! but different—and then looked ridiculously relieved when she pointed him to the refreshments table.

It was only then that she looked at the paper and saw that Shanna had written in big bold letters: DO NOT LET ELIA'S DAD BRING PASTRIES. NONORGANIC!!!

The rest of the Snowflake breakfast went . . . fine. Most people were really worn down by the holidays—and it was a week before they would even *have* the holidays. The parents mingled, coffee was drunk, and the pastries riddled with nonorganic ingredients were quietly disposed of. The kids came in with their classes one at a time, Red Beard Santa did his duty, photos were taken, gifts asked for, and toddlers cried and screamed and peed.

All the while Shanna moved through the room, talking to all the parents, directing the volunteers—giving directions and saying things like "Aces!" and "Thumbs up!" It was part of a strategy she had read about, she'd told Daisy: leading through positivity.

It mostly looked like Shanna was exhausting herself trying to make something perfect that was meant to be low-key and fun.

And when the whole thing was done, Daisy was exhausted, too. But she still had her shift at the boutique, and what got her through both was the thought of her dinner-and-a-movie plans for that night. Time spent alone! With her husband! And no small child! An after-dinner snack of a bucket of popcorn and the chest-tingling trumpet blare of the opening notes of the *Star Wars* theme were in her future.

So much so that she didn't want her future to wait—so after work, she quickly grabbed Carrie from Little Wonders, handed her off to Grandpa Bob with the promise of ice cream and a movie night of her own, swiped on some lip gloss, and headed out the door to catch a train into Boston.

As she walked through the streets of the city, the cold didn't bother her—even though it was freaking frigid. (How did people live like this? Another check in LA's column, being able to feel her toes.) She felt alive in a way she hadn't in ages. The thrum of the city—even a freezing one like this one—gave her life. People bustled. Lights popped. New and interesting things were in shop windows. As she moved across a bridge into Cambridge, she found herself treading on more familiar turf.

There, amid the twinkly Christmas lights strung around Harvard Square, was a tattoo parlor—its neon lights red and green for the occasion. There were an alarming number of Red Sox and Harvard logos in their offerings, but otherwise it had some glorious art.

She passed by kids who looked like they went to Hogwarts, in long scarves, laughing with kids who had mermaid hair colors, Goth makeup, and metallic Doc Martens.

Down the street was an alternative bookstore, teeming with gift ideas in the window for your favorite nerd: urban fantasy own-voices novels, stacks and stacks of cooperative tabletop games from indie game makers, and clothing styled with the latest deep-dive memes. Daisy couldn't help but smirk at the vintage Frak Off shirt hiding behind a couple of Lying Cat tees.

She almost wandered into the alt bookstore . . . but then, she saw it: across the way—a comics shop, about the width of a hallway. So small, it barely had a front window. But in that window?

A *Dungeons & Dragons: Shadowplague* trade paperback.

She could spot it from a thousand paces. She had her own copy of the graphic novel, of course. Well-read and dog-eared, and sitting in a box somewhere in Grandpa Bob's garage. The first original D&D comic in ages, she had devoured it when it came out while she was in college.

But to see on the cover the familiar art of the characters on their quest . . . it was like seeing an old friend.

She was inside the little comics shop before she realized she had crossed the street. If possible, it was narrower inside than it was outside—like an anti-TARDIS—with a long row of bins on one wall stuffed to overflowing with comics, an island of more bins down the middle, and a long, high glass counter dominating the other side. Inside the glass counter were myriad dusty collectibles, from role-playing miniatures to some Funko Pop Avengers to a surprising Bart Simpson collection.

A dinky bell rang as the door shut behind her, which, after

her last few months of retail experience, should have set the salespeople into motion.

Not here though.

A single employee lounged behind the counter, his head buried in a horror comic that Daisy didn't recognize. When he finally did glance up, Daisy noted that he could have been thirty or fifty, she was unable to tell behind his massive beard and thick glasses. His shirt said something in Klingon. His eyes grazed Daisy behind thick glasses before returning to his book.

"Can I help you with anything?" he said in a monotone.

"No—just looking," she said.

"Hrmph," he said as he settled back down into his horror comic.

Daisy's eyebrows went up. Back in LA, when she went into comics shops or bookstores, she could count on getting sucked into a conversation for at least an hour.

But this guy couldn't even look up. Didn't he know it was the holiday season in retail land? Maybe he wasn't in a festive mood.

"What are you reading?" she tried brightly.

The guy sighed deeply. *"Infidel."*

"Oh. I haven't heard of it."

"No kidding, lady," he murmured under his breath.

Daisy's face fell. Oh, she got it now. He was That Guy.

That Guy was the one at the con who started off the Q&A segment with "Actually, I have more of a comment than a question . . ."

That Guy spent hours online railing against *The Last Jedi* because he didn't like how the Rey and Kylo Ren pairing was centered in his movie about blowing things up in space . . .

It went without saying that, to That Guy, the all-female *Ghost-busters* was sacrilege.

That Guy would go through Reddit threads and correct misspellings on a woman's post and get pissed off if she didn't "acknowledge his contribution."

And That Guy never believed a woman like Daisy could read, let alone read a comic.

Her eyes narrowed. She wasn't about to let That Guy get through his holiday season without a visit from the ghost of Christmas Reality Check. "That book in the window—the Dungeons and Dragons one."

He looked up again. "Yes. D&D, you mean."

"Uh-huh. *Shadowplague* is volume one. Do you have further volumes or just the one?"

He blinked at her. Daisy liked to think he was mildly impressed. "Looking for a gift for someone?"

"No—why?"

"If you are looking for a gift, we have all of our new releases and graphic novels up front."

"Up front," she repeated, trying to follow. Yes, one would think they kept gifts stocked up front in the holiday season. "Not the back?" she said as she attempted patient sarcasm.

"Yeah—the back is where we store all the collections we acquire, thumb through trying to find a piece of gold among the dross. But trust me, if you're looking for something for your boyfriend or whoever, up front is your best bet." He was looking at her now, seeming to remember that a sale was a good thing. "We can order most anything, too. If they gave you the name or title—or publisher, if possible."

"Boyfriend?" she said. She could feel the tips of her ears burning.

"Oh, sorry—" he said, glancing at her hand. "Husband."

A disbelieving guffaw left her lips. Daisy had met That Guys before. But usually, all she had to do was lift an eyebrow and drop a word or two about her latest module into conversation and That Guy dissipated into a puddle of his own prejudices before he could even mouth the words "fake geek girl."

Daisy could have thrown down against him. She could have leaned against the counter and told him that his Bart Simpsons were out of order (she had absolutely no idea if that was true, but it would annoy him). She could have commented on the cover art on the cover of his *Infidel* comic, and how it was reminiscent of seventies horror movies. She could have given him a dissertation-length monologue on how the Society for Creative Anachronism in Berkeley in the sixties led to Gary Gygax's *Chainmail* game then his true masterpiece Dungeons & Dragons, and or how John Rogers pulled on that connective tissue when he wrote *Shadowplague,* which was currently in the shop window.

She could have rolled up her sleeves and showed off her d20 tattoo, next to her galaxy, far far away tattoo. And then harrumphed out of the store, refusing to buy a single thing.

She had named her daughter after Carrie Fisher, for Christ's sake!!

But then—she caught a glimpse of herself in the reflection of the glass counter.

She couldn't say any of that stuff. Because she wasn't Daisy right now.

She was still Cosplay Daisy.

Dull, boring, blah.

She looked like her sister. Like her *mother.*

Not like Daisy.

It was as she was struck dumb by her own reflection that the dinky bell rang again, signaling a new arrival.

"Hey—I thought that was you," Rob said, stamping his feet as he came in. There was a light dusting of snow in his hair. A glance to the window told her that it had started snowing in the intervening minutes. The snow made Rob's dark hair take on a salt-and-pepper quality, and she suddenly realized what he would look like in five, ten years.

"Hey, man," said That Guy behind the counter, quickly acknowledging the newcomer in a way he hadn't for Daisy.

"Hey—cool place," Rob replied. "Love the Barts."

That Guy smirked and nodded and left Rob to Daisy as he took her by the waist and gave her a big kiss.

"I'm still getting used to this. I did a double take when I saw you from the window," he whispered as he fingered a piece of (dull, awful) brown hair. But judging by the kiss he gave her, in his eyes it was a good change.

"You shopping for something?" he said, looking around the store.

"Not really," she said with a grimace. But Rob didn't see that because he was obviously bursting with some news.

"What is it?" she asked. "What's happened?"

"I was wondering if you would like to go to a ball with me."

"A ball?" she asked, incredulous. "Like a for real, 'lords and ladies dancing the waltz' type ball?"

"Not quite. It's the New Year's Eve charity ball for the Greater New England Children's Hospital," Rob replied with a laugh. "Jo-Jo, on the show? He and his dad, Joe Sr., are big supporters of the hospital, and they bought a table. Gave me a pair of tickets."

Wow, she knew the stars of the show made a decent chunk

of change in secondary endeavors like their home improve-
ment businesses (PBS not paying too much) but enough to
buy a table at a fancy charity dinner? Who knew public television fame was so potent.

"Oooo, do I need a costume?" she said, lifting her eyebrows. Visions of a General Holdo lavender draped gown
flitted through her mind.

"You . . . need a dress?" he grinned at her, hopeful. "It's a
kind of swanky thing."

There was a hint of warning in his voice. Right. So, no
costume.

"So what do you say? Wanna swank it up with me?"

Rob was so excited, so obviously proud of his budding
friendship with Jo-Jo, brandishing this proof of it like a shiny
new toy. How could she possibly say no?

Over her shoulder she saw That Guy at the counter, somehow both bored and eavesdropping at the same time.

"Sure," she said, with a smile. "Sounds like fun."

"Great," Rob said, then checked his watch. "So . . . are you
ready?"

"For what?" she asked.

"For what," he scoffed. "Dinner? Movie? The most ecstatic
experience of your life?"

That Guy smirked into his comic, obviously not understanding what the ecstatic part of her evening would be.

She was suddenly so disgusted that she was in here, sully-
ing her evening with That Guy.

"Yeah, I'm more than ready to get out of here," she said,
taking his arm and walking to the door.

"Have a good night—have fun at your . . . charity ball,"
That Guy said, not even lifting his eyes from his comic.

Yeah—that's who she was to him. Suburban mom, having

her date night in the city. Fancy charity ball on the horizon. Utterly clueless.

It was on the tip of her tongue to tell him they were going to see *Star Wars*—and would have definitely seen it last night at midnight if she hadn't been second in command at the Snowflake Breakfast—but why bother? Why give him any more of her time?

Then, That Guy called out after them. Or rather, after Rob. "Hey, man—just so you know, we got the complete set of the D&D graphic novels that you see in the window. Volumes one through three, or as the *Fell's Five* compendium."

Rob looked at him for a second, blinked. Then glanced at Daisy. "Cool, man. Thanks."

And they were out the door.

By the time they got through dinner, Daisy told herself, she would have forgotten That Guy's looks. By the time they were getting their after-dinner popcorn, she would have completely forgotten his sneers, his tone. And by the time the trumpet blare of John Williams's score thrust her to the back of her seat, she would be entirely in another world, away from all the That Guys, Snowflake Breakfasts, and Needletons.

That's what she told herself, at least.

But even as the words solidified in her mind, they turned to dust. Even she knew she was lying.

CHAPTER NINE

The Greater New England Children's Hospital New Year's Charity Ball would go down in history as the most memorable event of the season for the Boston social scene. At least, it would for Quinn Barrett—but she hoped for everyone else, it would fade into a distant memory.

Of course, that hadn't been her aspiration. No, that only became her aspiration at 11:58 PM the night of the ball. She knew the exact time because of the large art deco clock that had been behind her in the video.

Not the Halloween video.

A *new* video.

A completely new and different way to destroy her life.

The night had started gloriously.

Quinn Barrett was justifiably proud of herself. The charity ball was beyond beautiful. She managed to deliver a grand, upgraded scheme at no (extreme) additional cost. And she did it during the holidays.

And the holidays. Did. Not. Stop. They were a mad race of gift shopping, holiday cooking, wrapping, decorating, planning, and that was before she even got to work in the morning.

But Quinn handled it all with her usual trademark perfection. She was determined that the charity ball planning would have no impact on her other responsibilities.

She still worked at getting Gina up to speed to help around the house.

She still had her daily Parcels devoted to potty training.

She still managed all her lunch dates with Stuart—but he was as busy as she was, work presumably preoccupying him. But they did manage twice weekly sex sessions, which was a miracle of planning, considering their individual schedules. (One or the other of them might have been asleep during the activity, but honestly, that was just optimal time management.)

And she still delivered a stunning Christmas Day. The likes on her Instagram were proof of that.

The tree was twelve feet of white and silver decorations— with a few of Ham's preschool decorations studded throughout. Ham had been a ball of three-year-old joy, and Stuart was gloriously rumpled—it was practically a holiday luxury car commercial.

The only thing missing from the photos was a golden retriever puppy with a ribbon around its neck for Ham. But she knew it was a nonstarter and didn't even broach it with Stuart.

The one little reprieve she gave herself was skipping the Snowflake Breakfast. She conspicuously decided to schedule a doctor's appointment for Ham to get his flu shot that morning.

Stuart's parents were back from their Riviera trip, just long enough to indulge in a Christmas Day breakfast and give Hamilton his present of a pure silver baby rattle (how old did they think their grandson was?) before they headed out to get some "well-deserved rest" on St. Lucia. It was the perfect length of time to be judged by them, found wanting, and then they left.

Ham had dived into his gifts like an Olympic swimmer: headfirst, no hesitation. Stuart gave her Cartier earrings to match her watch. They were gorgeous, but strangely, felt like an afterthought to her. Her gift to Stuart was a weekend in New York City, just the two of them—to be used when Gina was ready to assume overnight care.

Yeah, she killed it this Christmas. A perfect Quinn Barrett production, from start to finish.

And when she walked into the Wharf Room at the Boston Harbor Hotel, she knew that it had all been worth it.

Quinn Barrett—the indomitable, unyielding bitch on wheels who never settled for less than perfection—was back, and better than ever.

She had taken a nondescript hotel ballroom and completely transformed it into a winter wonderland, circa 1920s jazz club.

Quinn had pushed herself, the bounds of her imagination, her organizational prowess, her design skills, and the capacities of the hotel crew, until the final product looked more like one of the Great Gatsby's opulent bacchanalias had encountered a freak ice storm.

The trust's event coordinator had wanted to kill her.

The result was magical.

Quinn had no control over the music. She had no control over the food. But damn if it wasn't the most perfect 1920s ballroom anyone had ever seen.

And that was what everyone said.

"Darling, it's exceptional," Jerome said, as he entered the glittering, pulsating party, his eyes drawn up along the column lines to the ceiling. Beyond the firm taking on the decorations at cost, he had always donated generously to the hospital—at least since Quinn introduced him to Stuart and the benefits of cultivating connections in that circle. "It was a risk going so far; you know these old Bostonians."

Yes, she did know those old Bostonians. Ostentatious displays of their wealth were not de rigueur, as her mother-in-law might say.

But at the moment, those old Bostonians were living it up, utterly enraptured by the party and the festive mood.

"I know you've been under stress—and yet, you deliver this masterpiece. Well done, my girl. Well done."

Quinn felt the glow of her mentor's praise as keenly as she did when he'd first hired her all those years ago.

Stuart, at her side, put his arm around her shoulders. "Of course she did—I expect no less than perfection from my wife."

A kiss landed on her temple. She turned to Stuart and winked at him.

"Quinn!" Sutton's voice squealed over the jazz band playing from the other side of the room. "It looks amazing in here!"

"Thank you—so do you," Quinn replied. Sutton did a spin in a knee-length beaded-fringe gown that Quinn was certain was vintage. Quinn worked out hard—Pilates had brought her body back from pregnancy with zeal, but it still would never again be the body of a twenty-seven-year-old spin class enthusiast.

"Hi, Sutton," Stuart said, leaning forward to give Sutton a friendly peck on the cheek. "You missed spin class on Friday."

"I was with my parents," she said. "They're not really into the whole six AM athleticism thing."

"Wait . . . you are in the same spin class?" Quinn asked, surprised. "That's quite the coincidence."

"Not really—there's only one spin studio in the city worth your time," Stuart said, brightly. "Remember when I switched from the seven AM class to the six AM class? Well, who should be there in the front row making us all look bad but your protégé here!"

"Listen, just because you can't keep up—"

"I can't! No one can! I'm going to have you investigated for blood doping."

Quinn relaxed into a smile as they continued to rib each other like bratty siblings. Sutton then turned back to Quinn. "How did you do this all—I could never have pulled this off! I barely pulled off a kids' bathroom in the Beacon Hill house."

"Now, now, I saw the photos, that bathroom is delightful—perfect for kids," Jeremy said.

"Oooo . . . did you see the photos from the spread? The magazine just sent them over to the office."

"The Martha Stewart magazine?" Quinn practically danced with anticipation. "Not yet—did you get to read the article?"

"No, they only sent over the photos, but my god, Quinn, it's glorious. You are going to be so proud when you see it."

Quinn couldn't help beaming. Here it was, true validation. Standing in the middle of that ballroom, being feted for a job well done on two fronts, and a night of gaiety in front of her. It really couldn't get better than this.

Sutton suddenly grabbed her arm. "Oh my god—is that JAXXON LARUE?"

She was staring into the sea of people—Quinn had absolutely no idea which one had captured her attention, but she would have bet on the tall, dopey-haired blond one in the middle of a pack of younger women, taking selfies.

"Who on earth is Jaxxon LaRue?"

"I've told you about him!" Sutton replied. "He's a YouTube star—he does all of these crazy things, like BASE jumping with Tom Cruise and eating super-hot chicken wings with Chrissy Teigen."

"I understood about three words in that sentence," Quinn said, bemused. "How about you, Stuart?"

"I understood about two, but I do know he's here because he endowed a chair after we did a heart and lung transplant on his little brother."

Quinn was about to marvel at the fact that someone who was merely internet famous could have the kind of money required to endow a chair at the hospital, when Sutton's grip transferred from her arm to Stuart's.

"You saved his little brother's life?"

Stuart shrugged, nonchalant. "I was on the surgical team."

"Can you introduce me?" Sutton squealed.

Stuart glanced at Quinn. "If I can be spared from living in your opulent shadow for just a moment?"

She gave him permission with a look. Stuart offered Sutton his arm and guided her into the throng of people surrounding this YouTube star and his camera phone. Quinn snorted a laugh as she saw Stuart maneuver Sutton with a hand on the small of her back face-to-face with Jaxxon LaRue.

Really, it wasn't as if there weren't *actual* celebrities here. She'd spied an Affleck brother somewhere around and more than one Red Sox player. A few Patriots were in the crowd too, not to mention people with names older than Boston itself. The idea that a goofy blond YouTube star reduced someone as confident and poised as Sutton to a puddle of squeals was a little alarming.

She would have to have a talk with her about the best way to present herself to clients, Quinn thought. Especially if she was going to be graduating to her own accounts in the new year. It wouldn't do for the protégé of Quinn Barrett, partner at Crabbe, Barrett, & Co., to be completely cow-eyed around someone mildly famous.

And that was how most of the evening went. Quinn moved around the room, talking to acquaintances, people Stuart worked with, people who commented on the amazing décor. People asked for her card. She demurred at least twice before giving it to them, pretending she didn't bring business cards to a charity event, but oh look! She found one in the side pocket of her clutch!

Speeches were given—by the chief of pediatric surgery, the Affleck brother, the banal comedian they had hired to MC the event. The head of the trust—a pearl-encrusted grande dame who no doubt arrived in Boston on the back of Paul Revere's horse—came up and announced the grand total raised by the ball, more than any other previous year. Raffle tickets were still being sold, and the winners would be announced just before midnight.

Then the band started to play, and the dancing began. Quinn danced with Stuart. She danced with Jerome. She danced with someone who'd played for the Red Sox in the nineties.

It was nice, it was so damn nice to have this night. A night where her past was behind her. Where everyone saw her accomplishments and did not associate it with one bad afternoon in late October. (Because, come on—if anyone knew about bad afternoons in late October, it was the Red Sox.)

And one where no one from Little Wonders could come and make her feel small.

Although, for a quick second, Quinn thought she saw the little blue-haired mom—Daisy?—who was Shanna's shadow on the Parent Association board. But no—she blinked and saw that her hair wasn't blue, it was brown. It must have been someone else. And she went back to dancing.

After all that dancing she needed some refreshments, so set herself off to the bar.

Out of all the rooms she had done for the ball, the bar was definitely her favorite. It looked like a glamorous speakeasy. The bar was full service, with the requisite teacups and jam jars used for serving the whiskey-heavy mixed drinks. When she wandered in, the bar was fairly empty. There was only one other couple, who was leaving, and a pair of young adults gabbing at the far end of the bar, by the window.

The boy was white blond and painfully thin, but vivid as he spoke, talking about running track, a concert he attended, and whatnot. The girl was stunning in an Instagram model kind of way—large pouty lips, thin where she was supposed to be, pert where it was pertinent. She had that half-bored, half-interested gaze of someone who was okay with this until something better came along.

"Vodka martini, top shelf," Quinn murmured to the barman, still watching the kids. The barman went to the top shelf, but found the fancy frosted vodka bottle to be empty.

"Looks like I need a fresh bottle. In the back," he said to her. Did he have an invitational glint in his eye? She glanced up at him again—oh my goodness, he did! As if he wouldn't mind her coming back to the storeroom with him to find said bottle. He must have been twenty-five. He was decently good looking. And it was all she could do to not preen with delight.

Instead, she shot him a wry look, and waved her left hand to him, shooing him back into the storeroom with the power of her wedding ring.

And yet, it was still flattering. Her gaze found its way back to the kids at the other end of the bar. They were now posing into the girl's phone, held up high to give the best angle, her pout on full display.

God, had Quinn ever been that young? That totally invested in only herself? That happy and hopeful and stupid?

"Hey," said the boy to the girl in a low whisper that unfortunately carried. "Wanna actually enjoy this party?"

Little Miss Pout turned interested as soon as a thin, rolled joint was produced from the kid's pocket.

No, she was definitely never that stupid.

She marched over to their side of the room, just as a lighter's flame lit the end of the joint.

"Hey!" she said, as the girl sucked in her breath and held it. She turned to Quinn, and looked impossibly young—fifteen at most, with the fear of being caught by an adult quickly subsumed by her own bravado.

"Yeah?" the boy said.

"You can't smoke in here. This is nonsmoking."

"Yeah, but it's not really smoking, you know. Not like cigarettes."

"Is it smoke that goes into your lungs and then the atmosphere? Because that's smoking, regardless of the drug being delivered to your bloodstream," Quinn said.

"Jeez, *mom,* calm the eff down," the girl muttered, and then snorted a giggle. She handed the joint back to the boy.

"If I were your mother, I might remind you that this is a hospital function. And there are a lot of people here that have rebuilt spines and newly cancer-free lungs they want to keep healthy."

"Yeah, and he's one of them, so back off, dude," came a voice from the other end of the room. Quinn turned. It was that overgrown manchild who had Sutton all up in a twist, Jaxxon LaRue.

Up close, Quinn could tell that some of his appeal was his cuteness. Like a St. Bernard—fluffy and muscley and huggable. But beyond that first impression, there was something similar to a scoff on his face, as if his absurd height literally made him better than the people shooting their adoration up at him.

One of those adorers was the girl, who stood up straight immediately when he walked into the room. "Hey, Jax," she cooed. "Your brother and I were just talking about you."

"No, we weren't," the boy muttered, but went over to Jax anyway and gave him that half-handshake, half-manhug thing that bros did.

"Dude, you don't think I know you're talking about me all the time? Telling people about how your SAT scores were better than mine?"

The boy cracked up. "Hey, I gotta get one up on you whenever I can, man."

"It would've helped if I took the SATs."

The girl started giggling like a stoned, well-groomed hyena. "Like, right? Oh my god, how crazy."

"I thought you left already," the boy said to Jaxxon.

"Nah, dude, I promised I'd announce the raffle winner—some crazy-rich dude is gonna win a trip to South America."

"Sounds amazing," the girl said, hopefully.

"Eh. I've been. The women are hot, but otherwise, whatevs."

Quinn shook her head, trying to clear it of the confusion that was suddenly reigning in her brain. Maybe the fumes had drifted over her way and clouded her mind, but mostly it was just complete shock at the self-involvement on display. And the complete lack of understanding. But it was time to get back to the most life-pressing point.

"Excuse me—if you're his brother," she said to the blond boy, "then that means you had a complete heart and lung transplant, right?" The kid looked to his brother, who raised an eyebrow. The kid turned back to her and did the same. "Yeah, so?"

"Yeah, so?" echoed Jaxxon LaRue. "Wait, do I know you from something?"

"Maybe you saw me in the hospital, with my husband, who was one of the surgeons who saved your brother's life?" Quinn said, indignant. "But I doubt it, because if you did ever come to the hospital, you'd know your brother shouldn't be *smoking pot* with a heart and lung transplant!"

The boy and the girl (who seemed to be a little more cognizant of what was happening) were able to be cowed. But not Jax.

"Hey, it's medicinal. It's like, therapy?"

"A sixteen-year-old kid with a heart and lung transplant has a prescription for medical marijuana?"

"Dude, what made you such a tight ass?"

"*Dude,* someone has to be a sane adult for your brother's sake, and it sure as hell isn't going to be you."

Jax finally, finally looked a little sheepish. Unfortunately, sheepish was a good look on him, and he knew it. Likely knew how to use it, too. He looked up at her from underneath blonde bangs in desperate need of a trim, like a puppy dog hoping for forgiveness after chewing a shoe.

Little did he know that Quinn was immune to puppy dog looks from internet stars.

"The joint," she said in her most commanding mom voice, holding out her hand to the boy and girl, but never taking her eyes off Jax. *"Now."*

The girl suddenly realized she still had it in her hand and jumped and gave a little squeak when she saw it there, still smoldering. The joint flew out of her hand and landed in a dark corner.

A dark corner draped with raw, very flammable canvas.

"Oh my god, are you crazy?" Quinn hotfooted it over to the corner. She peered into the dark, finding tiny flashes of red ash.

"You can't just"—STOMP—"fling things around"—STOMP—"like that!"—STOMP—"Are you freaking insane?" STOMP.

When she was satisfied, she let out a deep sigh, brushed a strand of hair out of her eyes, and, after retrieving the now squished joint, straightened her gown, and turned around.

And found Jaxxon LaRue watching her, with a smile on his face.

The meanest smile she'd ever seen.

"I do know you!" Jaxxon was saying. "You're Halloween Mom!"

Quinn felt every nerve in her body ready itself for the next command: *What do you want us to do? Fight? Flight? Freeze?*

"I don't know what you're talking about," she said, as cool as she was able to be.

"That doesn't work on me, dude, I never forget someone who trends higher than me," Jax said. "Come on, say it."

"Say what?" she asked.

"Say 'The freaking food trucks!'" Jax replied.

And that's when she saw it.

Jax had been holding up his phone. This entire time.

From the second he'd entered. Like an easily forgotten shadow.

He'd been recording.

"Oh yeah—that was my favorite part!" his brother said. Then, an echoing parody. "'The freaking food trucks!'"

"Wait—" she said, her voice coming out raspy, barely a whisper.

"Mr. LaRue!" The voice came from behind them. It was one of the event organizers, in a subdued gown, holding the all-important clipboard of authority. "It's time to draw the raffle winner. Could you follow me please?"

"Sure, no problem. Hey, bro, wanna come draw a raffle winner with me?"

"On it," his brother said, bumping his fist.

"Oh, can I come?" said the girl.

"Nah, girl, you're okay where you are." Then he turned to Quinn. "Halloween Mom—see you on the internet!"

"Wait!" she said with more voice this time. But, Jaxxon LaRue and his brother were gone. Leaving Quinn alone with a pouting, slightly high Instagram model.

And an ominous foreboding that something really, really awful was about to happen. And she couldn't stop it.

CHAPTER TEN

It was when Quinn Barrett came rushing into the ballroom at the Greater New England Children's Hospital Charity Ball that Daisy McGulch Stone knew her past was coming back to haunt her.

Up until then, it had been a wonderful evening. Perfect enough that she could forget all the imperfect parts of life for a little bit and enjoy the moment.

When they arrived at the charity ball, Daisy could not believe the room. It was like walking onto the set of a Jimmy Cagney movie, and she loved it. The extravagance, the attention to detail—it was set design worthy of an Oscar.

"Oh my god," she murmured to Rob as they found their table. "This is the fanciest room I've ever been in."

"Oh come on, you say that like you haven't been to the Emmys before."

"It was the technical awards," she said, but squeezed his hand. "Where is our table?"

"Why? You can't be hungry already," Rob said, laughing. "You ate half of Carrie's mac and cheese."

"Eating half of Carrie's mac and cheese is my due as the

mac and cheese maker," she countered. Grandpa Bob had again been happy to babysit one last time before he flew west with Donna for the winter months.

"Besides," she said to Rob, "you would want to sit down too if your tux weighed as much as my dress."

Daisy was so pleased with the gown she was wearing. She'd dug deep into her boxes of stuff currently freezing into ice blocks in the garage and pulled out an Amazon warrior cosplay costume. Based on the one that (the forever awesome) Robin Wright wore as General Antiope in *Wonder Woman*. She took the leather corseted bodice and found a bronze silk and tulle prom dress at Goodwill that she used for the skirt. Luckily, she was short, and she could turn the almost foot she had cut off the hem into a short pelisse-type jacket, covering her arms and framing her neckline with a popped collar. She broke out a shimmery glitter palate for makeup, but in neutral tones.

She used every ounce of sewing skills she had to become this next level of Cosplay Daisy: Fancy Ass Party Cosplay Daisy, now with Battle Bodice.

The outfit would have looked perfect with a gold spray-painted top hat, but she restrained herself.

No one had told Daisy to cover up her tattoos, of course. And she wasn't the only one here with tattoos—it was New England, but it was still the twenty-first century. There were no doubt tiny affirmations written on wrists, bad college decisions peppered among the elite. Even Rob had a hidden Red Sox logo on his shoulder. Famously the Affleck she'd spied in the crowd had a pretty atrocious tattoo on his back. (Wait, or was it the other one?)

And Rob would never ask her to cover them up—at least not in so many words. But he'd been strangely nervous about the event. So Daisy decided it was best to err on the side of subtlety and covered her arms. Plus—it was darn chilly in Boston at the end of December.

As they approached a large twelve-top in the center of the space, Daisy felt Rob squeeze her hand. She smiled back at him and found him looking a little green around the gills.

Rob was usually so calm and centered, to find him nervous was disconcerting. But instead of letting it make her nervous, Daisy decided she would be the support system, holding him up so he could shine . . . not entirely unlike her Battle Bodice.

And for Rob, she was ready to do sunshiny cheery battle.

"Hello!" Daisy said, as she approached the completely full table. Heads looked up from their drinks and conversations.

"Well, hello, friend!" said the man she recognized as Joe Sr., giving his trademark greeting. When his eyes finally fell on Rob, behind Daisy, he realized Daisy wasn't just a random fan, and a wide smile spread across his face.

"Young Robert! You made it!" Joe Sr. jumped out of his seat to shake Rob's hand. His shock of white hair and Teddy Roosevelt mustache only emphasized his genialness. He was such a huge presence on the show, it was hard to believe he wasn't much taller than Daisy.

"Yeah, thanks for gracing us with your presence, Robbie," said the young man next to Joe Sr., who remained in his seat, smirking slightly. Daisy recognized him as Jo-Jo.

Even seated, she could tell he was a head taller than his dad. But he didn't wear the same kind of self-ease that his father did. It might have been because he was in a tux and not in a flannel work shirt and boots. It might have been because he was a grown man named Jo-Jo. But regardless, he looked almost as uneasy as Rob did.

"Completely my fault!" Daisy said. "I had such a time getting our daughter settled, and of course, this dress does not wear itself—hi! I'm Daisy!" she said in a rush, talking a mile a minute over any potential awkwardness. She didn't know who she was channeling then. Was it Shanna? Quinn Barrett?

Was it her old self?

Whatever it was, it did the trick, because Joe Sr. kissed her hand, and said "enchanté" like he was Maurice Chevalier. Which made Joe Sr.'s wife smack his arm playfully, and Jo-Jo crack up laughing at his parents.

Daisy eased into her chair, her battle bodice wheezing at the laces. If nothing else she would have perfect posture this evening, because any random movement and she was going to have a wardrobe malfunction. Rob found himself quickly in conversation with Joe Sr., so Daisy reached across the table and shook hands with Jo-Jo's wife, a sweet-looking woman not too much older than herself, who Daisy learned in quick succession had been high school sweethearts with Jo-Jo, was now a mother of four, and a DIY expert with a blog.

"Wow—you'll have to teach me some tricks!"

"Happy to," she said, smiling. "With four kids and a husband working on the show constantly, you have to know how to fix things on your own."

"I mean, I can sew a hem," she said (and a battle bodice and a jacket, but she kept that to herself), "but anything involving hammers and nails I leave to Robbie."

"Maybe that's what we should do, Robbie," Jo-Jo said, with a smile on his lips but not in his eyes, "keep you on the hammers and nails of things and leave the show stuff to us."

"Don't mind him," Jo-Jo's wife said, when she saw Daisy's surprised face. "He's just grumpy about—well, he's just grumpy."

"I am not grumpy, I'm—"

"What you are is at a party, and you're going to dance with me," she said, brooking no opposition. "Now."

She rose from the table, and reluctantly, he did, too. Once she led him to the dance floor, Daisy turned to Rob, who had gone from green at the beginning, to a normal color while he chatted with other people, to now gray.

"What was that all about?" she asked, keeping her voice low.

"C'mon," he said, after a quick glance around the table. "Let's grab a drink."

They made their way to a funky bar in a side room that had been done up to look like a cool hidden speakeasy. Once Rob had ordered a pair of whiskeys from the surprisingly eye-flirty bartender, Daisy turned to him again.

"Are you trying to get me drunk?"

"Absolutely," Rob replied.

"Okay, but it's not going to make me forget that weirdness back at the table," she said. Then, with real concern, "What's going on?"

Rob took a swig of the newly arrived whiskey and sighed. "It's nothing. I didn't want to bother you with it."

"It's not a bother," she said, softly.

"I know, it's just . . . things are a little tense at work right now."

"Why?"

"We delivered the first episodes to the producers, and they were hoping that it would be a little . . . sexier."

"Sexier? It's PBS. I didn't think they were allowed to be sexier."

"They meant sexier as in slicker. More production value, more segments to engage viewers. So, I pitched the idea that we delve into a sort of reality competition program arena, while the main show is still about building the house."

"How so?"

"In a new segment, we'd show how the home owners chose their contractors, their landscape gardener, their interior designer, and other artisans. We'd have several of each 'bid' for the job by designing a small project to woo the home-owner. So, like, the landscape gardeners would each design a planting bed, or an interior designer would design one small room."

"That sounds like a good idea," she said. "It would allow you to feature a lot of local craftspeople, and show what it's really like when you build a house from scratch. You have to go through a long process to find the people you like."

"That's what I thought—and about half of the staff thought. But Jo-Jo . . . it's his first show all by himself, out of his father's shadow. He doesn't want to share the spotlight."

"So he killed the idea?"

"No. While Jo-Jo is the star, Joe Sr. is still the executive producer. He's still weighing the idea."

"Ah," Daisy said, nodding.

"Yeah. It's made things a little tense with Jo-Jo at work," Rob said, taking another swallow of his drink. "Like freezing-me-out-of-meetings tense."

"Wow," Daisy said. "But still—it can't be that bad if you got invited to this fancy ball?"

"We got invited before I made the pitch," Rob said, rue-fully. "And our names were on the tickets, nontransferable."

"So . . . what are you going to do?"

"I don't know," he said, giving a slight chuckle. "But I've got my fantasy 'I Quit!' speech all prepared."

"What?" she practically screeched. Her heart began to thud excitedly. "Quit?"

"Winter slows down construction; we're lucky we already had the foundation poured—so there's plenty of time to create this segment," Rob was saying, talking faster and being more animated than he had about anything in ages. "Even if it doesn't work in the main show, it would be great for online."

"Rob, honey—back up a sec," Daisy said, taking him by the arm. "You want to quit? Is quitting . . . something you can do?"

"No," Rob said, after a moment. "I guess it isn't. Not with a house down payment to save up for and all. But it's fun to dream a little."

"Right," said Daisy, letting herself lean into the little kiss he gave her on the end of her nose, the corner of her eye. But somewhere in the back of her mind, an insidious little thought began to repeat over and over and over:

He isn't happy. He wants to quit. Maybe we can move back home.

"Come on," Daisy said, trying to quiet the thought. "Let's go dance."

And so they did. They danced the night away. Daisy danced with Rob. She danced with Joe Sr.—as politely as she could manage. She talked with Jo-Jo's wife some more and found her really delightful and shockingly energetic for having four kids. She bought a couple of raffle tickets (a trip to South America!) and shot whiskey out her nose when she saw the crazy items in the silent auction. She people-watched—mostly the Affleck, trying to figure out if he was the one with the tattoo, but also, she saw a few sports types, some very old-money types, some doctor types, and someone who looked like that internet idiot Jaxxon LaRue.

And still, that insidious little thought persisted.

He isn't happy. He wants to quit. Maybe we can move back home.

Stop it, she told herself. This is too nice an evening to be thinking like that.

And it was—it was a glorious evening. In spite of Rob's tenuous situation at work with Jo-Jo, he was having a marvelous time, dancing with her, drinking a second whiskey like a man who knew he was Ubering home, and cutting loose in a way he hadn't since their daughter was born. And she was having a great time, too—forgetting all the harder parts of their life, the transitions they had gone through, and rocking out to big-band standards and eating rubber chicken.

It was as if she were completely new. Shiny and fresh as spring. And come midnight, the year would be new, too—full of new possibilities. No matter the little thoughts that tried to creep in and take this (whiskey-fueled) joy away from her. She would forget them. She would forget everything except Rob's arms around her Battle Bodice waist, and the way he smiled at her.

A quick frisson went around the room, like a family of meerkats had been alerted to some sound from far away. Everyone's heads went up, looking around.

"What's going on?" Daisy asked.

Rob's brow furrowed, then he checked his watch. "It's five minutes to midnight."

Ah, so that was the commotion. And Daisy saw it—the people up on the small dais, in front of the band, conferring.

"Everyone! Everyone!" An official-looking woman holding a clipboard came to the front. The crowd murmured their way to settling. "The countdown is going to begin in just a few minutes, and it will be a new year! But before we say goodbye to the old and hello to the new, we want to draw our big raffle winner!"

That certainly had everyone's attention.

"And to pull the winner, we have asked a very special friend to the Greater New England Children's Hospital to come up here. We are all very excited to bring you the youngest premiere donor to the trust we've ever had, Mr. Jaxxon LaRue!"

"Seriously?" Daisy's eyebrows shot up. "Jaxxon LaRue? Does anyone here even know who he is?"

Judging by the crowd's lukewarm reaction . . . no, no, they did not.

"I think I remember reading something about his brother being sick," Rob whispered while dutifully clapping. "I guess he donated a lot of money to the hospital."

"Huh, maybe he's not a completely self-absorbed internet bro," she whispered back.

Jaxxon LaRue bounded on the stage like an overgrown sheep dog, taking the mic from a surprised clipboard lady, holding his phone out over the crowd with the other.

"WHADUPPPPPPPPP GREATER NEW ENGLAND CHILDREN'S HOSPITAL!!!"

The crowd cheered with polite, somewhat bewildered enthusiasm. But most of these people were not of the era to know that they were currently on camera and to go nuts accordingly. Daisy shot a look to Rob, and he rolled his eyes back at her. "YouTube stars and camera phones everywhere—it's like we're back home."

Back home.

There it was, that little pitch of hope, running though her blood. But she didn't let those words infiltrate her. Couldn't let them. And her attention was drawn back to Jaxxon LaRue soon enough, when he brought his brother—a thinner, baby-faced version of Jaxxon—up on the stage.

"Without you good people, without this hospital, my brother

would not be standing here right now. And my mom was like, you need to show your appreciation. So for once, I listened to my mom, and gave you all a bunch of money."

Nervous titters through the crowd. Even though this event was entirely about money, these were not the type of people to mention money.

"I mean, it's internet money, but it still spends—right, Affleck?"

The Affleck in the audience raised his glass slightly, but didn't want the focus on him. And that was fine with Jaxxon LaRue because he preferred the attention exactly where it was.

"Although I do have a bone to pick with you people," he said, addressing the audience. "I thought I was the only internet celebrity you guys had on the payroll. But who did we see out in the bar?"

He paused, and held his mic up to his brother.

And then, things started to feel like they were happening in slow motion. Daisy saw out of the corner of her eye . . .

Someone rushing in from the back bar area. A familiar stride, an alert frame.

And then she turned her head.

"Quinn . . . ," she breathed.

What was Quinn Barrett doing here?

Rob looked down at Daisy, caught her gaze. Looked over.

And then Jaxxon and his brother said into the mic, after the longest pause ever . . .

"HALLOWEEN MOM!"

Quinn froze, like a scared rabbit. Then, Daisy saw her melt. From the spine down. As if what was going to happen was going to happen and she just had to absorb whatever tsunami was about to hit.

"Seriously, she's here. You know her, right?" Jaxxon said to the bewildered crowd. "Bro, do the thing."

His brother pulled himself up, snickering. "The freaking!"—STOMP!—"Food trucks!"—STOMP!

The two LaRue brothers dissolved in a fit of giggles. The crowd was mostly perplexed, with a few people chuckling.

"Dude, what the hell, right? Why was she here?" his brother said.

"She said she was married to one of your surgeons. Like, that guy whoever he is, must live like, in complete fear of his life," Jaxxon replied.

"Right, oh my God!" his brother snickered. "Like, You didn't"—STOMP!—"take out"—STOMP!—"the trash!"—STOMP!

"You didn't"—STOMP!—"give me"—STOMP!—"an orgasm!" Jaxxon chimed in.

"All righty then!" said the woman with the clipboard, who made a grab for the mic. "We're coming up on midnight, let's pull that raffle winner for the big-prize trip to Argentina!"

As the clipboard woman guided Jaxxon over to the raffle bowl, the winner was chosen, and started screaming delightedly from somewhere in the crowd, the countdown for the New Year began.

But as everyone gave voice to their own "Happy New Year!" and gold and black confetti fell across the room, Daisy could only watch Quinn Barrett. Still standing there, alone in the crowd.

And having endured her entire life being broken into pieces all over again.

Little Wonders Preschool
January Newsletter

Hello, WONDER-ful Parents!

And welcome to the new year! We hope you ~~survived your kids~~ had a wonderful holiday with your loved ones! We at the Parent Association are so excited for what the new year is going to bring!

We were so happy to provide a wonderful Snowflake Breakfast, that we are doing it again! We will be celebrating MLK Day with a Build Your Own Pizza Party! ~~What Martin Luther King has to do with pizza, I don't know. Maybe the teachers can do his portrait in pepperoni.~~ Positive associations will help teach our kids our amazing history!

Sign-up sheets for volunteer hours will be posted in the lobby, and on the Parent Association website, and on the Facebook group, and on the PA's Slack. ~~God, no one uses the Slack—why do we still have it?~~ And of course any donations of supplies and ingredients are appreciated. ~~We want money.~~

Don't forget the Parent Association meeting on the first Wednesday of the month—we will start ramping up for our biggest event of the entire year—the FAMILY FUN FEST in the spring! The Parent Association is immensely excited about the new and innovative plans we have, ~~oh god, what is Shanna~~

~~going to make us do?~~ and with your help and your volunteer hours and money we will make this the best #FFF ever!

In other news, theme day this month will be HOMETOWN HEROES! On January 25th, have your kids dress up as their favorite service officer—policeman, fireman, etc! ~~Really there are only those two, unless your kid wants to dress up as an IRS agent. And who doesn't?~~

Lest we forget (and don't forget because otherwise you're a bad parent) the new year is a great time to change the batteries in your smoke detectors and double-check your fire extinguisher—thus we will be having our EMERGENCY PREPAREDNESS WEEK! Don't forget to update your child's comfort kits, your contact information for the emergency alert system ~~(you know, that thing that every couple of months sends out an alert and gives you a heart attack)~~, and a representative from the fire department will be coming to talk to the kids! ~~FIRE TRUCK. There will be a fire truck at the school. Do not miss this day or else your child will never forgive you.~~

Together in Parenting!
Suzy Breakman-Kang
Parent Association Secretary

Addendum: To those of you ~~Terry, AGAIN~~ who inquired about the chicken coop, I REMIND YOU that our little flock has been moved indoors to the barn until the spring—so those children worried about their demise need not be concerned. We will welcome back Cherry, Jelly Bean, and Candy Corn in just a few short months! ~~Cherry is now a different color though. Don't worry when they reemerge in April—no one will remember.~~

Second Addemdum: Holy shit, did you guys see there was another video? Really, I can only feel sorry for Quinn now . . . I mean, if she hadn't been such a demanding president. Although, Shanna's walking close to the line too—I don't know if we got the better deal there, guys.

CHAPTER ELEVEN

O n Friday, January first, Quinn cleaned out her closets. All of her closets. Her clothes closet, her linen closet, her cleaning supplies closet, her kitchen pantry. She went through all of Ham's clothes, removing anything too small that was still somehow in rotation, and integrated all the clothes he got for Christmas.

She went through the mudroom, and scraped and sprayed all the mud and dirt off the boots and galoshes that had been accumulating there. She moved everything off the counters in her perfect gray-and-white kitchen, and proceeded to ruthlessly rid it of every crumb that had fallen into every corner and cranny.

What she did not do was go online.

She didn't need to, of course. She knew without looking that a new video featuring her was online, posted by one of the most popular internet stars, with millions and millions and millions of followers.

She knew she would have to suspend her Instagram and her Facebook accounts again. But she would have to clean that house later. Right now, she was cleaning this one.

When Ham woke up, she made him a big beautiful breakfast, from all the organic whole foods they had in their fridge. An amazing spinach frittata with lemon zest was well within her repertoire.

Once he went into his playroom, she cleaned the kitchen (again) and got to work rearranging the living room furniture. The weight of the tufted gray couch was far off balance against the vintage William Morris spindly chairs by the fireplace; she absolutely could not stand it anymore.

Hopefully her lawyers were not somewhere in the Caribbean without cell phone reception. She'd called and left a message last night when she and Stuart arrived home, knowing that waiting was "not conducive to their goal of limiting damage."

Her phone was turned off but it was no doubt fielding massive calls, texts, and notifications from the looky-loos, the concern trolls, and the occasional interview request. But in truth, she knew there was not one real person in the bunch to call and ask after her. To ask how she was doing. No friends at all.

Because she didn't really have any. And at that moment, she missed it. Craved it. That mythical f-word: friends.

Where did they go? She'd had friends in the past. Yvonne from elementary school; they used to run around with braids in their hair, biking through the Ohio woods and pretending to be Brontë heroines defeating evil. Frances, Rachel, and Erica were her minions in high school, thriving on imaginary drama and gossip. Friendships from college that at the time felt like the kind of passionate relationships that would be sustained, roots wedging themselves down into the very center of a person, becoming the foundation of the adult.

But now? No one was there.

Everyone had gone quiet, invested in their own lives.

And . . . it was probably her fault.

Her life had gone in a decidedly "up" direction, while others stayed unimpressively level. When she'd announced her marriage to Stuart on Facebook, replete with professional engagement photos—that she'd arranged an entire weekend in Nantucket around, doing her best to look casual and perfect at the same time—she was met with congratulations from all corners. But had she invited those corners to the wedding? Mostly no. Mostly, she kept it to the people in her new life. The people she wanted to be like. Her mother had balked when she told her that she wasn't inviting any of her old high school crowd.

She'd argued at the time that they wouldn't be able to come anyway, seeing that they mostly all stayed in Ohio. But really, deep down, had she been worried about how they would have fit in? How they would have reflected on her?

Deep down, probably yes.

And now, she was left with phone notifications from people who gleefully wanted that high school drama and gossip, and wanted to see someone who got too big for their britches fall.

Once the living room was rearranged to her satisfaction, she started going through her office, and began to Marie Kondo the hell out of her desk drawers.

Hamilton wandered in once asking for a snack. She made him a plate with olives and several different types of cheeses, of which he ate only the American square cheese slice she'd wrapped around a small piece of salami. She'd settled him into the couch in the playroom, and turned the TV to the Rose Bowl parade.

She made to leave, to tackle those drawers. . . .

"Is Daddy awake yet?" Hamilton asked her suddenly.

She paused, turned at the door. "No, honey. He's not here."

Hamilton nodded. Then he turned back to the television, his attention caught by the high school marching band from Oregon, playing the theme song to *Jurassic Park*.

Hamilton was used to his father not being there when he woke up, she told herself. Stuart stayed late in the city so often when he was on call, sleeping in the doctors' quarters—a fancy name for a spare room with an empty bed—at the hospital. So, there was no reason to suspect that anything was different this time.

Except everything was different this time.

Because this time, she didn't know if Stuart was ever coming back.

They had managed to not have the fight until they got home. But at first, Quinn had been shocked that there was a fight to be had at all. She had just been humiliated. Again.

Stuart had found her quickly in the crowd. He'd had her wrap and purse from their table in his hands. They'd gotten their coats and were out the door to the valet before the last refrain of "Auld Lang Syne" was sung.

Anyone they saw on their way out the door was greeted with a patented romance hero smile, and an easy excuse about having to go home and relieve the babysitter. He'd kept his arm across her shoulder, either bracing her from falling, or keeping her from running away, she wasn't sure. But once they got into the car, his stony voice issued just one edict.

"Tell me what the fuck just happened."

She did. As best she could, keeping her voice even.

He didn't say a word. Not until they'd walked in the front door, and sent Gina home, with instructions to get a good night's sleep, and that she wouldn't be needed until Monday.

"Tell me again," he'd said. Turning to her. The romance hero smile was gone. The kind, understanding bedside manner he used on his patients was gone. What was left was pure anger.

"I told you—" she whispered.

"Tell me AGAIN."

"Shh!" she replied. "Hamilton is asleep upstairs!"

"He's three thousand feet away in this monstrosity of a house *you* wanted. He couldn't hear us if we used air raid sirens. Now tell me again why I was just fucking humiliated in front of all my colleagues and Boston society tonight!"

That was when she realized Stuart wasn't angry for her. He was angry *at* her. That the simmering rage, that festering tension that had been nearly snuffed out, stomped on by all of Quinn's hard work for the last two months . . . it came flaring right back to life in Stuart's anger.

"Damn it, Stuart, this isn't my fault," she'd said. "Not this time."

"Oh, so you admit it was your fault last time?" he asked, mockingly.

"Last time I . . . I don't want to talk about last time."

"Damnit, I told you to *fix it*," Stuart raged.

"I DID," she said. "I worked so hard. I gave up the Parent Association, because it was taking up too much of my time—"

"You got kicked off," he interrupted.

"No . . . I told you that it was mutual."

"Don't sugarcoat it. I may not have been there, but I know you, and you don't quit anything."

"It. Was. Mutual," she said. "And I threw myself into Hamilton's potty training—"

"He couldn't get through the Thanksgiving thing without an accident—"

"And focusing entirely on designing the charity ball. Which I *killed*. That room was stellar! I got so many compliments, I gave out so many cards—"

"And how many of those cardholders are going to hire you when they figure out you're the one Jaxxon LaRue was talking about?" Stuart took a step toward her. Then another. "And here's a little secret—the only reason they kept you on the charity ball was because *I* stepped in. I told the trust that you needed to be the point designer. They told Jeremy they wanted you."

Quinn sucked in a breath, tried to absorb that information. It made her wobble, uncertain.

"Well?" Stuart said.

"Well what?"

"How about *thank you*. 'Thank you, Stuart, for pulling strings, and putting my career before yours.'"

"Before yours???" she asked, bewildered. "You have never, ever, ever put anything before your career."

"I'm saving kids' lives, it's kind of an important—"

"—not Hamilton, not me, certainly not my job—which I had to fight with you to even keep!"

It was true—when she had decided to go back to work at Crabbe & Co., it was met by passive aggression, a laundry list of things she would have to do and arrange to make that feasible, and every iteration of "you don't really need to/ we have plenty of money/it's just vanity/being a surgeon's wife is work!" Stuart could think of. In the end, he had acquiesced.

"As long as everything else was taken care of," he said. "That was the deal—you could work as long as everything else was taken care of. And clearly, it hasn't been, if tonight is any indication."

"That's not fair—again, this time it wasn't my fault. I just got recognized by a pair of entitled assholes, and they—"

"And they decided to get up on the stage and say that your husband is henpecked."

She crossed her arms over her chest. "There are a lot worse things someone could say about you, Stuart—you got off easy."

"Like what?" he said, suddenly straightening. "What could people say about me?"

"They could say that you're not a good father."

He cocked his head to the side so violently she thought he might have pulled a muscle. "You think I'm not a good father? You think I don't *provide*? That I don't fulfill my role for our son?"

Quinn felt something get stuck in her throat. The words, the words that had bubbled up and were fighting their way free: *No—you're not a good father. You're not here enough to be.* She had enough wherewithal to force them back down into the bile of her stomach.

"That's not what I meant. But that's what people have been saying about me. Ever since that Halloween video—that I'm not a good mother." She managed to keep the tears out of her voice. "That Hamilton is going to end up an ax murderer and that video is going to be exhibit A. That someone is going to call Child Protective Services on me. That I'm a terrible, terrible person who is going to ruin my child—so I'm sorry if you got called 'henpecked,' but it doesn't even compare."

Stuart got very silent. Stewing. And she knew she had scored a point. But it was at her own expense, letting him know how much pain she had been in, how much the video had hurt. Because he could and would use it against her. Make her stop working. Take Ham out of Little Wonders. Tell his mother how she had screwed up. Scale back her world.

But to her surprise, he didn't use it—at least not now. He seemed instead to be chewing over something, working at the side of his cheek.

"I don't like having my marriage examined in front of everyone I work with," he said finally. "And it's not a problem I would have, if not for your mistakes."

"I'm sorry," she said on a sigh, "that they did that."

"I don't want it to happen again. I can't have it happen again."

"Neither do I," Quinn said. "But I can't promise that it won't."

"Because . . ."

"Because . . ." *Because I'm Halloween Mom,* she wanted to say. *And Halloween will come next year, and the year after that. And that video will come back. No matter what the lawyers say, or what motions they file. The internet is forever.*

"Because you married me," she said finally.

"I'm starting to think that that's the problem," he said finally.

Everything stopped, midair, midbreath. The snow outside hung suspended in the sky, unable to touch the earth. Because everything else had crashed.

"What?"

"I'm leaving," he said, quietly, ". . . it's something I've been thinking about for a while. This . . . this house, this town, Needleton—I never wanted it."

"I certainly didn't trick you into it."

"I thought we'd be able to still be us. Remember us from before? Our place in the city, our lives, going out, enjoying ourselves, and not having it be so much work."

"It's not work for you," she spat out. "I'm the one who does all that, who arranges everything, so we still have as much of a life as possible."

"Yeah, and it has to be perfect, all the time."

Because you made me be perfect, she thought harshly. *Because you decreed my life was only mine as long as everything else was taken care of.* But the words wouldn't come. They were drowned out by other words, more panicked words.

"No—Stuart . . . We can work this out. I love you. We have a great life together. I'm still the me from before! I'll Parcel my time better. I can . . . be spontaneous and arrange some more date nights for us!"

"You do realize that spontaneous and arranging date nights are a contradiction in terms?"

"What about Hamilton?" she tried. "He needs his father."

He didn't answer, just moved to the door—slow, tired, determined—and put on his coat.

"Where will you go?"

"I have surgery tomorrow morning, so I'll just crash in the doctors' quarters tonight. And I'll find a place from there."

"The roads are icy—and there's nothing but drunks out there this time of night. You don't want to drive now," she tried desperately.

"I'll be careful," he said, and opened the door to the frigid night. "I'll, uh . . . I'll call you."

And he was gone.

Quinn had crumpled herself on her couch and cried. Great heaving sobs that would have put any soap opera actress to shame. But when she finished, she felt oddly calm. It was the wee small hours of the morning. She could count on one hand the number of hours she had before Hamilton would wake up.

When she crawled into bed, she was convinced she was just lying down to rest her body, not that her mind would actually turn off. But she was asleep in seconds.

She woke up to a perfectly made Stuart half of the bed, a completely lucid memory of what had happened, and no earthly idea what to do next.

Which was not a common sensation for Quinn.

She just had this deep-seated feeling that absolutely everything in the house was completely wrong.

Hence the massive cleaning.

The cleaning lasted all weekend. Ham helped her as much as a three-year-old could, having fun going through all his toys, stopping to play with toys he'd forgotten he had.

It was a 3,000-square-foot house, there was plenty to be cleaned. A big beautiful new build, filled with all the beautiful things she'd acquired and lusted over as she created other people's dream spaces. An antique refurbished dresser here, a rare print wallpaper for the downstairs powder room there.

Well, this was her dream house, she thought, once she had run out of closets, basement storage, pantries, drawers, and corners to clean and organize. And what did she have to show for it but an empty half of her bed and a not yet quite potty-trained son who barely noticed his father was gone?

But she didn't have an answer. She couldn't think about Stuart right now. She couldn't think about what he was doing or why he was blowing up their marriage, or how she could convince him to, you know, *not*. She instead had to focus on what was positive. On what she still had going for her.

Which meant, conversely, she had to actually assess the damage.

Sunday evening, with a pristine house, a toddler sleeping away inside the pop-up castle tent he had forgotten he owned, and a large glass of wine at her elbow, Quinn Barrett fired up the internet.

She typed in "Halloween Mom, new year's." She discovered that she had made a couple of year-end "fail" lists—videos of people falling off water skis, and attempting parkour with painful results, and of course, her. She scrolled past.

It didn't take her long to find the video that Jaxxon LaRue had posted. It was on his channel, fed directly to his millions and millions of subscribers. He posted videos daily, along with supplemental channels for his music videos, diss tracks (whatever those were), and podcasts. He even had a web series he was producing, starring an ex–Disney Channel star. It looked like it had decent production values, she thought randomly.

The most recently posted video was titled PARTY FOR THE DOCS THAT SAVED MY BRO (WITH SPECIAL SURPRISE GUEST!). It was about eight minutes long—medium length for his videos—and it started off mildly enough. Jaxxon LaRue prepping for the charity ball in his hotel room with his brother, doing excited intros into the camera about where they were and why they were attending this party. She saw the Instagram model girl in the background, being used basically as set dressing, and making Quinn feel an uncomfortable pang in her chest when she remembered what the girl had been like when they briefly met—vulnerable, defiant, young, and not entirely aware of what she was doing.

Then the video moved into the party—she recognized all her gorgeous work in dressing the massive room, and mentally preened. At least the décor shone to advantage. He talked to a couple of doctors, the lady from the trust with a clipboard. When he was done talking to them, he mocked them lightly to the camera, making fun of them in all the ways they were not a young twenty-something YouTube billionaire. He then goes on to point out celebs on his phone, the Red Sox players and the Affleck as they danced.

Then, about halfway through the video, he interrupts himself, with a talking head bit done later on that night.

"Okay, of all our celebrity sightings, I have to think that our favorite was this—"

And then—a bootleg of the Halloween video popped up. And Quinn was treated to a video of her stomping as she said "The freaking!"—STOMP—"Food trucks!"

The Jaxxon talking head came back. "Remember Halloween Mom? Well, guess who's going into the New Year the right way!"

And there was the whole interaction she had with Jaxxon and his brother, from the moment Jaxxon approached them at the bar. She got to see herself steel faced, taking the younger LaRue to task for the joint he had just lit.

She watched as Jaxxon joined the fight, and as he told her to back off his brother. As the joint flew through the air, and landed near the curtain. And of course, the stomping.

The video cut there, to Jaxxon and his brother snickering into the camera phone as they walked toward the stage.

The rest was their bit onstage, mocking her. She cringed when she heard the line about orgasms, knowing that Stuart would be apoplectic.

Then he closed it out, saying it was great and to check out his other channels, and the web series with the ex–Disney kid, and some Zen bullshit about having a blessed New Year.

And that was it.

It was less of a jolt to her system than the first video. As if she was almost resigned to the notoriety. Except for the fact that Jaxxon LaRue had such a massive following, such a media machine.

No doubt she could sue him. She could set her lawyers to the task, they would relish billing her the hours, and maybe even getting a decent settlement out of him. But she just didn't have the energy at the moment.

She took the Jaxxon LaRue video and downloaded it to her desktop. She'd learned how to do that on the advice of her lawyers—so she had a copy of the actual video, if the poster decided to alter it in some way, she could point to the original. She then went around to all of her social media sites and froze them again.

That's when she saw the one ray of light in a fairly shitty (so far) year.

A post from Sutton on her Instagram. In between all the pics from a sweaty spinning class, cute interior DIY looks she'd done to her apartment, or #bestlife photos from a beach or a theater or a restaurant, was a picture of a magazine cover.

The Martha Stewart magazine.

And there, on the cover, was the Beacon Hill house.

Specifically, a shot from its entry hall. Quinn had killed herself on that entry hall. Talking Mrs. Chafee out of the classic yet woefully outdated black-and-white-tiled entryway and into a beautiful salvaged marble floor threaded with green veining had been the work of her life, but it had been the basis for everything that came after, from the graceful sage on the walls to the antique oak-frame mirror with taper holders next to the Shaker chair. It was a master class in blending the old with the new, with setting the tone of the home via the entryway, and It. Had. Made. The. Cover.

A rush of pride filled her as she quickly went to her tablet.

The hard copy of Martha Stewart would be arriving this week sometime, but she had the digital subscription too and she would sip the rest of the wine and revel in the triumph of a year's worth of work.

But as she pulled up the magazine and found the article, all of that happiness dropped off her, like a banana peel, revealing the bruises beneath.

Her name was nowhere to be found.

The house was a Crabbe and Co. renovation, according to Jeremy. And it had been a team effort—led by himself. He'd taken special care of the house, learning its history, working closely with the architect to preserve and highlight its heritage.

Quinn would bet money that Jeremy didn't even know the architect's name. And that in between his trips to Morocco and Spain he had stepped into the Beacon Hill house maybe twice. While she had spent nearly every day there from the moment she met with Mrs. Chafee to the second she was shoved into the background.

She didn't understand—she'd been interviewed by the reporter. She even recognized some of her phrases and quotes, but they were attributed to "a Crabbe and Co. designer."

It would be one thing if Jeremy took all the credit for the company. Attributing it all to Crabbe and Co. was gauche, but at least she would be underneath that banner. But he hadn't confined it to that.

No—he had given a special shout-out to someone.

"Crabbe and Co. actively fosters talent, and so when young assistant Sutton Van Ness had a proposal for a child-friendly bathroom, she was given leave to run with it—turning the bland, beige Jack and Jill into a pop of bright joy in the stately house, perfect for the family's young ones."

The bathroom was pictured, along with some adorable moppets (no doubt on loan, because if Mrs. Chafee had kids she had never mentioned it) diligently washing their hands.

Sutton. Sutton, who admittedly had designed a very nice, if a bit generic bathroom, was the designer called out in the pages of Martha Stewart. In Quinn Barrett's bible. The indignity didn't end there.

No, the cherry on top was on the last page of the spread. In the very far corner was a photo, of Jeremy, his hand on Sutton's shoulder. The mentor and his new protégé.

It was as if Quinn Barrett the designer—along with Quinn Barrett the wife—no longer existed.

She had done everything for the Beacon Hill house. She had done everything to prove herself to Jeremy, to Crabbe and Co. Just like she had done everything to show Stuart she was the best and most perfect partner for life.

She had doubled down on perfection, and it had—totally and completely—blown up in her face.

And try as she might, there was just no way to design her way out of that.

CHAPTER TWELVE

O h my god, I can't. I just can't."

Daisy whipped her head around as she heard Shanna's words. But Daisy couldn't stop, as she was being pulled down the hall by Carrie at full speed, her little body tilted forward trying to drag her mother to her classroom.

Shanna was stage-whispering with Suzy Breakman-Kang and one of Charlie and Calvin's moms. The twins' mom was holding back a little bit while Shanna and Suzy broke down into giggles. Shanna caught sight of Daisy as she passed.

"Oh, Daisy!" she said. "Come here!"

"Can't stop, hit you on the way back!" Daisy said as Carrie increased her speed. Daisy didn't have to stop and question what Shanna had been so dramatically gasping over.

She knew.

Hell, she had been there.

She had seen the video, of course. The new one. She had immediately texted her friends in Los Angeles as soon as appropriate (read: as soon as she thought they might feasibly be awake on New Year's Day) to—well, mostly to freak out.

Sarah Prime had texted back first.

Sarah Prime: Hey, Daze – Happy New Year! What's going on?

What's going on? Daisy thought desperately. Only that she had *just* started to think she maybe hadn't completely destroyed someone's life, when—nope! Turns out Quinn's life was now Destroyed 2: Destroy Harder.

Then her other friends jumped in.

Allie: Girl, only you would text at this hour. How are you?
   It's been so long!

And that's when Daisy realized . . . she hadn't spoken to her friends in a very long time. Not since her initial panic over the first video.

She'd told them what was going on, but over the course of the conversation, Daisy realized she wasn't going to find any advice or absolution from her friends, because they were so removed from this. They loved her, they cared about her (actually, it turned out that Allie was a little worried that Daisy hated her, since they hadn't really spoken since the Halloween video situation), but they didn't live the same lives anymore.

They didn't even know about her hair color.

So, she had gone through the New Year's weekend friendless. Enjoyed by herself the blind panic and chewing her nails to the quick over her role in Quinn's latest debacle. And mostly, she just felt tired and sad. And guilty. So deeply guilty over her role in it. And the truth was becoming alarmingly clear.

The Halloween video was never going to go away. Not completely.

And she was just going to have to live with it.

When they got to the Tadpole Room, Daisy was on alert. She hadn't seen Quinn in person since New Year's (and Quinn certainly hadn't seen her there) and she knew she wouldn't be able to look her in the eyes. It was Wednesday—she had managed to avoid being in the same drop-off window. To be fair, yesterday she had spotted Quinn's car in the parking lot and had circled the block a few times until it was gone. She was late to the boutique, but she'd done so well over the holidays for Elaine, she'd earned a little grace.

Luckily, Quinn and Hamilton were nowhere in sight. Time for Daisy to do a quick drop-off and trot out the door.

But as Carrie gave her a big squeeze (a bit clingier than normal, but Ms. Rosie said that coming back to school after two weeks off was always a little tough) and shuffled off to join Jordan playing dolls (Jordan, issuing what doll Carrie got, and Carrie meekly submitting. Strange, Carrie was never meek . . .), Daisy was held from her quick retreat.

"Daisy, right?"

It was Elia's dad, who had just entered, Elia leading the way and straight into a hug for Ms. Rosie.

"Um, yes, hi," Daisy said.

His eyes flicked to her hairline, and she knew he was remembering her old color, reconciling the two. "You work at the Cranberry Boutique in town, right?" At her nod, he said, "My aunt Elaine runs it—she just absolutely gushed about you."

"Oh—that's very nice to hear." Wow, Cosplay Daisy must really make the right Needleton impression.

"Listen, I know it's last minute, but Elia's having her birthday party at the Bounce Palace in Depford next weekend. Is Carrie available to come? I know Elia would love it, I see her give Carrie a hug every morning."

Daisy blinked—true, Elia gave Carrie a hug every morning. In fact, she was hugging her right now. But Elia hugged *everyone*. To a degree that made Daisy hope someone would have a talk with her about bodily autonomy in the nearish future. That didn't mean they were special friends.

But then she realized, this was the first time Carrie, or Daisy for that matter, had been invited to anything, outside of Shanna's beneficence, since coming to Needleton.

Carrie, and Daisy, were being included.

"Um—sure. I think so," she said, and nodded.

"Great, I'll send you the Evite."

They exchanged emails, and Daisy deposited Carrie's heavy coat in her little cubby before she headed out. As she headed out the door, she heard Elia's dad saying to his daughter, "No, honey, you have to let go. Oh, that's—that's a great hug, your best ever, but I still need to go to work—"

The little thrill of being invited to the party fled the minute she hit the hall, and ran smack into the still lingering Shanna and Suzy.

Damnit, her goal of Quinn avoidance and a quick getaway was again under threat.

"Daisy, good to see you," Suzy said, turning an anticipatory smile to her. "How was New Year's for you?"

". . . Oh, it was great." She watched warily as Shanna and Suzy exchanged a glance. "Really nice and relaxing . . ."

"Okay, we can't stand it anymore. You have to tell us everything," Shanna said.

"Tell you what?"

"About the ball!" Suzy replied. "Shanna said you went to the hospital charity ball."

"Oh—it was also nice. We had a good time."

"And then . . . ?" Shanna said. "We want details. About,"

and here she dropped her voice and mouthed the words, "Quinn Barrett."

"Oh . . . it was . . . it was . . . ." But as her eyes registered their eager faces, Daisy lost her placid words. It was what? It was unfortunate. And more than that, it was cruel. And she hated that she was feeding the trough of gossip that Shanna was currently feeding from.

But before she could find any words, Quinn Barrett herself walked in the door.

Quinn didn't look perfect, for the first time ever in Daisy's experience. She wasn't a hobo, or anything like that, but she was wearing a puffy jacket over a paint-flecked work shirt. And her shoes were not three-inch heels—instead she had on snow boots, like the rest of them, with yoga pants tucked in. She looked . . . like a mom who hadn't showered.

She looked *normal*.

She still had on the big dark glasses that hid her gaze, but now she wasn't holding her chin in the air, making it impossible for people to meet her eye. Now, she had her gaze down, stomping snow off her boots and dusting off Hamilton, who looked like he'd rolled around in the fresh powder outside the door.

"Come on, Hammy," she was saying. "I'm sorry I overslept, but you gotta help me here. What's our Mommy Ham mantra?"

"Try for perfect," Daisy thought she heard the little boy say, in a subdued voice, as he was pulled down the hall and disappeared into the Tadpole Room.

"*Oh, my,*" Shanna said with relish. "How the mighty have fallen."

"Looks like the remnants of a three-chardonnay night," Suzy said, with a—as far as Daisy could tell—sincere look of shock. Then, her smart watch beeped. "Damn, I'm late already."

"Okay—see you tonight at the Parent Association meeting," Shanna said. "And don't forget to bring the temp flyers, and the schedule for the vendor calls—oh, and the map of the layout from last year's Family Fun Fest—and all that other stuff I texted you."

"Right," Suzy said, with a brittle smile. "But now I have to go to my actual job."

Shanna's eyes narrowed a little, but she air-kissed Suzy and gave her a little wave as she pulled the hood of her heavy coat up and prepared to do battle with the out-of-doors.

Daisy was about to say that she should get going too, when Shanna leaned over and whispered, "She got fired, you know."

"Suzy?" Daisy said, alarmed.

"No—*Quinn*."

Daisy's eyes went wide.

"Because of the New Year's video?"

"Must be—or because of her atrocious behavior."

"But that doesn't make any sense," Daisy reasoned. "She didn't do anything wrong."

Daisy had watched the New Year's video, several times. And from what she could see, all Quinn did was prevent a fire, and dissuade a stupid kid from compromising his recent organ transplant. And she wasn't the only one who had felt that way—the vast majority of the comments were on Quinn's side.

"Hold up—are you telling me your bro was SMOKING UP? He's lucky to have those lungs!"

"Jax—I love you but LISTEN TO THE MOM. Don't be a jackass."

"Do you know how many people are waiting on the transplant

list? Your bro got his cuz you're famous—don't go rubbing it in every-
one else's face."

But something else didn't fit in Daisy's brain.

"How do you know?" she asked suddenly.

Shanna ripped her gaze away from the Tadpole Room door, waiting for Quinn's reemergence.

"How do you know she got fired?" Daisy asked.

"Oh—" Shanna said, a little sheepish. "Well . . . to be frank, I called her office. And they said she was no longer with them."

Just then, the Tadpole Room door opened, and both heads turned automatically to watch as Quinn emerged, freed from the weight of Hamilton and his stuff. When she saw Daisy and Shanna, she started—as if she had been waiting for them to be gone, and was unpleasantly surprised to see them still there. But it was only for the briefest of seconds. Almost immediately, her sunglasses were back over her eyes and a neutral expression frozen on her face.

Daisy immediately dropped her gaze to her toes, guilt sweeping over her.

"Don't forget, Parent Association meeting tonight," Shanna said, as Quinn hustled past. "Everyone is welcome."

Quinn Barrett turned on her heel, cocked her head to one side, and blithely flipped Shanna the bird.

Daisy felt a surge of pride. *Good for you.*

And then she realized—it wasn't guilt that had swept over her as Quinn walked by. It was premonition. It was the queasiness that comes from knowing something awful is inbound—and that awfulness emanated from Shanna.

"Well, really—that was unnecessary!" Shanna said, aghast. "Why would you do that?"

"Seriously!" Shanna took out her phone and began furiously texting. "She has gone off the deep end."

"No, I mean, why would you call her office?" Daisy asked.

Shanna's head came up. Her alarm softened into a look of faux concern.

"Okay, Daisy—I know you feel guilty for your role in this situation, but—"

"Yeah, I feel guilty. But you—you're relishing her pain," Daisy said, eyes narrowing. "That's just cruel."

Shanna's thumb had frozen over her phone. Her jaw dropped, and her eyes seemed incapable of blinking.

"Daisy . . ." There was a warning in her voice. But Daisy decided not to hear it.

And without an excuse (oh, I'm going to be late, too!) or a goodbye, Daisy turned on her heel and walked out the door.

As she clicked away on the bright linoleum, Shanna called back after her:

"Don't forget, Parent Association meeting tonight! See you there!"

Needleton's Main Street still bore the hallmarks of the recent holidays: strands of Christmas lights were still wound around the trees, there was a garland and wreath strung across the main intersection that likely wouldn't come down until they got a few days off from constant snowfall. But in the shop windows, time had definitely moved on. After-holiday sales dominated the front of the stores, everything that had a Santa on it was designated to a clearance rack, as well as anything with long sleeves. Believe it or not, the shops were getting ready to make room for spring and summer.

"Thank goodness I had you," Elaine had said, as she moved some over-embellished holiday sweaters to a circular rack in the back. "You were my top salesperson. You have a very bright future in sales. Why, without you, I might have gone the way of the Knick Knack Nook."

The Knick Knack Nook was the narrow, dusty store next to the coffee shop on the corner. Despite the stellar location (because who doesn't like coffee) there was now a Going Out of Business sign in the window, next to a For Lease sign. Tragically, they hadn't sold enough shell-shaped soaps and carved whale tealight holders over the holidays to keep surviving.

But despite her stellar sales record, almost no one was coming through the door on a random Wednesday morning in early January. Maybe it was the after-holiday malaise. Maybe it was the fresh six inches of snow on the ground, and more that was still falling. Either way, by ten-thirty, Daisy had rearranged the entire store, had updated the computer's inventory, and was basically twiddling her thumbs.

"You might as well head home," Elaine said, on a sigh. "If this snow keeps up, no one is going to feel like shopping."

Great—now she was facing a whole day without earning even her meager precommission salary. But while she regretted the money—every penny she made went into their down payment fund, and the holidays had been such a boon—she was a little giddy to have the free time.

Seriously, what did someone without kids—with time to kill—*do*? Should she go home and prep dinner? Binge-watch something? Take an exercise class? Paint the Sistine Chapel?

Contemplate the hell she might have wrought with Shanna?

No—she didn't want to do that. She didn't want to obsess about Shanna, or Quinn, or any of that mess for once. A few hours to herself were too precious, she had to take advantage . . .

Daisy suddenly had a vision of the glossy, oversized Fifth

Edition hardcover sourcebooks buried in a box in the garage somewhere. Their gorgeous illustrations, their tantalizing details. An afternoon wasn't long enough to put together an entire campaign, but she could plot an adventure. Nothing big, a one-shot for three or four players—four, maybe five hours of game play, max.

Of course, she didn't have anyone to plan an adventure *for*. But the idea of immersing herself back in her happy place fueled her enough to have her smiling as she strode into the coffee shop on the corner for a quick caffeine refuel.

And ran smack into what she had been hoping to avoid.

Because Quinn Barrett was at a table.

She had her back to the door, so didn't see Daisy. Her attention was held by the front window, where she was gazing blankly at the snow, an empty coffee cup in front of her. For once, her sunglasses were elsewhere. But it was definitely her.

Even with the snow, they were not the only people in the coffee shop—although it was close. There was the dedicated typist in the corner, working away at his laptop, who seemed to come preinstalled at every Starbucks (although, this wasn't a Starbucks—the Needleton town council had voted against allowing a Starbucks into their main street as "too corporate").

Daisy could have turned and hightailed it to her car, parked behind the Cranberry Boutique, and fishtailed her way back to the house. But then fate intervened, and the barista caught her eye.

"Hi there!" he said, a dopey ray of incredibly ill-timed sunshine. "What can I get for you today?!"

She had no choice but to move from the doorway, and up to the counter.

Daisy froze, fearing that Quinn would turn her head at

the words, the movement. But she didn't. In the quietest whisper possible, she ordered a small black coffee, the drink that would take the least amount of time, get her out the door the quickest. But of course, after the barista had taken her money, he said—

"The carafe is empty! Need a new pot! Be right back!"

And he disappeared into the back storeroom.

As seconds ticked into minutes, Daisy became convinced that Quinn would notice her. That she would look at her, recognize her, and then all of Daisy's insides would be revealed. And then what would happen?

Just as Daisy was panicking herself into a small heart attack—what the hell was the barista doing back there, *growing* the freaking coffee beans?—the inevitable happened.

Quinn did look up.

She *did* see Daisy.

And then, she turned her head back to the snow.

"Here's your coffee!" The barista's mellow voice broke through her haze.

Slowly, she took the cup. And . . . then, what happened next, Daisy would never be able for the life of her to explain. But she found herself walking toward Quinn's table.

Because . . . because Daisy realized she'd been so worried about Quinn seeing through her that she'd never actually seen Quinn. Not really. Not until their eyes had just met.

And what she'd seen was a mirror.

"Excuse me, Quinn?" she said, her heart going a mile a minute.

Quinn turned her head, a look of frank surprise on her face.

"Hi, I'm . . . I'm Daisy? Carrie's mom? From . . . from Little Wonders?"

"I know," Quinn replied, blinking. "Hi."

"Hi." It came out on a push of breath, Daisy more nervous than she'd been when running her first game. Hell, *giving birth* had been easier than this—and Carrie's birth hadn't been easy.

The pause must have been interminable, because Quinn eventually said, "Can I help you?"

"I just wanted to say I'm sorry." She thought she'd have to force the words out, but once started they just spilled.

"What for?" Quinn said, her head cocking to the side.

"For the . . . for the video," she fumbled. "Videos, plural now, I guess. It sucks that it happened, it's . . . it's total bullshit, and nobody deserves it. Least of all you. And . . . I'm sorry."

There it was. All of her guilt, laid on the table—if not the whole truth, at least it was the whole feeling.

"O . . . okay," Quinn said, blinking.

"Okay. Well . . . ," Daisy replied, awkwardly. Now what? Full confession? Could she do it?

No. No she could not.

"See you around then!" And she scurried to the door before she could stop herself.

Coward, she berated herself as she hurried down the street—as fast as she could go in the snow. Which was unaccountably letting up. The wind had died, and only a few flakes were falling now.

And thus, she could hear the voice calling after her.

"Wait!"

Daisy turned, and there was Quinn—her jacket hastily thrown on, shivering against the rush of cold that smacked her after leaving the warm cocoon of the coffee shop.

Daisy stopped, let her catch up. Then took a deep breath. "Look, I—I need you to know—"

But she was cut off when Quinn threw her arms around her and gave her a hug.

Okay. That's completely normal, Daisy thought.

"Thank you," Quinn said as she let Daisy go. And though shivering and sniffling, for the first time, Daisy realized it wasn't because of the cold. Quinn had tears in her eyes. "That was the first time someone said that."

"Seriously?" she said.

"Well . . . no, but that was the first time someone meant it."

Daisy didn't know what to say to that. So they just stood there for a minute, shivering in the cold, as the sky lightly dropped snowflakes in their hair.

"Um, listen, this is going to sound weird," Quinn stuttered, "but do you know where I could get some pot?"

"What?" Daisy asked. "Pot? As in marijuana?"

"Yeah—do you know where I could get some?"

"No!" Daisy replied, astonished. "Why do you think I would know that?"

"I . . . I haven't smoked pot since college, and back then, the girls that knew where to get it, they looked like you."

"Like me?" Daisy asked, quickly going from alarmed to offended. "What does that mean? I look like a pothead?"

"No!" Quinn said suddenly. "You look cool!"

Daisy lifted a wary eyebrow. "Cool?"

"Cooler than I've ever been," Quinn mumbled. Then, she kicked the snow. "Well, I fucked that up, didn't I?"

Daisy in spite of everything, gave a slight chuckle. "If you want pot, it's legal in Massachusetts now. I'm pretty sure Mr. Happy Barista back there can point you to a good dispensary."

"No, I don't actually want pot—I just . . . I wanted to hang out with someone," Quinn said. "With you."

I wanted to be your friend. The words were unspoken but heard clear across the cold air.

"I'm not that cool. The one and only time I ever got high I ended up on the bathroom floor of my high school for five hours communing with the cold tile," Daisy said, relenting a little. "It wasn't my cup of tea."

"Ah," Quinn said. Then, after a moment of shuffling, her eyes lit upon something behind Daisy.

Daisy turned her head, to see a bar/restaurant, Ye Olde Needleton Pub, with an "Open" placard in the window next to a sign that said "Brunch Served Daily."

"Okay! It's Daisy, right?" Off Daisy's nod, she took her by the arm, and started dragging her down the block. "Well, Daisy—let's get drunk instead."

CHAPTER THIRTEEN

Quinn had no idea what had come over her. Other than that the idea of getting drunk with Daisy, Carrie's mom, sounded in that moment like the best idea in the history of ever.

Ye Olde Needleton Pub was, if possible, emptier than the coffee shop had been. Maybe because it was ten thirty in the morning, maybe because of the storm, which, as they had crossed the street, had kicked up again with a strange fury—the slowed gentle snowfall had gusted into wickedness in the space of half a block, so they were practically pushed through the door by Mother Nature. But for whatever reason, they were the only customers in the pub, if not the only people in the world.

"How do you people stay in business if a snowstorm shuts you down?" Daisy muttered, stamping her feet.

"You people?" Quinn asked.

"New Englanders," Daisy replied. "I don't get it—it's cold, it's dark by three PM, it snows all the time—how do you live like this?"

"Usually people don't let the snow stop them. I bet everyone is still in post-holiday hangover mode. Staying home where it's warm and cozy instead of going out and doing what needs to be done," she snorted. "Please. Like the world is going to wait for them. January is here and it's time to get moving."

Quinn glanced around the room—she'd never been here before, but it was a place that was absolutely dedicated to maintaining its authenticity, which according to the very large EST. 1799 painted under the name, was the common-variety quaint history at which Needleton excelled. So, the ceiling would never be higher than seven feet, the long wooden bar would never be updated, the plaster in between the heavy wood beams would constantly be patched, and the fireplace would always emit low-grade smoke.

"Hello!" she called out. A shuffle from the back, the sound of a plate crashing to the floor. A tall, reedy young waiter stuck his head out from the back. "Your sign says you're open. We're just going to take a table."

She grabbed Daisy by the arm, and dragged her to a table near the front bay window, the only natural light in the low, dark space. The reedy waiter scurried over to meet them.

"Hi, can I interest you in our—"

"Actually we are interested in whatever drinks you can make that have the highest level of alcohol content," Quinn said. "What would that be?"

The waiter goggled at her, then said . . . "Um . . . we can do a Long Island iced tea? But it's kind of early . . . brunch service doesn't technically start until—"

"Great, we'll have two of those, please," Quinn said, before he could protest further. "Okay by you?" she said, turning to Daisy, who nodded. She turned back to the waiter. "Fabulous—and just so you know, we are going to be here awhile, ordering a lot of stuff, and we are excellent tippers. Thank you so much!"

With that, their waiter gave her a little salute, and trotted off to the bar.

Only then did she realize Daisy was staring at her.

"What?" Quinn said, taking the plastic-covered menu from its spot wedged between the pewter salt and pepper shakers.

"You are really . . . intense. Like a human starter pistol."

Quinn suddenly felt cowed—usually, she prided herself on comments like that. In being the go-getter, the Get-Shit-Done mom. But coming from Daisy . . . it felt like she was doing something wrong.

Was she doing this wrong? She felt that old impulse—that repulsively female training to apologize for little more than existing. But she didn't give in to it. Nor did she swing the other way, and bristle against it, and get defensive and protest that she *wasn't* that way, no, not at all.

Instead, she met Daisy's eye, and . . . and laughed.

"Yeah," she chuckled, throwing up her hands. "Yeah, I am. But it's the only way anything in my life ever gets done, you know? Or that's what I convinced myself, anyway."

"I get it, believe me," Daisy said, smiling. "I just . . . I'm kind of in awe."

"Why?"

"Like . . . with the waiter. I would have waited politely for him to take us to a table, politely listened through his specials, and politely waited until brunch is officially served to order drinks."

"And we'd still be standing at the door," Quinn replied.

"I know, and I'd be silently pissed off about it, and worried that you were judging me."

"And I would be silently judging you. Modulating myself to

make you more comfortable, when I know what would make us most comfortable would be sitting down, ordering what I know we want, and relaxing in this . . . historic environment," she said. "I wasn't *im*polite. I said please and thank you. I just . . . wasn't passive about what I wanted. Also, politeness is for suckers who want to stand by the door waiting to be seen."

Daisy blinked twice. Then let out a guffaw of laughter. "Wow, you are honest."

"Honey, we haven't even gotten our drinks yet," Quinn said, her eyes falling to the menu, and the little paragraph about the pub. "Oh, look: Ye Olde Needleton Pub was founded by a husband and wife who met in the town's original needle factory."

"Aw, love among the iron filings."

And as their drinks arrived at the table, they both burst out laughing.

It was one of the strangest, easiest conversations Quinn had ever had. There was no "get to know you" small talk. No, they dove right in.

They ordered appetizers of fried cheese. They discussed the ridiculousness of preschool expectations.

"Ridiculous!" Quinn said. "But what are we supposed to do, *not* give our children every experience life has to offer?"

"I just don't understand the name."

"The name?"

"Of the school. Needleton Academy for Potential Prodigies and Little Wonders," Daisy said in between sips. "What if your kid turns out to not be a prodigy? What if they're . . ." she pitched her voice low, conspiratorial, "normal?"

"Oh, then you get kicked out of course."

Daisy almost dropped her drink.

"I'm kidding! God, it's just a name—and by sending your

kid there you can pressure them for the rest of their lives, letting them know they once had the potential to be prodigies."

"Well, I'm just glad the holidays are over," Daisy said. "Talk about pressure. We can finally dig ourselves out from decorations and candy."

"Oh nooooo. No we can not!" Quinn laughed. "There is always another holiday. They do not end. Preschool. Is. Relentless."

"Okay, but Valentine's Day is six weeks—"

"Not Valentine's. We have Martin Luther King Jr. Day, Groundhog Day, the Super Bowl if the Patriots are playing, Lincoln's Birthday right before, and President's Day right after. Then it's Read Across America Day on March first, Mardi Gras, and before you know it we are all hunting for that one green T-shirt your kid has for St. Paddy's. There is a party and decorations for each of 'em."

"Jeez Louise," Daisy said, looking as green as that mythical T-shirt.

"And that's just to March."

The fried cheese appetizers arrived, and they talked about their kids.

"You *drove* across country? With a three-year-old?" Quinn sputtered. "How? I can't take Hamilton to the mall without three pairs of underwear and knowing where every bathroom is."

"We stopped a lot, looked at corn mazes and very large balls of twine. We also played *The Sound of Music* sound track about forty thousand times."

"Yeah, but why? There are airplanes."

"When we moved . . . well, it happened really fast," Daisy said. "We just wanted to leave."

Quinn sobered slightly. "Why?"

Daisy took a long, slow sip of her drink, draining it almost to the bottom. "I could tell you that Los Angeles is cynical, that it chews people up and spits them out—but really, it was one moment when I wasn't on the parenting ball that had us getting out of Dodge."

Quinn waited.

"There's a park, close to where we lived, that Carrie loved. And one Sunday morning she woke up really early, was bouncing off the walls by the time the sun came up, so I took her out to the park, to burn off some energy. She'd just been potty trained, and looooooved to use the potty. The second we got to the park, she ran for the public bathroom that was there.

"I was six seconds behind her, but it was just enough time for the homeless drunk in there to grab her with one hand and his penis with the other."

Quinn sucked in her breath so loud their waiter popped his head out of the back.

"Yeah. I grabbed her and ran home, called the cops. The guy was gone by the time they got there. We never went back to that park. And ever since then, we just called it the Scary Thing.

"I know in the grand scheme of things I shouldn't have let it destroy my confidence as a parent. But it did. And Robbie already wanted to move, and this . . . made me want to live somewhere safe. So when Robbie got this job, we packed up immediately and we were off.

"But I think about it now, and I wonder if I . . ." Daisy stopped. Sucked in a steadying breath. "Robbie never blamed me. And I do *not* fit in here in Needleton. But I know that if I was *seven* seconds behind her, I . . . I . . ."

Quinn reached over, and put her hand over Daisy's.

"I've never told anyone this story. Not even Shanna knows."

Quinn's mouth quirked at the mention of Daisy's cousin-in-law. "Why me?"

"I don't know. I think, maybe, because I already know your biggest parenting fail. You deserve to know mine."

Their waiter came back. Quinn waved him away, while Daisy regrouped.

"Come on," Daisy said, finally. "Let's talk about anything else."

"Like what?" Quinn said.

"The weather? Home towns?"

"Well, we've covered weather. Might as well dish on small town Ohio."

"Ah—outside Houston in my case."

"Sounds desperately boring. Let's dig in."

And so, they talked about their upbringings. Their origin stories, as Daisy called it. By the time their lanky waiter (who turned out to be a history major at Boston College named George) came back to try and take their food order again, they had argued the length and breadth of who had the more dissatisfying upbringing.

"Not bad—just . . . dissatisfying," Quinn rationalized.

"Exactly!" Daisy replied. "I love my parents, my sister, my brother . . . I'm just not like them. They never got me."

"My mom to this day doesn't know where I came from. And I can point to her, all her unfinished projects, the fact that I always filled out all my school forms and just had her sign them, and say . . . *that* is why I am the way I am."

"I . . . guess, I'll be back for your food orders after another round of Long Island iced teas?" George said.

"Yes, thank you, George," Quinn said, waving him away as she slurped at the last drops of her drink.

"That's amazing," Daisy said, shaking her head, once he was gone. "Do you realize how completely deferential he was to you? Like, all of his body language. So what if they are jeopardizing their liquor license—Quinn Barrett wants another round, she gets it."

Quinn tilted her head, regarded Daisy. "You know, if there was actually anyone else in this place, they would look at the two of us and think that he was deferring to you."

"Why?"

"Because you're the cool one," Quinn said, pointing to Daisy's hair. "Or, at least, you used to be."

"Thanks," Daisy said, drily. "This is just . . . I've been calling it Cosplay Daisy."

"Cosplay?"

"Costume play," Daisy explained. "Where you dress up as a character. From comics, or a movie, or anime? Usually at a comic convention or the like."

"So . . . it's not you, it's a character?"

Daisy nodded. "Basically."

"Then why do it at all?"

Daisy sighed, seemed to consider. "Because I change my hair, and my daughter gets invited to a birthday party at the Bounce Palace. I wear a sweater set covering up my tattoos and I get promoted to the sales floor where I can make commissions and earn money toward a down payment on a house that my husband loves but that hasn't been updated since the sixties." Daisy looked forlornly out the window. "I can get my family everything they want or need, as long as I give up what I want and become someone else entirely."

Quinn held Daisy's gaze. "What is it that you want?"

"I want . . . a good multiweek D&D campaign. One where I am creating a story with my friends for hours at a time and you come off it feeling like that's the real world and this is the strange one. I want to know what I'm doing. I never know what I'm doing anymore," Daisy said, half laughing. Then . . . "What do you want?"

"I . . . I thought I knew what I wanted."

"Which was?"

"My life back."

At that prescient moment, their second round of Long Island iced teas arrived. And Quinn raised her glass to Daisy.

"But that ain't happening, so I better get a new dream," she said, clinking her glass to Daisy's. "For what it's worth though, I liked your blue hair."

"No you didn't," Daisy said, after a minute.

"Yes I did."

"What did you think the first time you saw me?"

Quinn thought back to the first time she'd seen Daisy Stone. Oh yeah—the Halloween parade. "I thought . . . you were a nanny or a mother's helper."

"Right. Not a parent with a kid at Little Wonders."

"That . . . was more because you were not like everyone else," Quinn said defensively. "Not that I didn't like it!"

Daisy just raised an eyebrow.

"I just . . . I don't understand it. That and the tattoos," Quinn admitted, sheepish.

"Oh, I can explain them to you," Daisy said rolling up her sleeves. "This is a rebel alliance symbol, on the side of a d20—a twenty-sided die. And on the other sides are a light saber, an empire insignia . . . over here is my version of a dryad, a sort of tree nymph creature from Greek mythology, that got co-opted into D&D. I put one in my first campaign that I just—"

"I only know about a tenth of those words. But what I meant was . . . tattoos are *permanent*."

Daisy rolled her eyes. "You know I'm not the only person in this town with tattoos, right? I'm not the only parent at Little Wonders—Charlie and Calvin's moms have matching tattoos."

"True, but yours are blatant. Your hair you can change, but your tattoos—I can see that they are objectively beautiful, but I just don't get it."

Daisy's eyes fell to Quinn's wrist. "That watch. You wear it every day?"

"Yes," she replied, looking at her vintage Cartier, trying not to tear up thinking about the day Stuart gave it to her. Darn alcohol.

"Because it represents you."

"But I can take it off," she said. "In fact . . ." She slipped the watch off her wrist. She didn't want to wear it at the moment. Not if she had to think about who gave it to her.

"And I can cover my tattoos with makeup if I need to."

"Well . . . that makes a certain kind of sense, I guess," Quinn replied. "At least you were an individual, not the carbon-copied blondish-blowouts everyone strives for around here. Me included."

Daisy looked down at her arms, lovingly. "The stories that these tell are so much a part of me that I don't want to take them off. It'd be like taking off my stretch marks."

"You . . . wouldn't want to take off your stretch marks?" Quinn asked, aghast.

"When I'm faced with a bikini model on a billboard, yeah . . . but most of the time, no." Daisy shrugged. "Carrie is a result of said stretch marks. It's kind of hard to regret them."

Quinn looked down to her trim waist. All those hours spent in the Pilates studio, all those half-empty cream jars in her cabinet she'd slathered over her stomach to prevent any lines when she was swollen with Hamilton. Not that they actually prevented them. They were still there.

"Do you regret yours?" Daisy asked.

"Right now . . . I'm regretting all the time I spent trying to maintain perfection." She sighed. "I am an interior designer. My whole life is about shaping things to look a certain way. To look perfect."

"You look great," Daisy said, trying to placate.

"Thanks. But it's kind of blown up in my face."

Daisy bit her lip. "With the videos, you mean."

"I thought my work would speak for itself. I thought my drive to create perfect spaces for my clients would be enough to show my design firm that the videos didn't matter. But no."

"Did you get fired?" Daisy asked. She seemed strangely fearful of the answer.

"No," she answered honestly. "After they broke their promises to me, I left."

It had been so easy to walk out the door of Crabbe and Co. on Monday. It was a mere few minutes after she had walked in, and thrown her hard copy of the latest issue of *Martha Stewart Living* on the table.

Jeremy protested, of course. Saying that the work that got highlighted was the *firm's* achievement. That she should really be thanking Jeremy for keeping her name out of the pages. "After that last video came out, I did what I thought would protect you—would protect our firm."

"The problem is that the text for the article has been set for weeks. I may not know the magazine business, but I know that these copies are printed well in advance of release."

Jeremy had the gall to look affronted.

"And the firm is going to take credit for the charity ball too, no doubt," she added.

"I doubt the hospital trust is going to want your name anywhere near it," Jeremy said, bristling. "Now, Quinn—" he tried, coming around the desk, conciliatory. "I know you feel thrown around. But we at Crabbe and Co. are still on your side."

"So you're going to make me a partner? You're going to put my name on the door and back in front of clients?"

Jeremy looked at her like she was a stupid child. And she'd realized that he'd been looking at her that way for a decade.

So she left. On the way out, she ran into Sutton.

"Quinn!" she said, startled. "I . . . I had no idea that he'd do that. I mean, you've been my mentor here, and I—"

"Congratulations on the magazine, Sutton."

"Oh, I . . . thank you."

"You have a lot to offer." Her eyes shifted to the side, to Jeremy's door. "Just beware what he'll take from you."

She'd cried the entire drive home.

Now, a little shaken, she looked at Daisy across the table. But Quinn's eyes traveled down from Daisy's to the Cartier watch sitting next to her sweating glass.

"That's not the only thing that blew up on me. Because apparently my pursuit of perfection still wasn't perfect enough for my husband. Who left me New Year's Day."

Daisy's jaw dropped.

"He *left*?"

"He's taking some time, to figure out what he wants. And I do not get it, because . . . I gave him *everything* he wanted. A beautiful home, a kid, and absolutely no demands about either."

"No demands?"

"He has a really important, stressful job, and it takes priority. So the house, Hamilton, our schedules, all of that falls to me. And I think I might have done it too well."

"How so?"

Now it was Quinn's turn to get silent and contemplate her drink. "The Halloween thing, that wasn't my biggest parenting fail. I'm pretty sure that my biggest parenting fail is that my son has only asked me once where his father is."

And now it was Daisy's turn to reach across the table and hold Quinn's hand.

"So, yeah, trying to be perfect has kind of screwed me over. Okay, time for another subject change," Quinn said, forcing herself not to cry. This morning was turning into afternoon and this conversation was swinging wildly between heart-rendingly cathartic and endlessly silly. She needed more silly. "Oh, I know! Should I get a tattoo?"

"Nooooooooooo," Daisy said immediately. "I mean, not unless you want one."

"Not really—besides, what if it turns out imperfect?" Quinn said, mock serious. "I would not be able to handle that. It would be like . . . shiplap in a town house."

"What?" Daisy said, choking on a laugh.

"As a designer, I have a personal vendetta against shiplap."

"But . . . what if your client really likes it?"

"Seriously?" Quinn said. "We've had this discussion, people! It's wall board! We killed this off in the eighties, but suddenly we put it on the horizontal and a little whitewash and you all think it's so effing quaint. I will never put shiplap in a home as long as I live."

"Ohhhkay. I think we might want to moderate our drinking a bit," Daisy said. "If only because we have to drive our cars through a blizzard and pick up our kids in about five hours."

"Fair," Quinn replied, reaching for the menu. "Then we are going to need more terrible-for-us food to cement our friendship."

"Friendship?" Daisy said tentatively.

"A lot of strange things have happened to me since the video came out—but one of the only good ones is this lunch today, so yes," Quinn said, decisively. "You are my friend now, whether you like it or not."

Daisy took a moment, seemed to digest that. As if she was deciding something. And Quinn couldn't help but hope she decided in her favor.

Then, with a tentative smile, she raised her glass. "To friendship."

Little Wonders Preschool
February Newsletter

Hello, WONDER-ful parents!

First a big thank you to everyone for making the Martin Luther King Jr. Day Pizza Party a rousing success! We are so very grateful to the Giordano family for their donation of pizza supplies from their restaurant—"I Have a Dream" spelled out in pepperoni was truly inspirational for our kids. ~~who can't read, but hey, pepperoni.~~

For those of you whose kids ~~TERRY~~ are pining for the chicken coop, I assure you, again, that the chickens are safe roosting in the barn. Please don't attempt to visit without express permission from Ms. Anna, and the accompaniment of Francisco, our chicken wrangler. ~~AKA, keep your kids out of the locked barn unless you want to find frozen chickens all over the play yard, TERRY. We will not tell you again!~~

A reminder to check the attached calendar: Spring Break is the last week of February. ~~(because that's as long as most of us can take these winters before we need to hit the beach for some vitamin D).~~ But while we still shiver away in the ~~gray wasteland~~ snow, it's a great time to perform your volunteer hours at Little Wonders! We have a number of planned celebrations and ample opportunity for you to get involved! First up is the Groundhog Day Puppet Theater and Cookie

Party—I highly recommend signing up! ~~Seriously none of you have signed up for this and we need stage hands. Come on.~~

And of course, we hope to see as many of you as possible at this month's parent meeting! We are deep into planning the Family Fun Fest and need your help! We need all of our regular helpers, official and unofficial, to make this the best—and most lucrative—Family Fun Fest ever! ~~Seriously, where the hell were you, Daisy? Shanna is a horror monster if she doesn't have you to boss around.~~

We look forward to seeing you ~~and your money~~ at the first Wednesday of the month!

~~If you don't show up, you don't want your kids to have the best and you might as well just let them watch *Teen Titans Go!* all day for all the importance you place on their care and education.~~

Together in Parenting!
Suzy Breakman-Kang
Parent Association Secretary

CHAPTER FOURTEEN

Quinn: Good morning! You've got everything together.

Daisy's phone buzzed. Her body gave a reciprocating flutter when she saw it was Quinn. Even when she was standing in the middle of the morning madness, the house a complete wreck—the basement being torn to shreds on weekends, but the work on it was stagnant during the week. Carrie was running around without her glasses bumping into things, Rob was on the phone with work while he tried to find his socks, she hadn't showered in two days and had to be at the boutique in an hour—she still smiled to herself.

It was exactly what she needed in that moment. And somehow Quinn had known it. It was one of the drunken promises that they had made during that first fateful lunch.

"Let's text each other inspirational crap every morning!" Quinn had said, still tipsy from the Long Island iced teas they had finished off an hour previously. "I go online and see all these inspirational mom things and I hate them so much but I want them, too."

Daisy deliriously agreed. After she sobered up, picked up Carrie at school, adamantly skipping the Parent Association meeting, drove home and phoned in dinner with mac and cheese in order to nurse the most horrific hangover she'd had since college, Daisy didn't think she'd ever hear from Quinn again. But there, first thing in the morning (after she'd gone to bed at eight PM and woke up at two to wander around the kitchen for forty-five minutes agonizing over her life choices), there was a text message dinging into her phone.

Quinn: Your hair is shiny like a new kitten.

Baffled, Daisy had texted her back.

Daisy: Is new kitten fur especially shiny?

Quinn: I have no idea. Go get 'em today, mama!

After a few seconds, Daisy texted her back.

Daisy: Thanks. And you have the tolerance and iron stomach of a binge-drinking college athlete.

Quinn: Awwww . . . I'm touched.

That had been the beginning. Every day since then they had been texting like junior high school crushes—both enjoying the thrill of a new friendship. Its intensity and its fun.

It almost made Daisy forget that she was the one who'd caused Quinn's life to break into itty-bitty pieces.

Almost.

Because of course Quinn's life wasn't perfect. She was dealing with the weight of a lost career and an MIA husband and (Daisy learned at that lunch) a son who refused to be potty trained and an entire support system that had broken down. And in the middle of all that, Quinn had decided the best thing to do first thing in the morning was to send ridiculous texts to her.

She began to crave them like a junkie craves their smack of choice.

It had been three delicious weeks of silliness. Of grabbing a coffee after dropping off the kids. Of having a friend. A real friend. Here! In Needleton!

"You texting with Shanna again?" Robbie said as he wandered through the kitchen, shoving his phone in his pocket. "Hey, sweetie!" he said, picking up Carrie as she blew in, swinging a screwdriver she had grabbed from somewhere. "Wow, okay, can I see that screwdriver? Thanks!" he said, disarming his daughter and sending a wide-eyed look to Daisy. "I gotta lock up Grandpa Bob's tools."

"As long as you let her in the basement with you, she'll find them. We gotta close it off until it's all fixed up for Grandpa Bob."

"So—Shanna?"

"Hmm?" Daisy said. "Oh, no—just another mom."

"Jamie says Shanna's getting a little overwhelmed."

"With what?" Daisy replied.

"Well, she's five months pregnant. On top of everything else. Gotta be overwhelming, right?"

"Hmm, right. I'll give her a call later," Daisy said, as she thought of the perfect pep talk for Quinn that morning and texted it to her.

Daisy: Your taste is impeccable and shiplap will destroy
   itself under your withering glare.

"We got the paperwork from my uncle's lawyers. The down
payment will go into a trust—where do we stand on that?"

"A couple more months of good sales at the shop, and no
car emergencies, and we'll have ten percent," Daisy said.

"Good—we're on track," Rob said, lifting his cereal in one
hand and his daughter in the other. "Right, sweetie? Everything is going perfectly."

Daisy took a swig of coffee, wrinkling her nose. Huh,
more bitter than she expected. "Yup. Perfect." Her stomach
swished a little. "Okay, ready to go to school!" she said, grabbing her bag. "Let's get in the car!"

"Um, well—Carrie needs to find her glasses," Rob said.
"And you are still in pajamas."

Daisy looked down to see her ratty Carrie Fisher History
Has Its Eyes on You tee and a pair of Rob's flannel Red Sox
sweatpants.

"Okay—not quite ready, but will be in five—three—
minutes."

As she trotted down the Little Wonders hallway that morning, Daisy's good mood ceased as soon as she saw Shanna at
the other end of the hall, moving toward her.

"Daisy! There you are!" Shanna said. "You are a hard person to get hold of these days."

"Oh, I've just been putting in a lot of hours at the boutique."

"I thought you were a seasonal employee."

"I was a good one so they decided to keep me on."

"Must be a lot of sweater sets to sell this time of year," Shanna replied, sarcastically.

Daisy set her jaw at the dig. "Well, we have a down payment to save for. I'm doing everything I can."

Shanna shifted her eyes to Carrie, and gave her a big smile. "Jordan's in class already, she's waiting for you!"

Carrie, strangely for her, hid behind Daisy's leg.

"We're having a shy morning," Daisy said by way of explanation.

"Of course," Shanna replied. "Daisy, I wanted to run some Family Fun Fest ideas by you, a couple of figures and projections from last year don't make any sense at all and I—"

"Um, yeah, sure—but I need to get Carrie to class."

"Oh, that's no problem, I can wait."

This was the point at which Carrie was usually dragging her down the hall, trying to get to the Tadpole Room and the fun therein. But today, Carrie was holding on to her like she was Luke Skywalker about to swing them across a Death Star ravine.

Daisy bent down, picked her up (only a little pee at this unexpected dead lifting), and began to step down the hall.

"Actually, I've got to open the shop in twenty minutes. Can I call you at lunch?"

"Right—of course," Shanna said. "I'll email you the stuff I'm talking about."

As Daisy opened the Tadpole Room door, she absolutely intended to call Shanna. She did. She knew she was remiss in their particular friendship. Although, is that what it was? It hadn't felt like friendship—not the text-heavy jokey one she had with her friends back home, or that she was developing with Quinn. She never saw herself turning to Shanna with a problem.

Although ever since Shanna took over the Parent Association, she sure as heck turned to Daisy with all her problems.

When Daisy hadn't shown up at the January meeting, Shanna had been livid. Oh, she'd gracefully accepted Daisy's cover story about feeling under the weather (more like under the table, but whatever) and been willing to move on, but . . . Daisy wasn't. She couldn't help remembering how Shanna had been so gleeful about Quinn's downfall. How she had sunk her teeth into schadenfreude like it was a delicious German pastry.

She'd asked Quinn about it, once they had moved on to the dessert portion of that first brunch.

"Why doesn't she like you?" Daisy blurted out, enjoying a surprisingly decent crème brûlée from Ye Olde Needleton Pub.

"Nobody likes me," Quinn replied after her own spoonful. "As I have learned."

"But Shanna's dislike is . . . different."

"I don't know." Quinn shrugged. "I honestly don't. When Jamie and I were copresidents, he always said she was amazing, and how well we'd get along, and that we should have dinners and be couple friends."

"I don't get their marriage sometimes," Daisy said, surprising even herself. The alcohol might have worn off but her tongue was still loose.

"Trust me, neither do I. Jamie's so great," Quinn said quietly. "He's always there."

"Always there?" Daisy had asked.

"You know . . . for Parent Association stuff. Shanna's going to have an easy go of it planning the Family Fun Fest, as long as she's got Jamie helping her."

But Jamie wasn't going to help her, and Daisy knew it, because he was helping Robbie rebuild their basement in his rare free time. Shanna wasn't happy about that either. And Daisy thought it best—at least for a few weeks—to keep an arm's-length distance.

But now, glancing back at Shanna, standing by herself in the Little Wonders hallway as Daisy hauled Carrie into the Tadpole Room, she wondered if she'd kept her distance long enough.

No reason she can't be friends with both, right?

But that desire flew right out of her head the second she set Carrie down in her classroom.

"Carrie, sweetie—keep your glasses on."

"Carrie, my friend!" Ms. Rosie said as she knelt down. "You know you have to wear your glasses to see, sweetie."

Carrie obeyed the will of her teacher—albeit unhappily.

"How do you get her to do that?" Daisy asked with a grin. But Ms. Rosie didn't return the grin.

"Actually, I wanted to speak with you about this. Carrie is taking off her glasses every chance she gets. It frustrates her to not see during reading time, art time—but still she fights wearing them."

"It's so strange," Daisy said, shaking her head, "she's had them for over a year, and when she first got them, she was ecstatic to be able to see clearly. She'd wear them to sleep."

"Kids go through changes; the important thing is to be consistent in the messages she is receiving, about how her glasses are good for her," Ms. Rosie said. "Is there any change that has happened recently, anything that has made her uncomfortable wearing them?"

"Well—the move . . . ," she began, but stopped. The move was months ago now. Carrie hardly ever mentioned their old apartment, or the dog that used to live below them, or going to Disneyland. That wasn't a part of her world anymore.

Her world was Grandpa Bob's house, Little Wonders, her cousin Jordan, and . . .

And that's when Daisy saw it. Carrie had wandered over to where Jordan was holding court, among the dolls and the wooden train tracks. Jordan was holding two dolls. She leveled a look at Carrie.

Carrie took off her glasses.

And then Jordan magnanimously handed her a doll.

It was one of those cinematic moments, a rack focus that brought everything smack in front of Daisy's face.

Thanksgiving. Jordan made fun of Carrie's glasses.

After Christmas. Carrie clinging like a barnacle to Daisy every day at drop-off, not wanting to go to school. To navigate the ups and downs of the preschool social structure.

When Jamie came over to help Rob in the basement, Carrie was a wire of tension until she learned whether Jordan was coming or not. Daisy consoled her child when she learned that Jordan wasn't coming.

But she hadn't needed consolation. She'd been relieved.

It took everything she had to not rush over to Jordan right now and smack the doll out of her hands and put the fear of god into the girl's heart, before making her sit down and learn the entirety of Dorothy Parker's body of work.

But she couldn't do that. Ms. Rosie was on it—she had moved to the girls and was whispering to Jordan. If she did intervene, Carrie would cling to her for another half an hour before she could be extracted, and she had to open the store. The only thing Daisy could do in that moment was leave her daughter in Ms. Rosie's care, and leave the room.

Shanna was gone by the time she emerged from the room,

her car no longer in the lot. Daisy couldn't focus on the *Fear Initiative* podcast (a horror-based RPG that was delightfully filling her commute), not with her head trying to make sense of her daughter—her fearless, loud, amazing daughter—and what she was going through.

Did kids do this? At *three*? Judge each other, exclude each other? Or was Jordan just a mean-girl potential prodigy?

And from whom did she learn that?

It wasn't hard to trace this particular apple's nearby tree. Daisy thought back to every single interaction that she'd had with Shanna. Shanna leading her through the halls, telling the administration that Daisy's daughter was going to go to school there. The Halloween parade, ordering her around. Heck, ordering her around at every single Parent Association meeting. Putting her into sous-chef mode at Thanksgiving.

Even with the Halloween video—she'd taken over, and made Daisy her coconspirator.

And Daisy was tired of it.

But she had absolutely no idea what to do about it.

Her phone dinged. She checked it at a stoplight.

Quinn: I need coffee. You?

Daisy was dialing the number before she knew what she was doing.

"Hey," Quinn said, picking up on one ring. "I have no job and my son is at school, wanna get a latte with me? I've been thinking about the layout in your grandpa-basement suite, and I know this is your husband's project but I—"

"I have to open the shop this morning," Daisy said.

Her tone must have given her away, because Quinn immediately jumped in. "What's wrong?" she said.

Daisy gave a little hysterical sigh. "I'm pretty sure my daughter is being mean-girled by her cousin and I don't know what to do about it."

She gave Quinn a quick rundown of everything she had seen that morning, and seen since Thanksgiving. Okay, it wasn't that quick, but Quinn listened to it all.

"Man, I'm glad I have a boy," she said once Daisy ran out of breath.

"What do I do?" Daisy replied. "How do I tell my daughter that she needs to wear her glasses? That it's important that she does? No matter what anyone else says?"

"You don't do that," Quinn said. "That's just gonna have her throwing them out the window."

"Then what?"

"I don't know . . . ," she sighed through the phone. "Ham fought me on underwear for the longest time. Alba—my old nanny—she told me that to get Hamilton potty trained I needed to get him Superman underwear."

"Okay . . . sure, why not?" Daisy said, completely lost as to where this was going.

"You have to understand, I was adamant that I would raise my son without branding. He didn't have any toys with Thomas the Tank Engine on them, no shirts with Mickey Mouse."

"Okay, I'm more of a Marvel girl than DC myself, but . . . it's underwear," Daisy said.

"Yeah, and Ham loved them. They made him feel powerful. So any mortification I felt when my mother-in-law saw them peeking out of his waistband had to be swallowed. And yeah, he's still got his off days—but every day he's Superman because of that underwear."

"And how does that translate to my daughter?" Daisy asked.

"You have to figure out a way for her glasses to make her feel powerful. To make it okay—to make it the best thing ever—for her to wear them."

"And how do I do that?"

"I don't know," Quinn said on a laugh. "That's more prudent parenting advice than anyone has ever asked of me before."

Daisy hung up after a thank you, a promise to meet up tomorrow for coffee. And sat in her car, thinking.

How could she make her daughter love her glasses again? They were so much a part of Carrie, a part of who she was.

How did she convince her daughter it was okay to be herself?

A horn honked behind her—the light had changed. She jumped, decided to pull over. She turned into a strip mall—snow piles melted in the lot, edging a nail salon, a Chinese food place, and a chain drugstore.

And then, she caught sight of herself in the rearview mirror.

Cosplay Daisy. Dressed up to pretend to be someone else.

How long could she pretend that she wasn't becoming that other person?

And how could she teach her daughter to love being herself if she didn't show her how?

Daisy hauled herself out of the car before she knew what she was doing. She waded into the snowbanks, heading directly for the drugstore.

Somewhere inside, there was a box of electric blue hair dye with her name on it.

CHAPTER FIFTEEN

Oh shit, kid, don't make me do this. Not to Percy. You love Percy.
The evening had started so well. Quinn had picked up Ham from school—there had been enough of a melt lately to go play outside. They'd run around together in the balmy forty degrees of the falling evening, and gotten good and muddy.

Yes, Quinn Barrett was muddy. It was a glorious feeling. But it didn't last when they came in and Gina had dinner on the table.

A dinner that a muddy Hamilton had promptly ignored, and run right to his recently acquired Percy the green engine toy, and was now playing with in the playroom. The cream-carpeted playroom.

That, she decided, she was fine with.

One of her first steps in becoming a less perfect parent was giving into her son's desire for a specific branded toy. A toy that seemed innocuous. A toy that seemed possibly good—one that was mechanical and worked with the wooden train track he already owned. And Percy, as Thomas's best friend, was not the lead of the show, and she was actually proud that

Hamilton wasn't blown away by star power. He was, instead, blown away by the color green.

So, when he had managed an entire two weeks without a potty accident, Percy came into their lives. And while Quinn had been blissfully redecorating Hamilton's room in her mind, pulling together a sage and forest palate and bunk beds replacing his toddler bed, instead Percy had been insidiously taking over Hamilton's mind.

It was as if Chucky were a naive green train.

This had been going on for the last two weeks, and inevitably it fed directly into what Quinn called the Dinnertime Fight.

It was his new thing. His new way of pushing back.

Here's how it went.

Gina would spend the better part of the afternoon putting together a healthy, organic meal.

Hamilton would deny its existence.

Quinn would make a really big deal about the meal.

Hamilton would play with Percy.

Quinn would bribe Hamilton to come to dinner with promises of a delicious, less than healthy but still organic dessert.

Usually by now, Hamilton would abandon Percy, dutifully come to the table, take three bites of whatever was presented and demand dessert, and go back to Percy until it was pajama time.

But not tonight.

"Percy wants mac and cheese!"

"Dinner is pork chops and brussels sprouts," Quinn tried one last time. "Now come to the table."

"Mac and cheeseeeeeeeeeee Percy!"

"Hamilton Franklin Barrett," Quinn tried one last time. "Come to dinner. And leave Percy."

And then . . . then the screaming began.

"NOOOOOOOO!!!!!!!!!" Hamilton was screaming. "NOOOOO! You, you . . . POOPYBUTT!"

Given her son's behavior, embracing imperfection had not been the cure-all she'd hoped it would be.

Poopybutt no longer felt like a slap in the face—not after the past week of being called a poopybutt at every "no" she uttered. No, now it was just the continual turning of the knife already in her gut.

Well, aren't you a horrible mom, it said, with each creaky wrist turn. *You can't even get your child to eat dinner. You're the worst parent ever.*

Maybe they had been playing outside too long. Maybe Ham was tired. Maybe she was tired. She looked over at Gina in the kitchen, quietly cleaning up the meal she had slaved over, her posture adamantly not listening to Quinn and Ham. Gina stepped away.

If Alba was here, she would have cajoled Ham to the table.

If Stuart was here, his very presence would have been such a big deal that Ham would have been ready to eat ten minutes ago—after he showed off Percy for the umpteenth time.

But it was just Quinn and her son, facing off in what had become a massive struggle of wills between them since the beginning of the year.

So much for Quinn Barrett, the Get-Shit-Done mom.

"If you don't come to dinner, Hamilton, Percy has to go on the shelf."

Don't make me do this. Not to Percy.

The shelf was time-out for Hamilton's toys. Too high up for him to reach, but within view. Usually toys went up there for only a few minutes—if at all. The mere threat of the shelf was enough to send Ham scrambling.

Not today.

Hamilton's "NOOOOOOO!!!!!!" was followed by a guttural cry of many vowels and clutching at the little plastic Percy.

"Hamilton. HAMILTON!" Quinn cried, grabbing his arm. "Come on, we have to—"

WUMPH!

Hamilton, slippery little eel, wriggled out of her grasp, and they both ended up on the floor. Ham on his pillow pile. Quinn with a wooden train track up her butt.

Quinn lay there, staring at the ceiling, more surprised than she was sore (and her butt was stinging something fierce). Wondering how the hell she was allowed to have a kid. How the hell she had fallen this low, and how she was going to get through spring break next week, where Ham would be home with her every day . . . and Gina had requested the time off.

She was so lost in her own reeling thoughts, it took her a minute to realize that the buzzing at her side was not from the wooden train track, but was actually her phone.

> **Daisy:** I never saw Ham grin so hard as when he saw you at pickup today.

Quinn felt the smile spread across her face. The same time that a suspicious stinging began in her nose and a tear leaked out of the corner of her eye.

Somehow, Daisy knew what she needed to hear, and that she needed to hear it at that exact minute.

Oh, all right, the fact that it came at that moment was more than likely a coincidence. But Daisy had been the one to hear about all her efforts toward imperfection, the one to listen while she talked about the latest needle she had to thread with Hamilton's behavior.

Being without Stuart was so much easier and so much harder than she had expected. To be the one in charge of the schedule, to no longer be deferential to his needs . . . that was both freeing and frightening. It upended Hamilton's life as little as possible. Stuart spent a weekend or two stopping by the house to spend time with Ham, but never more than an afternoon. And after that afternoon it was always . . . challenging.

I never saw Ham grin so hard as when he saw you at pickup today.

Quinn just had to think about that moment. How he'd lit up and run to her.

Quinn began to chuckle. And then it became a full-on laugh. Loud and long.

Hamilton, who had been sitting in shock on his pillow pile, began to giggle, too. Then, he came over and pig-piled Quinn, both of them giggling madly, like broken Tickle Me Elmos.

They stayed like that until Gina tiptoed over to the playroom door. "Uh, Ms. Quinn?" she said, looking at them like they were utterly loony—which they no doubt looked. "Everything okay?"

"Everything's fine," Quinn said. "Everything okay with you, Hammy?"

Hamilton suddenly jumped to his feet. "I have to go potty." And he took off like a shot, holding his butt.

"He has to go potty," Quinn said, hauling herself up off the floor.

"He's been doing well with that," Gina said.

"Yes, he has," Quinn said, musing. In fact, Ham hadn't had an accident in . . . how long? Quinn opened up her phone, checked her calendar. She had given him Percy after two weeks of no potty accidents, but that was a couple of weeks after New Year's. Awhile ago now.

In fact, according to the log she'd kept on her calendar, Ham hadn't had a potty accident since the beginning of the year.

"Holy shit," she murmured. Then, catching Gina's surprised look, "Er, proverbially speaking. But holy shit!"

He'd been accident free since the first week of January. He'd gone both number one and number two in the potty every time! No naptime or overnight accidents! Today, he'd even run in to use the potty while they were playing outside!

Nothing was perfect. Absolutely nothing was perfect, except . . . this one thing was actually, maybe, finally solved.

A flush was heard from afar, followed by the thumping of small running feet. Ham appeared, pulling up his pants.

"Ham!" Quinn rushed over and swept him up into her arms. "You did it!"

"Did what?" he asked, confused.

"You went potty! Yay!"

"Oh, okay," he said, going along with it. "Yay!"

"Yay! And you deserve a great big present," Quinn said. "What do you want? Anything!"

"Mac and cheese?!"

"Um, I was actually thinking something bigger than that, but okay," Quinn said, and turned to Gina. "There's a box of organic mac and cheese somewhere in the back . . ."

"I got it," Gina said. "And I'll put the pork chops and brussels sprouts in the oven to keep them warm?"

"Thanks," Quinn said. Then, "But you can box those up and take them home if you want. Mac and cheese sounds good to me, too."

Gina nodded and moved off.

"What else would you like?"

"Dessert?"

"Think bigger."

"Disney World?"

Quinn blinked; trust her son to go from dessert to Disney in one swing. She was about to negotiate him back down to earth, but then she thought . . . *why not?* The coming week was spring break. She didn't have any work to report to. And Grandma had a condo in Orlando.

Besides, she deserved to spend some of Stuart's money.

It was utter madness. It was probably, according to the books, really bad parenting. No doubt he would think that if he washed his hands after using the potty he'd get a trip to the moon, but the only words that she found coming out of her mouth were . . .

"Why not, buddy? Why not!"

One week later, Quinn and Hamilton were on their way back from Logan airport, hurtling along in freshly fallen snow, incongruously tan and wearing oversize Mickey Mouse apparel. Quinn even had a row of braids with beads on the side of her head, her sad attempt at a Bo Derek impression. Hamilton loved them—almost as much as he loved the Goofy baseball cap that he refused to take off.

After a three-hour (and fifteen-minute) flight, they were tired. They were horrifically tacky. They were on their millionth replaying of "It's a Small World."

But even in the midst of all that, they were happy.

The trip had been amazing. True, it hadn't been without the regular difficulties that come with the air travel and toddler combo. Quinn had tried to adhere to her parenting rules on the flight down (limit screen time, only educational games), but by the time they landed, Hamilton was watching "Baby Shark" for the umpteenth time and the people behind them were ready to destroy her.

The rest of the trip . . . all the rules went out the window. Oh, mealtimes and bedtimes were held to, but only kinda. Mostly, if they wanted to do something, they did it. Dinner of corn dogs? On it. Stay up late to watch the light show? Absolutely. Ride It's a Small World seventeen times in a row? Why the hell not, Quinn had headphones and an audiobook.

When Quinn Barrett decided to pursue imperfection, she went full tilt.

Ham had a marvelous time. It took him a minute to loosen up too, but once he figured out that it was okay to run around and have fun here, he went into it with the gusto of . . . well, a three-year-old at Disney World.

It was a blur of junk food and cartoon characters and castles and sunshine. A week of specific memories that she couldn't remember at the moment, just the overall sense of good feeling.

There were a couple of tantrums, brought on by too much sun and not enough naptime. (And one Quinn tantrum as the result of a really inadequate wine at the resort.) But there were no potty accidents. And more than anything, every time Quinn thought the chaos was going to get to her, she looked at the text that Daisy had sent her.

Daisy: I've never seen Ham grin so hard as he did when he saw you at pickup today.

And remembering that made her just . . . embrace the chaos.

Her mom, who they spent a few nights with at her condo before they decided it was better to get a hotel at the resort, noticed the change.

"You seem happier than I expected you to be."

They were on her mom's balcony, overlooking the green vistas of a very average golf course as night fell. Ham had conked out after a long day in the park, dreaming no doubt of swimming with the Little Mermaid or something similar. And Quinn had come out here to restrain herself from rearranging her mother's living room furniture (which was laid out *horribly,* she practically tripped over footstools with every step).

Her mother knew about the videos. And now, she knew about Stuart. No amount of Quinn saying, "Everything's fine, Mom" on the phone could keep her from inferring the truth.

"Happier than you expected?"

"More relaxed."

Ah. Well. She supposed throwing all the rules out the window and letting her son go crazy in Fantasy Land helped with the relaxation.

"I gave up on . . . something I thought was important. Took a page out of your book," Quinn replied.

Her mom cocked her head to the side. "What do you mean?"

"You know, Mom . . . you took up knitting for six months and I have one holey scarf to prove it. You tried stained glass art, guitar, clock making, Argentine tango, American Sign Language, and three different boyfriends my freshman year of high school. No wonder I craved perfection."

"That's not very fair. I was always pursuing a passion."

"Really? How's your Etsy shop going?"

Her mother slanted her a side eye and took a deep breath.

"I'm sorry, I didn't mean to get into a fight—"

"I never gave up on what was important," her mother said stiffly.

"You mean the pursuit of passion?" Quinn tried gently. "I suppose that's not . . . ignoble . . ."

"No, sweetie. I mean you," her mother said, coming over and planting a kiss on Quinn's furrowed brow. "I wanted to give you a full life. And me as well. Was it chaotic? Yes. Did I fail at some things? Yes. But I never *never* gave up."

Her mother gathered up the glasses, made to go inside.

"Mom," Quinn said, calling her mother back. "You didn't fail. I . . . I turned out okay."

Her mom had smiled at her, sniffling up a few tears.

"In the end, that's all any parent wants."

Quinn had thought about that conversation the entire rest of the trip, the three-hour (and fifteen-minute) flight home, and the drive from Logan.

She *was* okay. The weight of judgment from the world didn't come from her mother, she certainly hadn't felt it as a child. When had she started letting the world dictate what she was going to be?

She glanced to the backseat. Ham was singing along to the horrific earworm of "It's a Small World."

"It's a world of laughter a world of tears . . . it's a world of hopping, a world of fins . . ."

He definitely dreamed about the Little Mermaid.

She didn't want this to end. Well, she wanted the "Small" concert to end, but not really. She wanted a full life. Not one structured and rigorous, not one where she fought against the tide of chaos, but one where she embraced it. Being on vacation had been a break from reality, how to continue this feeling when they had a schedule to hold to?

"How you doing, Ham?" she said into the rearview mirror.
"Good."

"Ready to be home?"

"Yeah. But I miss Mickey. And Goofy."

"And Donald and Pluto."

"We didn't see Pluto."

"We didn't?" she replied as they took the off ramp to Needleton. There was a billboard there for the local ASPCA. Ham always barked at it when they passed.

He didn't this time, his focus was out the other window, thinking of the missing Pluto, no doubt. The ASPCA.

She nearly swerved, her eyes unable to break from the sign until the last second.

A dog. How long had she wanted a dog? But she never even floated the subject with Stuart, knowing he would grumble objections.

But Stuart had removed himself from the decision.

This was just the kind of chaos she'd been looking for.

"Where are we going?" Ham asked, as she turned down an unfamiliar road.

"We're going to go see Pluto, buddy."

Hamilton and Pluto, a two-year-old, housebroken (they promised he was housebroken) mostly Ridgeback-mixed-with-something-unknown mutt, had become best friends the second they laid eyes on each other. It was as if Hamilton's heart said, "That's my dog!" and Pluto's said, "That's my boy!"

They were allowed to take the dog home for fostering that day. There would be a home visit later in the week, but when she gave her address (a nice street, with lots of nice acreage to run around on) and the ASPCA worker saw Hamilton with the dog, they made allowances.

The donation she pledged no doubt didn't hurt.

They stopped by the pet store on the way home, picking up a dog bed, food, bowls, and a bunch of fun toys that Hamilton decided were absolutely necessary.

She was driving blissfully along, trying to remember what was in their pantry that they could have for dinner, listening to her son comfort the dog whimpering in the carrier in the back.

"Don't worry, it's going to be okay. You're going to come home with us. And my mommy will be there, and my daddy will too—"

Well, there was the knife twist. Ham obviously knew his daddy hadn't been home, but she hadn't told him anything other than he was working. He hadn't even picked up the phone when she'd called to tell him about their Disney trip. She'd left a half dozen messages on his voice mail, and then finally one with Charlene, his scheduler. It was the only way she had any assurance that he actually got the message.

Stuart was absent. Had made himself absent. And she knew, after two months, she needed to start telling her son something.

But as she turned into their driveway, she realized she couldn't tell a three-and-a-half-year-old after a week at Disney and getting a dog named Pluto that his dad wasn't coming home anytime soon. She wasn't that brave.

"Ham, sweetie. You know Daddy has to work a lot . . ."

"Daddy!!!"

"Ham, sweetie—"

"See, Pluto? I told you! Daddy's here!"

Quinn slammed on the brakes, squealing to a halt.

Because Stuart Evelyn Barrett was waiting on her—well, their—doorstep.

Shivering in his wool coat. A bunch of flowers in his hand.

Her husband had come home.

CHAPTER SIXTEEN

The first day after the Little Wonders spring break, Daisy McGulch Stone strolled into the Cranberry Boutique, threw off her heavy jacket, and took her place on the sales floor.

She stood there for approximately thirty seconds before Elaine came running in from the back.

"Daisy!" Elaine said, unable to hide her alarm. "Your hair!"

"Yes, I had it done. About time too, my mother would have been livid if she saw the number of grays I was letting see the light of day."

"But it's . . . it's . . ."

"Purple," Daisy said. "Well, actually the color was called Lavender Shock."

Elaine let out a breath. "Shock is not inaccurate."

When Daisy had pulled into that drugstore, she had been met with a rainbow of choices from white blond to auburn to pitch black. But an actual rainbow was harder to find. So, she had held on to her conviction but resorted to the internet for her favorite LA-based salon supply shop (Juliana the makeup genius had hooked her up with that) and decided that blue was so last season. This year, she was going Holdo purple.

Her internet order—in a sleek black box with an obscure name, Robbie probably thought she was ordering sex toys—had arrived the day before spring break, which strategically was ideal. She had taken off work for the week since Carrie didn't have school. The first day they were left home alone, they broke open the box, and dyed Mommy's hair.

Carrie was so excited to watch. She was even more excited when Daisy gave her a purple stripe.

Yep, Daisy was the mom who dyed her three-year-old's hair. And Carrie *loved* it.

So did Quinn—Daisy had texted her a picture while Quinn was in Florida, and Quinn flipped out, in a good way. Then texted back pictures of her mom's octogenarian purple-haired neighbors.

Quinn: You think you're soooooo avant garde. ☺ ·

And the strategic upside? Was that it gave Carrie an entire week to love her purple hair without anyone else's influence. Shanna had taken Jordan to Hilton Head to visit her parents for the break, so there were no cousin playdates, no family dinners to contend with. It was just Daisy and Carrie, playing dress-up and having fun with makeup and getting cabin fever. They went into the boxes in the garage, untouched in months, and pulled out all of Carrie's favorite board games (and some of Daisy's).

They had probably every board game ever made for the preschool set.

Basics like Chutes and Ladders, Candy Land, Hi Ho! Cherry-O, that game with the loud motor and the snapping fish. Kid-size Jenga, Velcro balls and felt dart boards, and so many, many more. Daisy looked at all of these as primers for the day she introduced her daughter to D&D, and they spent all of the break enthusiastically geeking out over the old things they loved, and the new things they would.

After a week of immersion in fun games, and a not insignificant number of *Star Wars* books, she and Carrie walked into the Tadpole Room at Little Wonders that morning. With her glasses on, a purple streak in her hair, and wearing her favorite *Star Wars* shirt, Daisy was disheartened to see Carrie clutch her hand instead of running down the hall. She was going back into herself, in a way that made Daisy fear the entire week off had been a mere fantasy.

But the second Carrie walked into the room, she was surrounded by the other kids. Hugs were given (by Elia of course) and then the exclamations began.

"You have purple hair!"

"It matches your glasses!"

"I want purple hair!"

When Daisy left, Carrie was being admired far and wide. And she was grinning madly, tugging at Elia and Charlie and Calvin to go play with the train sets.

Seeing her daughter glow gave Daisy the confidence she needed to walk into the boutique and smile placidly at Elaine, like she was doing right now.

Although the longer Elaine stared, the less placid Daisy felt.

"And . . . what are you wearing?"

"Do you like it?" she said, fingering the off-the-shoulder silk T-shirt and twirling her maxi skirt. "It's from the new spring stock—trying to will warm weather into existence."

"Daisy, you cannot wear that," Elaine said, stiffly. "It will turn off customers."

"I thought it looked good on me."

"You want me to speak plainly, fine," Elaine said, brittle. "It shows off those tattoos. And our clientele does not respond to this . . . costuming."

Daisy nodded, swallowed. "It's interesting that you say costuming. Because this isn't the costume. The sweater sets, the brown hair, that was my Clark Kent disguise."

"Regardless, I need you to—"

"Tell you what," Daisy interrupted. "Let me on the floor today. If I beat your best sales for a February Monday, you concede that it's not the tattoos and hair and makeup—"

"And your nose piercing."

"And the piercing," she said, willing herself to not touch the tiny silver ring she had put back in her septum. "If I don't . . . you can let me go."

Elaine sucked in her cheeks. Then she threw up her hands. "I don't have anyone else who can cover your shift, so you're going to have to work today."

Daisy smiled her biggest, brightest smile. "I won't let you down!"

"Seriously. What happened?" Robbie said, later on that evening.

"Nothing happened. I . . . I quit," Daisy replied, as she put together the various pieces of Carrie's lunch. Carrie had come home from school in an absolute daze of exhausted happiness. She had conked out right after dinner.

Which gave Robbie plenty of time to freak out over what Daisy had told him at dinner. That she was no longer working at the Cranberry Boutique.

"You didn't just quit. You love that job."

Daisy shot him an unparalleled *are-you-serious?* glare. "I did not love that job."

"You didn't?" Robbie asked. Daisy could see he was genuinely perplexed. "But you were always so . . . enthusiastic."

Damn, maybe Cosplay Daisy had been a better disguise than she'd ever imagined if Rob couldn't spot the performance.

"Well, Elaine wasn't all that enthusiastic about me," she said on a sigh, indicating her hair. "The real me."

Daisy had hoped that she would get through her shift victorious, she really had. But then . . . well, she knew it the moment it happened. She'd been on a roll, really doing well. Monday foot traffic was always horrendous, but she had put out a witty quote on their chalkboard, threw open the door to invite people inside . . . and everyone who did left with a purchase.

Until that one customer came in.

It wasn't just one actually, it was a mother-daughter duo. The mom was a customer she had waited on before, who came in semiregularly, browsing for the latest in clean-cut casual wear. Her daughter was about middle school or early high school age—the Little Wonders spring break might have been last week, but the grade schools had this week off.

Daisy smiled wide when she saw them.

The daughter's jaw dropped, like she'd just seen a comic book come to life.

The mom's face froze.

"Hi there," Daisy greeted them cheerfully. "We have some wonderful new spring stuff in, check it out!"

The mom nodded stiffly. The daughter eyed Daisy with unconcealed interest. And then after a thirty-second mute circuit of the store, the mom pulled her daughter (who had been looking at the jewelry rack) to the door.

It didn't matter what her sales were for the day, if she beat every other February Monday. She saw that mom leave and she knew what Elaine was going to say.

"You're a very good salesperson. Your sales today are no doubt stellar," Elaine had said, once she clocked out. "Imagine what they would have been if you'd been dressed normally."

"This is normal," Daisy had replied. Then, unable to hide the pleading in her voice, "You don't really want that mom and her judgmental attitude as a customer, do you?"

"Yes. I do," Elaine said, not unkindly. "She's exactly who this store caters to, and there are a lot of her around here."

"There are a lot of people who bought from me today who don't care what my hair or arms look like." But it was no use. Elaine just shook her head.

"I don't want to lose you. But if you insist on looking . . . not normal, I can't have you on the sales floor—it's not the image the Cranberry Boutique needs to project. You can do the inventory, and the books—"

"No," she said flatly. "Thank you for the opportunity, Elaine, but I don't want to work somewhere that thinks I'm not normal."

She'd walked out of the store, her head held high. It only took the walk to the car for the anxiety, worry, and regret to set in.

The anxiety was for what she would tell Rob.

The worry was for how were they going to make ends meet now?

But the regret . . . the regret had been not for dying her hair. It was for staying with the boutique for so long.

"I still don't understand . . . why did you do it?"

"I told you, I didn't—"

"No, I mean—you knew they had a policy about how

salespeople looked. So why did you dye your hair?" Robbie said, his voice raised. "Why jeopardize your income—which we really, really need—for purple hair? What, were you that bored over the break?"

Daisy didn't often get mad at Robbie. He was too nice—as a person, as a husband. Sure there were those times when Carrie was a newborn and she was doing night feeds and he was snoring seven hours straight that she contemplated murder, but other than that, it was really rare. But at that moment, with Robbie's myopia and raised voice, her entire vision went blood red.

"Why? WHY?" she said, gritting her teeth. "I did it for our daughter! I don't know if you'd noticed—oh, that's right, you *haven't*—but she wasn't wearing her glasses at school."

"She wasn't?" he said. "Why? And what's that have to do with—"

"Because she didn't have anyone showing her that it was okay to be herself." Daisy didn't say "you idiot," but it was implied. "Another kid told her the glasses were stupid. And since then, our daughter—our brilliant, delightful, whirling dervish of a daughter needed someone to show her how to be confident being herself. Because I certainly wasn't doing it. Changing every last thing about myself to support you and your GODDAMNED dreams!"

"My dreams? MY dreams?" Robbie fired back. "I thought these were our dreams!"

Daisy threw her hands into the air. "Are you INSANE? You think it was my dream to move to your hometown? To be three thousand miles away from everything I know and love? To be sneered at by moms at preschool and unemployable because I don't dress like a Daughter of the American Revolution?"

God, it felt so good to finally let all of this out, it was practically spewing out like hot lava and volcanic ash.

But all that lava singed her husband.

Robbie looked stricken. "So, what? You have one foot out the door? I thought you liked it here."

"I miss *everything* about Los Angeles. The weather, my friends, my work, the atmosphere of creativity . . . But mostly, I miss myself. I miss feeling confident. I miss feeling like I'm not a freak. And I tried to fit in here—you know I tried. Wear the clothes, hide my tattoos—but that just made me feel worse. Like I was hiding out here even more."

Robbie took off his Red Sox hat to run his hand through his hair. He looked as if she had slapped him—and she had, metaphorically. "I'm sorry. I didn't know you felt this way. I mean—I knew it was going to be an adjustment, but . . . I thought you were happy."

"No, you *needed* me to be happy, so that's how you saw me."

"Well . . . at least one of us was."

He said it so forlornly, Daisy found herself sitting down next to him, drawing his eyes to hers.

"Are you happy?" she asked.

"Yes . . ." Then, "Sometimes. Mostly I'm . . . disappointed, I guess."

"How so?"

He rubbed his hand over his face, blowing out a long sigh. "I think I expected to pick up where I left off. That my friends would be here. My family. But everyone is busy, has kids, jobs. Jamie can't even make it to a football game. I just . . . sometimes feel alone here."

"You were barely twenty-two when you left. No responsibilities."

"Yeah, it turns out being an adult sucks no matter where

you are," he said with a grimace. "I miss my friends from LA. I know you miss yours. And work is . . . not what I had hoped."

"I thought Joe Sr. went with your idea. Adding in a mini competition for the other contractors?"

"He did. But Jo-Jo is like the king of passive aggression. I'm out on a limb on my own, and I don't have long relationships with any of the staff . . . they all have worked with him for a decade or more. Every day it's eggshells. If the competition idea flops, I don't think I'm back for next season. And then we're really screwed."

"We're not screwed," Daisy said. "You'd find other work. They're not the only show produced in Boston."

"They almost are." Then, he cocked his head to one side. "Boston? You wouldn't want to go back to LA?"

"I don't think we can," Daisy said after a moment.

"You mean because of the house?" he asked. "We don't have to—"

"No . . . not just because of the house," she admitted. "If you had asked me a couple of months ago, I would've told you that I was secretly hoping you would want to."

"You were?"

She nodded. Then, she thought about everything that had happened since then. She had made her first real mom friend. And she had resolved to be herself, living out loud. Just making that decision had brought her so much relief, all the hard puritan edges of Needleton seemed to lose their pointiness.

"But now," she continued, "we came to Needleton, we set ourselves on this path. I think we'd regret it if we gave up. Especially for Carrie—she loves it here. She loves Grandpa Bob, loves the school. I think . . . this is the right place for her to grow up."

"It is a good place to grow up," Robbie said. "I should know. But that doesn't mean Los Angeles is bad. We . . . we might have judged it too harshly. It's where you basically came into being."

"No, it's not bad. And I am going to work my ass off to make certain my daughter is as weird as she wants to be. Because I am going to be myself here. Tattoos, hair . . . overelaborate celebrations every time a *Star Wars* movie comes out. And that might mean she doesn't get invited to some birthday parties—but I can't exist any other way."

Robbie leaned over and kissed her. A deep and grateful apology.

"I'm sorry if I ever made you feel like you had to be someone else."

She kissed him back. "I'm sorry if I ever made you feel like you are alone here."

"So . . . you don't have one foot out the door?"

"No, you're stuck with me for the long haul. But," she said, after another long, lingering kiss, "I need your help—to remind me that it's okay to be myself. If you ever see me slipping."

"You got it."

"I'm just sorry that I had to lose a job to get to this point," she sighed. "I don't know what we're going to do about the down payment."

"Honestly—I'm not worried about that now," Robbie said, leaning back with a smile.

"Why?"

He took her hand. "Because I know we'll figure it out, together."

Together. Daisy and Rob. With Carrie. In Needleton.

What a wonderful, wonderful place to be.

Little Wonders Preschool
March Newsletter

Hello, WONDER-ful parents!

Well, we are MARCHing right along into the year! Soon enough this in-like-a-lion month will be out like a lamb and we will welcome spring! ~~Ha. Wishful thinking. I can't feel my toes.~~ But while we wait for that first breath of warm weather, don't forget that we are celebrating Literature Week at the beginning of the month! Parents are encouraged to come in and read to the whole class ~~if you don't you are shortchanging your children and no it doesn't count toward your volunteer hours~~. The highlight of the week is always Dress as Your Favorite Literary Character Day, so we look forward to seeing your little Harry Potters and Alice in Wonderlands! ~~And no, PJ Masks are not literary characters, I don't care how many books of theirs your kid has. Stick to the rules.~~

Also, don't forget St. Patrick's Day! ~~I know you won't, this is Massachussetts.~~ Send your kid to school in green clothes, lest they get pinched! ~~Just kidding, we don't allow pinching. Any kid caught pinching will end up in the calm down corner . . . but green clothes, just in case.~~

And mark your calendars for the Parent Association meeting on the first Wednesday of the month! The Family Fun Fest is a little over a month away, and we will be handing out assignments for volunteers on a first come, first serve basis! ~~So if you don't want to be stuck cleaning up the puke behind the cotton candy machine, better show your face at the meeting.~~ Also, our ~~exhausting annoying bitchy clueless~~ indomitable leader, Shanna Stone, has an exciting announcement to make, so attendance is highly recommended!

We will also be addressing the recent contagion that has infected our school. That scourge we no doubt all know and love by now: the word "poopybutt." We have been assured by Ms. Anna and all of the teachers that this is a normal developmental moment in a child's vocabulary and expression, and that they all eventually learn insults such as "poopybutt" from other kids. ~~Whatever. If I find out it was your kid who taught my kid "poopybutt" I swear to god I am GOING TO COME FOR YOU.~~

Ms. Anna and the Tadpole Room's Ms. Rosie will be on hand at this month's Parent Association meeting to address parent concerns related to "poopybutt," and discuss strategies to return our children to a more loving form of self-expression.

~~It was your kid, wasn't it, Terry? They've got older siblings, learned it from them? I AM GOING TO KILL YOU TERRY.~~

Together in Parenting!
Suzy Breakman-Kang
Parent Association Secretary

CHAPTER SEVENTEEN

Everything was fine. Perfectly normal. In fact, Quinn told herself, it was a relief to have things back this way. She just . . . needed to sleep.

Her internal alarm—which usually went off precisely at 5:45 AM—decided that having her wide awake by four and staring at the wall for two hours was the absolute best use of her time.

This is what she got for abandoning her Parcel Method in fits of imperfection.

Stuart snored lightly, blissfully beside her. Well, not exactly beside her. In their king-size bed a wall of pillows had been erected in the middle. Ostensibly it was because she wanted to read in bed, and didn't want to disturb his sleep with even her tiny reading light. But really, it was because the strangeness of having him back in their bed had not worn off, even after more than a week of having him home.

The closeness of him, the weight on his side of the mattress, was both foreign and heartbreakingly familiar. After that first night—where they negotiated his returning to not just the house, but to their bed ("It would confuse Ham otherwise" was the argument), she woke up in the middle of the night, and found that she was spooning him, pressing her body up against his.

After that, the pillow wall came into effect.

She felt massive amounts of guilt for it. And then she hated herself for the guilt. And then she felt guilty for hating the guilt. Because honestly, Stuart had done everything right. Absolutely everything, from the moment they'd pulled up to the door, and saw him sitting there, flowers in hand.

"Hey, buddy!" he'd said, as Ham jumped out of the car and ran through melting slush to hug his dad.

"We got Pluto!" Ham had cried.

"You met Pluto? At Disney World?" Stuart had replied.

"No, at the doggy store!"

At that moment, Pluto—who had somehow gotten out of his cage; this dog might have been more than Quinn had bargained for—burst out of the open car door and galloped up to Hamilton on the front steps.

"You got a dog?" Stuart said, his attention turning to Quinn for the first time.

Her heart tripped over itself the second his eyes met hers. It was like a body blow, knocking her back on her heels.

Stuart let go of Ham, whose joy at seeing his father was quickly replaced with the joy of having his dog at home.

"Come on, Pluto! I'll show you my room!" Ham said. He climbed up the steps and through the front door that had been opened by Gina, who had arranged her life to meet them when they got back.

Gina met Quinn's eyes, questioning. Quinn nodded, letting her know everything was okay.

"Hamilton!" Gina then cried. "How I missed you! Who is your friend?"

With Hamilton chattering, and Pluto snuffling and woofing, Gina ushered them inside, leaving Quinn and Stuart to freeze their toes off in the melted slush around their feet.

Oh man, Ham and Pluto's muddy feet were going to destroy her floors.

The fact that such a thought raced through her mind at *this* moment caused a bubble of hysteria to creep up her throat. Dear god, honestly, who cared? She didn't. Not when Stuart was standing in front of her after two long months.

How many times had she imagined this exact situation since New Year's? Stuart, on her doorstep, flowers in hand, an intense expression of remorse on his face. It was her favorite falling-asleep fantasy, when she was trying to convince herself everything would be okay. That he would come home, that he would beg for her forgiveness, and that they would have another baby within the year and small sick children would only need surgery during regular business hours and he'd be home for dinner every night.

She never told anyone about this fantasy, not even Daisy. Because she never believed it would happen.

But there he was, his romance novel face and his spin class–trained body and those hands holding flowers. Those hands. That had held hers in front of an altar at the First Episcopal Church five years ago. Those hands that liked to lace hers, pinning her down, when he was inside her.

There he was.

And here she was, travel weary, her hair was a mess, and wearing leggings and a Mickey Mouse T-shirt under her open jacket.

And she'd had absolutely no clue as to how to proceed.

"Gina wouldn't let me inside," he said.

Well, Gina was getting a raise.

"You look . . . nice," he tried.

That was a reasonable start. Very soft, cordial, a way to ease into the eggshell conversation they were no doubt about to have.

But Quinn—Quinn was done with eggshells.

"What are you doing here?" she asked, blunt. A little snort of air blew out her nose when she saw the look on Stuart's face.

It goes both ways—she could pull the rug out from under him too, she thought.

"I . . . ," he started, then stopped himself. "You went to Florida."

"Yes. To see my mother. And Disney World."

"You . . . willingly saw your mother?" Stuart asked.

She crossed her arms over her chest. "Yes, I did," she said, putting her chin up in the air. "What about it?"

"Nothing!" Stuart said. "It's just, she usually drives you crazy."

"Well, I've been doing a lot of unusual things lately."

"Like getting a dog?"

"Actually, that is perfectly normal. I've always wanted a dog."

"You have?" Stuart asked, his nose wrinkling in distaste. "I didn't know that."

"No, because I knew you hated dogs, so I never brought it up."

"I don't hate dogs," he said. "But . . . they do take a lot of work."

"You're not the one who's going to do it, so what do you care?" she challenged.

"I care because you are the one who took on so much stuff that your life basically imploded. And now you want to take on a dog?"

"Okay, so we're back to blaming me for everything," she said, throwing up her hands. "Thanks for the flowers, great seeing you, Stuart, I'll tell Ham you had to go back to work."

She marched past him, making for the door, but his hand slid gently down her arm and clasped her hand.

Oh, that hand. That touch. It had been so long since he'd touched her.

"I don't want to fight," he said, soft.

"Then what do you want?" she breathed.

He licked his lips. "I . . . I didn't know that you were going to Florida."

"I called you. A half dozen times."

"I know."

"Sent you emails. Texts. Left word with your parents' household and with Charlene."

"I know—I just . . . I got busy and I didn't check my messages. And when I figured out you had taken Ham and left the state, I . . . I freaked out."

"Yeah, I know," she replied. "Unlike you, I check my messages."

It had come after a long day at Epcot. Her heart had leaped when she saw it, because her phone glitched and said it was coming from a Crabbe and Co. number. But it wasn't Jeremy, or Sutton, or anyone begging her to come back. It was Stuart who left a message. Telling her that he was upset—no, *livid*—that she took Hamilton to Florida without talking to him first. She could practically hear his gritted teeth on the recording.

But those teeth weren't gritted anymore.

"I just took him on vacation. We don't have an official separation agreement, no custody arrangements, so you have no—"

"It wasn't that," Stuart said. "I realized . . . I realized I didn't like not knowing where you were. Not knowing what you were doing."

"You haven't known where I was or what I was doing for two months." Not to mention, she had no idea what he was doing, where he had been. She didn't even know where he had been living. The doctors' quarters at the hospital would have been for a night or two, not months. Did he get a sublet? Did he . . . did he stay with someone else? A female someone else?

"I knew you were here," Stuart was saying. "In Needleton. I knew you were taking care of our son. It shook me to my core—to think that you were out in the world somewhere and I wouldn't know what you were doing. I realized I never wanted to not know.

"I want to come home." He sighed. "Nothing makes sense in my life without you. I can't find my socks, I don't know what Hamilton's doing in school. You're my home base. I can have the worst day at work, the world can go cockeyed, but as long as you're here, I know everything is okay.

"I miss you. I love you." He took a deep breath, stepping into her warmth. "And, I'm sorry."

He was so . . . there. So warm, smelling so good, so present, and so *there*. And she'd missed him.

Really, really missed him.

"Okay," she said.

"Okay?" he said, a hopeful smile breaking across his face. "Okay, I can come home?"

"Okay, you can come inside . . . and we can talk about it."

As they crossed the threshold, a cacophony greeted them inside. The sound of paws and little feet on hardwood, Gina calling after them both.

"Mommy! Daddy!" Hamilton said, when he saw them. "Pluto went potty on the floor!"

"I'm on it, Ms. Quinn—" came Gina's voice from the playroom.

Quinn's eyes darted to Stuart, who was frowning, and looking like he was choking on an "I told you so." The second he saw Quinn's eyes though, his expression cleared.

"Really, buddy?" Stuart called back to Hamilton. "Then . . . let's get Gina some more paper towels."

So, they'd talked. And talked and talked and talked. And they'd cried (well, Quinn cried) and laughed, and talked some more.

And then they'd had sex.

Really, really, mind-bending sex, full of longing and anger and fighting for control. Quinn had no idea who won— although her orgasms plural put her in the plus column.

But she had a suspicion that the winner was truly Stuart, because from that moment on, he'd be sleeping in their bed. Having breakfast at the kitchen nook, leaving, coming home after work to have dinner with them, and then doing it all again, as if nothing had happened.

But nothing was normal. Nothing felt right. How he managed to snore next to her, sleeping deep, threw her for a loop. There was so much that no longer fit into the spots it used to.

The clock next to her blinked 4:26 AM. She let out a long sigh, and tried to shuffle into a more comfortable position.

On the other side of the pillow wall, Stuart grumbled, "C'mon . . . stoppit."

She wasn't going to be able to toss and turn, so she might as well use these predawn hours for something.

Usually, Quinn wasn't very good at introspection. In her previous incarnation, whenever she had the downtime necessary for self-reflection, she would instead parlay that into completing another task, or adding a Parcel to her day. She could have tried therapy, but . . . according to her in-laws, that was just for people who liked to talk about themselves. But ever since New Year's—hell, really, ever since Halloween, self-reflection popped up uninvited—so if she couldn't stop it, she might as well multitask and get something done at the same time.

She made herself a cup of coffee (she was NOT frothing milk in fear of the noise waking up the house), checked on Hamilton—who was snuggled in bed with Pluto—and settled in at her desk in her office. Her drafting table, where she played with her designs at home, had been untouched since the fiasco at the charity ball. What was she going to do with all of her ideas, anyway, now that she didn't have Crabbe & Co. to make them real? But . . . she wasn't able to forgo her designs entirely. Like self-reflection, they kept creeping in at the worst time. She'd find herself doodling a dresser shape or a lamp on the edge of a paper, or walking into a room and immediately redoing the color scheme or the layout in her mind.

So, when Daisy had told her about the basement being made into a grandfather suite, she finally had an outlet for some of her ideas—and she might have gone overboard. She had filled an entire notebook with sketches. She'd surreptitiously gotten the measurements from Daisy. And then double-checked them that one time they went over to her house for a playdate. (And she also took the measurements for that kitchen, because my god.)

She played with her sketch for a little while, sipping her coffee and enjoying the silence. Right now, she could pretend that everything was okay. That everything was like it was before.

But which before? Before Stuart left . . . or before Stuart came back?

It was strange, because Quinn was used to being alone—Stuart had an odd schedule, so she was often alone. So why had it felt so lonely when he left?

And why did she feel even lonelier now that he was back?

Maybe because she still had so many questions.

He'd given her answers—in their long conversations (which tended to get cut off by sex). But she didn't know how much she believed him.

She wanted to know where he'd been staying.

Answer: friend's sublet apartment for a couple of months, and pretty much working all the time.

She wanted to know what he did for Valentine's Day.

Answer: three spin classes around a ten-hour workday.

She wanted to know what she'd done that was so horrible he felt that leaving was his only option.

Answer: . . .

Yeah. She still didn't have a lot of answers.

She pulled out a couple of fabric swatches, and was matching them to colors in her sketch, when she heard the soft swing of the door behind her.

"Hey," Stuart said, groggy, in the doorway. "I was wondering where you were."

"Couldn't sleep," she replied. "Do you want some coffee?"

"I want you to come back to bed," Stuart growled, turning his romance novel face on. Although, since he was squinting against the light of her desk lamp, it was not at its usual potency.

"I'm not gonna sleep."

"I wasn't talking about sleeping," he replied, coming over

to kiss the back of her neck. He settled into the chair next to hers, and let his eyes fall to her drafting table.

"What's all this?"

"It's a basement redesign," she replied, shuffling the papers so he couldn't look at them. It felt . . . invasive for some reason.

"I thought you weren't doing design anymore."

"I . . . I left Crabbe & Co. I couldn't work there after the magazine article. But that doesn't mean I'm not designing."

Stuart let out a long sigh. "I read the article, you know. And you worked magic on that place."

"You read the article?" she asked, surprisingly touched.

"Yes. When you think about the way it looked before . . ."

"Did I show you pictures of before?" she asked, her brow furrowing. Normally, she didn't show Stuart the before pictures. He always wrinkled his nose at things that were a complete mess—writing them off as unsaveable. So she eventually just stopped showing him.

"You must have. Or they were in the article," he said, then cleared his throat. "The point is . . . you're really good at what you do. And what Jeremy did was absolutely wrong. But maybe . . . it was actually the best thing for you."

"How so?"

"You don't need to work. You married a Barrett—and a surgeon to boot. Yes, you can absolutely design and decorate as a hobby, but working . . . it took up so much of your life you could devote to other things."

"Such as?" she asked.

"You could get involved at the school again," he suggested. "And this time have the ability to devote yourself to it. You could give back, work with the hospital trust. Or you could just take extra Pilates classes and plan our summer vacation. I just want you to be happy."

Quinn looked at her drawings, snorted. "I haven't been to a Pilates class in a while."

"Well, you should," he said. "You need to take care of your body."

"The Pilates studio was convenient to work."

"So find something here. A healthy body is a healthy mind."

"I'll try to remember that," she said, letting the sarcasm drip. "What if designing makes me happy?"

"Does it? Now? It's so public."

"Public," she said, letting the word hit the floor like a lead brick.

He obviously keyed to the dryness of her voice because he sighed, and then bit his lip. "You're different."

Her arms came across her body. "Yeah, I am."

"I didn't expect you to be different. You didn't used to . . . never mind."

"I like being different," she said, defiant.

"I like that you are, too," he replied instantly. "But I think I need some time to get to know this new Quinn."

His hand came out, and gently uncrossed her arms. Held them in his own. "I have a proposal for you. Week after next, I can free up my schedule. Take a couple days off, and you and I can just hang out. Get to know each other again. How does that sound?"

Quinn looked at his hands on hers. Those hands. On the one hand, taking a week off to spend time working on their marriage seemed like a massive weight he was putting on her shoulders. On the other, she knew she had to give him a chance.

Because he was her husband.

And she loved him.

And maybe she could finally get some of those answers.

"Yes," she said. "That sounds like a great idea."

"Wonderful," he said, kissing her on the forehead. Then he glanced out the window. "Sun's coming up—might as well be awake. Let's go have some breakfast. I'm starving . . . could you make me a green smoothie?"

CHAPTER EIGHTEEN

When Daisy knocked on Quinn's door, she was walking on air. She was having an A+ mega awesome supercalifragilisticexpialidocious day, and she could not wait to tell her best mom friend about it.

She could not believe the score she'd just made. It was epic. In the annals of geekdom, it was akin to Mario finding an unknown question mark box with a fire flower right before fighting Bowser in his castle.

It started when she'd gone into the city to run some errands. Well, one errand specifically.

"I'd like to return these."

The D&D *Fell's Five* graphic novel compendium hit the counter, still wrapped in its cellophane. That Guy barely looked up from the comic he was leafing through. (He licked his fingers as he turned the pages! Licked them! She hoped that was a personal copy, he had better not try to sell it.)

Then his eyes fell to Daisy. She'd thought that her purple hair and wearing a shirt that showed the edges of her tattoos would have had him standing a little straighter, realizing he was in the company of his brethren . . . but that was wishful thinking.

That Guy sighed, put down the comic, and slid the book toward himself.

"D&D not your cup of tea?" he said.

She subtly pushed the sleeve of her jacket up, exposing her forearm and the d20 tattoo.

"I already have a copy," she said. "Signed. By the author."

That Guy merely turned back to the register. "You have a receipt?"

It had taken her until after their fight for her to get up the courage to ask Robbie for the receipt. He'd been so proud of himself when she'd opened the gift at Christmas that she didn't have the heart to tell him that she already had *Fell's Five.*

"I thought you wanted it . . . that's why the comic book guy told me about it as we were leaving the store?" Robbie had said, his brow crinkling adorably.

"Not exactly." She'd smiled at her husband, remembering That Guy's condescension. "But it is the perfect gift for me—as proven by the fact that I already have it."

Now, That Guy's condescension was on full display again as he examined the receipt.

"Hold on," That Guy said. "This was purchased back in December?"

"Yes, it was a Christmas gift."

"We can't do returns after thirty days—store policy."

"Seriously?" That was such bullshit. "It hasn't been touched—the cellophane is still on it."

"Store policy."

"I don't get into town a lot—this was my first chance to come in."

Maybe her pleas made some headway. Maybe he finally looked at her and saw a comrade in nerd arms. Maybe he only saw a foolish woman who needed a break, but either way, he relented a bit.

"Best I can do is store credit."

Daisy forced herself to not roll her eyes. She didn't want to leave her money with That Guy. She didn't want to give him the satisfaction. But . . . she was behind on the brilliant comic *Saga*, and surely there was something or other that could pique her curiosity.

"Let me look around."

"Sure. And if you find anything for you or your husband, let me know."

Yeah—now she really didn't want to leave her money with him. But she didn't have much of a choice.

She'd gone through the shelves, perusing, nothing really sparking her interest. She grabbed the latest *Saga* trade, but still had plenty of store credit left over.

Then . . . she wandered to the back.

"You're not going to find anything back there!" That Guy called out, not looking up from his finger-lickin' book. "That's just where we keep the overstock from our acquisitions."

Long boxes, short boxes, file boxes piled to the ceiling, defying the will of gravity to stay vertical. She knew that comic book stores often acquired whole collections from people who have decided to clean out their garage, but to see it in front of her was a little daunting. Usually, 97 percent of what was in those boxes wasn't worth the paper it was printed on anymore, but sometimes, you ran across a mint condition *Action Comics #1* and could send your kids—and their kids—to college from its proceeds.

She'd moved over to a long box on the top of a pile marked "Reviewed." She guessed that meant they'd already gone through it and picked the needles out of the haystack. But as she thumbed through a bunch of musty Bronze Age comics, she stopped short.

Was that what she thought it was?

Was that . . . a copy of *Chainmail*? Gary Gygax's early foray into creating a fantasy role-playing game? It was in shockingly good shape. Except for the smudge on the corner.

Then, she peered closer.

That was no smudge. That was a signature—one, as a D&D devotee, she knew pretty well.

She glanced over her shoulder. That Guy wasn't paying her any attention, still behind the counter reading. Her heart pounding a mile a minute, she hauled the box up (nearly upsetting the delicate structural balance) and marched to the front.

"How about this?" she said to That Guy. "Can I have this?"

"You want one of the overstock boxes?" Well, it seemed like she finally had his full attention.

"It was in the pile marked 'Reviewed.'" Then, the coup de grace, "There are some old X-Men comics in here that my husband would just die for. He loves the yellow guy. With the claws?"

". . . You mean Wolverine?"

"Yes!" she said, batting her eyes for good measure. "Hugh Jackman's so hot, amirite?"

That Guy looked from her, to the box, back to her. Then he shrugged. "Go for it—we don't have room in the back for that anyway."

She flashed That Guy a full-wattage smile, and got out

of that store before he could change his mind. She practically skipped to the car, and spent the entire car ride back to Needleton trying to get her heart rate under control.

So by the time she'd pulled up at Quinn's house, she was in a state of absolute giddy joy, smiling like a drunken ferret.

"Hey," Quinn said, when she answered the door, and then she gave Daisy a once-over. "You look amazing. What's going on?"

"Hi, I *am* amazing, I had a total win, and I will tell it to you later if you're into meeting up," Daisy said so fast it sounded like she was on speed. Or at least on sugar.

"Sure," Quinn said, her brow furrowing. "You want to come inside now?"

"No, I have to go to the Parent Association meeting tonight. I know," she said to Quinn's raised eyebrow. "But I promised Shanna." Shanna had sent at least a dozen texts that week, all saying that she really needed Daisy's help and to please, please come to the meeting. Daisy was a little skeptical, but Shanna was family. There are some things you can't escape.

"So, what's up then?" Quinn said.

Daisy dug into her bag, to find what had really brought her here. "I was hoping to see you at pickup or drop-off, but I had so much to do today—anyway, you know how Robbie works for *The Brand New Home*?"

Quinn nodded.

"And you know how I told you they are incorporating a competition element for craftsmen, designers, landscape artists?"

"Yes . . ." Behind Quinn, Daisy heard barking, and then a shadow moved.

"Pluto, NO! Quinn, can you do something about Pluto,

he's—" Suddenly Stuart appeared in the hall. "Hey. Can we help you?"

"Stuart, you remember my friend Daisy? Carrie's mom, from Little Wonders."

"Right." Stuart's gaze went from Daisy's hair and her septum ring to finally meeting her eyes. He gave her a very easy, practiced smile. "Nice to see you again. Quinn, when you have a second, the dog. That you got for our son."

Stuart disappeared back into the house. Daisy met Quinn's eyes. She had a feeling Stuart didn't go very far. "How's that going?"

"Oh! Um . . ." Quinn bit her lip. "You know . . . great. Getting back to normal."

Yeah. He definitely hadn't gone very far.

"So, anyway—something about the show?" Quinn said, pulling Daisy's mind out of the hallway and back to the conversation.

"Right! They need interior designers to enter the competition, and I think you should apply."

"What?" Quinn blinked.

"Actually, I showed Rob those designs for the basement that you texted me, and *Rob* thinks you should apply."

"I . . . I'm not with a firm anymore, I don't have associates or their infrastructure . . ."

"You'll have the show's infrastructure to help," Daisy replied. "Here's the paperwork if you decide you want to apply. Callbacks will be week after next. And I have a feeling you'll get one—you're probably the most qualified person they've got. But that's inside info—the benefit of knowing the producer's wife."

Daisy practically shoved the application into Quinn's hand. Then she checked her watch. "I have to go. Shanna awaits."

"Okay, bye," Quinn said, and as Daisy leaned in for a cheek kiss (god, she'd become so very bougie but she was feeling so good she couldn't be mad about it), she saw a shadow move in the dark hall behind her.

"And call me so we can meet up," she said. Quinn nodded, and waved as she shut the door.

But before the door closed, Daisy heard Stuart's voice float out on the cold air, setting Daisy's jaw and putting a tarnish on her amazing day.

"Who on earth is she and what was that about?"

"Shanna, where are you?" Daisy whispered harshly into her phone.

She had been late to the Parent Association meeting, hoping to sneak into the back of the auditorium without being noticed, get first crack at one of the better volunteer jobs at the Family Fun Fest, and make sure she said hi to Shanna on her way out.

But instead of finding a room full of parents intently listening to Shanna give a PowerPoint presentation breaking down their needs for the upcoming festival, she walked into the hum and murmurs of a room full of people annoyed at having to be kept waiting.

And when the door shut loudly behind her, every eye flew to Daisy.

"Finally!" Suzy Breakman-Kang said in a rush, as she came down from her spot at the main table on the dais. "We're going to be starting soon, everyone! Thank you for your patience!" The clickety-click of her kitten heels sped up as she broke into a trot.

"Suzy, what's going on?" Daisy had said when Suzy reached her side. "Where's Shanna?"

"She's not with you?" Suzy said, alarmed. "She called me, said she needed to talk to you before tonight."

"I . . . I haven't heard from her," Daisy said, a trickle of worry going down her spine. This was not like Shanna. Something must be wrong. "Do you think she's okay?"

"Can you call her?" Suzy asked. "I'll try and stall everyone."

Daisy stepped out into the hall, avoided the questioning glares from other parents (it could have been about the meeting, it could have been about the hair, she decided to not care), and dialed Shanna's number.

"Daisy!" Shanna sounded so relieved when she picked up.

"Shanna, where are you? Are you okay?" Daisy said.

"I am much better now that I'm talking to you," Shanna said, sighing. "You would not believe the day I've had . . ."

"Um, yeah, and I would love to hear about it, but I'm here at the Parent Association meeting—the one you're supposed to be leading?"

There was a pause. A possible penny dropping. And an "Oh my god . . ." from the other end of the phone.

"Did you forget?"

"No, I . . . there was a lot of stuff that happened the past couple of days, it slipped my mind. I called to tell you about it but you never called me back."

"I'm sorry—"

"No, I know you're busy . . . I just thought since you aren't working anymore that you were a bit available."

"I am," Daisy found herself saying. "I am available." Guilt swamped her. Yes, she'd been avoiding Shanna, but clearly something serious was happening, and she should have been a better friend.

"Is it the baby?" she asked.

"Partly. I need to bring my blood pressure down, according to the doctor."

"Oh dear," Daisy breathed. There was a choke in Shanna's voice. Blood pressure in pregnancy was no joke—preeclampsia was life threatening to both mom and baby. Which Daisy knew from her own pregnancy. She knew that Shanna had been stressed, but this . . . this news meant that she needed to do everything in her power to protect her health and the health of the baby.

Shanna would have to quit the Parent Association.

And Shanna wasn't a quitter.

"Shanna, listen—nothing matters except taking care of yourself. Nothing. There are people who can take over. You know, help you out."

Shanna gave a sad little laugh. "You have no idea how good it is to hear you say that. Can *you* help me out?"

"Absolutely," she replied immediately.

"Great—I need to address the Parent Association. Can you facilitate that?"

Daisy tried not to grind her teeth at the word "facilitate" and instead reminded herself that sometimes Shanna's lawyer/boss lady snuck back into her vocabulary.

"Of course."

Daisy crept back into the room, where Suzy Breakman-Kang was very slowly addressing a question from the floor. "Thank you for asking that, *Terry*—I would like to remind everyone that the chickens will move out of the barn and into their yard coop *after* the frost melts, but in time for the kids to enjoy the new chicks at the Family Fun Fest—"

This time Daisy slipped inside and moved quickly down

the aisle to the stage. She caught Suzy's eye, and Suzy beckoned her up to the dais.

"All right, everyone—Daisy Stone has something to share!" Suzy said.

"Actually, it's not me who has something to say," Daisy said, addressing Suzy, who jerked her head toward the crowd. So she turned, and faced the audience.

It wasn't the most crowded Parent Association meeting she'd been to (that record was still held by the post-Halloween debacle) but it was close.

"Uh, hi, everyone." For the first time since she had gone back to her old appearance, she wished she was still Cosplay Daisy. But then, she realized, she could still channel Cosplay Daisy's confidence. "Hello, and thank you for coming tonight. Obviously there's been a little bit of a kerfuffle, and Shanna isn't here tonight. So she's asked me to help her out. Shanna, take it away."

Daisy held up her phone, put it on speaker mode. She grabbed a mic from behind the currently unused podium, switched it on. A loud wince of feedback, and then it was working. She held it up to the phone's speaker.

"Hi, everyone, I'm so sorry I couldn't be there tonight," Shanna said, sounding calm, confident, and passably contrite. "As most of you know, I'm about six months' pregnant. And I had my checkup earlier this week, and my blood pressure was a little too high for the doctor's liking."

The crowd shifted a bit in their seats. Yes, parents of small children tend to have less in the way of conversational limitations, but it's not often you get a neonatal update at the preschool parent meeting.

Shanna paused, either to gather her courage or to up the

audience's suspense. Either way, Daisy wished she would just rip the Band-Aid off. It would be a lot easier once she said she was resigning.

"So," Shanna said, after clearing her throat. "I would like you all to thank my best friend and cousin, Daisy Stone, for stepping up to act as my unofficial deputy."

See? That was so much bett . . . wait, *WHAT*?

"While I'm still your devoted Parent Association president, Daisy will be point person on all things organizing for the Family Fun Fest, reporting directly back to me. She's got all of the volunteer position breakdowns—Daze, I just emailed them to you—as well as the CBAs for each event station and stall—"

"Shanna, I just want to note that due to objections from some parents as cruel," Suzy interjected, "that the goldfish toss is going to be replaced with a cultural music performance/ hula hoop hop."

"Duly noted—Daisy, take that down. Also, Daisy will be organizing and soliciting the donations and gift baskets for the silent auction, which has historically been our biggest fundraiser." Shanna gave a slight chuckle. "Although I have no doubt that Daisy's and my combined genius will take those totals to new heights."

"Wait—Shanna," Daisy finally managed to interject, "what do you mean, unofficial deputy?"

A pause on the other end of the line. "You know, you're absolutely right. I shouldn't be appointing a deputy willy-nilly."

"Thank you—"

"We are a democratic institution. Positions like that need board approval."

"Wait, I—"

"I nominate Daisy Stone to act as deputy president of the Parent Association," Suzy Breakman-Kang said immediately.

"I second the nomination," came from Jay, the VP, who looked horribly relieved.

"Wait—"

"All those in favor?"

The room resounded with ayes.

"Opposed."

Not a peep. Of course not. Because no one else wanted to be saddled with the responsibility.

"Everyone thank Daisy for now being my *official* deputy!" Shanna said. "Now, I should get back to my meditation. Daisy, take me off speaker?"

Daisy dropped the mic that she had forgotten she was holding like it was made of lava, swiftly pulling the phone up to her ear.

"Shanna, what the hell—"

"Daisy, I cannot thank you enough for helping me out. Like you said you would."

"That's not what I meant—"

"Oh, it will be fine. Don't worry, half the work is done already anyway, you just have to collect all the donations, call all the vendors, take all the deliveries, pay all the invoices, oversee setup and breakdown—honestly, it's nothing. Come over tonight and we'll go through everything."

"I—I have things to do."

"Really?" Shanna said, brightening. "You got another job?"

"I . . . I have Carrie, and Rob's schedule to consider, and—"

"Bring Carrie with you! I know Jordan would love to see her. She really misses her best friend."

Daisy pulled up short. "Best friend?"

"I know you *think* that Jordan might have been causing

Carrie some . . . growing pains, but really, Jordan is just a dynamic leader, one that we should all aspire to be," Shanna said, brooking no argument. "Can't wait to see you! Take a lot of notes!"

And with that Shanna hung up.

Daisy stared at her disconnected phone. The Family Fun Fest was a month away. The entire production had just been dropped, half finished, in her lap. And if Daisy didn't step up, April ninth was going to be the preschool equivalent of the Fyre Festival.

And she would be the one going down for it. Because you can't blame the pregnant lady for needing to protect her health. But you can blame her hapless purple-haired cousin for not being up to the job.

Daisy looked up. She was still on the stage. Every eye was turned to her, as it seemed she was now leading the meeting.

"Okay . . . um, let me pull up all the stuff that Shanna sent me, and we'll get to, erm, handing out volunteer posts," she said, as she quickly went into her phone, and sent a single text.

QUINN. HELP.

CHAPTER NINETEEN

Quinn Barrett had three things she needed to accomplish in the remainder of March.

1. Give her marriage the attention and care it needed to repair itself.

2. Talk Daisy off the ledge and help her pull off the Family Fun Fest that was unceremoniously dropped in her lap.

3. Audition for the interior design challenge of *The Brand New Home*.

These tasks were listed in order of importance, because obviously her marriage came first . . . and auditioning for the show was just a foolhardy lark. Just a "Well, let's see if this is even possible, and if it's not, then don't worry about it!"

Of course, these items were on top of her normal everyday accomplishments—including but not limited to the care and feeding of Hamilton, getting the home ready for spring, putting all of her winter clothes away in the closet, paying bills, making doctors' appointments, readying their taxes, making dentist appointments, attempting a workout regimen again (this fits into making her marriage work, so double!), calling a plumber to deal with the tankless water heater when Stuart discovered there was no hot water one *really* cold morning, and begging their plowing service to come out one last time and plow their driveway. (Damn that last snowfall! Come on, it was March already!)

And while said tasks were listed in order of importance, they were not listed chronologically, which was why Daisy was in her house, freaking out, while the plumber banged around in the basement and Quinn dug through her closet.

"She just dumped it all on me! But she's not stepping down, just . . . delegating. So I have to report everything back to her." Daisy was chugging green juice at Quinn's kitchen counter, like she was three whiskeys in and not about to slow down anytime soon. "God, this is horrible, what's in this?"

"The blood of your enemies," Quinn called back from the closet. She was digging through her file boxes from last year, looking for a particular folder. She was as meticulous about her filing as she was everything else, but it was eluding her. Damn, she had just gone through these boxes a few months ago—where was it?

"She's got me coming over once a week," Daisy was saying, "to quote unquote 'check in.' But I know it's going to be more than that—it already has been! She had me come over last night after the meeting *and* this morning, to go over some things she'd forgotten. And she's wants me to bring Carrie, because Jordan misses her 'best friend.' Which is just a whole other level of manipulation, because Carrie has to see Jordan all day and I feel like she only just got her confidence back. But Shanna won't take no for an answer."

"Because she's lonely," Quinn said, then, "Aha! Here it is."

She hauled the box she had been looking for out of the closet, and into the kitchen, where she saw the shocked look on Daisy's face.

"What?" Quinn said.

"You think she's lonely? That's . . . more charitable of you than I expected."

"Oh, I'm sorry, was this just a venting?" Quinn asked, sincerely. "Was I supposed to commiserate and not empathize?"

"You were supposed to hate her more than I do right now, so I could say, 'She's really not that bad, she's family,' and feel superior for my largesse."

"Got it. I'll try again? 'Grrr! That Shanna! She's terrible! I curse her with hyperactive triplets!'"

Daisy gave a weak smile, but then fell silent. "Do you really think she's lonely?"

"Being a stay-at-home mom isn't easy." Quinn shrugged. "I've only been doing it for a couple of months, and I crave adult conversation."

"Hence you're lowering your standards to hang out with me."

"Ha-ha. But really. She's also the one in charge. And often that means you're talking to people, not *with* people. If you don't have a copresident, or a friend to share it with . . . Heavy is the head that wears the crown."

"I have been blowing her off a lot, recently," Daisy admitted.

"I hope not for my sake," Quinn said. "I know Shanna and I have had our issues, but that doesn't mean—"

"It wasn't because of you—well, only kind of, and it's part of a bigger thing, but . . ."

"But . . ."

Daisy bit her lip, then shook her head. "But . . . it doesn't matter. It doesn't matter. What does matter is how am I going to do this? I've never done anything like this before."

Quinn scoffed. "Don't be ridiculous, of course you have."

Daisy looked at her like she had just claimed she was from Tatooine (yes, Quinn had seen a movie too). "I promise, if I ever organized a preschool Family Fun Fest, I would remember it."

"What did you do at the Cranberry Boutique again?"

"Sales associate, but—"

"And before they let Cosplay Daisy on the floor?"

"Invoices and inventory. Straightening out the books."

"Wow," Quinn said, mock facetiously. "Sounds like you have strong experience convincing people to give you money, and then allocating that money and resources to their purposes. Which is basically soliciting donations for the auction and baskets, and ordering supplies and keeping track of needs."

"Okay, fair point, but that's certainly not everything, and not in such a short time frame," Daisy argued. "You should see what Shanna handed me the other night—she said it was half done, but NOTHING is done."

"Oh? As someone who worked in independent film production you don't have experience pulling together the impossible on a significantly shortened time line?"

Daisy shot her a level glare. "There's a saying in film production. 'You can make something quickly, cheaply, well: pick any two.'"

"Daisy, I am here to tell you that you are going to beat the odds, and manage all three."

"Again, the question is how."

Quinn grinned.

"With me, of course."

Quinn handed her the folder she had disrupted her entire filing system to find. A simple red folder, divided into subjects, tasks, and subcommittees, neatly labeled with all the relevant information and broken down into easy-to-follow instructions.

She handed it to Daisy with the reverence usually reserved for the Ten Commandments, inscribed on stone.

"What is this?" Daisy asked, her voice barely a whisper.

"Everything you need to pull off a festival. All of my vendor lists, my donor lists—and the people you need to talk to at those organizations that are receptive to donating—all of my builder and handyman workers to help with something complicated like the auditorium build last year—"

"You . . . built the auditorium last year?"

"We built the little stage," Quinn qualified. "And a cross-reference list of costs of party supplies so those bastards at party supply stores can't jack up the prices on a bouncy house on you."

"I . . . Does Shanna have access to all this stuff via Jamie?"

Quinn smirked. "Not all of it. Not my personal notes."

"And this is so well organized! Shanna basically threw a box of handwritten invoices at me. You're amazing."

"Yes, I am." Quinn checked her vintage watch. "I have a couple of Parcels to spare. Let's start calling vendors, and then we can start dividing up the parent volunteers and conquering. Conscript them into serving on a subcommittee. Most parents would love to be able to burn their involuntary volunteer hours on something they can do during their lunch break."

Daisy hesitated. "I don't like bothering people."

"People are there to be bothered," Quinn said. "They are there to be *told* what to do. You get to be a total bitch over email, demanding people contribute to their community and their children's education. You gotta strut down that preschool hallway and own it. Congratulations! You're the boss now!"

Daisy eyed her dubiously. "You scare me sometimes."

"And the rest of the time I inspire you."

"You know, the real problem is money," Daisy said. "No matter that the kids will have fun, but we have to beat the fund-raising number from last year—"

"You mean my number?" Quinn said. "It's okay, I appreciate the irony."

"And if I don't, it's me that fails. Not Shanna."

Quinn leveled a frank look at her friend. "Then let's not fail. Come on, let's dive in."

They flipped through the folder, Daisy taking the food vendors (because history has shown that everyone loves a food truck), and Quinn taking the list of the Main Street shops for gift basket donations.

"If you're this organized in your designer life, then you are a shoo-in for the show," Daisy said, as she picked up the phone and started to dial.

"Hmm," Quinn said, as she stared very, very intently at whatever paper was in her hand.

Daisy lowered her phone.

"You are going to apply, right?"

"I'm . . . I haven't really thought about it."

"What is there to think about?"

What was there to think about? How about Stuart? After Daisy had dropped off the papers the other day, she and Stuart had a slightly heated exchange about their contents. She mostly brushed off his concerns by saying that she wasn't all that interested in it. That seemed to placate him.

The problem was . . . she was interested. She read over the forms, she had all the requisite experience and accreditations to be considered. And, before Stuart had moved back in, she'd been idly researching what it would take to open her own small company.

Nothing big. Not yet. But something where she could express her creativity, her organization, and make beautiful rooms for people who needed the help finding their style. Needleton and the surrounding suburbs were awash with big new construction houses that were blank slates. Surely some new homeowner needed guidance picking wallpaper.

Unfortunately, the internet was the twenty-first-century yellow pages . . . and how was she supposed to have a website for her work without her old videos creeping back in to shame her? And if she made her comeback on *television*? They might as well run the Halloween Mom video in a picture-in-picture display.

It was . . . daunting.

"I . . . have a lot of things to consider, that's all," Quinn said, pasting a serene smile on her face. It was her "this is my final say on the matter" smile, and worked great with wait-staff and receptionists, but was apparently completely ineffective on Daisy.

"Don't consider too long," she said. "The deadline for applications is Monday." Quinn knew that. It was flashing in red in her mind every time she had a spare moment to herself. "And I don't want you to let something as stupid as an internet video keep you from doing what you're meant to do."

A warm rush of pride flooded Quinn's chest. "What I'm meant to do."

"Clearly you get a rush from organizing other people's lives," Daisy said, indicating the papers in her hands. "And your house is like walking into a magazine spread, but like, a lived-in one."

"Thank you?" Quinn cracked a smile.

"The point is . . . don't let anyone tell you who to be," Daisy said, earnestly. She flipped a lavender length of hair over her inked shoulder. "Anyone. Not . . ." She hesitated. "Not Stuart, and least of all the internet. You are Quinn Barrett. You gotta strut down the preschool hallway and own it."

Quinn rolled her eyes, but couldn't help feeling the words.

"The preschool doesn't really apply to the situation, but . . . okay. I'll think about it."

And she did. She thought about it for the next two days, over the weekend. Thought about it as the snow melted and Hamilton and Pluto rolled around in the mud. Thought about it when Stuart came back from his morning spin class freshly showered and smelling amazing. Home. She should be more focused on home. On Hamilton's progress, on Stuart and building their marriage to a stronger place, to where they became an unbreakable unit, talking about their problems, his successes reflecting on her. And vice versa?

That was the problem. For her to have successes that reflected well on him, she had to have successes. And yes, having a smooth-running, beautiful home and a happy, well-adjusted child were massive, massive successes. Nearly impossible in this day and age. But . . .

There was that "but."

She and Hamilton would be building with blocks, and she would be thinking about the design of the Lego house in her hands.

She and Stuart would be idly chatting about how many weeks she and Hamilton would spend at his family's house on Nantucket this summer (Stuart's schedule would only allow him to visit on the weekends) and she would be mentally scouring the shops in town for beautiful island pieces to incorporate into some future design.

There was this part of her that she couldn't turn off. And she didn't want to.

Quinn did not think of herself as a controversial person. In the narrow life she led in Needleton, she might come off as "strong willed" (or another euphemism for brash, bitchy, or blunt), but in the grand scheme of things, she was truly insignificant. And she didn't want significance. She didn't even want perfection, not anymore. She just wanted to have a happy home, and a fulfilling existence.

Going on television to enter a design contest . . . that was courting significance. But success there might overcome the only other impression the world had of her—that of Halloween Mom.

In fact, other than an unknown length of time, it might be the only thing that could.

So, Sunday night, after Stuart was asleep, she got up, booted up her computer, found the form and instructions beneath some sketches on her desk, filled out the online application, and hit Send before she could change her mind.

She was certain that nothing would come of it.

They were probably overloaded with applicants, and as it was last minute, they had likely already chosen their next round.

So imagine her surprise when, a few days later, she learned that the next round would include her.

The next round, which occurred during the week that Stuart had decided to take off. So they could work on their marriage.

And she did want to work on their marriage. But Stuart . . .

Stuart seemed to think that working on their marriage consisted mostly of sex and talking about grand future plans.

They planned their summer vacation (Nantucket, obvs), they talked about what schools they wanted Hamilton to go to (Groton was Stuart's alma mater, but Quinn blanched at the thought of Hamilton going to boarding school), what kind of volunteering Quinn could do (Stuart's mother apparently had ideas, and a few charities with openings on their boards—once her little scandal was well and truly over, that is). The idea of her designing was not brought up.

And they adamantly did not talk about the past. Which was the only thing Quinn wanted to talk about. Because her big questions still had no answers. And Stuart dodged every attempt she made to approach them.

She still wanted to know *WHY.* Why he'd left. Why he thought it was remotely okay to do that to her, to Hamilton. Why did he have so little faith in her? Why did he think it was all in the past?

Why did she still want him after all of it?

So while they did not talk about the past, the only thing that kept Quinn from going crazy was thinking about *her* future, and the TV competition callback burning a hole in her brain.

The second round consisted of submitting plans and photos of a recently completed project, as well as an interview. The one bit of luck that she had was that it would be a phone interview, and she wouldn't have to sneak out of the house. Unfortunately, for the other half of the requirements, she would have to contact Crabbe and Co., and ask for copies of official plans with her name on them as project manager and lead designer.

Which she really, really didn't want to do.

Stuart was in the basement, trying to figure out the tankless water heater, which didn't work that morning *again*. While he pretended to be handy, there was nothing for Quinn to do but dive right in, so she lifted the kitchen phone off the receiver and dialed the number before she had a chance to chicken out.

"Well hello there," Sutton's voice purred on the other end of the phone. "Bored yet?"

"Funny you should ask, Sutton," Quinn said. "I have a favor to ask of you."

Sutton paused for a second. She heard a shuffling noise. "Of—of course, Quinn . . . Gimme a sec."

"Sutton, did you just drop the phone?"

"No! No, I was . . . ducking into the hall. Um, I didn't want Jeremy to overhear. Hi! How are you? Bored of, ah, being at home yet?"

"'Bored' isn't the right word," Quinn said, taking a deep breath. "But I am working on a little something at the moment, and . . . could you send me copies of the comprehensive plans for the Beacon Hill house?"

". . . the Beacon Hill house?" Sutton asked. "Why?"

"I . . . well, it's silly, but I'm applying for a . . . well, it would sort of be a job. And they need to see previous work." Her name was all over the official plans, she knew. Because she had designed and drawn them. Jeremy might have erased her from the magazine article, but she knew he was too lazy to bother erasing her from the paperwork. "It's all completely aboveboard, I promise."

"I would never think it wasn't!" Sutton said quickly. "So you're applying to a new firm? I didn't think you were . . . going to go back to work."

"Why not?"

"Just . . . ," Sutton hedged. "That it seemed like you were done with designing. To, you know . . . focus on your family?"

Quinn's brow came down. Really, she expected this kind of attitude from Stuart—not from her smart young female former protégé to whom she tried to impart the basic tenet of fighting for everything you want.

"Well, it wasn't really done with me. Besides, it's not a firm, it's a . . . TV show. I have no doubt I won't get it and this is all for nothing."

"A TV show?" Sutton said. "Wait, are you applying to *The Brand New Home*? The PBS show?"

"Yes . . ." Oh god, was Sutton applying, too? That would be terribly awkward.

"I heard about that! Actually, I know the homeowners—friend of a friendish. Good luck. From what I'm told, you'll need it."

"So, you'll copy those designs for me?"

"Absolutely, I got you covered."

"Great—so," Quinn said, awkward. "How are things going there?"

"Good—it's a lot of work. Jeremy gave me my own project. Lead designer. Small, but it's all mine."

Quinn tried to listen with interest, but in truth, she was waiting for that vague knife-in-gut feeling to pass. It was unseemly that she still felt this way. She should be happy for Sutton's successes. But the idea that she was flourishing in the place that had kicked Quinn to the curb . . . well, it wasn't going to stop hurting anytime soon.

"That's great. I'm sure you're going to do fine," Quinn said, cutting Sutton off mid-description of the two-bedroom beachside bungalow she was in charge of. "Listen, I've got to go—email me those plans as soon as you can?"

"Sure, and . . . and say hi to Stuart for me. Haven't seen him at spin class in a couple of weeks. Good luck with the show!"

It turned out that she didn't need luck. Because after her phone conversation with the producers, one of whom was Robbie (who made a disclosure at the beginning of the meeting saying that he knew Quinn via his daughter's preschool and was therefore abstaining from the interior designer decision), she knew, without a doubt, that she had advanced to the next round.

They laughed at the right moments. They asked the right questions about the Beacon Hill house. They asked about her creative process, her work history, her favorite part of designing (figuring out a solution to an impossible problem), and her least favorite part (when that solution didn't work, grr!).

As they talked, she became more and more enlivened. She went from "oh this is nothing more than a lark" to "I want this so badly my blood is screaming" in the space of fifteen minutes.

It wasn't an hour after she hung up the phone that she got a call from the production office.

"Hey, Quinn." It was Robbie, on speakerphone. "Got a sec?"

"I'm on my way to Little Wonders to pick up Hamilton," she said. "So you have ten glorious minutes of child-free convo time."

"Excellent! Well, it's my pleasure to tell you that you have made the final round."

"I did?" She smiled wide, and tried not to swerve the car with her chair dancing.

"The clients loved the sample you sent. Our producers—minus myself, who abstained—unanimously voted you in. All you have to do now is come on the show, and give your final presentation to the clients, and they choose the winner."

"On the show," she said. Actually on camera. Nerves began to swamp her again. Was she courting more notoriety? But, she rationalized . . . they knew about the video. Granted, it hadn't come up in the meeting—and it wasn't something that she'd figured out how to put on her resumé, but Robbie knew about it, he must have disclosed it to his coworkers. And if they knew about it, and didn't care . . . maybe, just maybe it didn't matter.

"Yep. We'll be filming the client meetings this Friday. So you need to present a design idea for a nursery."

Friday . . . three days. She could mock up some ideas for a nursery in three days. During the week that Stuart had taken off so they could focus on their marriage.

But honestly . . . yes, she could do it. And she wanted to do it. It wasn't as if they were spending the week doing nothing but drinking mai tais, either. Stuart still checked in with the office, worked out. And she was helping Daisy—which Stuart didn't mind in the least. In fact, he encouraged it, saying it was a good way to get her feet wet back with the school, without sticking her neck out too far.

Which was an odd thing to say, but he meant well.

So, if she worked on a nursery design while he thought she was going over a Family Fun Fest budget, then no one got hurt.

There was one close call, when he leaned over her computer and saw a file marked "nursery ideas."

"Nursery ideas?" he asked, with a smirk. "Is there something you have to tell me?"

Quinn gave a little laugh, but at that moment, she knew, yes . . . she did have something to tell him. She couldn't go to the interview on Friday—she couldn't appear on a television show—without him knowing.

On Friday morning, she came down the stairs, dressed and made up, portfolio in hand, ready for her proverbial close-up.

"Morning, Ms. Quinn!" Gina said from the sink, where she was washing out the remnants of a green smoothie from the blender. "You look very nice."

"Thank you. Hey, buddy!" She bent and kissed Ham's head as he slurped up said green smoothie. "Where's your dad?"

"Riding his bike," Ham said in between slurps.

In the basement, where he had set up his fancy new stationary bike. She made her way down there, her nerves staying eerily calm with each step.

She found Stuart working away on the bike, sweating up a storm. When he saw her, he stopped, pulled the earbuds out of his ears.

"Morning," he said, dubiously. "Where are you going?"

"I have an interview."

"An interview?" He stepped off the bike now. "Where?"

"For the television show *The Brand New Home*."

Stuart sighed deeply.

"I have to head into the city, so I need you to drop Hamilton off at school today."

Stuart wiped off his face with a towel, taking the moment to regather himself. "I thought you weren't going to pursue that."

"I know that's what you thought. And I know what all your arguments are against it," Quinn said. "But I decided that this is something I want to do. It's important to me."

"Damnit, Quinn," he said softly, shaking his head. "You're going to put yourself out there again. And you're going to be humiliated again."

"I don't believe I will be," she said, as calm as she could manage. "But if I am, that is my choice."

"I just want you to be happy, okay?" he said, heat coming into his voice. "I want us to be happy."

"Having a career makes me happy."

"And if I end up humiliated with you?" he bit out.

She froze. Those words, among all of his others, were a slap in her face.

The look on her face must have told him how *way* out of bounds that was, because he sighed deeply, held up his hands in surrender. "You . . . could you just do one less thing? Could you focus on our family and do one less thing?"

"Maybe you should focus on our family and do one *more* thing," she shot back, surprising herself. "Which is take our son to school today." She breathed deep, digging for that well of composure all the self-help books swore she had. "You want to repair our marriage. And you think taking a week off here and there is enough to get us back on track. But I need a partner every day. I need a partner, right now."

He was silent for a moment.

"I'm not asking for your permission. This is my decision. I'm going in to the interview. I'll be back before lunch. And when I get home, we can have a wonderful afternoon together, and maybe . . . maybe talk about what we *actually* need going forward."

She left him there, stunned. And as she walked away, she was stunned herself.

It would be easy to assume that Quinn Barrett had already done the hardest thing she would do that day. Confronting Stuart was not something she liked doing, or was used to, but it had been absolutely necessary, because now, she was free.

Freed from the uncertainty that had been plaguing her for weeks, free from trying to fit herself back into the role Stuart wanted her to play.

Therefore, the on-camera interview should be a breeze.

And it pretty much was . . . until she was actually on camera, sitting across from the homeowners she had to impress.

"You'll sit here, Quinn," the producer was saying, ushering her from hair and makeup (she had thought her hair and makeup were already done, but she was grateful for the touch-ups). Robbie had popped in earlier to wish her luck, but for obvious reasons he would be sitting out the interview. This producer was female, with a no-nonsense attitude, a headset on, and the all-important clipboard of authority in her arm. She placed Quinn on one end of a low couch. A stone coffee table was in front of her and beyond that, three cameras were set up, and a big lighting display with white bounce boards. They were going to go for a casual vibe with the setting, but the set was anything but casual.

"And the homeowners will sit next to you—if you could try and cheat a little to the camera, that would be helpful," the producer said. "Do you need water, or anything?"

"I'm fine."

"You look so relaxed," she said. "You're gonna do great. Oh, and here they are now. George, Sybil, this is Quinn Barrett."

They were a young professional couple in their early thirties. He was genial, with an easy smile and an expensive watch. She was impeccably dressed, swollen to about six or seven months, and honed in on Quinn with an intense gaze.

And suddenly Quinn knew exactly who she was dealing with. She was staring at herself, four or so years ago.

Quinn stood to shake their hands. George pumped hers enthusiastically, while Sybil's was more tepid.

They sat down, and Quinn was about to launch into her design plans when the producer spoke.

"All right, George, Sybil, why don't you start this time? Tell Quinn a little bit about yourselves."

"Okeydokey," George said, projecting a goofy charm. "We're the Hendersons. We are moving from our apartment in the city to our first new house and we are looking for—"

"We're looking for perfection," Sybil interrupted. "Somebody smart, coolheaded, and able to deliver perfection. That's all."

"That's all?" Quinn said, cracking a smile.

"Yes," Sybil replied, her chin going up.

"Okay," the producer interrupted. "Quinn, your turn. Why don't you tell us a little bit about you."

"Happy to. I am a designer who loves an updated traditional esthetic. I worked for a major firm for over a decade, taking on a variety of projects, learning and loving every minute of it. And I'm a mother to a three-year-old, so everything you're doing right now, I've been through."

"That's good to know," George replied. "You can give us pointers."

"Oh, I have no doubt there are a ton of people in your life giving you pointers. And a ton of people just randomly on the street throwing advice at you."

George threw his head back, laughing deep. But Sybil remained straight-faced.

"Is that all?" Sybil asked. "Is that the only thing we should know about you?"

Quinn met Sybil's gaze. Her stomach dropped. And she finally, finally understood.

"You recognize me, don't you?"

Sybil's chin went up higher, accompanied by an affirmative eyebrow.

"Recognize you?" said the producer, who Quinn had sort of forgotten was in the room. "From what?"

Quinn sighed. She felt the weight of the silence, of everyone's stares. She could laugh it off, try and deny it. But no. This was happening, and she had to face it.

"Last fall, I was the inadvertent star of a viral video. I'd had a very long and stressful day, and lost my temper with my son, and destroyed his Halloween costume. Someone was recording."

She saw the producer mouth the words "Halloween Mom" and then start typing furiously on her phone.

Quinn turned back to the couple. George, who was blinking in surprise, and Sybil whose pink cheeks were the only sign that she had any emotional reaction to, well, anything.

"When you walked in here, I . . . I actually saw a version of myself a few years ago."

"I . . . I do *not* think we're alike," Sybil said, almost laughing.

Quinn leaned in, forced Sybil to hold her gaze. "I hope we're not. I hope that you never lose it with your child, and certainly never have it broadcast across the internet. I don't mean to alarm you. But it wasn't that long ago that I was embarking on some of the same massive changes you're facing. First new house. First new baby. And you think that you can maintain control. That you *have* to. Just as long as everything is perfect."

Sybil held her stare, but gave the smallest most imperceptible nod.

"For how long?"

"I'm sorry?" Sybil replied.

"For how long do you want it to stay perfect?" Quinn asked. "An hour? A day? How long can you hold your breath?"

Sybil blinked, unable to come up with an answer.

"One thing I've learned over the past three years as a parent—and especially over the past six months as a person— is that perfect is static," Quinn said. "It's an Instagram photo. You can't live in it—and if you try, you'll suffocate because there's no air in a vacuum.

"You want a nursery that is going to help your life work— and match how beautiful that life is going to be. That's what I can do. I can give you something that will grow with your child, that will be easy to clean, that will help you endure the days as much as enjoy them.

"But if you want perfect, and someone else promised it to you—then you should choose them. I am a very good de- signer. I'm also a mother, I'm a friend, I'm a wife, and I am very publicly not perfect. If that is going to be a problem for you, I completely understand, and I will be on my way."

When neither of the Hendersons moved, Quinn slowly rose to her feet. "Thank you for the opportunity," she said, and was about to maneuver herself back past the cameras and lights to the exit when Sybil reached out and caught her arm.

"I'm curious . . . about what you mean by a room that will help make our lives work," Sybil said. "Can we see your de- signs?"

"Absolutely," she said, sitting back down and flipping open her portfolio. Her heart was singing. "These are obviously just first ideas, impressions. I will go over every detail with you, and explain anything you need. I want to know about what textures and materials you like and dislike, we are going to talk about blackout curtains and modular lighting, and the world's best invention that I have long wished I'd done in my own nursery, washable wallpaper."

She practically floated on the drive home. Not even horrendous traffic bothered her. They didn't announce anything, but she knew without a shadow of a doubt that she had won. The prize? Designing the nursery, of course. And she was champing at the bit to get to it.

While they hadn't given her the job, the producer pulled her aside after, and told her to keep the week of April the sixth available. She nearly laughed when she heard that—it was also the week of the Family Fun Fest. But if anyone was going to be happy for her, it was Daisy.

She could only hope that Stuart would be happy for her, too.

Her mood came down from the clouds as she thought about the second part of the conversation she and Stuart needed to have. But after laying it all out there with Sybil and George (they were totally on a first-name basis now), Quinn felt like, surely, she was on such a roll that she could lay it all out there with Stuart, too.

She had done it—she had accomplished all her March tasks. She had helped Daisy. She had auditioned for the show. And she had finally managed to really work on her marriage.

Man, she was killing today. It was like the day Dolly Parton wrote both "Jolene" and "I Will Always Love You." But, you know, more important.

"Stuart!" she called out when she walked through the door. "Hey, hon!"

"Ms. Quinn!" Gina said, as she popped her head out from the kitchen. "Good meeting?"

"Very." She smiled. "Stuart in the basement again? Is the water heater still acting up?"

"He's gone into the hospital, Ms. Quinn," Gina said, apologetically.

"What?" Quinn's face fell. "But he had today off."

"Apparently they called him with an emergency."

Quinn must have looked crestfallen, because Gina came toward her. "Come, Ms. Quinn—you've had a lovely week together. He had to go and save someone's life! And he left you a note, here."

He had to go and save someone's life. It was the excuse to end all excuses. Something that couldn't be argued with. Everyone accepted it—even Gina! Even Hamilton. Because he didn't even miss his dad when he was gone.

She was so, so tired of accepting it.

Quinn picked up the note, written on Stuart's personalized letterhead.

> *Had to go to the hospital. I'm sorry. We'll talk when I get home.*

She crumpled the note in her hand.

Well . . . Quinn guessed she finally had one of those answers she'd been waiting for.

Why did Stuart think he could just leave her like that?

Answer: because he did it all the time.

Little Wonders Preschool
April Newsletter

Hello, WONDER-ful Parents!

Spring has finally sprung ~~yes we breached 50 degrees break out those speedos~~ and with it, the advent of our biggest event of the year, the Family Fun Fest! We are expecting quite the crowd on Friday, April 9th, so make sure you come early before we run out of raffle tickets. ~~We have unlimited raffle tickets. Come early if you want to be saddled with extra work and the chance for a decent parking spot.~~ The children are very excited, and have been working on their hallway displays ~~Glitter. Glitter everywhere~~ to show off their creativity and Little Wonders to everyone!

There are lots of new and awesome things ~~that were added at the very last minute~~ in this year's festival. We are very excited to announce that not only will we have three bouncy houses, we will be having a petting zoo, courtesy of Needleton Farms. Goats, horses, and other farm animals will be ~~destroying~~ gracing our lawns. Don't worry, they won't get in the way of the train route! And a schedule of the cultural musical performances is attached!

And—this year, we have reached epic heights with the silent auction! The ever popular restaurant vouchers are back, as is the weekend at a beach house on the Cape! ~~The weekend~~

is in November and the house is termite-infested, but have at it, folks. However, there were also some very specialized items donated—so the Parent Board has decided to open up select items to be auctioned online. Check out the link below if you want a sneak peek of the Little Wonders special online auction! I have no idea what any of this crap is but I'm told it's cool.

Also, for those parents asking, TERRY yes, the chickens have moved back into their outside coop! Your little ones are already eagerly observing the new chicks we have brought into the flock, and picking out names! try getting them to eat chicken nuggets after this. Just try.

The Parent Association cannot pull off this event without every single volunteer, so your help is greatly appreciated. Don't show up late or else you don't get your hours counted. Don't test me. We cannot wait to see everyone on the afternoon of April 9th!

Together in Parenting!
Suzy Breakman-Kang
Parent Association Secretary

CHAPTER TWENTY

When Daisy McGulch Stone looked back over her life, she should have known that the inflection point, the moment her life would be divided into before and after, would happen at the Little Wonders Preschool Family Fun Fest (and Silent Auction).

Not that any one thing went wrong at the Family Fun Fest itself. Because, in fact, everything went wrong.

Not through any fault of Daisy's, of course! After her pep talk from the human starter pistol known as Quinn Barrett, she dived into the madness of making the Family Fun Fest the funnest damn fest in the history of Needleton—nay, in the history of Massachusetts!

She'd wrangled down prices on bouncy houses. She'd drawn up the schedule of musical events. She'd double- and triple-checked the audio equipment they had in the Parent Association closet for the musical acts, and borrowed Robbie's old amp as a backup. She'd reinstituted the goldfish toss, animal cruelty complaints be damned, because according to last year's financial breakdowns, it made *bank* for the school. She'd arranged for the food trucks. She'd gotten permits from the Needleton town hall, and she'd reported everything back to Shanna, who reclined on the couch when she and Daisy met. Every freakin' night.

"Thank you so much for taking all this on," Shanna always said. "I would never have been able to do this without you—I swear, if this baby's a girl, I'm naming her after you." Then, she would look over the day's spreadsheets and say something like, "Martino's Bakery is where we are getting the cakes for the Cake Walk? Not Bedford Farm and Cafe? Oh *my*."

But not even Shanna's nitpicking could stop the train of Daisy's production skills coming to the fore. She analyzed, she brainstormed, she went over the breakdowns with a fine-tooth comb, looking for ways to maximize their budget, their profit, and the kids' fun.

Damn, she was on fire. When she wasn't dying of sleep deprivation, that is.

And the most important thing Daisy had done was to follow Quinn's command and *delegate*. She sent emails to various parents who were low on their volunteer hours for the year, saying they could burn them off by soliciting donations for the silent auction and raffle baskets.

And they delivered. In spades.

Suzy Breakman-Kang was absolutely livid when she learned about this—Suzy, being the warden of all things volunteer hours. She had placed herself in that role when Shanna had taken over from Quinn, and she had relished the authority it gave her.

"You can't just give away volunteer hours!" she practically screeched. "That's my job!"

"For everything *not* related to the Family Fun Fest, yes," Daisy had said. Okay, maybe it wasn't Daisy. Maybe she was channeling Cosplay Daisy, the way she did on the phone. But it turned out that Cosplay Daisy very much enjoyed flaunting her authority. "But you all *officially* appointed me deputy to deal with the Family Fun Fest. And to complete that task, I'll dole out volunteer hours as I see fit."

Suzy was left with her mouth hanging open, no doubt composing the world's meanest newsletter in her head.

But as the items that the volunteers managed to procure came in—and began to overwhelm—Daisy might have had her most genius moment yet.

"Quinn, why did you never do an online auction?" she said over coffee, as she stared at the spreadsheet in front of her. They were at the café on Main Street, taking up Quinn's favorite table by the window, getting dirty looks shot their way by computer-lugging caffeine addicts coveting their good table with outlet access. Ostensibly they were here to do anything but work, but Quinn had so artfully dodged any questions about her reunification with Stuart that they had no choice but to work.

On top of the pile of papers was a list of all the items that had been collected for the silent auction. It included but was not limited to Red Sox tickets, passes to goat yoga, breakfast with the Needleton firefighters, a signed headshot of an Affleck brother, and a new-in-box pair of size seven Christian Louboutin ankle boots.

"We looked into it," Quinn replied. "But ultimately decided that we didn't have the kind of items that would do any better online than in person, so the effort wasn't worth it."

"Well, we have some items this year that would be worth it," Daisy said. The Louboutins were made for eBay (curse her size nine feet, else they'd be hers!). As was the Affleck headshot, and . . . maybe the goat yoga? But that wasn't enough to justify making a separate online auction. And she knew, without a doubt, that she could sell stuff online. She had plenty of retail experience, and hadn't she made ends meet in between production jobs with some judicious selling of her geek stockpile? She just needed more product . . .

She contemplated it as they left their coveted table (it was quickly scooped up by laptop junkies).

And started to make their way up the street. But then, she stopped in her tracks, right in front of the empty storefront that used to be the Knick Knack Nook.

"What?" Quinn asked, but Daisy didn't hear her. Her mind was caught on an idea. It was only when Quinn waved her hands in front of Daisy's face that she snapped out of it.

"Are you okay?" Quinn said with concern.

"I'm better than okay," Daisy said, grabbing her friend's hand, a maniacal grin spreading across her face. "I just got an idea that is absolutely terrifying!"

"Terrifying?" Quinn asked. "For whom?"

"For me . . . and if I can convince him, probably for Rob."

Indeed, it wasn't terrifying for Rob. Or if it was, he certainly didn't say so.

"I know what I want to do." It was one week after her initial idea had formed. One week, where she had done some research, priced her options, and formulated a rough-draft business plan. It had been the most nerve-wracking, exhilarating secret she'd ever kept from Rob, and considering all the strange looks he'd given her this past week, he probably thought she was cheating on him.

Now, Rob looked up at her, dubiously, from the circular saw he was setting up. They were in the basement, which was swiftly being transformed. Currently he was working on some cabinets for the corner kitchenette, but he stopped the second Daisy came down the stairs.

"Carrie go down for her nap?" he asked.

"Yes," she said, and then repeated, "I know what I want to do."

"I was hoping to start the new *Great British Bake Off* season, but if you've got something else in mind . . ."

She laid down the copy of *Chainmail* in front of him. The one from the long box she'd gotten in trade for Rob's well-intentioned Christmas present. She held her breath, waiting for his reaction.

"Is this a new adventure module?" Rob asked. "You want to play D&D? I mean, I'm all for a campaign, but there's only two of us and Carrie will be awake soon—"

"That is a copy of *Chainmail*—it's Gary Gygax's first published rules for medieval fantasy wargaming, basically his proto D&D. I found it in a long box at that comic shop in Cambridge. It's in great condition, and see that squiggle there? . . . it's signed by Gygax."

"Wow," Rob said, with proper reverence. "I take it that's quite the find."

"I have friends in Los Angeles, people from games I've run, who would pay over a thousand dollars for this."

Rob finally looked up from the booklet to her face.

"A thousand dollars?" he said. "Seriously? What else was in that box?"

"Stuff That Guy at the comic store wouldn't have recognized as worthwhile in a million years," she said. "But I did. And it got me thinking—if That Guy can have a successful store, why can't I?"

Rob blinked at her. Waiting.

"I figured out what I want to do—here, in Needleton. I want to open up my own comic and game store."

Rob looked down at the booklet. Ran his finger across the (plastic-covered) title and signature.

"This is a great find, and I'd put you up against any professional nerd any day of the week, but . . . do you really think you can run a store?"

"Yes," she answered definitively. "I have retail experience, I know how to order and inventory stock. And having run around like crazy trying to put this Family Fun Fest on I know what it takes to get something on its feet. Not to mention more than a passing acquaintance with the permit office at town hall. But instead of selling sweater sets or ordering bouncy houses, I'd actually be doing something I care about.

"There's nothing like this store in Needleton—comic lovers stuck in the suburbs have to go into the city to get their in-person comic fix; I can siphon them off. I know the market and what customers are looking for. I have connections from my D&D groups in LA; one bookstore owner even offered me a monthly column on his website, which is good promo and offers credibility. I would have a physical store for weekly releases and to hold stock—there's a storefront on Main Street that's an amazing location, right next to the coffee shop, and we will turn it into something beautiful and classy, not junky and dusty like most comic shops—but a good portion of my business would be online. Selling things like that." She pointed to the book.

She had a bunch of other points in her business plan. She could have kept going—a parent/kid comic book club was something she was really excited about—but the look on Rob's face told her to hold off.

Because Rob looked . . . intrigued.

Daisy's heart swelled. Maybe . . . maybe this was possible.

"I love this idea, Daze," he said, rubbing his chin. "Trust me, I would have died for a comic shop in Needleton when I was a kid."

"But . . ."

"But . . . where are we going to get the money?" he rationalized. "We are so tight as it is."

"Well . . . we kind of do have the money," Daisy replied. "The down payment fund."

"You want to use the money we are saving up to buy this house?" His eyebrows disappeared under his baseball cap. Then he snorted a laugh. "Where would we live?"

"I don't want to move out—just delay the purchase. See if Grandpa Bob would hold off on his gift for a year, if your uncle could wait for the purchase to go through. And then if the store isn't viable, we'd know it."

"Daze . . ." Rob's face lost all trace of humor. "You're talking about risking our future. For—"

"For our future," she finished for him. "A different version of it. The more I've thought about this, the more I'm convinced it's what I need to do."

"I . . . I think we're going to need more than your assurance that you can do this to sell Grandpa Bob and my uncle on the idea," Rob replied. "I don't know how to convince them. My uncle especially. They don't really understand this kind of stuff. When I made the move to LA my uncle thought I was insane for pursuing a dream."

"Your uncle understands money, right?" Daisy challenged. "How about this—if I sell *Chainmail* for over a grand—over fifteen hundred—in the Family Fun Fest silent auction, would that be proof enough?"

"It would certainly go a ways to show your knowledge and the fact that there's money in comics and games," Rob replied. Then, after a moment, "Okay."

"Okay?"

"Okay." He leaned over and kissed her. "Better get to selling that book."

The way she kissed him back . . . well, suffice it to say, it was a good thing Carrie took a long nap that day.

But Daisy found she didn't have time for many such interludes. Because March quickly gave way to April and Daisy spent the time running running running to get everything done and perfect for the Family Fun Fest.

So by the night before the big day, Daisy was just about out of juice. She had done everything she could. Workers would begin arriving in the morning, bouncy houses, miniature trains, and goldfish would be arriving shortly thereafter. The big yard had been cleaned and cleared yesterday, ready for its transformation. Everything was going to be perfect. Daisy had nothing left to do but sleep.

She woke up the next morning well rested, utterly focused, ready to go. She opened up the kitchen blinds as she started the coffeemaker, ready to greet the day she had been killing herself for.

And it was pouring.

Daisy stood there, utterly gobsmacked, long enough for her coffee to burn, one single thought running through her mind.

Oh FUCK.

How . . . how was it raining? There wasn't any rain in the forecast! It had been nothing but clear, bright blue sky on every single weather update she'd been tracking. There wasn't even a hint of wind! This was supposed to be the perfect early April weekend!

It would be one thing if it was a drizzle that would clear up by midmorning—basically a little spritz just to clear the dirt away. But no, this was a full-on, straight-down pour, and the darkness of the sky indicated that it wasn't going anywhere anytime soon.

Snapping out of it, she quickly moved to the living room, and flipped on the TV. She sat through three minutes of early morning news (Red Sox fans were lining up for opening day already, and traffic was abysmal) before they got to the weather.

". . . cold pressure system moved in swiftly overnight, and parked itself over the southern Boston region. Keep those rain boots handy, because it's going to be hanging around for a while—"

Daisy turned the TV off. No need to belabor the point—it was raining, it wasn't stopping, and the Family Fun Fest was going to be soaked.

Daisy checked her clock: just 6:00 AM. The first deliveries were slated to begin at the school in an hour. She had to start reacting. She had to start canceling everything.

First thing first, though, she had to tell Shanna.

Shanna picked up the phone with a muffled and sleepy, "Hello?"

"Shanna, it's Daisy. Look outside."

". . . Daisy?" Shanna replied. "What's wrong?"

"What's wrong is that it's raining! Like, really really raining!"

"It's raining?" Shanna sounded awake now. Even alarmed. Daisy could hear her leveraging herself out of bed and the footfalls across the floor, presumably to a window.

"Oh, my god . . . ," Shanna said, after a few moments. "Oh my god—what are we going to do?"

"We have to cancel," Daisy replied. "We have insurance policies for most of the rentals—we can reschedule to the backup date. There will be a small penalty for the move but at least—"

"Okay . . . what's the backup date?" Shanna asked.

Daisy nearly dropped the phone.

"Are you telling me you never set a backup date?" Before dropping *everything* in my lap, she wanted to scream.

"Are you telling me you didn't?" Shanna's voice bit out.

"No, Shanna, I didn't. If there's no backup date, then we have to cancel the whole festival outright."

"No! Daisy, we can't cancel!" Shanna cut in. "We are *not* canceling the Family Fun Fest."

"But . . . everything is outside! There's a petting zoo!"

"Figure out how to make it inside," Shanna snapped. "Really, didn't you plan for this contingency?"

"*Me?*" she practically screeched. *This isn't my job!* she wanted to scream. *You made me do this!* But she couldn't. Partially because, at this point, she had taken over so completely, it was her responsibility. And partially because . . . she hadn't planned for this. She'd assumed there was a backup scheduled. And, as she tracked the weather, it just continually listed sun, sun sun sun sun . . . so she didn't concern herself with less and less likely scenarios.

Because up until yesterday, it wasn't going to rain—so why bother planning for it?

"I am not giving up. People are expecting a Family Fun Fest today, they are getting a Family Fun Fest. Shanna Stone does not fail. Understood?"

"Shanna, it's going to be awful . . . impossible . . ."

"You can't cancel anything, because as Parent Association president, I'm the one who signed all the leases you brought me, I would have to be the one to cancel them. So start figuring out how to make this an inside festival. Now, if you'll excuse me, according to my doctor I need another hour of sleep."

Daisy stared at the phone for several seconds after Shanna hung up.

Daisy could have chucked it all. She could have walked away, washed her hands of it, called Shanna crazy and let the Little Wonders gossip mill eviscerate her. In fact, that sounded like the best possible option at the moment. But . . .

But . . . Daisy wasn't a quitter, either. The kids, the teachers, the parents—they were all looking forward to this day so, so much. Heck, the auction website had already started. Bids were being placed. In some ways the Family Fun Fest had already begun.

And . . . Daisy had an idea forming. Something that she could do to make the Family Fun Fest unforgettable. And if not unforgettable, at least fun, and dry.

Swiftly, she dialed her phone again.

"Daisy?" Quinn said, picking up on the second ring. She too sounded sleepy, but the call had alarmed her. "Are you okay?"

"I'm fine. I'm sorry to wake you," Daisy said.

"I finished *The Brand New Home* nursery last night. I am exhausted," Quinn said on a yawn. "But nothing some coffee can't cure. What's up?"

"What's up is that I have eight hours to save the Family Fun Fest."

Eight hours later, the rain was still coming down, but the Little Wonders Family Fun Fest (and Silent Auction) was absolutely rocking. And Daisy was riding a high of adrenaline and caffeine that should be regulated by the FDA. But she had done it. Somehow, she had taken an outdoor festival and managed to shove it inside, without losing many of the events, or any of the fun.

"This is amazing," Robbie said, as he walked down the Little Wonders hall, now done over to look like a board game. Each primary-colored tile was part of the Candy Land-esque path, leading the kids from one event to another in each of the different rooms.

"Thank you," Daisy said, taking his hand. "It was . . . a challenge."

"You rose to it."

Things had to be pared down, of course. The three bouncy houses became one, the train and the soccer league were both gone, not to mention several of the carnival-esque games that simply did not fit inside buildings, and the food trucks were converted to stalls, walking back and forth to the trucks for freshly made tacos, sandwiches, and chipped ice.

In between fielding phone calls and texts from parents asking if the festival was still on, posting updates to the Facebook group and the Slack saying, "Yes, we are still on" but not adding "because Shanna is a slave-driving lunatic," Daisy and Quinn managed to rearrange the entire event.

Half of the festivities found a new home inside the large, historic barn on school grounds. Interestingly, since it was a historical landmark, it was not nearly as decrepit on the inside as she had been led to believe by the outside. It was structurally reinforced and very sound. And since the chickens had moved to their outdoor coop at the beginning of the month, it was unoccupied.

The petting zoo and the remaining bouncy house were very happily ensconced in there, as well as some of the games that needed the space: the strongman striker game, the milk bottle toss, the corn hole game. Anything that involved hitting, or throwing more than a Ping-Pong ball, was not going to make it inside Little Wonders itself.

The inside of Little Wonders had been transformed by Quinn's hand—which was no mean feat, considering they did it in less than a day, and *while* school was in session.

Once Quinn and Daisy had hung up that morning, Quinn chugged down some coffee and dug out her crafting supplies. Untouched since the creation of the ill-fated Halloween spaceship, she and Hamilton loaded every can of paint, brush, cardboard frame, and tube of glitter she had into the car and drove over to the school. They made a pit stop at the craft store on the way, the very first customers inside, and cleaned out the fabric section.

Meanwhile Daisy loaded up her car with every single board game, action figurine, poster, and costume that she had (that was age appropriate, that is). They convened at the school. While Quinn began to transform the auditorium, Daisy had stood outside the school, under her umbrella, basically accosting parents dropping off their kids, begging them for help. She was practically giving away two-for-one deals on volunteer hours—no doubt once the final tally came in, Suzy Breakman-Kang's head was going to spin around *Exorcist* style.

She didn't have much luck—most people had to go to work, after all—until Charlie and Calvin's moms came, and with them ladders, sewing kits, and a working knowledge of how to put things together. They also had the help of the teachers, who ducked out of class when they could to give them a hand. Because nobody but nobody knows how to wield construction paper and a wall stapler like a preschool teacher.

And once Daisy had convinced Ms. Anna to let the class-rooms "visit" each other, Quinn got access to the Tadpole Room, the Iguana Room, and the Rainbow Room, and turned them into their themes.

The Rainbow Room became a princess's tower. Pink and white fabric hung from the ceiling like a circus tent, giving the entire space a "PG-rated harem" vibe. It was where the dress-up house and face painting were set up, as well as a backdrop for a "photo booth." Daisy, with all of her cosplay experience, was the lead makeup artist, and all the little kids were happy to trade their tickets to be transformed into a unicorn or a tiger, or in the case of one enterprising young man, a Sharknado.

The Iguana Room became a jungle. Green streamers and cloth (left over from St. Patrick's Day) hung from the ceiling tiles, making a path for kids to pass through. The smoke ma-chine (left over from the dance party portion of the Happy Halloween Parade and Dance Party) made a reappearance, and Robbie was sent out on a mission for dry ice. In the Jungle Room, they managed to relocate the few carnival games they could accommodate inside—the Goldfish Toss, renamed the Piranha Toss, and the Cake Walk, now called a "Trek Through the Amazon." Everyone had an amazing time exploring the jungle.

But the third room was Daisy's favorite. She'd reimagined the Tadpole Room into the Dungeon Room. Quinn had found at the craft store a fabric patterned with large stones, so when hung all around the room, it looked like they were in the belly of a massive underground dungeon. And Daisy had one of her cosplay outfits that looked the most like a suit of armor posted at the door on a mannequin she'd bor-rowed from the Cranberry Boutique—what Elaine didn't know wouldn't hurt her.

This was the Escape Room.

Tickets were paid for at the entrance. To get out, you had to play a game—board games like Candy Land, Chutes and Ladders, Sneaky Snacky Squirrel, Uno Attack, Don't Wake Daddy, Mousetrap, kid-size Jenga. Or a game of Simon Says, Red Rover (not easy to play inside but when needs must), or the game where you fished rubber duckies out of a kiddie pool, whatever that was called.

When you won, you were given a small prize and allowed out—only to have most of the kids come running back in, eager to play again.

However, while those rooms were filled with fun, all paths led to the auditorium/multipurpose room, where the stage had been given over to the musical acts. Currently, a young woman with a rainbow wig named Zuzu who played nursery songs at everyone's third birthday party in the Needleton area was currently on the stage, and the kids were enthralled, clapping along with a silly version of "Wheels on the Bus."

While the kids grooved out to the classics, their parents could peruse the silent auction items and the raffle baskets, where they had been placed in long rows for easy bidding and ticket entering. And at the far end of the room, was the pièce de résistance . . . the Easter Bunny.

Aka, Robbie, in a rental Bunny Suit.

Daisy had snuck over to him as he finished handing out jelly beans to Elia. He broke free from the little girl's hug and made his way over to Daisy.

"Where's Carrie?" he asked.

"In the Dungeon Room, of course," Daisy replied. No doubt making sure everyone played by the rules of each game. "Quinn is keeping an eye on her."

Quinn was running the Dungeon Room. While it might

have been more Daisy's speed, she was needed for her face-painting skills in the Princess Room, and Quinn was also impressively capable of running multiple games at once.

Daisy should take her to Vegas.

"How's the face painting going?" They'd ducked behind the stage curtain, where Rob could take off his bunny head, and take a drink of water, without scaring the kids.

"Did you see the lizard I did on Hamilton? He looked like he was in the remake of *V.* I think that's my pièce de résistance."

"Seriously," Rob replied. "You should consider making geek game parties part of your business plan. This turned out amazing."

"Are . . . are you serious?" she asked. "You're going to back my plan?"

"After this, how could I not?" Rob replied. "Besides, I checked the online part of the auction about a half hour ago. *Chainmail* is already up over three grand."

"It is?" Daisy squealed in excitement. "Yes!!"

"One day you'll have to explain to me why we donated that to a preschool auction instead of selling it for ourselves. That could have gone a long way toward outfitting your store."

"Don't worry," Daisy replied. "You don't know what else was in that box."

"Really?" His eyebrows went sky high. "Like what?"

Daisy was about to tell him about the Dave Arneson–signed original *Blackmoor* campaign–setting booklet, but they were interrupted when Jamie ducked his head behind the curtain.

"Hey, Rob—you'd better get back out there. A line of sugared-up toddlers is forming. Mutiny is on the horizon."

"On it." And with one last very sweaty kiss, Rob ducked back into the auditorium, to his adoring fans.

Daisy remained behind the curtain for an extra couple of seconds. Just to take a moment, to take a breath, and enjoy the fruits of her crazy, crazy day.

"Thank you," came Jamie's voice from beside her. She jumped slightly—she'd forgotten he was there. "I know that Shanna can be a bit crazy these days, but you really, really came through for her."

Daisy smiled up at Jamie. Daisy actually hadn't seen much of Shanna since the start of the festival. She had obviously been texting her all day long, blowing up her phone with "Just checking in!" and "I'm sure everything will fit inside, just talk to Ms. Anna." Daisy texted back with unspecific but firm re-assurances, but eventually was so busy she could barely do more than text back a thumbs-up emoji. Then, about fifteen minutes before the doors opened, Shanna arrived, hoping to put the final touches on everything. When she saw just what had been pared down, and what state the rooms were in with only fifteen minutes to go, she nearly broke down in tears, such was her panic.

Luckily Jamie was there, and he took her for a walk in the afternoon drizzle, telling her everything was going to be great. They must have snuck back in while Daisy was knee deep in toddler faces in want of paint.

"You've really only known her since she's been pregnant," Jamie was saying. "But I promise, she's usually a normal person. Funny and smart and holds our lives together. You really helped her out, stepping up like this."

Daisy put her hand on his arm. "She's just taking care of her health, and the baby's health. It's completely understandable."

He looked at her strangely for a moment. Then, as if a lightbulb went off over his head, "Oh—you mean the blood pressure thing? Yeah, it really freaked her out when it was slightly elevated. But then they took it again and she was normal."

"Normal?" Daisy asked, a strange sour feeling in her stomach.

"Yeah—and normal every time since. But it's so great of you to be aware of it, and to give her a break from her Parent Association duties."

"Hmm, yeah. That was . . . awesome of me," Daisy said. She must have come off as self-deprecating because Jamie just laughed.

"Well, you were there. You knew she bit off more than she could chew with the Parent Association. Like I've told her, it's not a one-man job. So, you stepping up to help—that was really clinch. Good cousin vibes."

Jamie, like the darling oblivious man that he was, extended his fist for a bump. Daisy hesitated before dully bumping him back.

Daisy made her excuses—the Princess Room and face paint awaited—and Jamie ducked away, on the hunt for his wife.

But, Daisy did not head back to the Princess Room. No, she made a furious beeline straight for Quinn and the Dungeon Room.

She could not beLIEVE that Shanna had used her health to mock up an excuse to shove off the entire festival onto Daisy's already stressed shoulders. She was trembling with rage.

However, she didn't need to go as far as the Dungeon Room, because just then, Quinn appeared in the auditorium. She had Hamilton and Carrie at her side, Gina trailing behind, having been conscripted to watch the kids while the moms worked the festival.

"Hey," Quinn said. "What's going on?"

"Do I look that pissed off?" Daisy said. Quinn raised her eyebrows, alarmed.

"Come to think of it, yes you do—but everyone was just told to come in here for an announcement."

Daisy blinked and looked around. The room was being crowded by people streaming in from the other rooms and outside.

"Daisy, what's going on?"

"I don't know, I just know I'm going to K-I-L-L"—spelled out because Carrie and Hamilton were looking at her with decided interest—"Shanna when I see her."

Quinn glanced over Daisy's shoulder. "Well, if you want to begin your homicidal spree, I'd start up there."

Daisy turned around, looking up to where Quinn indicated. Shanna was on the little stage, Suzy Breakman-Kang at her side. Shanna looked glowing, resplendent, neat as a pin—not covered in face paint and her hair a mass of frizz. She confidently took the microphone once Zuzu with the rainbow wig had finished "The Itsy Bitsy Spider."

"Everyone? Everyone!" Shanna said into the microphone. The crowd settled. "Hi—for those of you who don't know me—all two of you"—pause for light chuckles—"I'm Shanna Stone, the Little Wonders Parent Association president."

She paused for applause. When only a smattering was forthcoming, she barged ahead.

"I just wanted to take a moment and say thank you. Because of you, not only did we have a great festival, but according to the tallies," here Suzy Breakman-Kang held up a clipboard, "we have earned more for the school than any previous year!"

That earned hearty applause from the audience. Daisy felt

a hot glower come up over her face. Of course they earned more money—her *Chainmail* was netting them thousands! The online auction was inspired! They could do bake sales and sell cookie dough from here to the next Family Fun Fest and they wouldn't touch that amount.

And there was Shanna, up on the stage, taking in the applause that belonged to Daisy.

"That means more fun events for our kids, more supplies for our teachers, and a better Little Wonders!" Shanna beamed. "Now, this festival was not easy to pull off, especially considering our little rain difficulty. But we did manage it, didn't we?"

Oh, sure, Daisy thought. *We* absolutely did.

"So I want to especially thank Daisy Stone, my cousin and my bestie, for creating the impossible, and giving us this amazing indoor festival!"

As the applause turned to her, Daisy felt her face heating up—but this time with pride. From the stage, Shanna motioned her to come up.

Daisy made her way up to the stage, completely in shock, people applauding around her. So this is what it would have been like if she'd ever won an Oscar, she thought. She could hear the announcer now: "Daisy Stone is the first person to win this award for playing a non-cosplay version of herself in a preschool. This is her first nomination."

"And . . . a little bird told me that Daisy is soon going to be opening up her own business," Shanna said into the mic as Daisy climbed up the short steps to the stage. "So if you like comic books and pop culture as much as she does, keep your eyes peeled for her new shop!"

Daisy met Shanna's eyes, shocked. She hadn't shared her business plan with anyone but Rob—how did Shanna know?

But Shanna was beaming and handed Daisy the mic. She whispered, "Just say thank you!" in Daisy's ear.

And for some reason, that made Daisy's brain start to burn. Daisy had killed herself for Shanna, not just today, but for the past month, and Shanna dared to dictate that she should simply say "thank you"?

Daisy had a lot more to say than that.

"Hi, everyone," Daisy said into the mic. "I appreciate everything and everyone in this room for coming together as a community to pull off this festival, and have a great time doing it. Everything we do is for our kids and seeing them have a blast today makes it all worth it, amirite?"

Applause at that, and the kids whooped along with their parents.

"All of the volunteers worked their butts off, but I know I wouldn't be up here today without the faith and support of one person in particular." Daisy turned and looked at Shanna, who touched a hand to her heart.

Daisy smiled directly at Shanna as she said, "Quinn Barrett—thank you so much for everything! Your dedication, creativity, and hard work made today possible—yours, and yours *alone*."

Quinn looked like she was trying to blink SOS in Morse code at Daisy, but Daisy didn't care. She allowed the applause to transfer to Quinn, and satisfactorily watched as Shanna's jaw dropped.

But only for a second, because Shanna was well aware of the stage she stood on. She quickly shook off her shock and grabbed the mic back from Daisy. With an unceremonious, "Suzy is going to pull the raffle basket winners. Have a great festival everyone!" Shanna shoved the mic in Suzy's hands.

As the bowls with the raffle tickets and the baskets were

brought up to the stage, Shanna grabbed Daisy by the arm and pulled her behind the curtain, just off to the side of the stage.

"How could you do that to me?" Shanna whirled on Daisy the second they were out of sight.

"How could I do that to you?" Daisy said, chuffed. "How could you do that to me?"

"I just wanted to say thank you—and to plug your business idea, Robbie is so excited about it! And you go and . . . and . . ."

"And thank Quinn for her help?" Daisy asked. "Why is that a bad thing?"

"Because . . . you know why!" Shanna blurted out.

"No, I don't!" Daisy shot back.

"Hey, um, guys?" It was Quinn as she ducked her head back behind the curtain. "I think we should move this conversation? People can hear you."

Daisy glanced at Quinn. Over her shoulder, she could see the room beyond—so quiet you could hear a pin drop—not even the kids were making noise. And Suzy certainly wasn't handing out raffle baskets. No, every ear was tuned to what was happening stage left.

"God, Quinn, could you just for once get out of my life?" Shanna bit out.

"Oh, I'm happy to go . . ."

"No," Daisy said. "No! You don't get to talk to her that way. She came through for me when you decided to drop everything in my lap for the Family Fun Fest."

"I didn't *drop* everything. I needed help," Shanna replied, her hand going to her swollen belly.

"No you didn't," Daisy replied. "Jamie told me. Your blood

pressure is normal, but you used your pregnancy as an excuse to offload your responsibilities onto me. I had no idea what I was doing. I needed help, and it was Quinn who stepped up."

"*I needed help, too!*" Shanna exploded. "I need help all the time! I need someone to give me a *house*, Daisy. And I could have used someone to help me acclimate to Needleton when I first moved here. I need someone with a child who can be Jordan's friend—you think I don't know that she's a bully? You think I don't *know* she's the one who spread 'Poopybutt' like a virus? I have absolutely no idea how to stop it! I don't know how I'm going to manage a second kid, because no doubt I'm going to screw this one up, too. I need friends. You were supposed to be my friend. But then you went and decided that Quinn was better than me. Just like Jamie did."

Daisy mouth fell open like a fish. Shanna's nose had gone all red, and tears were threatening her eyes. Quinn was stock-still. Daisy made a few noises before she managed to form a coherent thought.

"Jamie . . . Jamie doesn't think Quinn is better than you. He was just telling me about how you keep his life together, how you're his best friend."

"He thinks Quinn is better." She turned her heated gaze to Quinn. "He spent every waking hour raving about you last year. He got so mad when I took on the president position, saying that if Quinn couldn't do it, no one could. He was crazy about you."

"I . . . I don't have an answer for that," Quinn said, bewildered. "Other than to say that nothing went on between Jamie and me—he was my copresident."

Pieces began to fall into place for Daisy. Jealousy. Shanna's driving motive for hating Quinn was jealousy. But not over her perceived perfection, doing all and being all as a wife, mother, and career woman—it was over something much more fundamental.

"No," Shanna said. "He was—*is*—my husband. But you never thought of him as that—as made very clear by your own husband!"

"*What?*" screeched Quinn. "What does Stuart have to do with this?"

"Last year, when you invited us over for dinner—"

"You turned us down."

"Because your husband had let it drop what kind of dinner it would be. What kind of marriage that you had. He said he had no problem with your interest in Jamie, because he had his eye on me."

"That . . . that's not true," Quinn sputtered. "Stuart would never say anything like that. You—you must have misunderstood!"

Gasps and rumbles were making their way from the room beyond the curtain. Daisy was suddenly very, very aware of how public the conversation had become.

"Guys, let's take a breather; Shanna, come with me—"

But Shanna wasn't listening. She had fury and triumph written all over her face, no doubt the only thing in her vision the sputtering Quinn.

"What, you didn't know you were in an open marriage?" Shanna sneered at Quinn. "Oh my, how sad. *Oh. My.*"

Quinn's sputtering stopped. She grew uncomfortably silent. Uncommonly still.

It took a moment for what was happening to sink in.

Oh. My.

Daisy could practically see Quinn's mind working. It was turning over and over what Shanna had just said. But the moment Quinn looked up, Daisy knew she hadn't focused on the content. No, she'd focused on . . .

Oh. My.

"It was you," Quinn said softly.

"What?" Shanna replied.

"It was you—'Oh. My.' You said that, on the Halloween video, exactly like you just did. You . . . you're the one who made the video."

Shanna stared at her for a moment, and then . . . a great puff of laughter left her chest. Followed by snorts and giggles of growing hysteria.

"No . . . Quinn, no . . . ," Daisy tried, stepping her body in between Shanna and Quinn.

"You . . . you think this is *funny*?" Quinn was saying. "You ruined my life! Why? Because you thought my husband made a pass at you?"

"No— No, Quinn, she didn't!"

But Quinn just advanced on Shanna, Daisy stopping her from getting more than a half step.

"You're lucky you're pregnant, or else I'd . . . I'd . . ."

"It wasn't me," Shanna said, getting her laughter under control.

"Seriously? You think I'd believe that?"

"It wasn't me," Shanna said again, this time more sober. And as she slid her eyes over to Daisy, Quinn's eyes followed.

"I didn't make that video, Quinn," Shanna said, biting out the words. "I didn't post it online. I didn't ruin your life."

But Quinn didn't even look at Shanna. She had her eyes firmly on Daisy's.

Daisy could hardly believe how easily the words came out of her mouth.

"Shanna didn't do it. I did."

CHAPTER TWENTY-ONE

Quinn wasn't entirely sure how she got home. She only knew that she managed to find Gina and a lizard-faced Hamilton, got them into the car, and started driving. Hamilton may or may not have pitched a fit about leaving the festival. The truth was, Quinn was so focused on getting home, she couldn't think about anything other than getting there.

Now they were back in their house, and Hamilton was upstairs washing off the lizard in a Gina-supervised bath.

Quinn couldn't help but think of her life only twenty-four—nay, *twelve* hours ago. She had finished a hard week's work on the install of the nursery just the night before. She was flush with success. She was awakened by her friend calling, who needed her help. She had been driven by the desire to be of use and the pride that she was the right person for the job.

And Daisy . . . Daisy had been the best friend she'd been craving her entire adult life.

She was happy and fulfilled.

Wasn't she?

As Quinn wandered through her still, quiet house, that question hung in the silent air.

There was no denying the elephant in the room—or rather, the missing elephant.

Because Stuart wasn't there.

He'd texted earlier in the day, saying he'd gotten pulled into assisting on another surgery, and he wouldn't make the festival. To be honest, Quinn had been working so hard, she didn't care very much. Having Stuart there meant she would have had to focus on him—on pleasing him. And it was a bit of a relief to not have to worry about that.

Because previous to this, it was all she had been focused on.

After the *The Brand New House* interview, when Stuart finally came home from his impromptu visit to the hospital, Quinn had been anticipating their conversation. The one she had been begging for, spoiling for, to finally put them on the same page about their marriage. She had waited patiently for him to talk.

And he did.

"I'm sorry," he'd said. Stuart had gotten home late from the hospital and climbed on the bike in the basement right after dinner. When she'd emerged from Hamilton's room after an extra half hour of reading time before he was willing to fall asleep, Stuart was halfway through a biathlon. So she'd waited some more, until after he got off the bike, until after he'd taken a shower, until after they were both about to crawl into bed.

"I'm sorry," he repeated, when her face didn't register a change. "You're right, I need to start doing more around here. I need to be more present, more supportive. On a daily basis, not just when I can make it fit in my schedule." He looked at her with love, with that romance novel gaze.

"It's . . . it's good to hear you say that," she said, solemnly. "But I don't understand why you thought it was okay to leave in the first place."

He blinked, the romance novel face falling away. No doubt he thought the argument was over. But it wasn't that easy this time. "Because I didn't feel like I had your support."

"You . . . didn't have my support?" Quinn couldn't believe what she was hearing.

"My job—it's stressful, and I just want things to be happy and calm when I get home—it's my escape."

"It doesn't work like that," Quinn had said. That's what she had been doing before—striving for perfection, making Stuart's and her life Instagrammable and amazing. And it had nearly broken her.

"I know, because you always seemed like you were focused on other things," he'd said.

"Now, hold on—"

"Okay, please don't get upset," Stuart said, holding up his hands, trying to make peace. "I'm just answering your question. Now I'm going to be more involved. I promise. But . . . can we continue this discussion tomorrow? Or later?" He sighed deeply. "The surgery today, it didn't go well."

"I'm so sorry," she'd said automatically. Surprisingly she hadn't picked up on it—usually she could tell immediately when a surgery had been unsuccessful. But she had been so intent on having this conversation, no doubt she had missed his mood.

"The patient is still in critical care. I have to go back tomorrow to check on him, see if we'll be able to go back in."

"Tomorrow?" Which was Saturday.

"Yes—and I'm on call all next week. So please, let's get some sleep. We both need it."

The argument, her questions, the sour pit of it still burned her stomach. But he had said he was going to try harder, and that's what she had asked of him. He was tired, she was tired, and as long as there was progress, she could wait a little more to have the whole discussion.

But Stuart ended up spending the whole Saturday in the city, at the hospital. Sunday, he managed to avoid their conversation by taking Ham out for a hike in the melty, salty cold air. He got his son so worked up that Ham skipped his nap and had become a bear by bedtime.

Then Monday rolled around, and Stuart was back at work, on call, coming home late . . . and she'd told herself, after his week on call, that they'd address their issues for real. She'd find a family therapist, they'd go and talk to someone about how to meet each other's needs. They would start to walk a path to meeting those needs.

Everything would be fixed.

She'd convinced herself of this as Stuart fell back into the old pattern of leaving everything to Quinn.

How many times had this happened? Quinn expressed some frustration, Stuart said he'd be better, and they just went back to the way it had been? How many times had she let this pattern play out?

She was disgusted with herself, but as more time went on, the more she felt like she had missed her shot to have the talk. The day-to-day of Life overwhelmed the sense of urgency to face their situation.

Meanwhile, she'd gotten the call from *The Brand New Home*—she'd been chosen by the Hendersons to do the nursery. She was ecstatic. Even texted Stuart, who texted back a "Great. Congratulations." While her marriage was at a stalemate, at least she had this nursery to focus on.

And she pulled off the greatest, most functional, cutest nursery the world had ever seen, if she did say so herself. Her modular wall lighting was inspired, voice or touch operated, adjustable to mimic sunrise and sunset as necessary. Her low built-in shelves were exactly what she'd wished she'd had as a new parent. She'd filmed sequences for the show, letting them watch the messiness of the making rather than just the amazing finish. She'd had paint in her hair on camera. She'd been a mess in public. And she'd loved it.

That was just twenty-four hours ago.

Which betrayal hurt her more? Stuart's? She didn't know if she believed he would ever make a pass at Shanna like that—because . . . that was ridiculous, right? No doubt she'd misinterpreted something that he said. But it's absolutely true that he wasn't present now. He hadn't committed himself to his family like he'd said he would. He'd just . . . gone back to the way it was.

And then there was Daisy. The one person who had made things a little okay after everything fell apart was actually the cause of it. She thought back to the Halloween parade. She barely remembered seeing Daisy there—just something about Daisy picking up chairs she shouldn't have. Surely that wasn't enough to destroy someone's life, right?

Daisy had tried to tell Quinn what had happened, in the auditorium.

"I . . . I didn't mean to—I had just moved here," Daisy was blubbering, trying to grab Quinn's arm. "I was telling some friends back in LA what it was like, and showed them the video—after that I was so scared—"

But Quinn's brain could not really hear any of it. The weight of it rested on her chest, suffocating. She was just numb. And she just wanted to get Ham and go home. She shook off Daisy, ignored the crowd, and got out of there.

When she thought of all the times Daisy and she had met up, hung out in the last few months. How many times could Daisy have told her? How many times had Daisy been laughing behind her back?

No . . . Quinn knew Daisy hadn't been laughing. She wouldn't do that.

But she hadn't been honest, either.

Oh god—had she become Quinn's friend out of *guilt*? Quinn had long suspected that there might have been some pity involved when Daisy first approached her at the coffee shop, but she was at such a low point, pity was almost acceptable. Besides, their friendship quickly evolved beyond that.

But guilt? Guilt was something else altogether. Guilt made their friendship a penance. Something that could absolve. Guilt added a layer of unease to every single phone call, text, and Long Island iced tea and just weighed her down into sadness.

"Mommy? Why're you crying?" Ham appeared in the archway of the living room, wearing his royal blue monogrammed bathrobe.

Quinn touched her hand to her face. She hadn't realized that tears were streaming down her cheeks until that moment.

"Just . . . just because I'm a little sad, buddy," she said.

"You're sad? I'll give you a hug!" And Ham came over and wrapped his arms around her. She gathered him up and squeezed him tight.

"Thank you, Hammy," she said. "You give the very best hugs."

"Did the video make you sad?" he asked.

She froze. "The video?" she said, pulling back to look at him.

"Carrie's mommy said she made a video," Ham replied. And Quinn realized horrifically that not only did every adult in the auditorium hear every word of her exchange with Daisy and Shanna, but every kid did, too.

Including Ham.

"It's kind of about the video," she replied.

"Is it a bad video?" he asked. Hamilton equated bad videos to things that were too violent for him to be allowed to watch. Like Road Runner cartoons.

"No . . . it's a video of Mommy being silly. Having a tantrum," she qualified.

"Ohhhhh," Hamilton said. "Can I see it?"

Quinn was about to open her mouth to automatically tell him no, but she stopped herself. Maybe he deserved to see it. It had been the cause of such a huge shift in her—and consequently his—life. Yes, he was three years old, almost four. Yes, he might not understand the full impact of it. But as Ms. Anna had said all those months ago—kids are smart and sensitive enough to know when something is going on.

"Okay, buddy. Grab me my computer?"

Hamilton trotted over to the dining room table and very, very carefully brought back Quinn's laptop. She hoisted Ham onto her lap, went into that file she'd hidden deep in her computer that housed the video, queued it up, and pressed Play.

There it was, that brisk October day. The camera swung wildly, settled on Quinn and Hamilton, hiding behind the barn. Shanna's voice (how had she ever not known it was Shanna's voice, she could hear it so clearly now) said, *"Oh. My."* From somewhere off to the side.

"Mommy, is that you?" Hamilton asked.

"Yes," Quinn answered calmly. "And that's you I'm talking to."

Hamilton took that in like he'd been told a massive important secret. He leaned in, watching the screen even more intently.

And then, on the screen, Quinn began stomping.

"I did"—STOMP—"All of this"—STOMP—"For you!"—STOMP—"The parade!"—STOMP—"The Party!"—STOMP—"The freaking food trucks!"—STOMP—

Quinn couldn't bear to look. She turned away. But Ham, Ham was transfixed . . . and then she felt his body shaking.

He was laughing.

"Mommy, you're so silly!" Ham said in between delighted cackles.

"Yeah," she said, feeling a smile dawn on her face. She felt a laugh bubble up in her chest. It was pretty silly, when you looked at it.

On the screen, she nearly fell, windmilling her arms. Ham burst out in renewed laughter. And this time, Quinn joined him, her joy full and fat. God, all the terrible things that had happened, all the criticism, all the worry over how this would affect her son, and Hamilton . . . he thought it was the most hilarious thing.

"Why are you so silly, Mommy?"

"I was really upset that day," she said, gasping for breath.

Ham immediately sobered. "Why?"

". . . I don't remember anymore," she replied. "I'm very sorry I yelled at you, though."

"It's okay," he said, and gave her another hug. "I don't remember either."

"Bud, you should patent those hugs. You'd make a mint," she said after she absorbed his love into herself.

"What's a mint?"

"A lot of money."

"Oh. Hey, there's Daddy!"

Quinn's head came up. Ham was looking at the computer, where the second video in her hidden file—the Jaxxon LaRue video from the New Year's ball—had begun to play. They had gotten past the beginning bit, where Jaxxon and his brother talk in the hotel room, and into the montage of the party.

Jaxxon was on the screen, talking to the event coordinator from the Children's Hospital Trust. And there, in the background, where Ham was pointing, was Stuart.

Dancing.

With Sutton.

She'd seen it before. She'd watched them dance together at the ball itself. Thought very little of it at the time, because Stuart had always had that young Clooney vibe. He leaned into it, that wasn't a crime. He and Sutton knew each other through Quinn. They'd coincidentally ended up in the same spin class. So they were understandably friendly.

But now, watching it again with new eyes, the dance was obviously more than friendly.

Quinn started to get the sinking feeling that Shanna hadn't misinterpreted what Stuart had said to her last year.

Pieces began to fall into place. Stuart's ease in finding a place to stay in the city when he'd left her. The voice mail she'd gotten from him when she'd been at Disney World. She thought her phone had malfunctioned, saying she'd had a call from Crabbe & Co. But Sutton's cell was a Crabbe & Co.

phone, and if Stuart had unintentionally picked up hers to call . . .

Other things . . . deeper clues. The strange way Sutton spoke when Quinn had called her, to ask for the plans to the Beacon Hill house. Now Quinn realized that she'd sounded oddly familiar, then surprised, that it was *Quinn* on the other end of the call.

Speaking of the Beacon Hill house . . . Stuart knew what state the Beacon Hill house had been in before it was refurbished and photographed for the Martha Stewart magazine. The Beacon Hill house was on the walk back from the spin studio to the office. Sutton could have easily let Stuart in to take a peek. And . . .

And it would have to have been before Stuart left. Because by New Year's, the Beacon Hill house was completely done.

Scales were falling from her eyes. Pennies were dropping. And Quinn refused to fall down with them.

"Excuse me." Gina's voice broke through Quinn's concentration. "Hamilton, there you are."

Quinn snapped the computer shut.

"Hey!" Hamilton protested.

"Sorry, buddy," Quinn said. "But that's enough computer."

"Awwww . . . ," Hamilton said, pouting.

"Now, why don't you go with Gina to get your PJs on, and then you can play Legos until it's time for stories."

The promise of Lego time before bed perked Ham right up, and he trotted over to Gina without a backward glance.

"Gina—can you stay a little late tonight?" Quinn asked. "I think I need to run an errand."

"Absolutely," Gina said.

"Thanks—you've been a lifesaver these past couple of months. I really appreciate it, more than I've told you."

Gina blushed, and went off with Ham, who was pulling at her hand.

And Quinn turned to her phone, dialed.

It took two rings for Quinn to formulate her plan. And on the third ring, Charlene, Stuart's surgery scheduler, picked up.

"Hi, Charlene," Quinn said, her voice that miraculous combination of perky and soothing that masked all homicidal thoughts. Charlene was always all business—she would never presume that Charlene would knowingly cover for Stuart in committing infidelity, but that didn't mean she didn't cover for him. "I was wondering if Stuart had left yet? He was supposed to meet me for dinner, and the restaurant is about to give our reservation away."

"Er, yes, Mrs. Barrett," Charlene said. "He clocked out two hours ago."

"Really? He's not picking up his phone."

"Perhaps he's at his spin class."

"That's where he was going first, but it would have been over by now," Quinn said, putting some worry into her voice. "Oh god, do you think I should start calling emergency rooms?"

"Mrs. Barrett, I'm sure everything is all right. Did you try his other number?" Charlene answered.

"Other number?" Quinn's mind sparked, she quickly scrolled through her contacts. "You mean . . . his 617-555-7751 number?"

"Yes, that's the new one," Charlene replied.

It wasn't a new number. It was Sutton's number.

"Would you like me to try him?" Charlene was saying.

"Um—oh, he just walked through the door! Thank goodness."

"That must be a relief."

"And he has a very prettily wrapped present under his arm."

Charlene chuckled. "Mystery solved. Enjoy your evening, Mrs. Barrett."

"You too."

Quinn hung up.

But before the cold fury could settle over her, the doorbell rang.

She marched over and wrenched open the door. Surely the UPS man would see the absolute freaking-out/exhaustion/ recent life alteration on her face, and drop his package and flee for the hills.

"*What,*" she spat out. And then pulled back her snarl when she saw Daisy and Shanna standing on her doorstep, shivering in the falling night and the remaining light rain.

"Oh. Hi."

"Hi," Daisy replied.

"Hi," Shanna echoed, after a quick nudge from Daisy.

"What are you doing here?"

"We wanted to make sure you're okay." Daisy's voice was choked with emotion. "Are you okay?"

"I'm fine. Not that you really care."

"I do care though," Daisy said earnestly. "Quinn, I'm sorry. I'm so, so sorry. You have to know, I never, *ever* intended for that video to get out. I sent it to some friends because . . . I thought it was funny and I didn't think about you at all, and I should have. I should have thought about you, how you were just having a bad moment, and we all have them. And after . . . after it got out, I was just so scared. So scared that the school was going to kick out Carrie, scared that a place that already thought I was a freak would think I was a bitch on top of it."

"So you were okay with the world thinking I was a bitch?" Quinn replied, crossing her arms over her chest.

"No! No . . . I just . . . I didn't know how to fix it."

"Well, one way not to fix it was to back Shanna in taking over the Parent Association," Quinn said, her eyebrow going up.

Now, Daisy nudged Shanna again, harder. And reluctantly Shanna spoke up.

"Daisy didn't know I was going to do that." Shanna sighed. "And for what it's worth, I'm sorry I did. It was a lot harder job than I thought it was going to be and . . . and I know now that you didn't deserve what I did."

"I just want to know one thing," Quinn said, turning her gaze back to Daisy. "Did you hang out with me all this time because you felt guilty?"

"No! No . . . I hang out with you because you're my friend and I need you," Daisy sputtered. "I was *lost* in Needleton until you. I thought I was never going to fit in, I'm the weird mom, the weird cousin you all tolerate—sorry, Shanna, but that's how I felt—until you became my friend and I realized we are all pretty much winging it. You're the person who made being in Needleton okay."

Quinn felt wet on her cheeks, and she knew it wasn't the rain.

"Okay," she said, sniffling. "Thank you both for coming."

"Can we come inside?" Daisy replied. "Shanna and I would really like to beg for forgiveness some more."

"Actually, I'm about to head out," Quinn said. "My husband is cheating on me, and I need to catch him in the act."

Daisy's and Shanna's jaws dropped in unison.

"Do you guys want to come?"

They were going against rush hour traffic, so the drive into Boston went fast—almost as fast as Daisy and Shanna had said yes to Quinn's bold proposal.

Phone calls were very quickly made to spouses saying they'd be a little later than originally thought. Game plans were laid out, addresses looked up, phones were set to record, and Quinn climbed behind the wheel.

"It's so clean in here," Shanna said, from the backseat of Quinn's SUV. "How is it this clean in here? My car looks like Willy Wonka's factory after a nuclear blast."

"It's annoying, right?" Daisy said from the passenger seat.

"This is because I cleaned out my car so I could haul all my craft stuff to the Family Fun Fest," Quinn answered, as she merged onto the Mass Turnpike. "But Hamilton doesn't like it to be messy back there, so he keeps it pretty clean."

"Really?" Shanna replied. "Can you come and teach Jordan your ways? I can't get her into the car in the mornings without the bribe of an Oreo."

"You give Jordan Oreos to get in the car?" Daisy asked.

"Yes. And it keeps her happy and quiet on the drive, too. I'm a horrible parent and she's a total jerk. Please pass your judgments."

"No judgment," Quinn said, and she reached over and opened the glove box, revealing her emergency box of Fig Newtons. "There are days these are necessary, for us both."

"Ohhh," Shanna said, lighting up at the sight of the cookies. "Do you mind if I have one? This baby is screaming for sustenance."

"Feel free."

As Shanna munched on the cookies, Quinn looked over at Daisy, who was grinning into her hand.

"What?"

"Nothing," Daisy said. "I just . . . in my wildest dreams, I never imagined tonight including the two of you sharing your Nabisco child-bribing secrets."

Quinn caught Shanna's eyes in the rearview mirror.

And suddenly, the three of them were all laughing.

Their mood stayed that way, swapping three-year-old horror stories, until they exited the turnpike and made their way to a nondescript brownstone in Back Bay that had been broken up into apartments.

"You know what you're going to do?" Daisy asked as they parked the car.

"Uh-huh." Quinn nodded. She'd expected butterflies in her stomach. Instead it felt like a ball of cold lead had settled there, giving her the weight she needed to make an impact.

"What if he's not there?" Shanna asked.

"He is."

Quinn had texted Stuart, asking if he wanted to meet for dinner. He'd lied and said he was just grabbing a bite before he headed back into the hospital, it was apparently going to be "a long night."

They were just out of the car when one of the building's tenants was exiting.

"Hold the door! Wait! Hold the door please!" Shanna started yelling, as she trotted toward the door, conspicuously holding her belly as she did so. "I have to pee so bad!"

The bewildered tenant's latent chivalry kicked in and he held the door wide open for Shanna. Quinn and Daisy slipped in after her.

"No one ever questions a pregnant lady's need to pee," Shanna said, flipping a lock of hair over her shoulder. "Now . . . which floor?"

They climbed the stairs to the third floor in silence. Quinn steadied herself as she knocked on the door.

Which creaked on its hinges as she did so.

"It's open," she mouthed to Daisy and Shanna. And motioned for them to follow her.

Daisy, for her part, had lived in a major city long enough to put her keys in between her fingers before she followed. She also, smartly, whipped up her phone, set to Record.

The apartment was cozy, and to Quinn's eye, well designed. Sutton wasn't with Crabbe and Co. for nothing. A lamp was on in the corner, and a speaker playing a pert, throaty ballad by a no doubt young, hip singer. A bottle of wine was open on the counter in the kitchenette. They could hear the shower on in the bathroom, and a feminine laugh emanating from that direction, followed by a low chuckle.

That lead ball in Quinn's stomach dropped to the floor.

He really was here. They really were together.

" . . . oooookaaay . . . ," Daisy whispered. "Are we going to . . . I dunno, go into the bathroom?"

"No!" Shanna whispered back. "Are you crazy? We just wait for them to . . . finish?"

"What if it takes a while?" Daisy whispered back. "They could be . . . you know . . ."

Luckily, Quinn didn't have to listen to her friends debate whether or not her husband and Sutton were fucking in the shower and the length of time it would require. Because just then, they heard the shower door opening, and Sutton stepping out.

". . . hold on, I'm just getting the wine," she laughed as she opened the bathroom door, tying a short robe around her waist.

She gave a little yelp, jumping back, when she saw the trio standing there.

"Hi, Sutton," Quinn said.

"Q . . . Quinn . . . ," Sutton stuttered. "What are you doing here?"

"I came to talk to you," Quinn said. "Your door was open, you really need to be more careful."

"The lock sticks," Sutton said dully. "How did you know where I live?"

"I have your address. You're on my Christmas card list."

"I'm sorry, but now's not a good time, I . . . have company."

"I know," Quinn said indulgently. "Why don't you call Stuart to come out here? He should probably hear this, too."

It was as if she could see Sutton's heart stopping. But to her credit, she didn't try to bluff anymore. She just called over her shoulder, "Stuart, come out here!"

The shower turned off. "What?" Stuart called back. "Why?"

"Don't ask questions, honey," Quinn replied. "Just do as she asks."

The small space was silent, with Sutton staring at three random women in her living room, until Stuart slowly pulled open the bathroom door, and came out, a bathrobe wrapped around him.

A monogrammed royal blue bathrobe that matched Hamilton's.

"Quinn," Stuart said, trying to convey calm, and control. "Daisy, too. And . . ."

"Shanna. Surely you remember me? Jamie's wife? You propositioned me last year?"

"I . . . I don't believe I did, but if that is what this is about—"

"Honey," Quinn interrupted, "you're here in Sutton's apartment in a bathrobe I got you for Christmas, you don't get to argue about whether or not you tried to cheat on me with Shanna."

"I . . . all right. I suppose there is something you should know," Stuart said. He reached his hand out to Sutton, who took it gratefully. "Sutton and I . . . when you and I were separated, we started seeing each other, it just happened—"

"Actually, I'm not here to talk to you," Quinn interrupted, definitively. "I'm here to talk to Sutton."

Sutton looked from Stuart to Quinn. "Quinn, I want you to know, I never wanted to hurt you—you were my mentor, for chrissakes! I wouldn't have a career if not for you. But what happened was—"

"Sutton, I know what happened," Quinn said with a look of pity. "He's very charming. You're very pretty, flirtatious. Maybe you didn't start seeing each other 'officially' until after the New Year's ball, but it had been headed that way for a while, hadn't it? I bet he turned up on your doorstep that night, having walked out of our house an hour before."

The look on Sutton's face told them all it was true.

"But when I took Hamilton to Florida for spring break, Stuart lost it, and you saw him lose it. You two fought, and either you kicked him out or he left, it doesn't matter. He ended up back on my doorstep, ready to make amends. But the person he came back to wasn't the same person he left."

"Sutton, don't let her make you feel bad," Stuart whispered, "you didn't do anything wrong."

"No, but you did," Daisy muttered.

"Excuse me, who the hell asked you?" Stuart barked out.

"HEY," Quinn said, and then, taking a deep breath, returned to her steely calm. "Again—you are not here to talk. You are here to listen. What I have to say is to Sutton."

"So say it," Sutton piped up. "Say it and leave."

Quinn took one step forward. Sutton flinched, but refused to back up.

"If you want him," she said, her voice turning soft—softer than she thought possible, "if you want him, you had better not want anything else for yourself. Not your career—not if it's going to get in the way of his. And not kids—not if you expect him to take part in the mundanity of family life. Because if it's not about him, he's not going to be there.

"You had better not want to even be human, to make mistakes! But if you can maintain the pretense of perfection, if you can twist yourself into a pretzel trying to please him, walk on eggshells the rest of your life . . . Oh, and ignore it when he'll likely cheat on you, according to my friend Shanna over here . . . then enjoy him. He's yours."

"I . . . I . . . thank you?" Sutton said after a moment.

"Stuart," Quinn came over to stand in front of him. "You can come to the house over the weekend to see Hamilton and pick up your things. Don't bring Sutton."

"That's . . . surprisingly mature, Quinn," he said.

"Did you expect me to be devastated?" she replied. "Don't worry, we have plenty of time for that—the divorce is going to take forever and be an absolute nightmare. But I recommend you roll over and give me everything I ask for because not only do I have witnesses to your infidelity, but Daisy here has proof on video."

Daisy gave a little wave. And for the first time, it seemed that Stuart and Sutton looked beyond Quinn to notice Daisy holding up her phone.

"Wait—she can't just—"

"I'm a lawyer," Shanna piped up, "and this topic has recently been under debate, but the camera phone was in plain view . . . so pretty much yes, she can."

"I have to get home to my son," Quinn said, as they all moved toward the door. "Have a lovely rest of your night."

And with that, they left the two dripping-wet lovers, and got the hell out of there.

The drive home was alternately solemn and hysterical. They were silent until they got on the turnpike, when Quinn couldn't take the silence anymore and blasted the radio. They found an old hair metal song from the eighties, and they sang along, loud and terribly, as if they'd learned the lyrics in the womb.

The carpool karaoke lasted until they turned into Quinn's driveway.

"That was amazing," Daisy said, as they exited the car.

"I do a decent Bon Jovi," Quinn quipped.

"You know what I mean," Daisy said. "The way you stood up for yourself. The way you stood your ground and kicked him to the curb. Oh, before I forget—"

Daisy dug out her phone, her fingers flying.

"What are you doing?"

"I'm emailing you this video."

"Do us all a favor and don't send it to anyone else this time," Shanna said drily, stepping around the car.

Daisy looked up, soberly, her eyes finding Quinn's. "I am so very, very sorry about that. I hope you know—"

"Oh, shut up and hug me," Quinn said. "Thank you," she whispered in Daisy's ear. "I don't think I would have been able to do this if you hadn't been there."

When Daisy pulled away, there was a decided shine to her eyes.

"Or you," Quinn said, calling over to Shanna, "thanks for your help."

"Are you kidding? That was the most fun I've had in ages. Let's do it again next Friday."

"Oh god, whose marriage should we destroy next week?" Daisy laughed.

"Please not mine," Shanna replied.

Now it was Quinn's turn to sober up. "Shanna, you know Jamie and I never—"

"I know," Shanna said, cutting her off. "Jamie chewed my ear off about it tonight. I mostly agreed to come over with Daisy just to get away from it for a minute."

"But the thing is . . . you weren't wrong," Quinn admitted.

". . . I wasn't?"

"I did want Jamie—or rather, I wanted what you have in Jamie."

Shanna was silent, waiting.

"You have a partner—not just a husband, but a real partner who knows and understands what is going on in your lives and does his share. I was so jealous of that. No doubt, I leaned on Jamie more than I should have, especially considering he was—is—your husband."

Shanna bit her lip, and then nodded.

"I just hope you appreciate it. That you both do," Quinn said. "Because that's special."

"Thank you. I do," Shanna said. "Or at least, I certainly will more now."

"Me too," Daisy said, and squeezed Quinn's hand.

"So . . . ," Quinn said, sniffling away any errant tears. "See you at drop-off on Monday?"

"See you at drop-off."

Daisy and Shanna departed in Daisy's old car, decorated

with all those nerdy decals she really needed Daisy to explain one day. Quinn watched them until their headlights disappeared in the trees.

Then she headed inside.

"Mommy!" was the cry that greeted her. Little feet padded down the stairs and across the floor as Hamilton flung himself at her knees.

"I'm sorry, Ms. Quinn," Gina said, coming down the stairs. "He refused to fall asleep until he could give you a good-night kiss."

"It's all right, Gina," Quinn said. "I'll take it from here."

She hugged her son back fiercely, picking him up in one smooth motion and making for the stairs.

"Where'd you go, Mommy?"

"I just had to go into the city to tell your daddy something," she said into his soft hair.

"Oh. I'm glad you're home."

"Me too, buddy," she sighed. "Me too."

Little Wonders Preschool
May Newsletter

Hello, WONDER-ful Parents!

Congratulations everyone! We made it through another school year! ~~Yay . . . only a dozen or so more to go . . .~~ So, the time has come to CELEBRATE! Graduation and Moving Up ceremonies will commence on Friday, May 7th, just the right way to kick off Mother's Day weekend. Our five-year-olds in the Iguana Room will be graduating to Needleton's fantastic kindergartens, while all our other classes get ready to move up to the next room. ~~LOL, let's pretend this means anything because we all have our kids signed up for the summer session, right?~~

We look forward to making this the most delightful graduation ceremony our kids have ever experienced, ~~only one they've ever experienced~~ so we are calling on our WONDER-ful parent volunteers to assist with refreshments, tent and chair setup, audio visual needs, and of course, balloon maintenance.

As always, the sign-up board for volunteers is in the main lobby, via the portal on the website, on the Facebook group, and you can send inquiries and special requests via the Little Wonders Slack. ~~I better not see you making any special requests, TERRY.~~

As we prepare for the big changes to come, we at the Parent Association are reflecting on the past. We have had a ~~dramatic ridiculous telenovela-esque~~ momentous year, unlike any in our history, and we have all ~~barely survived~~ been enriched by the experience. But it is time for a new board to take the reins, so elections will begin in June with the onset of the summer session. All positions are open ~~because none of us want to do anything like this again~~ and I cannot recommend enough getting involved in our WONDER-ful school by serving on the school board!

As this is my final newsletter as your Parent Association secretary, I say to you one last time . . .

Together in Parenting!
Suzy Breakman-Kang
Parent Association Secretary

Addendum: if you are planning on donating baked goods to the refreshment table at graduation, and you are unable to make your own organic treats, please make certain that the treats you purchase are made in a nut-free commercial kitchen, and that there are no food colorings—repeat, NO FOOD COLORINGS—in the frostings. ~~Seriously, guys, after St. Patrick's Day my kid pooped green for a week.~~

CHAPTER TWENTY-TWO

It was Daisy's firm opinion, seconded by Quinn, and confirmed by Shanna, that you really hadn't lived until you witnessed a preschool graduation on a balmy May day.

It was too nice outside to be cooped up in the auditorium/multipurpose room. A day with the wild, blue, cloud-speckled skies that made you breathe deep and tip your face to the sun.

It was entirely possible that Daisy was adjusting to the vagaries, and the delights, of New England weather.

They were all seated together in the big yard. The same yard where, seven months ago, lives and spaceship costumes were forever altered. The irony of being here now did not escape anyone because it was all the same, and all so different.

Daisy, Rob, Quinn, Jamie, and Shanna had their own row—Shanna on the aisle because she was eight and a half months pregnant, and in her own words, "about to explode like a water balloon on hot pavement." They watched as their almost four-year-olds and their classmates sang a song about their school (to the tune of "Bingo").

We're Little Wonders at our school,
And we are safe and happy
Learn our A-B-Cs
Colors, 1-2-3s
Manners, thank you, please
Becoming smart and strong.

It was not an exaggeration to say that there was not a dry eye in the yard.

"Thank you to our Tadpole Room!" Ms. Anna said, taking the stage once their class had finished their song, and all received their flowers (in lieu of diplomas) from Ms. Rosie. "They will be advancing to Ms. Mariet and the Iguana Room in the near future, and we are so happy to have been able to provide a loving and warm environment for them to learn and grow."

The crowd burst into applause as the kids were ushered off the stage. It took a herculean effort by their teachers to keep the kids in line and not running to their parents they could see in the audience, but they managed to corral them, while the Iguana Room stood up, one by one walked across the stage and received their "diplomas" . . . which Quinn had told Daisy were gilt edged, because Needleton parents demanded a level of class to their preschool certificates.

As soon as the Iguana Room had been allowed to throw their painted-blue cardboard hats into the air, the graduation ceremony was officially over and the kids sprinted to their parents. Daisy was practically tackled by Carrie.

"Mommy, did you see me sing?"

"Yes, baby, you sang beautifully!" Daisy replied.

"Daddy, did you see me?" Carrie said, releasing Daisy and throwing herself at Rob.

"You'd think we hadn't heard them singing that song every day for the last month," Quinn said, as Hamilton let go of his mother's neck and grabbed Carrie's hand, and started singing again.

"You might have," Daisy replied. "I've heard nothing but buzz saws."

Daisy had spent the past month in a constant state of construction. Not only was the basement of the house in its final stages of refurbishment, because Grandpa Bob was due back from Arizona in just a few days, but Rob had begun making display shelves for Daisy's storefront.

She had managed to get a pretty decent lease for the old Knick Knack Nook space on Main Street. Elaine at the Cranberry Boutique even vouched for her with the town council, saying that she would bring a new variety to their local independent shops. She hoped to open up sometime in June—dependent entirely on when they managed to get the space fully refurbished. There were plenty of issues that needed addressing, and Rob was as handy as they come, but as *The Brand New Home* was wrapping up its first season and actively beginning work on its second, Daisy knew that Rob's time was precious. The fact that he had started the shelves made her feel terribly guilty for taking him away from his other work.

"I'm in this with you, kid." Robbie had just shrugged, and kissed her forehead. "Besides, Quinn designed these shelves and she scares me, so I'm going to get them done."

The one good thing was that they hadn't—yet—had to tap into their down payment money. They likely would when Daisy started ordering inventory—and Rob's uncle and Grandpa Bob had both approved a delayed time frame for payment—but for now, the money she made from the Dave

Arenson *Blackmoor* and other items in that gold mine of a long box was enough for the first and last month's rent and shelf-building supplies.

Daisy, meanwhile, was busy building the party-planning aspect of her business. She already had three preschool birthday parties on the books, and had done one just last weekend for Jordan's fourth birthday, at a family rate. Jordan wanted her basement playroom transformed into a combo dungeon-princess birthday party, as in she wanted all the pink and fluffy décor and face painting of the Princess Room, and all the ordering about and war mongering of the games in the Dungeon Room.

Daisy looked forward to the day she got to sit her niece down and introduce her to the world of D&D. Jordan was made to rule a kingdom. Or at the very least, organize a small band of scrappy adventurers.

Shanna was more than happy to leave all the work up to Daisy. But for once Daisy didn't mind—since she was getting paid. And every penny that she made was a penny she didn't have to take out of the down payment fund.

Future parties would be far more geek-tastic as her business expanded. But this was a good start. Quinn had helped her with the party planning, showing her how to rig all the decorations, and of course was there with Hamilton at Jordan's birthday, but she had been busy herself.

Yes, she was in the early stages of her divorce, with volleys being thrown, visitation being worked out, and lawyers exchanging paper. It was a massive task, pulling apart the life they had built, but with every step, so far, Quinn had felt better and better. Lighter. More free.

And . . . she had started therapy. Her friends were amazing, but it wasn't their *only* job to help her through this. She didn't have to feel guilty about monopolizing a therapist's time. And it really helped her focus on herself, not all the stuff outside she couldn't control.

Her mother was coming to visit in a few weeks. For once she wasn't worried about it.

Her in-laws hadn't said word one about the divorce from whatever island they were vacationing on. She didn't mind that either.

Stuart had made one initial threat, in their divorce proceedings. His lawyers had intimated that there was proof of her unfitness as a parent from the Halloween video, and as such, attempted to use it as leverage in their negotiations.

But Stuart hadn't expected her to embrace the video, and put it in her bio on her new business website.

Yes, Quinn was starting a business, opening up an interior design firm of her very own. Honestly, she didn't have much choice, because after her episode of *The Brand New Home* aired, she'd gotten so many calls for work she needed a way to organize it all.

When the episode had aired, just a few weeks ago, Quinn had expected it to garner notice. To once again be brought up in conversation, or on the design blogs, as a subject of ridicule. Maybe even Jaxxon LaRue would be inclined to comment (although, given the recriminations he got from the New Year's video, maybe not). And yes, there was some of that. But there was also a surprising amount of praise.

For the way she was honest about parenting with the Hendersons. For how she owned up to her internet infamy. But mostly, for how *awesome* the nursery turned out to be.

There was even an Instagram post that made Quinn nearly pass out.

It was a photo of the finished nursery, the corner where

she had set up the low shelves and the soft toys. And it was posted by none other than the queen of casual elegance herself, Martha Stewart.

It's hard to go from career woman to internet joke and back again, but Quinn Barrett (the mom in the Halloween costume stomping video—remember that? Me neither) proves she's made of sterner stuff. Learning lessons about her own pursuit of perfection, she left her career at the rigidly traditional Boston interior design firm Crabbe & Co. to hang up her own shingle, Messy Life/Lovely Home Interiors. And her debut on the new design show The Brand New Home proved a triumph—turning in the best baby room we've seen in ages. We can't wait to see what her Messy Life brings next.

3w   Like   Reply   👍⚪14

It wasn't the eight-page spread in the magazine she'd spent her career dreaming about. And it certainly wasn't the great public resurrection she'd imagined for months. There would be no morning shows where she owned her Uptight Mom narrative, no apology from the world at large for what she had been through.

But in many ways, it was better, because instead of focusing on the past, it made room for what was to come.

And what was to come was the Iguana Room, and the last year of preschool.

"Are you guys ready to have four-year-olds?" Quinn asked.

"I already have one, thanks," Shanna piped up. Newly four Jordan was off with Jamie, taking his phone and posing for selfies. "And she's terrifying."

"I wonder what's going to happen with the Parent Association," Daisy mused. "Are you going to run again, Shanna?"

"Are you insane?" Shanna guffawed. "Have you noticed the liquid-filled beach ball under my shirt? It's going to become a human being in a few weeks. I'm not doing anything other than that for the foreseeable future. But after . . . I've been thinking about going back to work, and letting Jamie scale back on his hours. He might be willing to run again. He actually enjoyed it." She slid a glance to Quinn. "But probably only because you were there to do the hard stuff."

"Well, I have officially retired from preschool presidency. I'm not diving back into that. Besides—new business, remember? I've got plenty of upcoming projects and commissions to keep me busy. But you could do it, Daisy."

Daisy blinked. "I have a new business, too! Let's . . . let's leave the Parent Association to new blood. There will be a bunch of parents bringing their kids to the Baby Bear Room, eager to overinvolve themselves with Little Wonders. If any of us were there it would no doubt just ruin their fun."

"Wow, that is exceedingly generous of you," Shanna said drily.

"Yeah, you're such a giver, Daisy," Quinn added with a laugh.

At that moment, Ham and Carrie came sprinting back to their moms, Rob, Jamie, and Jordan close behind.

"Mommy, come on, it's time for your surprise!" Carrie said, tugging at Daisy's hand.

"Shhh . . . Carrie, you're not supposed to tell her yet," Rob said, unable to hide his grin.

"There's a surprise?" Daisy asked, looking from her friends to her husband and daughter.

"She's just talking about the pizza party," Rob said quickly.

"Yep, the pizza party!" Quinn added quickly. "At the restaurant on Main Street. Should we get going?"

"Pizza party?" Carrie asked her dad. "But you said—"

"Pizza party! Everyone, let's go to the pizza party!" Jordan and Hamilton started cheering along with Jamie.

"All right," Daisy said, laughing. "Let's go."

They parked on Main Street, near the front of Daisy's new store. Brown paper covered the inside of the windows, a sign on the door said New Business Coming Soon. She really had to think of a name for the place.

"Why are we here?" Daisy asked, as Rob opened up the trunk.

"I just wanted to drop off these before we hit the restaurant," he said, pulling a set of newly finished shelves out of the trunk. "Come on, Carrie!"

Daisy unbuckled Carrie from her car seat, and together they followed Rob into the store.

"Just let me get the lights . . ."

And the store—*her store*—appeared before her eyes.

"What . . . how did you? . . . when?"

The narrow space was transformed. The entire thing looked like a fancy gentleman's library. Woodwork reached to the ceiling—no musty, ratty old IKEA shelves in this place. But the wood itself was a light ash, a beautiful pale shade, giving the space a lift of femininity.

There was a long, low glass counter, edged in wood. There was the modular lighting that Quinn had insisted on, installed. Two refurbished, electric blue leather chairs sat in the front window, a little reading nook.

"I had a couple of guys from the show help out," Robbie said. "And you know . . . these guys gave me a hand, too."

Just then, bursting from the back storage room was Quinn, Hamilton, Shanna, Jamie, and Jordan.

"Surprise!" They cried in unison.

"Surprise!!!!" Carrie echoed. "Did I do it right?"

"Yes, sweetie, you did great." Robbie kissed his daughter. "Now, it's not complete. You still don't have a POS system, and you need internet, but . . .

"And some stock," Shanna piped up. "But hey, it's your store."

It was her store. She could see it. She could see the shelves full of trade paperbacks, the front-facing display shelves full of the newest comics every week. She could see exactly where she was going to put her Captain Phasma costume. The game wall, the figurines. It was all going to be here.

"I can't believe you did this," she said, turning to Rob, almost crying.

"Hey, I can't believe you moved across the country with me, so this is the least I could do. Besides, I had to get all of your stuff out of the basement and garage before Grandpa Bob came home. But there's more."

"There's more??"

Daisy was waved to the back of the store, to what she had thought would be the stockroom.

There, Robbie had set up an old round table, worn and secondhand. On it were a few bottles of wine, a recently placed pizza, and Daisy's D&D 5th Edition Dungeon Master's Guide.

"What . . . is this the pizza party?"

"No," Jamie replied. "We—Robbie and I—are going to take the kids down the street to the pizza place. You ladies are going to have your own party here."

"Here?"

"Yup," Shanna said. "That was Robbie's plan."

"Wait, what are we going to do—drink wine and unpack boxes?"

"I've heard a lot about this Dungeons and Dragons thing," Quinn said. "Let's give that a shot."

Daisy looked at her friend like she was crazy. "You. Want to play Dungeons and Dragons."

"Robbie said it was the one thing you would want for Mother's Day."

"He's not wrong," Daisy said. "But it's not what *you* want for Mother's Day."

"Oh, don't get me wrong," Shanna added. "I have a full spa day planned on Sunday. But you seem to think this is fun . . . so maybe it is."

"But . . . Robbie, I don't have anything planned."

Robbie dug into a box and handed her one of her binders. "Use something from your old campaign."

Her fingers tingled as she took the folder from him.

"So, it's settled. All right, kids, who wants to go get our own pizza?"

"WE DO!!!" Jordan cried, and started dragging her daddy to the door.

"Come on, Hamilton!" Carrie said, taking her friend by one hand and her dad with the other.

"Bye, Mommy!" Hamilton waved over his shoulder to Quinn, who blew him a kiss.

"Bye, Hammy—be good for Carrie and Jordan's daddies."

Daisy, Quinn, and Shanna waved them goodbye, watching their own Little Wonders skip and chatter, excited about the prospect of pizza, and whatever else the future held. (Maybe ice cream!)

"Okay, seriously?" Shanna said. "They're getting pizza, not

going to war. You don't get to cry—I'm the one with the hor-mones."

"I'm not crying," Daisy said, rubbing her eyes. "I just can't believe you guys agreed to this. I'm so glad you did, you're going to love it."

"Playing D&D or having a child-free afternoon?" Quinn said, as she opened a bottle of wine and poured out two glasses—and found a sparkling water for Shanna.

"Both," Daisy said, as she sat down at the table, began flip-ping through her notebook, rummaging and finding her DM screen.

"Don't get me wrong, I crave free time," Quinn was saying, her eyes going soft, "but those kids are kind of great, aren't they?"

"They are," Shanna agreed, her eyes going soft, too.

"Yeah," Daisy agreed. "But don't worry, I won't keep you too long. We'll play a short adventure, only about four hours, give or take."

"Four HOURS?" Quinn said, blinking in shock. "Do you know how many Parcels that is?"

"Seriously, think of what you could do with four hours." Shanna agreed, wild eyed. "You could write up an entire le-gal brief—you could do your *taxes* in four hours."

"I could cook an entire Thanksgiving dinner *while* design-ing a room and binge a sitcom on Netflix," Quinn countered.

"Or, you could play a short game of D&D," Daisy replied, laying all of her pages out in front of her. She pulled out a few sets of dice, and handed them to her friends. They looked at the sparkly purple (in Quinn's case) and fluorescent green (for Shanna) geometric objects with a mixture of amusement and awe. Daisy smiled as she rolled up her sleeves.

"Settle in, ladies. This is gonna be fun."

P.S.

About the author

Read on

Insights,
Interviews
& More . . .

Meet Kate Rorick

Stacey Cochrane

Emmy Award–winning writer KATE RORICK is the author of novels about modern motherhood. She is also a television writer and producer, most recently for *The Librarians* and *Marvel's Cloak & Dagger*. She is one of the writers behind the runaway YouTube sensation *The Lizzie Bennet Diaries* and authored its two tie-in novels. In her vast spare time she is a bestselling author of historical romance, under the name Kate Noble. She lives in Los Angeles with her family. ❧

Q&A with Kate Rorick

Q: You are a (fairly) new mother—without naming names or giving out details, did you base any of the situations in Little Wonders *on real life?*

A: If you're asking have I ever stomped on my kid's Halloween costume or witnessed a Parent Association meeting meltdown—no, sorry, those are wholly out of my imagination. I have attended my fair share of Halloween parades and school festivals, but they were much less dramatic than the ones depicted. But I did recently experience a preschool graduation ceremony for my first child, and am in the potty-training trenches with my second, so suffice to say . . . certain plot points in the book are incredibly present in my life.

When you become a parent, you are dropped into an entirely new world, with a different language, different customs, and different rules. It doesn't matter how much you've planned, how much you've read, how much advice you've gotten—You. Are. Not. Prepared. And as soon as you feel like you've found your feet, your kid grows, the rules shift, and you have to scramble to keep up.

When my first child began preschool, I was a wide-eyed doe of panic, trying to figure out how to navigate interactions with the teachers and the parents—how do you best advocate for your child? How do you set up a playdate? How do you get another parent to be friends with you? (It's not like you can pass them a note in study hall or arrange a parental hookup on Tinder.) So everything in *Little Wonders* about feeling out of your depth, about trying to balance who you are with what you need to be for your child, about navigating life with a three-year-old . . . that's all very, very realistic. ▶

Q&A with Kate Rorick *(continued)*

Q: Daisy has a hard time adjusting to her new life on the East Coast. Have you experienced life on both coasts? Or have you been strictly a West Coast dweller your entire life?

A: I've spent large chunks of my life on both coasts—having been raised in the East, plus spending the first decade of adulthood there. I moved west for work about ten years ago . . . and while it's home now, there is always the sensation of true home being where you were raised, three thousand miles away. So I have a great deal of sympathy for Robbie and his homesickness driving him all the way back east from LA. But it's a lot harder for Daisy, who is not a Needleton native, to feel the same sense of home. Especially when her sense of belonging to Los Angeles is so strong.

Q: Daisy is a self-declared geek, a Star Wars *aficionado, and a Dungeons and Dragons Dungeon Master. Does geek culture play a significant role in your life?*

A: Yes, geek culture plays a pretty significant role in my life— because in my day job I write for television, and very often the shows I work on are genre shows. But also because . . . I love it. Who among us doesn't remember the thrill deep in our chests when Luke Skywalker fired those rockets and the Death Star blew up? Or when Harry Potter caught that first snitch? When you and your merry band of adventurers face your first dragon? Geek culture has become mainstream culture because these experiences—and the feelings they evoke—are universal.

My experience of Los Angeles is that it's filled with geeks and nerds—far more so than it is with the beauty-obsessed beach dwellers that movies teach us live here. People who are so passionate about narrative, stories, world building that they'll spend hours upon hours learning and living those worlds. And so many—SO MANY—of those nerds are women, and mothers. It was incredibly important to me that Daisy be nerdy (in fact, there was a lot more in the book about her geek cred that had to be cut because I can get really boring when I go into detail), because all too often, the depiction of moms is that they *aren't* nerdy. They aren't given permission to be passionate about anything other than their kids. Sure, the dads can have hobbies, but the moms? Maybe they get a book club. (I have nothing against book clubs. I'm in one. But I've also played my fair share of RPGs and tabletop games, and think they deserve equal press.)

Q: *Do you feel the internet has taken over our lives to a point where it is out of control?*

A: Yes and no. The internet is an amazing tool—it has taken the place of the phone book, the encyclopedia, the Thomas Guide, your French-to-English dictionary, and your high school reunion. It has become absolutely essential for modern life and, in my opinion, should be considered a public utility.

But because it is such a one-stop shop, it absolutely has the potential to take over our lives. Especially as it facilitates social interaction. Why have friends in real life when you can just talk to a wall of the likeminded reinforcing your opinions? The dopamine rush you get from "likes" is as strong as the one you can get from an addictive habit. I should know—I crave Instagram hearts with every post. Unfortunately, the only thing you can really do about it is self-impose boundaries.

Q: *How do you feel the internet has changed parenting?*

A: I don't know how I would have gotten through the baby phase without it. There are so many resources available to scour in those wee small hours during feedings—parents have organized communities to offer advice, tips, and strategies. And crowdsourced parenting can be a social good—for instance, I am a member of a parenting Facebook group, and there is one woman on there who is a car seat expert. She will answer any car seat question you might have and she is a godsend!

However, it can easily—like almost everything else on the internet—turn toxic and cultish. (Mommy wars, or antivaxxing, anyone?) So, you have to tread carefully. ▶

Q&A with Kate Rorick *(continued)*

Q: Quinn has a run-in with an internet "Influencer." Do you think this is a new phenomenon, or are these people just getting their celebrity in a new and different way?

A: I'll be honest—Influencer culture kinda scares me. I know that at some point my children are going to be exposed to it, but the idea that someone with good screen presence and a camera angle that denotes intimacy will have sway over my kid is terror-inducing. But I don't think this kind of celebrity is in any way new—people have been chasing fame for fame's sake forever, with or without skills that warranted it. The difference is the speed with which someone can reach an audience, and how wide that audience can get.

Q: Any words of wisdom on Halloween costumes for kids?

A: Ha! Well, I do have some experience with cardboard construction for costumes, so I can give you spray painting tips. But my best advice is once your kid starts voicing an opinion, listen to what they want. If they want to be one of four hundred Elsas, let them be Elsa. If you don't, their memory of Halloween won't be fun and candy, it'll be "I felt bad because everyone else had a pretty Elsa costume and I didn't."

Take a Peek at Kate Rorick's Debut Novel

The Baby Plan

Available now from HarperCollins

CHAPTER 1

It was the mashed potatoes that did it.

The damned holiday mashed potatoes, made with nearly a pound of butter and cream cheese and onions and pepper and salt—and the occasional potato—that ruined Nathalie Kneller's announcement, three years in the making.

And worse, she had been the one to make the potatoes. So really it was her own fault.

Usually, the family didn't get together for Thanksgiving. Christmas was their big holiday. Ever since her dad retired and traded the house they grew up in for a condo with a parking space big enough for an RV, he'd spent more time ▶

exploring the great American roadways than not. But he would always be back in Santa Barbara for Christmas, and Nathalie and her sister would joyfully make the drive up from Los Angeles to gleefully welcome him home, and dutifully receive the gifts he'd picked up in his travels.

Never mind that Nathalie was not in need of any more turquoise jewelry, or tumbled rocks taken straight out of Carlsbad Caverns. Her dad had given her a rock tumbler when she was nine, and she'd loved it. But sometimes it seemed like she was stuck at that age, as that person, in his mind.

But this year Nathalie *begged* her father to be back by Thanksgiving. He had to be. Timing was everything.

"I don't know, kiddo," her father had hemmed on the phone. She could hear the radio playing in the background. *". . . Listening to 104.3 KBEQ Kansas City! Stay tuned for Blake Shelton, Faith Hill, and Dierks Bentley!"*

"Kathy really wanted to go to Branson this trip, see the sights . . ."

Nathalie had to bite her tongue to keep her annoyance at her stepmother's love of anything country in check.

"Please?" she'd said on the phone. "I'll even host!" Considering the postage-stamp size of the two-bedroom house she and David had just spent their life savings on, this was a card she'd hoped she wouldn't have to play. But she had to pull out all the stops against Branson and Kathy.

"Well . . ."

"Dad, it's . . . it's important."

"Important, how?" her father had asked, suspicious. "Is everything okay?"

It took everything in her to not blurt it out over the phone. But again, timing was crucial. So instead, she just said, "Everything's great, Dad. I just . . . I'd just really love to see you. And show off the house."

She'd heard him sigh on the other end of the line. "Okay. I'll talk to Kath about it, but . . . count us in."

Nathalie had smiled and mentally fist-pumped as she said her goodbyes to her dad.

Then, cold realization settled over her: she was going to have to host Thanksgiving dinner.

At the age of thirty-three, she'd never hosted a holiday meal. Their place had always been too small, they always had friends or family to go to . . . one way or another, it was something they'd always managed to avoid. Now, she had invited it on herself.

But there was nothing to be done about it. She needed to have her family there on Thanksgiving.

Because on Thanksgiving, she would be thirteen weeks and one day pregnant.

Thirteen weeks was the cutoff point, ending the queasiness and worry of the first trimester, and the beginning of the (supposedly) smooth-sailing second. But more importantly, it was the point at which it was universally agreed that it was safe to tell people. The chances of something going catastrophically wrong plummet, and you can tentatively share your good news—either quietly, in hushed tones over brunch with girlfriends, or by the trumpet blast of posting a sonogram pic on your Facebook wall.

Or, if you were like Nathalie, you could announce it in the Thanksgiving toast you'd had composed for three years, your family gathered around, your father sniffling away tears at the thought of his first grandchild.

So, for the next ten days, while her father took a meandering route back to California from the Midwest, and her husband David watched with silent bewilderment, Nathalie wrote lists, scoured Pinterest, and laid out a rational, detailed, and perfect plan for their very first Thanksgiving.

Number one on the list was they had to get an actual dining room table.

"What's wrong with our current table?" David asked as Nathalie dragged him through IKEA.

"The bistro table can go on the deck," *where it's supposed to*, she finished mentally. The little metal table was whimsical in their old tiny apartment, but they were well into adulthood now, in their thirties, with 401(k)s and homeowner's insurance.

Time for the black STORNÄS extendable table that showed it.

After acquiring chairs (NORRNÄS in white, for contrast), she gave David a six-pack of his favorite IPA and set him to the task of assembly while she went and bought matching fall-themed linens, serving dishes, utensils, decorations, and all the other things that ▶

people who have never had cause to entertain before might not have around the house. The gold-edged china plates she'd inherited from her mother and dragged from apartment to apartment but never used finally came out of their boxes, ready for their moment in the spotlight.

The one thing she was not worried about was the food. She had made almost every single dish, minus the turkey, having brought various sides to potluck Thanksgivings and even once, when she was eleven, doing the whole dinner on her own. Plus, she had her mother's recipe box, and knew exactly how to time the cooking to make everything in her small kitchen.

Although, she could use an extra pair of hands.

"Sorry, Nat, I can't," Lyndi said into the phone. Her little sister's regret was apparent in the tone of her voice, but it did little to appease Nathalie.

"But you said you had it covered!"

"I know, but . . ."

"It's just one little pie!" Nathalie exclaimed. It wasn't just one little pie. It was their father's favorite triple berry pie, and normally she would have done it herself, but timing the pie with cooking the turkey was tricky and good leaders knew how to delegate.

"Yeah, but our oven's totally crappy, and I don't even have, like, a pie plate. Besides, Marcus doesn't eat gluten so he doesn't want any of that stuff in our apartment."

Nathalie was glad Lyndi couldn't see the look on her face at the mention of Marcus's gluten sensitivity. It also didn't help that she was in the middle of mashing the potatoes.

And oh God, the potatoes. Her morning sickness, which usually confined itself to the mornings, decided to voice a strong objection every time the masher smushed another boiled potato. She dreaded adding the butter and cream cheese and the thick dairy smells it would create.

She had just about breathed through the worst of it when Lyndi said, "You got gluten-free stuffing for him, right?"

". . . I'm sorry?"

"For Marcus? Gluten-free stuffing?"

"You're bringing Marcus?" Nathalie asked, incredulous.

"Well, yeah. I mean, if that's okay," Lyndi said.

"I . . . I guess it is." Thank God she had bought that sixth chair. "But, surely your roommate has other places to go—friends, or a party?"

In truth, Nathalie would have rather not had Marcus there. She had met him once, when she was helping Lyndi move into the third-floor apartment in the bohemian neighborhood of Echo Park. And he was nice enough, helping Lyndi carry her bike up the stairs. But his niceness and splitting the rent with her sister didn't exactly warrant him being present at the moment of her big announcement.

"No, we're going out to our friend's pre-Thanksgiving bash tonight," Lyndi said. "And, besides . . . you know that Marcus isn't *just* my roommate, right?"

Nathalie blinked. "You're dating?"

"I mean, I guess you could call it that," she said, awkwardly.

This was news to her. And not just because she'd thought Marcus was gay.

Lyndi was twenty-four, and sometimes the years between them stood out—like when one tried to define "dating." Often Nathalie felt like a second mother, rather than a big sister. And obviously Lyndi felt the same way, because when she finally spoke her voice was small, like a little girl caught after misbehaving.

"Are you mad?"

"No, sweetie," Nathalie heard herself saying with a sigh. "But you could have told me earlier. Thanksgiving is tomorrow, and now I have to make the pie, *and* gluten-free stuffing!"

"So he can come? Yay!" Lyndi cheered through the phone. "And I'm sorry about the pie but hey, I'll bring the flowers, okay? Don't worry about that!"

Lyndi was off the phone before Nathalie could protest that she'd already got a centerpiece (a brass cornucopia she filled with tiny squashes), but as usual with her little sister, Nathalie let her get her way.

Having Lyndi there for the announcement was more important than fretting over the random guy she had with her.

Of course, what she didn't expect was Lyndi showing up the next day at noon, completely hungover.

"Oh my God, are you okay?" Nathalie said, seeing Lyndi's gray face. She tried to hide how she was feeling with a wan smile, but it ▸

didn't work when she was the same color as her flowy pale blue minidress.

"Happy Thanksgiving to you, too," Lyndi said breezily, giving her sister a quick hug and then slipping past her.

"Hey, Nathalie!" said the massive arrangement of flowers behind Lyndi. "Good to see you again!"

"Good to, er, see you, too," she replied, taking the flowers (oh God, the smell) and finally being able to actually see Lyndi's if-you-could-call-him-that boyfriend.

Marcus had a sweet smile, that was the first thing she realized. He was lean—likely from a lack of gluten—and achingly hipster, with the skinniest of skinny jeans, a narrow strip of a tie and a full sleeve of tattoos peeking out from his button-down shirt. He was also surprisingly nervous. As one hand extended to shake hers, the other went to his short dreads, twisting the dark hair tightly.

Nathalie decided to take pity on him. "Good to see you, too, Marcus," she said in the voice that she used with her shyest students. "Come on in, it's wonderful to have you."

"Hey, Marcus!" David came in from the living room, extending his hand and pulling Marcus into a bear hug. Marcus seemed only slightly surprised, considering he'd never met David before. "I've got the game on. Wanna beer?"

"Um . . . do you have any wine?" Marcus replied. "White?"

David only gave the slightest hesitation before he slapped Marcus on the back, and pulled him toward the TV. "Sure thing. Hon, can you open the wine?"

"You got it," Nathalie singsonged back. Luckily they had a bottle of white in the back of the fridge. She hadn't had a drink in three years, and she knew Lyndi was a red girl. The white was meant for Kathy, who, when confronted by a lack of Bartles & Jaymes (which Nat didn't know existed outside of, oh, the 1980s), would settle for a pinot grigio.

She put the flowers on the table. "These are gorgeous," she said to Lyndi. And they were. They put her brass cornucopia to shame. Fat seasonal blooms in earthy reds and oranges, with a trail of yellow orchids flowing out, still on the vine.

"Thanks. I designed them."

"Designed them?"

"The arrangement. It's what I'm doing at the flower co-op now."

"I thought you were a delivery girl at the shop."

"I still do some deliveries, we all do . . . but I sort of got promoted." Lyndi shrugged, then scowled. "And it's not a shop, come on. You know that."

"Of course," Nathalie replied, wanting to keep the peace. "And congrats! On the promotion." In truth, she didn't really understand what Lyndi did at her current job. It was a place that sold flowers— so that was a flower shop, right? Even if it was only online? Whatever it was, Lyndi had stuck with it for six months, so it was better than any other job she'd tried. Nathalie could only hope one of these days she'd focus on a career.

A timer dinged in the kitchen. Nathalie heeded its call like Pavlov's dog.

"Oh what is that smell?" Lyndi said, following her.

"The holiday mashed potatoes," Nathalie answered, taking them carefully out of the oven. "Can you help me with this?"

To accommodate the triple berry pie, she'd had to rearrange the timing on baking the potatoes . . . which meant she'd had to hit the pause button on cooking the turkey for an hour. But, she thought, as she and Lyndi shoved the bird back in and cranked up the heat, it would be fine in the end.

Totally fine. ∾